'You have no idea why I might be here, Lindsay? No reason to wonder why I might come looking for my errant wife?'

Errant wife. So he blamed her. Of course he did. And she knew he had a right to blame her, because she'd left him without an expl—————————— he'd said, a warning. ————————————————————ven if he couldn't or w——————————

'It's been six ————————————————— coolly, 'and you hav————————————————think it's reasonable for ———————————— to see you.'

'Didn't you think I'd ever come, demanding answers?'

'I gave you an answer—'

'A two-sentence email is not an explanation, Lindsay.'

He held up a hand to forestall her reply, although she couldn't think of anything to say.

'But don't worry yourself on that account. I have no interest in your explanations.'

Frustration bubbled through her and emotion burned in her chest. Maybe she hadn't had so many words when she'd finally left, but that was because she'd used them all up. Antonios hadn't heard any of them.

'The reason I'm here,' he continued, his voice hard and unyielding, 'is because I need you to return to Greece.'

Her jaw dropped and she shook her head in an instantaneous gut reaction.

'I can't—'

'You'll find you can, Lindsay. You pack a bag and get on a plane. It's that easy.'

The Marakaios Brides

Powerful Greeks meet their match!

Proud Greek blood flows through the veins of brothers Antonios and Leonidas Marakaios. With determination and ruthlessness they have built their family's empire to global heights.

It has been their sole focus—
even to the exclusion of love.

But now two women look set to challenge their pride, their passion and their marriage vows!

Read Antonios's story in:

The Marakaios Marriage

May 2015

And meet Leonidas in:

The Marakaios Baby

August 2015

THE MARAKAIOS MARRIAGE

BY
KATE HEWITT

Published in Great Britain 2015
by Mills & Boon, an imprint of Harlequin (UK) Limited,
Eton House, 18-24 Paradise Road, Richmond, Surrey, TW9 1SR

© 2015 Kate Hewitt

ISBN: 978-0-263-25061-9

Harlequin (UK) Limited's policy is to use papers that are natural,
renewable and recyclable products and made from wood grown in
sustainable forests. The logging and manufacturing processes conform
to the legal environmental regulations of the country of origin.

Printed and bound in Spain
by CPI, Barcelona

After spending three years as a diehard New Yorker, **Kate Hewitt** now lives in a small village in the English Lake District with her husband, their five children and a Golden Retriever. In addition to writing intensely emotional stories she loves reading, baking, and playing chess with her son—she has yet to win against him, but she continues to try.

Learn more about Kate at www.kate-hewitt.com

Books by Kate Hewitt

Mills & Boon® Modern™ Romance

Kholodov's Last Mistress
Undoing of De Luca

The Chatsfield

Virgin's Sweet Rebellion

Rivals to the Crown of Kadar

Captured by the Sheikh
Commanded by the Sheikh

The Diomedi Heirs

The Prince She Never Knew
A Queen for the Taking?

The Bryants: Powerful & Proud

Beneath the Veil of Paradise
In the Heat of the Spotlight
His Brand of Passion

The Power of Redemption

The Darkest of Secrets
The Husband She Never Knew

Visit the author profile page at millsandboon.co.uk for more titles

To Pippa Roscoe—
thank you for your invaluable feedback on this story.

CHAPTER ONE

'HELLO, LINDSAY.'

How could two such innocuous-sounding words cause her whole body to jolt, first with an impossible joy, and then with a far more consuming dread? A dread that seeped into her stomach like acid, corroding those few seconds of frail, false happiness as she registered the cold tone of the man she'd once promised to love, honour and obey.

Her husband, Antonios Marakaios.

Lindsay Douglas looked up from her computer, her hands clenching into fists in her lap even as her gaze roved helplessly, hungrily over him, took in his familiar features now made strange by the coldness in his eyes, the harsh downturn of his mouth. With her mind still spinning from the sight of him, she said the first thing that came into it.

'How did you get in here?'

'You mean the security guard?' Antonios sounded merely disdainful, but his whisky-brown eyes glowed like banked coals. 'I told him I was your husband. He let me through.'

She licked her dry lips, her mind spinning even as she forced herself to focus. Think rationally. 'He shouldn't have,' she said. 'You have no business being here, Antonios.'

'No?' He arched an eyebrow, his mouth curving coldly, even cruelly. 'No business seeing my wife?'

She forced herself to meet that burning gaze, even though it took everything she had. 'Our marriage is over.'

'I am well aware of that, Lindsay. It's been six months, after all, since you walked out on me without any warning.'

She heard the accusation in his voice but refused to rise to it. There was no point now; their marriage was over, just as she'd told him.

'I only meant that all the academic buildings are locked, with security guards by the door,' she answered. Her voice sounded calm—far calmer than she felt. Seeing Antonios again was causing memories to rise up in her mind like a flock of seagulls, crying out to her, making her remember things she'd spent the last six months determined to forget. The way he'd held her after they'd made love, how he'd always so tenderly tucked her hair behind her ears, cupped her cheek with his hand, kissed her eyelids. How happy and safe and cherished he'd once made her feel.

No, she couldn't remember that. Better to remember the three months of isolation and confusion she'd spent at his home in Greece as Antonios had become more and more obsessed with work, expecting her simply to slot into a life she'd found alien and even frightening.

Better to remember how depressed and despairing she'd felt, until staying in Greece for one more day, one more *minute*, had seemed impossible.

Yes, better to remember that.

'I still don't know why you're here,' she told him. She placed her hands flat on the desk and stood, determined to meet him at eye level, or as close as she could, considering he topped her by eight inches.

Yet just looking at him now caused her to feel a tug of longing deep in her belly. The close-cut midnight-dark hair. The strong square jaw. The sensual, mobile lips. And as for his body…taut, chiselled perfection underneath the dark grey silk suit he wore. She knew his body as well as her own. Memories rushed in again, sweet and poignant reminders of their one sweet week together, and she forced them away, held his sardonic gaze.

Antonios arched one dark eyebrow. 'You have no idea why I might be here, Lindsay? No reason to wonder why I might come looking for my errant wife?'

Errant wife. So he blamed her. Of course he did. And she knew he had a right to blame her, because she'd left him without an explanation or even, as he'd said, a warning. But he'd forced her to leave, even if he couldn't, or wouldn't, ever understand that. 'It's been six months, Antonios,' she told him coolly, 'and you haven't been in touch once. I think it's reasonable to be surprised to see you.'

'Didn't you think I'd ever come, demanding answers?'

'I gave you an answer—'

'A two-sentence email is not an explanation, Lindsay. Saying our marriage was a mistake without saying why is just cowardice.' He held up a hand to forestall her reply, although she couldn't think of anything to say. 'But don't worry yourself on that account. I have no interest in your explanations. Nothing would satisfy me now, and our marriage ended when you walked away without a word.'

Frustration bubbled through her and emotion burned in her chest. Maybe she hadn't had so many words when she'd finally left, but that was because she'd used them all up. Antonios hadn't heard any of it. 'The reason I'm here,' he continued, his voice hard and unyielding, 'is because I need you to return to Greece.'

Her jaw dropped and she shook her head in an instantaneous gut reaction.

'I can't—'

'You'll find you can, Lindsay. You pack a bag and get on a plane. It's that easy.'

Mutely she shook her head. Just the thought of returning to Greece made her heart start to thud hard, blood pounding in her ears. She focused on her breathing, trying to keep it even and slow. One of the books she'd read had advised focusing on the little things she could control, rather than the overwhelming ones she couldn't. Like her husband and his sudden return into her life.

Antonios stared at her, his whisky-brown eyes narrowed, his lips pursed, his gaze ruthlessly assessing. *In. Out. In. Out.* With effort she slowed her breathing, and her heart stopped thudding quite so hard.

She glanced up at him, conscious of how he was staring at her. And she was staring at him; she couldn't help herself. Even angry as he so obviously was, and had every right to be, he looked beautiful. She remembered when she'd first seen him in New York, with snowflakes dusting his hair and a whimsical smile on his face as he'd caught sight of her standing on Fifth Avenue, gazing up at the white spirals of the Guggenheim.

I'm lost, he'd said. *Or at least I thought I was.*

But she'd been the one who had been lost, in so many ways. Devastated by the death of her father. Spinning in a void of grief and fear and loneliness she'd been trying so hard to escape.

And then she'd lost herself in Antonios, in the charming smile he'd given her, in the warmth she'd seen in his eyes, in the way he'd looked at her as if she were the most interesting and important woman in the world. For a week, a mere seven days, they'd revelled in each other. And then reality had hit, and hit hard.

'Let me clarify,' he said, his voice both soft and so very cold. 'You *will* come to Greece. As your husband, I command you.'

She stiffened. 'You can't *command* me, Antonios. I'm not your property.'

'Greek marriage law is a little different from American law, Lindsay.'

She shook her head, angry now, although not, she suspected, as angry as he was. 'Not that different.'

'Perhaps not,' he conceded with a shrug. 'But I am assuming you want a divorce?'

The sudden change in subject jolted her. 'A divorce...'

'That *is* why you left me, is it not? Because you no longer wished to continue in our marriage.' He bared his teeth in a smile and Lindsay suppressed the sudden urge to shiver. She'd never seen Antonios look this way. So cold and hard and predatory.

'I...' A divorce sounded so final, so terrible, and yet of course that had to be what she wanted. She'd left him, after all.

In the six months since she'd left Greece, she'd immersed herself in the comforting cocoon of number theory, trying to finish her doctorate in Pure Mathematics. Trying to blunt that awful ache of missing Antonios, or at least the Antonios she'd known for one week, before everything had changed. She'd tried to take steps to put her life back together, to control her anxiety and reach out to the people around her. She'd made progress, and there had been moments, whole days, when she'd felt normal and even happy.

Yet she'd always missed Antonios. She'd missed the person she'd been with him, when they'd been in New York.

And neither of those people had been real. Their marriage, their love, hadn't been real. She knew that absolutely, and yet…

She still longed for what they'd shared, so very briefly.

'Yes,' she said quietly. She lifted her chin and met his gaze. 'I want to end our marriage.'

'A divorce,' Antonios clarified flatly. Lindsay flinched slightly but kept his gaze, hard and unyielding as it was.

'Yes.'

'Then, Lindsay,' he told her in that awful silky voice, 'you need to do as I ask. *Command.* Because under Greek marriage law, you can't get a divorce unless both parties agree.'

She stared at him, her eyes widening as she considered the implications of what he was saying. 'There must be other circumstances in which a divorce is permissible.'

'Ah, yes, there are. Two, as a matter of fact.' His mouth twisted unpleasantly. 'Adultery and abandonment. But as I have committed neither of those, they do not apply, at least in my case.'

She flinched again, and Antonios registered her reaction with a curl of his lip. 'Why do you want me to return to Greece, Antonios?'

'Not, as you seem to fear, to resume our marriage.' His voice hardened as he raked her with a contemptuous gaze. 'I have no desire to do that.'

Of course he didn't. And that shouldn't hurt, because she'd chosen it to be that way, and yet it still did. 'Then…'

'My mother, as you might remember, was fond of you. She doesn't know why you left, and I have not enlightened her as to the state of our marriage.'

Guilt twisted sharply inside her. Daphne Marakaios had been kind to her during her time in Greece, but it still hadn't been enough to stay. To stay sane.

'Why haven't you told her?' Lindsay asked. 'It's been six months already, and you can't keep it a secret forever.'

'Why shouldn't you tell her?' Antonios countered. 'Oh, I forgot. Because you're a coward. You sneak away from my home and my bed and can't even be bothered to have a single conversation about why you wished to end our marriage.'

Lindsay drew a deep breath, fighting the impulse to tell him just how many conversations she'd tried to have. There was no point now. 'I understand that you're angry—'

'I'm not angry, Lindsay. To be angry I would have to care.' He stood up, the expression on his face ironing out. 'And I stopped caring when you sent me that email. When you refused to say anything but that our marriage was a mistake when I called you, wanting to know what had happened. When you showed me how little you thought of me or our marriage.'

'And you showed me how little you thought of our marriage every day I was in Greece,' Lindsay returned before she could help herself.

Antonios turned to her slowly, his eyes wide with incredulity. 'Are you actually going to blame me for the end of our marriage?' he asked, each syllable iced with disbelief.

'Oh, no, of course not,' Lindsay fired back. 'How could I do that? How could you possibly have any responsibility or blame?'

He stared at her, his eyes narrowing, and Lindsay almost laughed to realize he wasn't sure if she was being sarcastic or not.

Then he shrugged her words aside and answered in a clipped voice, 'I *don't* care, about you or your reasons. But my mother does. Because she has been ill, I have spared her the further grief of knowing how and why you have gone.'

'Ill—'

'Her cancer has returned,' Antonios informed her with brutal bluntness. 'She got the results back a month after you left.'

Lindsay stared at him in shock. She'd known Daphne had been in remission from breast cancer, but the outlook had been good. 'Antonios, I'm so sorry. Is it…is it treatable?'

He lifted one powerful shoulder in a shrug, his expression veiled. 'Not very.'

Lindsay sank back in her chair, her mind reeling with this new information. She thought of kind Daphne, with her white hair and soft voice, her gentleness apparent in every word and action, and felt a twist of grief for the woman she'd known so briefly. And as for Antonios… he adored his mother. This would have hit him hard and she, his wife, hadn't been there to comfort and support him through her illness. Yet would she have been able to, if she'd stayed in Greece?

She'd been so desperately unhappy there, and the thought of returning brought the old fears to the fore.

'Antonios,' she said quietly, 'I'm very, very sorry about your mother, but I still can't go back to Greece.'

'You can and you will,' Antonios replied flatly, 'if you want a divorce.'

She shook her head, her hair flying, desperation digging its claws into her soul. 'Then I won't ask for a divorce.'

'Then you are my wife still, and you belong with me.' His voice had roughened and he turned away from her in one sharp movement. 'You cannot have it both ways, Lindsay.'

'How will my seeing your mother help her?' Lindsay protested. 'It would only hurt her more for me to tell her to her face that we've separated—'

'But I have no intention of having you tell her that.' Antonios turned around, his eyes seeming to burn right through her as he glared at her. 'It is likely my mother only has a few months to live, perhaps less. I do not intend to distress her with the news of our failed marriage. For a few days, Lindsay, perhaps a week, you can pretend that we are still happily married.'

'*What—?*' She stared at him, appalled, as he gave her a grimace of a smile.

'Surely that is not impossible? You have already proven once what a good actress you are, when you pretended to fall in love with me.'

Antonios stared at his wife's lovely pale face and squashed the tiny flicker of pity he felt for her. She looked so trapped, so *horrified* at the prospect of resuming their marriage and returning to Greece.

Not, of course, that they would truly resume their marriage. It would be a sham only, for the sake of his mother.

Antonios had no intention of inviting Lindsay into his bed again. Not after she'd left him in such a cold-hearted and cowardly way. No, he'd take her back to Greece for a few days for his mother's sake, and then he'd never see her again…which was what she obviously wanted. And he wanted it, too.

'A few days?' she repeated numbly. 'And that will be enough…'

'It's my mother's name day next week,' Antonios told her.

'Name day…'

'In Greece we celebrate name days rather than birthdays. My family wishes to celebrate it especially, considering.' Grief constricted his throat and burned in his chest. He could not imagine Villa Marakaios without his mother. Losing his father had been hard enough. His father had built the vineyard from nothing; he'd been the brains behind the operation, for better and definitely for worse, but his mother had always been its heart. And when the heart was gone…

But perhaps his own heart had already gone, crushed to nothing when his wife had left him. He'd thought Lindsay had loved him. He'd believed they were happy together.

What a joke. What a lie. But Antonios knew he should be used to people not being what they seemed. Not saying what they meant. He'd had hard lessons in that already.

'We are having a celebration,' he continued, just managing to keep his voice even. 'Family and friends, all our neighbours. You will be there. Afterwards you can return here if you wish. I will explain to my mother that you needed to finish your research.' He knew Lindsay had been pursuing her doctorate in Pure Mathematics, and when she'd left him she'd told him she needed to tie a few things up back in New York. He'd said goodbye in good faith, thinking she'd only be gone a few days. She'd already told him that her research could be done anywhere; she'd said there was nothing for her back in New York. But apparently that, like everything else, had been a lie.

Lindsay's face had gone even paler and she lifted one hand to her throat, swallowing convulsively. 'A party? Antonios, please. I can't.'

Fury beat through his blood. 'What did I ever do to you,' he demanded in a low, savage voice, 'to make you treat me this way? Treat my family this way? We welcomed you into our home, into our lives.' His insides twisted as emotion gripped him—emotion he couldn't bear Lindsay to see. He'd told her he didn't care about her any more, and he'd meant it. He had to mean it. 'My mother,' he said after a moment, when he'd regained his composure and his voice was as flat and toneless as he needed it to be, 'loved you. She treated you like her own daughter. Is this how you intend to repay her?'

Tears sparkled on Lindsay's lashes and she blinked them back, shaking her head in such obvious misery that Antonios almost felt sorry for her again. Almost.

'No, of course not,' she said in a low voice. 'I…I was very grateful to your mother, and her kindness to me.'

'You have a funny way of showing it.'

Her eyes flashed fire at that, and Antonios wondered what on earth she had to be angry about. *She'd* left *him*.

'Even so,' she said quietly, one hand still fluttering at her throat, 'it is very difficult for me to return to Greece.'

'And why is that? Do you have a lover waiting for you here in New York?'

Her mouth dropped open in shock. 'A lover—'

Antonios shrugged, as if it were a matter of no consequence, even though the thought of Lindsay with another man, violating their marriage vows, their marriage *bed*, made him want to punch something. 'I do not know what else would take you so abruptly from Greece.' *From me*, he almost said, but thankfully didn't.

She shook her head slowly, her eyes wide, although with what emotion Antonios couldn't tell. 'No,' she said in a low voice. 'I don't have a lover. There's only been you, Antonios. Ever.'

And yet he obviously hadn't been enough. Antonios didn't even know whether to believe her; he told himself it didn't matter. 'Then there is no reason for you not to come to Greece.'

'My research—'

'Cannot wait a week?' Impatience flared inside him, along with the familiar fury. Didn't she realize how thoughtless, how selfish and cruel she was being?

Even now, after six months of coming to accept and learning to live with her abandonment, he was stunned by how completely she'd deceived him. He had believed in her love for him utterly. But, Antonios reminded himself, they'd only known each other a week when they had married. It had been impulsive, reckless even, but he'd been so *sure*. Sure of his love for Lindsay, and of her love for him.

What a fool he'd been.

Lindsay was staring at him, her face still pale and miserable. 'One week,' Antonios ground out. 'Seven days. And then I intend never to see you again.' She flinched, as if his words hurt her, and he let out a hard laugh. 'Doesn't that notion please you?'

She glanced away, pressing her lips together to keep

them from trembling. 'No,' she said after a moment. 'It doesn't.'

He shook his head slowly. 'I don't understand you.'

'I know.' She let out a shuddering breath. 'You never did.'

'And that is my fault?'

She shook her head wearily. 'It's too late to apportion blame, Antonios. It simply is. Was. Our marriage was a mistake, as I told you in my email and on the telephone.'

'Yet you never said why.'

'You never asked,' Lindsay answered, her voice sharpening, and Antonios frowned at her.

'I asked you on the phone—'

'No,' Lindsay told him quietly, 'you didn't. You asked me if I were serious, and I said yes. And then you hung up.'

Antonios stared at her, his jaw bunched so tight it ached. 'You're the one who left, Lindsay.'

'I know—'

'Yet now you are attempting to imply that our marriage failed because I didn't ask the right questions when I called you after you'd left me. *Theos!* It is hard to take.'

'I'm not implying anything of the sort, Antonios. I was simply reminding you of the facts.'

'Then let me remind you of a fact. I'm not interested in your explanations. The time for those has passed. What I am interested in, Lindsay—the *only* thing I am interested in—is your agreement. A plane leaves for Athens tonight. If we are to be on it, we need to leave here in the next hour.'

'What?' Her gaze flew back to his, her mouth gaping open. 'I haven't even agreed.'

'Don't you want a divorce?'

She stared at him for a moment, her chin lifted proudly, her eyes cool and grey. 'You might think you can blackmail me into agreeing, Antonios,' she told him, 'but you can't. I'll come to Greece, not because I want a divorce but because I want to pay my respects to your mother. To explain to her—'

'Do not think—' Antonios cut her off '—that you'll tell her some sob story about our mistake of a marriage. I don't want her upset—'

'When do you intend on telling her the truth?'

'Never,' Antonios answered shortly. 'She doesn't have that long to live.'

Tears filled Lindsay's eyes again, turning them luminous and silver, and she blinked them back. 'Do you really think that's the better course? To deceive her—'

'You're one to speak of deception.'

'I never deceived you, Antonios. I did love you, for that week in New York.'

The pain that slashed through him was so intense and sudden that Antonios nearly gasped aloud. Nearly clutched his chest, as if he were having a heart attack, the same as his father, dead at just fifty-nine years old. 'And then?' he finally managed, his voice thankfully dispassionate. 'You just stopped?' Part of him knew he shouldn't be asking these questions, shouldn't care about these answers. He'd told Lindsay the time for explanations had passed, and it had. 'Never mind,' he dismissed roughly. 'It hardly matters. Come to Greece for whatever reason you want, but you need to be ready in an hour.'

She stared at him for a long moment, looking fragile and beautiful and making him remember how it had felt to hold her. Touch her.

'Fine,' she said softly, and her voice sounded sad and

resigned. Suppressing the ache of longing that trembled through him, Antonios turned away from the sight of his wife and waited, his hands clenched into fists at his sides, as she packed up her belongings and then, without a word or glance for him, slipped by him and out of the room.

CHAPTER TWO

LINDSAY WALKED ACROSS the college campus in the oncoming twilight with Antonios like a malevolent shadow behind her. She walked blindly, unaware of the stately brick buildings, now gilded in the gold of fading sunlight, that made this small liberal arts college one of the most beautiful in the whole north-east of America.

All she could think of was the week that loomed so terribly ahead of her. All she could feel was Antonios's anger and scorn.

Maybe she deserved some of it, leaving the way she had, but Antonios had no idea how hard life in Greece had been for her. Hadn't been willing to listen to her explanations, fumbling and faltering as they had been, because while she'd wanted him to understand she'd also been afraid of him knowing and seeing too much.

Their marriage, Lindsay acknowledged hollowly, had been doomed from the start, never mind that one magical week in New York.

And now the time for explanations had passed, Antonios said. It was for the best, Lindsay knew, because having Antonios understand her or her reasons for leaving served no purpose now. It was impossible anyway, because he'd *never* understood. Never tried.

'Where do you live?' Antonios asked as they passed several academic buildings. A few students relaxed outside, lounging in the last of the weak October sunshine before darkness fell. Fall had only just come to upstate New York; the leaves were just starting to change and the breeze was chilly, but after a long, sticky summer of heatwaves everyone was ready for autumn.

'Just across the street,' Lindsay murmured. She crossed the street to a lane of faculty houses, made of clapboard and painted in different bright colours with front porches that held a few Adonirack chairs or a porch swing. She'd sat outside there, in the summers, watching the world go by. Always a spectator...until she'd met Antonios.

He'd woken her up, brought her into the land of the living. With him she'd felt more joy and excitement than she'd ever known before. She should have realized it couldn't last, it hadn't been real.

Antonios stood patiently while she fumbled for the keys; to her annoyance and shame her hands shook. He affected her that much. And not just him, but the whole reality he'd thrust so suddenly upon her. Going to Greece. Seeing his family again. Pretending to be his wife—his *loving* wife—again. Parties and dinners, endless social occasions, every moment in the spotlight...

'Let me help you,' Antonios said and, to her surprise, he almost sounded gentle. He took the key from her hand and fitted it into the lock, turning it easily before pushing the door open.

Lindsay muttered her thanks and stepped inside, breathed in the musty, dusty scent of her father's house. It was strange to have Antonios here, to see this glimpse of her old life, the only life she'd known until he had burst into it.

She flipped on the light and watched him blink as he took in the narrow hallway, made even narrower by the bookshelves set against every wall, each one crammed to overflowing with books. More books were piled on the floor in teetering stacks; the dining room table was covered in textbooks and piles of papers. Lindsay was so used to it that she didn't even notice the clutter any more, but she was conscious of it now, with Antonios here. She was uncomfortably aware of just how small and messy it all was. Yet it was also home, the place where she'd felt safe, where she and her father had been happy, or as happy as they knew how to be. She wouldn't apologize for it.

She cleared her throat and turned towards the stairs. 'I'll just pack.'

'Do you need any help?'

She turned back to Antonios, surprised by his solicitude. Or was he being patronizing? She couldn't tell anything about him any more; his expression was veiled, his voice toneless, his movements controlled.

'No,' she answered, 'I'm fine.'

He arched one dark eyebrow. 'Are you really fine, Lindsay? Because just now your hands were shaking too much for you even to open your front door.'

She stiffened, colour rushing into her face. 'Maybe that's because you're so angry, Antonios. It's a little unsettling to be around someone like that.'

His mouth tightened. 'You think I shouldn't be angry?'

She closed her eyes briefly as weariness swept over her. 'I don't want to get into this discussion. We've both agreed it serves no purpose. I was just—'

'Stating a fact,' Antonios finished sardonically. 'Of course. I'm sorry I can't make this experience easier for you.'

Lindsay just shook her head, too tired and tense to argue. 'Please, let's not bicker and snipe at each other. I'm coming to Greece as you wanted. Can't that be enough?'

His eyes blazed and he took a step towards her, colour slashing his cheekbones. 'No, Lindsay, that is not remotely enough. But since it is all I have asked of you, and all I believe you are capable of, I will have to be satisfied.'

He stared at her for a long, taut moment; Lindsay could hear her breathing turn ragged as her heart beat harder. She felt trapped by his gaze, pinned as much by his contempt as her own pointless anger. And underneath the fury that simmered in Antonios's gaze and hid in her own heart was the memory of when things had been different between them. When he'd taken her in his arms and made her body sing. When she'd thought she loved him.

Then he flicked his gaze away and, sagging with relief, she turned and went upstairs.

She dragged a suitcase out of the hall closet, forced herself to breathe more slowly. She could do this. She *had* to do this, not because she wanted a divorce so badly but because she owed it to Daphne. Her own mother had turned her back on her completely when she'd been no more than a child, and Daphne's small kindnesses to her had been like water in a barren desert. But not enough water. Just a few drops dribbled on her parched lips, when she'd needed the oasis of her husband's support and understanding, attention and care.

'Lindsay?' She heard the creak of the staircase as Antonios came upstairs, his broad shoulders nearly touching both walls as he loomed in the hallway, tall and dark, familiar and strange at the same time. 'We need to leave shortly.'

'I'll try to hurry.' She started throwing clothes into her suitcase, dimly aware that she had nothing appropriate for the kind of social occasions Antonios would expect her to attend. Formal dinners, a huge party for Daphne… as the largest local landowner and businessman, Antonios's calendar had been full of social engagements. From the moment she'd arrived in Greece he'd expected her to be his hostess, to arrange seating for dinner parties, to chat effortlessly to everyone, to be charming and sparkling and always at his side, except when he'd left her for weeks on end to go on business trips. Lindsay didn't know which had been worse: trying to manage alone or feeling ignored.

In any case, she hadn't managed, not remotely. Being Antonios's wife was a role she had been utterly unprepared for.

And now she'd have to go through it all again, all the social occasions and organizing, and, worse, it would be under his family's suspicious gaze because she'd been gone for so long. Her breath hitched at the thought.

Don't think about it. You can deal with that later. Just focus on the present.

The present, Lindsay acknowledged, was difficult enough.

'You left plenty of clothes at the villa,' Antonios told her. 'You only need to pack a small amount.'

Lindsay pictured all the clothes back in their bedroom, the beautiful things Antonios had bought her in New York, before he'd taken her back to Greece. She'd forgotten about them, and the thought of them waiting for her there, hanging in the closet as if she'd never left, made her feel slightly sick.

'I'll just get my toiletries,' she said, and turned to go to the bathroom down the hall. She had to move past him in the narrow hallway and, as she tried to slip past his powerful form, she could smell his aftershave and feel the press of his back against her breasts. For one heart-stopping second she longed to throw herself into his arms, wrap herself around him, feel the comforting heat of his body, the sensuous slide of his lips on hers. To feel wanted and cherished and safe again.

It was never going to happen.

Antonios moved to let her pass and her breath came out in a shuddering rush as she quickly slipped towards the bathroom and, caught between relief and despair, shut and locked the door.

Ten minutes later she'd packed one small case and Antonios brought it down to the hired car he had waiting in one of the college car parks. Lindsay slipped into the leather interior, laid her head back against the seat. She felt incredibly, unbearably tired.

'Do you need to notify anyone?' Antonios asked. 'That you're leaving?'

'No.' Her research, as he'd so bluntly pointed out, could wait. She'd stopped her work as a teaching assistant for introductory classes after her father had died last summer. Only nine months ago, and yet it felt like a lifetime.

It *had* been a lifetime.

'No one will worry about you?' Antonios asked. 'Or wonder where you've gone?'

'I'll email my colleagues. They'll understand.'

'Did you tell them about me?'

'You know I did,' she answered. 'I had to explain why I left my job and house and went to Greece on the spur of the moment.'

His hands flexed on the steering wheel; she could feel his tension. 'It was your choice, Lindsay.'

'I know it was.'

'You said you had nothing left back in New York.'

'It felt like I didn't.'

He shifted in his seat, seeming to want to say more, but kept himself from it.

Lindsay turned her face to the window, steeled herself for the next endless week of tension like this, stalled conversations and not-so-veiled hostility. How on earth were they going to convince Daphne, as well as the rest of his family, that they were still in love?

They didn't speak for the rest of the three-hour drive to New York City. Antonios returned the rental car and took their suitcases into the airport; within a few minutes after checking in they'd been whisked to a first-class lounge and treated to champagne and canapés.

It seemed ludicrous to be sitting in luxury and sipping champagne as if they were on honeymoon. As if they were in love.

Lindsay sneaked a glance at Antonios—the dark slashes of his eyebrows drawn together, his mouth turned downwards in a forbidding frown—and she had a sudden, absurd urge to say something silly, to make him smile.

The truth was, she didn't know what she felt for him any more. Sadness for what she'd thought they had, and anger for the way he'd shown her it was false. Yet she'd been so in love with him during their time in New York. It was hard to dismiss those feelings as mere fantasy, and yet she knew she had to.

And in a few hours she'd have to pretend they were real, that she still felt them. Her breath hitched at the thought.

'Does anyone know?' she asked and Antonios snapped his gaze to hers.

'Know what?'

'That we're…that we're separated.'

His mouth thinned. 'We're not, in actuality, legally separated, but no, no one knows.'

'Not any of your sisters?' she pressed. She thought of his three sisters: bossy Parthenope, with a husband and young son, social butterfly Xanthe, and Ava, her own age yet utterly different from her. She hadn't bonded with any of them during her time in Greece; his sisters had been possessive of Antonios, and had regarded his unexpected American bride with wary suspicion. They'd also, at Antonios's command, backed off from all the social responsibilities they'd fulfilled for him when he'd been a bachelor. A sign of respect, Antonios had told her, but Lindsay had seen the disdain in their covert glances. What they'd done so effortlessly, maintaining and even organizing the endless social whirl, had been nearly impossible for her. They'd realized that, even if Antonios hadn't.

And now she would have to face them again, suffer them giving her guarded looks, asking her questions, demanding answers…

She couldn't do this.

'Is the thought of my family so abhorrent to you?' Antonios demanded, and Lindsay stiffened.

'No—'

'Because,' he told her bluntly, 'you look like you're going to be sick.'

'I'm not going to be sick.' She took a deep breath. 'But the thought of seeing your family again does make me nervous, Antonios—'

'They did nothing but welcome you.' He cut her off with a shrug of his powerful shoulders.

She took a measured breath. 'Only at your command.'

He arched an eyebrow. 'Does that matter?'

Of course it does. She bit back the words, knowing they would only lead to pointless argument. 'I don't think they were pleased that you came home with such an unexpected bride,' she said after a moment. 'I think they would have preferred you to marry someone of your own background.' A good Greek wife...the kind of wife she hadn't, and never could have, been.

'Perhaps,' Antonios allowed, his tone still dismissive, 'but they still accepted you because they knew I loved you.'

Lindsay didn't answer. It was clear Antonios hadn't seen how suspicious his sisters had been of her. And while they *had* accepted her on the surface, there had still been plenty of sideways glances, speculative looks, even a few veiled comments. Lindsay had felt every single one, to the core.

Yet she wasn't about to explain that to Antonios now, not when he looked so fierce—fiercely determined to be in the right.

'You have nothing to say to that?' Antonios asked, and Lindsay shrugged, taking a sip of champagne. It tasted sour in her mouth.

'No, I don't.' Nothing he would be willing to hear, anyway.

His mouth tightened and he turned to stare out of the floor-to-ceiling windows overlooking the runway. Lindsay watched him covertly, despair and longing coursing through her in equal measures.

She told herself she shouldn't feel this much emotion. It had been her choice to leave, and really they'd known so little of each other. Three months together, that was all. Not enough time to fall in love, much less stay there.

She was a mathematician; she believed in reason, in fact, in logic. Love at almost first sight didn't figure in her world view. Her research had shown the almost mystical relationships between numbers, but she and Antonios weren't numbers, and even though her heart had once cried out differently her head insisted they couldn't have actually loved each other.

'Maybe you never really loved me, Antonios,' she said quietly, and he jerked back in both shock and affront.

'Is that why you left? Because you didn't think I loved you?' he asked in disbelief.

'I'm trying to explain how I felt,' Lindsay answered evenly. 'Since you seem determined to draw an explanation from me, even if you say you don't want one.'

'So you've convinced yourself I didn't love you.' He folded his arms, his face settling into implacable lines.

'I don't think either of us had enough time to truly love or even know each other,' Lindsay answered. 'We only knew each other a week—'

'Three months, Lindsay.'

'A week before we married,' she amended. 'And it was a week out of time, out of reality...' Which was what had made it so sweet and so precious. A week away from the little life she'd made for herself in New York—a life that had been both prison and haven. A week away from being Lindsay Douglas, brilliant mathematician and complete recluse. A week of being seen in an entirely new way—as someone who was interesting and beautiful and *normal*.

'It may have only been a week,' Antonios said, 'but I knew you. At least, I thought I knew you. But perhaps you are right, because the woman I thought I knew wouldn't have left me the way you did.'

'Then you didn't really know me,' Lindsay answered, and Antonios swung round to stare at her, his eyes narrowed.

'Is there something you're not telling me?'

'I…' She drew a deep breath. She could tell him now, explain everything, yet what good would it do? Their marriage was over. Her leaving him had brought about its end. But before she could even think about summoning the courage to confess, he had turned away from her again.

'It doesn't matter,' he answered. 'I don't care.'

Lindsay sagged back against her seat, relief and disappointment flooding her as she told herself it was better this way. It had to be.

Antonios sat in his first-class seat, his glass of complimentary champagne untouched, as his mind seethed with questions he'd never thought to ask himself before. And he shouldn't, he knew, ask them now. It didn't matter what Lindsay's reasons had been for leaving, or whether they'd truly known and loved each other or not. Any possibility between them had ended with her two-sentence email.

Dear Antonios,
I'm sorry, but I cannot come back to Greece. Our marriage was a mistake. Lindsay.

When he'd first read the email, he'd thought it was a joke. His brain simply hadn't been able to process what she was telling him; it had seemed so absurd. Only forty-eight hours before, he'd made love to her half the night long and she'd clung to him until morning, kissed him with passion and gentleness when she'd said goodbye.

And she'd known she was leaving him *then*?

He hadn't wanted to believe it, had started jumping to outrageous, nonsensical conclusions. Someone else had written the email. A jealous rival or a desperate relative? He'd cast them both in roles in a melodrama that had no basis in reality.

The reality was his phone call to Lindsay that same day, and her flat voice repeating what she'd told him in the email. Maybe he'd been the one to hang up, but only because she'd been so determined not to explain herself. Not to say anything at all, except for her wretched party line. That their marriage was a mistake.

Disbelief had given way to anger, to a cold, deep rage the like of which he'd never felt before, not even when he'd realized the extent of his father's desperate deception. He'd *loved* her. He'd brought her into the bosom of his family, showered her with clothes and jewels. He'd given her his absolute loyalty, had presented her to his shocked family as the choice of his heart, even though they'd only known each other for a week. He'd shown how devoted he was to her in every way possible, and she'd said it was all a *mistake*?

He turned to her now, took in her pale face, the soft, vulnerable curve of her cheek, a tendril of white-blonde hair resting against it. When he'd first seen her in New York City, he'd been utterly enchanted. She'd looked ethereal, like a winter fairy, with her pale hair and silvery eyes. He'd called her his Snow Queen.

'Did you intend to leave me permanently,' he asked suddenly, his voice too raw for his liking or comfort, 'when you said goodbye to me in Greece?' When she'd kissed him, her slender arms wrapped around his neck, had she known?

She didn't turn from the window, but he felt her body tense. 'Does it matter?'

'It does to me.' Even though it shouldn't. But maybe he needed to ask these questions, despite what he'd said. Perhaps he would find some peace amidst all the devastation if he understood, even if only in part, why Lindsay had acted as she had. Perhaps then he could let go of his anger and hurt, and move on. Alone.

She let out a tiny sigh. 'Then, yes. I did.'

Her words were like a fist to his gut. To his heart. 'So you lied to me.'

'I never specified when I was coming back,' she said, her voice tired and sad.

'You never said you were going. You acted like you loved me.' He turned away from her, not wanting her to see the naked emotion he could feel on his face. She wasn't even looking at him, but he still felt exposed. Felt the raw pain underneath the anger. Still, one word squeezed its way out of his throat. 'Why?'

She didn't answer.

'Why, Lindsay?' he demanded. 'Why didn't you tell me you were planning to leave, that you were unhappy—?'

'I tried telling you the truth but you never heard it,' she said wearily. 'You never listened.'

'What are you talking about?' Antonios demanded. 'You never once said you were unhappy—'

Lindsay shook her head. 'I don't want to go into it, Antonios. It's pointless. If you want an explanation, it's this: I never really loved you.'

He blinked, reeling from the coldly stated fact even as he sought to deny it. 'Why did you marry me, then?' he asked when he trusted his voice to sound even. Emotionless.

'Because I thought I loved you. I convinced myself what we had was real.' She turned to him, her eyes blazing with what he realized, to his own shock, was anger or maybe grief. 'Can't you see how it was for me? My father had died only a few weeks before. I went to New York because I wanted to escape my life, escape my loneliness and grief. I wandered around the city like a lost soul, still feeling so desperately sad and yet wanting to be enchanted by all the beauty. And then you saw me and you told me *you* were lost, and when I looked in your eyes it felt like you were seeing me—a me I hadn't even known existed until that moment.'

She sank back against her seat, out of breath, her face pale, her shoulders rising and falling in agitation. Antonios's mind spun emptily for a few stunned seconds before he finally managed, his voice hoarse, 'And that was real.'

'No, it wasn't, Antonios. It was a fairy tale. It was playing at being in love. It was red roses and dancing until midnight and penthouse suites at luxury hotels. It was wonderful and magical, but it wasn't *real*.'

'Just because something is exciting—'

'Real was coming to Greece—' she cut across him flatly '—and discovering what your life was like there. Real was feeling like I was drowning every day and you never even noticed.' She bit her lip and then turned towards the window; he realized she'd turned to hide her own emotion, just as he'd tried to hide his. The anger that had been a cold, hard ball inside him started to soften, but he didn't know what emotion replaced it. He felt confused and unsteady, as if someone had given him a hard push, had scattered all his tightly held beliefs and resolutions.

'Lindsay…' He put a hand on her shoulder, conscious once again of how small and fragile she seemed. 'I don't understand.'

She let out a choked laugh and dashed quickly at her eyes. 'I know, Antonios, and you never did. But it's too late now, for both of us. You know that, so let's just stop this conversation.'

A stewardess came by to take their untouched champagne glasses and prepare them for take-off. Lindsay took the opportunity to shrug his hand from her shoulder and wipe the traces of tears from her eyes.

When she turned to look at him, her face was composed and carefully blank. 'Please, let's just get through this flight.'

He nodded tersely, knowing now was not the time to demand answers. And really, what answer could Lindsay give? What on earth could she mean, that she'd been drowning? He'd taken her to his home. His family had welcomed her. He'd given her every comfort, every luxury. Just the memory of how she'd responded to his touch, how her body had sung in tune to his, made a bewildered fury rise up in him again. What the hell was she talking about—*drowning*?

And if she truly had been unhappy, why hadn't she ever told him?

CHAPTER THREE

As soon as the sign for seat belts blinked off, Lindsay unbuckled hers and slipped past Antonios. She hurried to the first-class bathroom, barely taking in the spacious elegance, the crystal vase of roses by the sink. She placed her hands flat on the marble countertop and breathed slowly, in and out, several times, until her heart rate started to slow.

Telling him that much, confessing to even just a little of how she'd felt, had depleted every emotional resource she had. She had no idea how she was going to cope with seven more days of being with Antonios, of pretending to his family.

She pressed her forehead against the cool glass of the mirror and continued with her deep, even breathing. She couldn't panic now. Not like she had back in Greece, when the panic had taken over her senses, had left her feeling like an empty shell, a husk of a person, barely able to function.

How had Antonios not seen that? How had he not heard? Maybe her attempts at trying to explain had been feeble, but he hadn't wanted to listen. Hadn't been able to hear. And he still couldn't.

She'd refuse to discuss it any more, Lindsay resolved.

She couldn't defuse his anger and she wouldn't even try. Survival was all she was looking for now, for the next week. For Daphne's sake. Her mother-in-law deserved that much, and Lindsay wanted to see her again and pay her respects.

But heaven help her, it was going to be hard.

Taking a deep breath, she splashed some water on her face and patted it dry. With one last determined look at her pale face in the mirror, she turned and headed back to their seats.

Their dinners had arrived while Lindsay was in the bathroom, and she gazed at the linen napkins and table-cloth, the crystal wine glasses and the silver-domed chafing dishes, remembering how they'd travelled like this to Greece. How luxurious and decadent she'd felt, lounging with Antonios as they ate, heads bent together, murmuring and laughing, buoyant with happiness.

Utterly different from the silent tension that snapped between them now.

Antonios gestured to the dishes as she sat down. 'I didn't know what you wanted, so I ordered several things.'

'I'm sure it's all delicious.' And yet she had no appetite. Antonios lifted the lid on her meal and she stared at the beef, its rich red-wine sauce pooling on her plate, and twisted her napkin in her lap as her stomach rebelled at even the thought of eating.

'You are not hungry?' Antonios asked, one eyebrow arched, and Lindsay shook her head.

'No.'

'You should eat anyway. Keep up your strength.'

And God knew she needed what little she had. She picked up her fork and speared a piece of beef, putting it into her mouth and chewing mechanically. She couldn't taste anything.

Antonios noticed, one eyebrow lifting sardonically. 'Not good enough for you?' he queried, and she let out a little groan.

'Don't start, Antonios.'

'I can't help but wonder, when you had every luxury at your disposal, how you still managed to be so unhappy.'

'There is more to life than luxuries, Antonios. There's attention and support and care.' So much for her resolution not to talk about things.

'Are you saying I didn't give you those?' Antonios demanded.

'No, you didn't. Not the way I needed.'

'You never told me what you needed.'

'I tried,' she said wearily. She felt too tired to be angry any more, even though the old hurt still burrowed deep.

'When? When did you try?'

'Time and time again. I told you I was uncomfortable at all the parties, never mind playing hostess—'

His brow wrinkled and Lindsay knew he probably didn't even remember the conversations she'd found so difficult and painful. 'I told you it would get better in time,' he finally answered. 'That you just needed to let people get to know you.'

'And I told you that was hard for me.'

He shrugged her words aside, just as he had every time she'd tried to tell him before. 'That's not a reason to leave a marriage, Lindsay.'

'Maybe not for you.'

'Are you actually saying you left me simply because you didn't like going to parties?'

'No.' She took a deep breath. 'I left you because you

never listened to me. Because you dumped me in Greece like another suitcase you'd acquired and never paid any attention to me again.'

'I had to work, Lindsay.'

'I know that. Trust me, Antonios, I know that. You worked all the time.'

'You never acted like it bothered you—'

She let out a laugh, high and shrill, the sound surprising them both. 'You never change, do you? I'm trying to tell you how I felt and you just keep insisting I couldn't have felt that way, that you never knew. This is why I left, Antonios.' She gestured to the space between them. 'Because the way we were together in real life, not in some fairy-tale bubble in New York, didn't work. It made me miserable—more miserable than I'd ever been before—and that's saying something.'

He frowned. 'What do you mean, that's saying something?'

'Never mind.' She'd never told him about her mother, and never would. Some things were better left unsaid, best forgotten. Not that she could ever forget the way her mother had left.

This isn't what I expected.

A hot lump of misery formed in Lindsay's throat and she swallowed hard, trying to dislodge it. She didn't want to cry, not on an aeroplane, not in front of Antonios.

'*Theos*, Lindsay, if you're not going to tell me things, how can I ever understand you?'

'I don't want you to understand me, Antonios,' she answered thickly. 'Not any more. All I want is a divorce. And I assume you want that, too.' She took a shaky breath. 'Do you really want to be with a wife who left you, who doesn't love you?'

Fire flashed in his eyes and she knew it had been a low and cruel blow. But if that was what it took to get Antonios to stop with his questions, then so be it.

He leaned forward, his eyes still flashing, his mouth compressed. 'Do I need to remind you of how much you loved me, Lindsay? Every night in New York. Every night we were together in Greece.'

And, despite her misery, desire still scorched through her at the memory. 'I'm not talking about in bed, Antonios.'

'Because you certainly responded to me there. Even when you were supposedly *drowning*.'

She closed her eyes, tried to fight the need his simply stated words caused to well up inside her. Sex had always been good between them, had been a respite from the misery she'd faced every day. Maybe that made her weak or wanton, to have craved a man who'd hurt her heart, but she had. From the moment they'd met, she had. And some treacherous part of her still craved him now.

She felt Antonios's hand on her knee and her eyes flew open. 'What—?'

'It didn't take much to make you melt,' he said softly, the words as caressing as his hand. His hand slid up her thigh, his fingers sure and seeking. Lindsay froze, trapped by his knowing gaze and his even more knowing hand. 'I knew just where to touch you, Lindsay. Just how to make you scream. You screamed my name, do you remember?'

Heat flooded through her and she had to fight to keep from responding to his caress. 'Don't,' she whispered, but even to her own ears her voice sounded feeble.

'Don't what?' he asked, his voice so soft and yet also menacing. 'Don't touch you?' He slid his hand higher, cupping her between her legs. Just the press of his hand through her jeans made her stifle a moan as desire pulsed insistently through her.

'What are you trying to prove, Antonios?' she forced out, willing her body to stay still and not respond to his caress. 'That I desire you? Fine. I do. I always did. It doesn't change anything.'

'It should,' Antonios said, and he popped the button on her jeans, slid his hand down so his fingers brushed between her thighs, the sensation of his skin against hers so exquisite she gasped aloud, her eyes fluttering closed. Couldn't keep her hips from lifting off the seat.

Lindsay pressed her head back against the seat, memories and feelings crashing through her. He always had known just how to touch her, to please her. He still did, but there was no love or even kindness behind his calculated caresses now. With what felt like superhuman effort she opened her eyes, stared straight into his triumphant face, and said the thing that she knew would hurt him most.

'You might make me come, Antonios, but you can't make me love you.'

He stared back at her, his expression freezing, and then in one deft movement he yanked his hand from her, unbuckled his seat belt and disappeared through the curtains.

Lindsay sagged back against her seat, her jeans still undone, her heart thudding, and swallowed a sob.

Antonios strode down the first-class aisle, feeling trapped and angry and even dirty. He shouldn't have treated Lindsay like that. Shouldn't have used her desire, her body against her.

Shouldn't have been that pathetic.

What had he been trying to prove? That she felt something for him? He stood in the alcove that separated the first class from business and stared out into the endless night. He didn't know what he'd been trying to do. He'd just been acting, or perhaps reacting, to Lindsay's assertion that she didn't love him. That their love hadn't been real.

It had sure as hell felt real to him. But he'd told her he didn't love her any more, and he needed that to be true. He'd made sure it was true for the last six months, even as he'd maintained the odious front to his family that their marriage was still going strong. He'd had to, for his mother's sake as well as his own pride.

Or maybe you were just actually hoping she'd come back. Fool that you are, you still wanted her back. Because you loved her. Because you made promises.

And was that what was driving him now? The desire, the need to have Lindsay back in his life? Back as his wife? Or was it an even more shameful reason, one born of revenge and pride? Did he want to make her hurt the way he had, to pay for the way she'd treated him?

Antonios had no answer but he was resolved to stop this pointless back and forth, demanding answers that he knew would never satisfy him. The reasons she'd given him for leaving their marriage had been ridiculous. Maybe he had been working too hard, maybe he'd even ignored her a little, but that didn't mean you just walked out.

Except to Lindsay it seemed it did, and nothing, no revenge or explanation, could change that cold fact. His mouth a grim line of resolution, Antonios headed back to their seats.

Lindsay had tidied herself in his absence, her jeans buttoned back up, her face turned towards the window. She didn't move as he slid into the seat next to her. Didn't even blink.

'I'm sorry,' Antonios said in a low voice. 'I shouldn't have done that.' Lindsay didn't answer, didn't acknowledge his words in any way. 'Lindsay...'

'Just leave me alone, Antonios,' she said, and to his shame her voice sounded quiet and sad. Broken. 'It's going to be hard enough pretending we're still in love for your family. Don't make it any harder.'

He watched her for a moment, part of him aching to reach out and tuck her hair behind her ear, trail his fingers along the smoothness of her cheek. Comfort her, when he'd been the cause of her pain and he knew she didn't want his comfort anyway.

'I'm going to sleep,' she said, and without looking at him she took off her shoes, reached for the eye mask. He watched as she reclined her seat and covered herself with a blanket, all with her face averted from him. Then she slid the eye mask down over her eyes and shut him out completely.

Lindsay lay rigid on her reclined seat, her eyes clenched shut under the mask as she tried to will herself to sleep and failed. She felt a seething mix of anger and regret, guilt and hurt. Her body still tingled from where Antonios had touched her. Her heart still ached.

Forget about it, she told herself yet again. *Just get through this week*. But how on earth was she going to get through this week, when being in Greece had been so hard even when Antonios had loved her, or thought he had, when she'd thought she'd loved him?

Now, with the anger and contempt she'd felt from Antonios, the hurt and frustration she felt herself...it was going to be impossible. Something had to change. To give.

She slipped off her eye mask, determined to confront him, only to find him gazing at her, the hard lines of his face softened by tenderness and despair, a look of such naked longing on his face that it stole her breath. She felt tears come to her eyes and everything in her ached with longing.

'Antonios...'

His face blanked immediately and his mouth compressed. 'Yes?'

'I...' What could she say? *Don't look at me like you hate me?* Just then, he hadn't. Just then he'd looked at her as if he still loved her.

But he doesn't. He doesn't even know you, not the real you. And you don't love him. You can't.

'Nothing,' she finally whispered.

'Get some sleep,' Antonios said, and turned his head away. 'It's going to be a long day tomorrow.'

They arrived in Athens at eleven in the morning, the air warm and dry, the sky hard and bright blue, everything so different from the damp early fall of upstate New York. Being here again brought back memories in flashes of pain: the limo Antonios had had waiting outside the airport, filled with roses. The way he'd held and kissed her all the way to his villa in the mountains of central Greece, and how enchanted Lindsay had been, still carried away by the fairy tale.

It wasn't until the limo had turned up the sweeping drive framed by plane trees with the huge, imposing villa and all of the other buildings in the distance that she'd realized she'd been dealing in fantasies…and that she and Antonios would not be living alone in some romantic hideaway. His mother, his brother, Leonidas, his two unmarried sisters, an army of staff and employees—everyone lived at Villa Marakaios, which wasn't the sweet little villa with terracotta tiles and painted wooden shutters that Lindsay had naively been imagining. No, it was a complex, a hive of industry, a *city*. And when she'd stepped out of the limo into that bright, bright sunshine, every eye of every citizen of that city had been trained on her.

Her worst nightmare.

She'd seen everyone lined up in front of the villa—the family, the friends, the employees and house staff, everyone staring at her, a few people whispering and even pointing—and she'd forgotten how to breathe.

Antonios had propelled her forward, one hand on her elbow, and she'd gone, her vision already starting to tunnel as her chest constricted and the panic took over.

She hadn't felt panic like that since she'd been a little girl, her mother's hand hard on her lower back, shoving her into a room full of academics.

Come on, Lindsay. Recite something for us.

Sometimes she'd managed to stumble through a poem her mother had made her memorize, and sometimes her brain had blanked and, with her mouth tightening in disappointment, her mother had dismissed her from the room.

After too many of those disappointments, she'd dismissed her from her life.

This isn't what I expected.

And, standing there in the glare of Greek sunshine,

Lindsay had felt it all come rushing back. The panic. The shortness of breath. The horrible, horrible feeling of every eye on her, every person finding her wanting. And she'd blacked out.

She'd come to consciousness inside the house, lying on a sofa, a cool cloth pressed to her head and a white-haired woman smiling kindly down at her.

'It's the sun, I'm sure,' Daphne Marakaios had said as she'd pressed the cloth to Lindsay's head. 'It's so strong here in the mountains.'

'Yes,' Lindsay had whispered. 'The sun.'

Now, as she slid into the passenger seat of Antonios's rugged SUV, having cleared customs and collected their luggage, she wondered if he even remembered how she'd fainted. He'd certainly been quick to accept it as her re-action to the sun, and she'd been too overwhelmed and shell-shocked to say any differently.

And she'd have to face his family again in just three hours. How on earth was she going to cope?

They drove out of Athens, inching through a mid-morning snarl of traffic, and then headed north on the National Highway towards Amfissa, the nearest town to Antonios's estate in the mountains.

With each mile they drove, Lindsay's panic increased. This time she knew what she was facing, and it would be so much worse. Now everyone would be suspicious, maybe even hostile. She could picture his sister Parthenope eyeing her with cool curiosity, her husband by her side and dark-haired, liquid-eyed little Timon clinging to her legs; Leonidas, Antonios's younger brother, giving her one of his sardonic looks; Ava and Xanthe, his younger sisters, eyeing her with sceptical curiosity, as if

they'd already decided she didn't belong. And the questions…she would have to answer so many questions…

'Antonios,' she said, his name little more than a croak,
and he glanced at her briefly before snapping his gaze
back to the road.

'What is it?'

She focused on her breathing, tried to keep it even.
'Would it…would it be possible for me to come to the
villa quietly? I mean, not have everyone waiting and…
I'd rather not see anyone at first.' *In. Out. In. Out.* With
effort she kept her breathing measured and her heart
rate started to slow. She could do this. She'd managed
to control her anxiety for most of her life. She could do
it now. She had to.

'The point,' Antonios returned, 'is for you to see people and be seen. No one thinks anything is wrong between us, Lindsay.'

But they would have guessed. Of course they would
have guessed. His siblings weren't stupid, and neither was
Daphne. Lindsay had been gone for six whole months
and then Antonios had come all the way to New York to
fetch her. Everyone would be wondering just what had
gone wrong between them.

'I understand,' Lindsay said, her eyes closed as she
pressed back against the seat and kept concentrating on
those deep, even breaths. 'But I'd rather not have everyone there when we arrive.'

'What am I meant to do? Send them away?'

She opened her eyes as she tried to suppress a stab
of irritation or even anger, wondering if he was deliberately being difficult. Or was he just obstinately obtuse,
as usual? 'No, of course not. I just don't want them all

lined up in front of the villa, waiting to welcome me.' Or not welcome, as the case well might be.

Antonios was silent for a moment, his gaze narrowed on the road in front of them, the sun glinting off the tarmac. 'You mean like last time.'

'Yes.'

'You fainted,' Antonios recalled slowly. 'When you got out of the car.'

So he had remembered. Just. 'Yes.'

Antonios's expression tightened and he turned back to the road. 'I'll see what I can do,' he said, and they didn't speak for the rest of the journey.

Two hours later they'd left the highway for the narrow, twisting lane that curved its way between the mountains of Giona and Parnassus. They came around a bend and Villa Marakaios lay before them, nestled in a valley between the mountains, its many whitewashed buildings gleaming brightly under the afternoon sun.

Antonios drove down the twisting road towards the villa, his eyes narrowed against the sun, his mouth a hard, grim line.

As they drove through the gates he turned to the left, surprising her, for the front of the villa, with its many gleaming steps and impressive portico, was before them. Instead, Antonios drove around the back of the complex to a small whitewashed house with an enclosed courtyard and latticed shutters painted a cheerful blue. It looked, Lindsay thought in weary bemusement, like the villa she'd once imagined in her naive daydreams. A honeymoon house.

'We can stay here,' Antonios said tersely, and he killed the engine. 'It's used as a guesthouse, but it's empty now.'

'What?' Lindsay stared at him in surprise. Last time

they'd stayed in the main villa with all the family and staff; only Leonidas had his own place. Since his father's death, Antonios had been appointed the CEO of Marakaios Enterprises and essentially lord of the manor.

Now he shrugged and got out of the car. 'It will make it easier for us to maintain the pretence if we are not so much in the public eye.' He went around to the boot of the car for their cases, not looking at her as he added, 'And perhaps it will be easier for you.'

Lindsay stared at him, his dark head bent as he hefted their suitcases and then started walking towards the villa. He was being thoughtful, she realized. And he'd given credence to what she'd told him, if just a little.

'Thank you,' she murmured and with a wary, uncertain hope burgeoning inside her she followed him into the villa.

CHAPTER FOUR

ANTONIOS PUT THE suitcases in the villa's one bedroom, tension knotting between his shoulders. Coming back to Villa Marakaios always gave him a sense of impending responsibility and pressure, the needs and concerns of the family and business descending on him like a shroud the moment he drove through the gates. But it was a shroud he wore willingly and a duty he accepted with pride, no matter what the cost.

He could hear Lindsay moving behind him, walking with the quiet grace and dignity she'd always possessed.

'Why don't you rest?' he said as he turned around. Lindsay stood in the doorway, her pale hair floating around her face in a silvery-golden cloud, her eyes wide and clear, yet also troubled. 'Everyone is coming for dinner tonight,' he continued. 'I need to see to some business. I'll come back before we have to leave. But I suppose you don't mind me working all hours now, do you?'

The less they saw each other, the better. Yet he still couldn't keep a feeling of bitterness or maybe even hurt from needling him when she nodded, and wordlessly he walked past her and out of the villa.

He walked across the property to the offices housed separately from the family's living quarters, in a rambling whitewashed building overlooking the Marakaios groves that stretched to the horizon, rows upon rows of stately olive trees with their gnarled branches, each neatly pruned and tended, now just coming into flower.

He paused for a moment on the threshold of the building, steeling himself for the demands that would assail him the moment he walked in the door. Ten years after his father had told him of the extent of Marakaios Enterprises' debt, he'd finally brought the business to an even keel—but it had taken just about everything he had, both emotionally and physically.

Now he greeted his PA, Alysia, accepted a sheaf of correspondence and then strode into his office, perversely glad, for once, to immerse himself in paperwork and answering emails and not think of Lindsay.

Except he *did* think of Lindsay; she was like a ghost inside his mind, haunting his thoughts with both the good memories and the bad. The week in New York—that intense, incredible week when they'd shared everything.

And yet nothing, because he was realizing afresh just how much of a stranger she was.

In New York he'd thought he'd known her. She'd told him about her research, and he'd watched how animated she became when she talked about twin primes and Fermat's Last Theorem and Godel's proof for the existence of God. He hadn't really understood any of it, but he'd loved seeing her passion for her subject, intelligence and interest shining in her silver-grey eyes.

She'd told him about her father, too, who had died just a few weeks before they met. She'd cried then and he'd comforted her, drawing her into his arms, fitting her body around his as he'd tenderly wiped the tears from her face.

He thought about the first time they'd made love, how

her eyes had gone so wide when he'd slid inside her and she'd said in wonder, 'It's like the most perfect equation,' which had made him laugh even as pleasure overtook them both. With Lindsay he'd felt happier than he ever had before. He'd felt *right*, complete in a way that made him realize just how much he'd been missing.

And then he recalled the emptiness that had swooped through him when he'd talked to her on the phone and she'd told him in that lifeless voice that it was all a mistake.

'Welcome back.'

Antonios looked up from his laptop to see his brother, Leonidas, lounging in the doorway of his office. Fourteen months younger, half an inch taller and a little leaner, Leonidas had been mistaken more than once for his twin. They'd been close as children, united in various boyish escapades, but since Antonios had become CEO the gulf between them had widened, and Antonios's vow of secrecy to his father made it impossible to bridge.

No one is to know, Antonios. No one but you. I couldn't bear it.

'Thank you,' he said now with a nod to Leonidas. He tried to offer his brother a smile, but the memories of Lindsay that had assailed him just now were still too poignant, too painful.

'Good trip?' Leonidas asked, one eyebrow cocked, and not for the first time Antonios wondered how much his brother knew, or at least guessed, about him and Lindsay.

'Fine,' he said briskly. 'Short. I thought about stopping in New York to see the new clients but there was no time.'

'I could do it,' Leonidas offered and Antonios shrugged.

'I'll travel back to New York next week, with Lindsay. I'll see them then.'

Leonidas's expression turned neutral as he gave a careless nod. 'So you're both returning to America in just one week?'

'Lindsay has research to finish.'

'I thought she could do it here.'

Antonios shrugged, hating the deception he was forced to maintain. First with his father, and now this. He'd accused Lindsay of lying to him, but he was the greater liar.

Soon, he told himself. Soon enough he would come clean. All too soon, when his mother was past knowing. The thought made him close his eyes briefly, and he snapped them open. 'She has to wrap up things with her house,' he said dismissively. 'You know how it is.'

Although of course Leonidas didn't know how it was. He was a determined bachelor and besides his private villa here he kept an apartment in Athens. Their father had appointed him as Head of European Operations before he'd died, and since then Leonidas had spent most of his time travelling to their various clients in Europe, working on new accounts because Antonios didn't want him to see the old ones. Couldn't let him know how close they'd come to losing it all.

'So she'll return when?' Leonidas asked and Antonios forced himself to shrug.

'We haven't decided on a date,' he answered coolly. 'Now, don't you have work to do? I just saw an email from the Lyon restaurant group. They're concerned about their supply.'

'I'm on it,' Leonidas answered, his voice terse, and he turned from the office.

Antonios sank back in his chair, raking his hands

through his hair. Maintaining this deception was going to be even harder than he'd realized. And when he came clean...he burned to think of the disbelief and pity he'd face from his siblings.

Burned to think that it had come to this, and why? *Because Lindsay never loved you. And you didn't know her well enough to love her like you thought you did.*

Grimacing, he turned back to his laptop. He'd wasted enough time thinking about Lindsay today.

Lindsay managed to sleep for a couple of hours, waking muzzy-headed and disorientated to the sound of someone knocking on the door.

She stumbled out of bed, reaching for a robe hanging from the bathroom door to cover herself; it had been too warm to sleep in anything but her underwear. A maid whose face she vaguely recognized was standing outside, a man behind her carrying several suitcases.

'What...?' Lindsay began, confused and still only half awake.

'Kyrios Marakaios wanted your clothes to be brought here,' the maid explained in halting English. Lindsay knew only a few words of Greek. 'He asked for me to help put them away.'

'Oh...thank you.' She stepped back to let the woman in, and then watched uncomfortably as the man deposited the suitcases in the bedroom before leaving and the maid began unpacking the clothes she'd barely worn and then hanging them in the walk-in closet.

Lindsay offered to help but the woman insisted she'd do it herself, so she left the bedroom and went to the living area of the villa, gazing through the sliding glass doors that led to a private pool. If she were in the deep end of that thing, she thought disconsolately, she couldn't be more out of her depth.

Dinner, she knew, would be in just a few hours. She needed to get ready, and not just her clothes and make-up. She needed to prepare emotionally. Mentally.

Lindsay made herself some tea and took it outside to the pool area, sitting in one of the loungers and cradling the warmth of the mug between her hands as she closed her eyes and focused on her breathing. She pictured the ornate dining room where the family gathered for more formal meals, imagined each chair, each face, and focused on keeping her breathing slow and even.

Visualization, her therapist had told her, was meant to be helpful when trying to manage new or difficult situations. And she'd become good enough at it that she could picture it all and still stay calm.

It was when she was actually *in* the situation, facing all those people, all their stares and questions, that she started to panic.

'What are you doing?' Lindsay's eyes flew open and she saw Antonios standing by the gate that led out to the drive, his eyebrows drawn together in a frown. 'You sound like you're hyperventilating.'

'No, just breathing.' She felt a blush heat her cheeks and she took a sip of tea. 'Trying to relax.' And not succeeding very well.

Antonios's mouth twisted as he glanced around at the pool, the water sparkling in the bright sunlight, the whitewashed villa looking cool and pristine, everything beautiful and luxurious. Lindsay braced herself for some cutting remark about how difficult she must find it to relax in such a paradise. But to her relief he said nothing, just nodded towards the villa, his mouth tight.

'You should get dressed,' he said as he walked past her. 'We need to be at the main house in an hour.'

The maid had gone when Lindsay went back inside, and she spent a long time in the huge, sumptuous shower, as if she could postpone the inevitable moment when she faced Antonios's family.

He'd told her it was casual, which meant full make-up and a nice dress. The Marakaios family didn't do casual the way she'd ever understood it, and that just added to her stress and tension.

An hour later she stared at her reflection in the bath-room mirror, wiped icy palms down the sides of the lav-ender linen shift that Antonios had bought for her in New York. She remembered the joy of trying on new clothes, parading them for him, laughing at his deliber-ately lascivious expressions. An ache of longing swept through her and she leaned her forehead against the mir-ror. They'd had so much fun together, for such a short while. No matter if it hadn't been real or lasting, she still missed that. Missed him, and missed the woman she'd been with him, before he'd taken her back to Greece. Be-fore everything had gone wrong.

A sharp knock sounded on the bathroom door. 'Are you ready?' Antonios called. 'We need to go.'

'Okay.' Lindsay lifted her head from the mirror and stared at her reflection once more. Her heart was starting to beat fast, her chest to hurt, and she had that curious light-headed sensation that always preceded a full-blown panic attack.

Breathe, Lindsay. You can do this. You have to do this.

She gripped the edge of the sink, focused on her breathing and willed her heart rate to slow.

'Lindsay...' Antonios called, impatience edging his

voice, and, after a few more agonized seconds of trying to keep the panic under control, she straightened and opened the door.

'I'm ready,' she said as she walked out of the bathroom. She was feeling light-headed enough to have to focus on her walking, the way a drunk person would. She didn't think she was very convincing because Antonios regarded her silently for a moment. She didn't look at him, just kept her chin held high, her shoulders back. *Breathe.*

'You look lovely,' Antonios said finally. 'I remember that dress.'

'Thank you.' It was hard to get words out of her throat, but she just about managed it. 'Why don't we go?'

She started out of the villa and Antonios followed. She stumbled slightly on the gravel drive and he took her arm, exclaiming as he did so.

'You're freezing.'

She always went cold when she had a panic attack, a result of her blood pressure dropping, but she wasn't about to explain that now. 'I'm fine—'

He stared at her for one long, fathomless moment, his arm gripping hers. He felt warm and steady and strong and the temptation to lean into him was nearly unbearable. She stood straighter.

'Let me get you a wrap. The nights are chilly here.'

'Fine.' Not that a wrap would actually help.

He came back a few minutes later with a matching lavender pashmina and draped it over her shoulders. 'Thank you,' Lindsay murmured, and they kept walking.

The quarter mile to the main villa felt like a trek across the Sahara, and yet Lindsay would have willingly walked it forever rather than face what was inside.

All too soon they had arrived; Lindsay paused before the huge double doors that led to the enormous marble foyer with its sweeping double staircase. Antonios greeted the manservant who opened the front doors, and then several other servants who circulated through the foyer, trays of canapés and glasses of champagne held aloft.

Definitely a casual dinner, then.

Lindsay managed to murmur a few hellos, offer some smiles. After a few minutes Antonios led her into the living room where his family waited; Lindsay saw his brother, Leonidas, by the window, Parthenope sitting on a sofa, her lips pursed and her eyes narrowed as she stared at her. Xanthe and Ava stood together by the window, heads bent together. Lindsay watched as one of them whispered something to the other.

Her chest constricted so much it felt as if she were having a heart attack. She stopped where she stood, flung one hand out to brace herself against the doorway as Antonios walked into the room to greet his family.

'Lindsay,' Daphne Marakaios said and, rising from her chair, she walked towards Lindsay, her arms outstretched.

Lindsay accepted the woman's embrace, felt how much thinner and more fragile she seemed from the last time she'd seen her. 'Daphne,' she murmured, and pressed a kiss against each of her mother-in-law's wrinkled cheeks.

Daphne eased back, her gaze sweeping over Lindsay. 'It's so good to have you back, my dear.' She squeezed her hands. 'I hope it is good to be back?'

The questioning lilt in Daphne's voice made Lindsay wonder just how much her mother-in-law knew about the state of her son's marriage.

'Of course it is,' she murmured. It was good to see

Daphne again at least, and she hoped her mother-in-law knew it.

'Come sit by me,' Daphne instructed, and led Lindsay to a sofa in the corner of the room. She was grateful for her mother-in-law's attention; it kept everyone else from besieging her with questions, even if she felt their speculative stares from across the room. Still, she'd got one of the worst parts of the evening over with: the grand entrance that being with Antonios had always entailed, that had always reminded her of those unbearable evenings with her mother's friends.

Daphne chatted with her briefly, asking surprisingly pertinent questions about her doctoral research; in Lindsay's experience most people's eyes glazed over when she started talking about the abstract details of number theory, but Daphne seemed genuinely interested.

And talking about mathematics was the most calming thing Lindsay could have done; explaining the impossible and even mystical beauty of transcendental numbers made her breathing slow and her body relax.

From across the room she caught Antonios glowering at her and her mind blanked.

'I find your work so fascinating, my dear,' Daphne said and Lindsay realized she'd just stopped speaking, maybe even in the middle of a sentence. 'You have such a lively mind, such a fierce intelligence.'

Lindsay smiled, or tried to, because the sincerity in Daphne's voice made her suddenly feel near tears. If she'd stayed, perhaps if she'd just tried harder, she could have developed a relationship with this woman that would have gone a long way to addressing the absence of a mother in her own life since the age of nine. Maybe she would have made friends with Antonios's sisters, rather than having them now staring at her stonily from across the room.

And just like that the panic swamped her again. She pressed one hand to her chest to ease the pain, and Daphne laid a hand on her arm.

'Lindsay, are you all right?'

'I'm fine.' Those two words had become her mantra. Lindsay forced herself to drop her hand from her chest and smile at Daphne. 'Sorry, just tired from the flight. But how are you? Antonios told me—'

Daphne smiled wryly. 'Then you know I'm not so well. But I've lived a good life. I have only a few regrets.'

Which was, Lindsay thought, an extraordinarily honest thing to say. Most people defiantly declared they had no regrets whatsoever.

And as for her? Did she regret marrying Antonios? Loving him, even if it hadn't lasted? Leaving him? All of it?

'Shall we go into the dining room?' Antonios asked. He'd crossed the room without her realizing it and now stood in front of her, his smile perfectly in place although the expression in his eyes was veiled. In his dark suit and crisp white shirt and navy silk tie he looked impossibly beautiful, everything about him reminding her of how happy she'd been with him. For such a little while.

Lindsay stood up and took his arm, grateful for the support even though she could feel Antonios's tension. His forearm was like a band of iron under her hand.

It wasn't until everyone was seated at the dinner table, the first course served, that the questions started. The interrogation.

Antonios's sister Parthenope began it. 'So, Lindsay, how was America?'

'Fine. Cold.' Lindsay dabbed her mouth with her napkin, pressing it against her lips as she took a deep breath.

'You were gone a long time,' Xanthe chimed in, her eyes narrowed, mouth pursed. They were suspicious of her. Angry, too. Antonios might not have told his family what had happened, but they clearly guessed some of it.

'Yes…I had to continue my research.' She forced herself to return her napkin to her lap, pick up her fork. Her knuckles shone white as she clenched it and she made herself relax her grip.

'I thought you could do this research anywhere.' This from Ava, who was the same age as her, twenty-six, yet now looked at her as if she were an alien and inferior species—a wife who had left her husband to do mathematical research. A freak.

'I can,' she answered, her voice seeming to echo in her own ears. Her chest was starting to hurt again. 'But I had a few things I had to wrap up in New York.'

'Then you're finished there? You won't be returning?' Parthenope again, her voice sharper this time, as she shot Antonios a concerned glance.

Lindsay swallowed. And swallowed again. She couldn't think of anything to say. She didn't want to lie, but telling the truth was just as unpalatable an option and would only invite more questions. More disapproval. She could feel everyone's stares on her and her vision started to swim.

'Lindsay's not quite done in New York,' Antonios said, his tone carefully bland. 'But she knows her home is here.'

At this Parthenope nodded approvingly because, unlike Lindsay, she was a good Greek wife and would never even imagine leaving her husband for six whole months.

Lindsay blinked back the dizziness and reached for her wine glass, but her hands were so icy and damp with sweat that the glass slipped from her fingers and fell to the tiled floor, shattering into a million pieces and splashing red wine all over the pristine white tablecloth and her dress.

A ringing silence ensued as a staff member sprang to attention to clean it up. Lindsay stared at the mess in horror, felt her head go light again as everyone's gaze swung to her and the enormity of the situation and just how much of it she couldn't handle crashed over her once again.

'I'm sorry,' she managed through her constricted throat.

'Not to worry, my dear,' Daphne said. 'It could happen to anyone.'

But it happened to me. Lindsay clenched her hands in her lap, dug her nails into her palms and hoped the pain would distract her from the full-fledged panic attack she could feel coming on. Dizziness. Trouble breathing. Chest pain.

She'd tried so many different things to control the attacks while she'd been here. Breathing techniques, reciting prime numbers in her head, the desperate measure of alcohol. Nothing worked, and pain didn't either.

Spots danced before her eyes.

'Excuse me,' she murmured, and rose unsteadily from the table. She could see Antonios frowning at her but she was past caring. If she didn't leave now, she'd embarrass herself—and him—far more than this.

Somehow she made it to the bathroom. She doubled over the sink, rested her cheek against the cool porcelain. Her head spun and her chest hurt.

After a few long moments the dizziness thankfully receded and she started to feel a little better. She washed her face and blotted her dress as best she could. She looked, she realized, terrible. Her dress had a large red stain on the front from the wine. She couldn't go back into the dining room like this.

She sank onto the floor, drew her knees up to her chest and wondered whether she could spend the rest of the night—the rest of her life—in the bathroom.

A knock, an impatient *rat-a-tat-tat*, sounded on the door. 'Lindsay, are you in there?'

Lindsay pressed her face against her knees. 'Go away, Antonios.'

'Open the door.'

She almost laughed at that. He was like a bulldozer, steamrolling over everyone and everything to get what he wanted. She'd been charmed by his determination when they'd met in New York; no one had ever showed such an interest in and desire for her.

Now she just felt tired. 'Please go away.'

'Are you all right?'

This time she did laugh, wearily. 'No.'

Antonios jiggled the door and then pushed his shoulder against it. The door sprang open, and Lindsay wondered if *anything* could hold out against her husband.

He swore at the sight of her sitting hunched on the floor, and then crouched down so they were at eye level and peered into her face. '*Theos*…what's wrong, Lindsay? Are you ill?'

'No, I'm not ill, Antonios.' She straightened, every muscle aching from the exertion of the panic attack and her own futile resistance to it.

'Then what—?'

And suddenly she was so very tired of it—of him not understanding, of her trying, perversely and at the same time, to explain and to hide. He wanted to know? Fine. He could know. Everything. And she didn't even care whether he believed her or not any more. 'I was having a panic attack,' she told him shortly. She washed her hands and face in the sink, even though she'd already done so once. At least it was something to do.

'A panic attack…' Antonios was staring at her in amazement.

'Yes, a panic attack. I suffer from a social anxiety disorder. Being in strange situations, or being the centre of attention, can cause me to panic.'

Antonios continued to gape at her. 'And you…suffered from this during our marriage?'

'Yes.'

'But you never—'

'Said? I tried, Antonios. I tried to explain, but you never wanted to listen.'

'I would have listened if you'd told me something like that!'

She eyed him wearily. 'Are you sure about that?'

He stared back at her, his expression unreadable. 'Let me make my apologies to my family,' he said finally. 'Will you be all right for a few minutes?'

'I'll be—'

'Fine? I'm not buying that one any more.' His voice was flat, toneless. 'Will you be all right?'

Lindsay let out a shuddering breath. 'Yes.'

Antonios stalked towards the dining room, fury coursing through him, although what or whom he was angry with he couldn't say. Wasn't ready to think about. He had a terrible feeling it was himself.

Six questioning faces turned to him as he came through the double doors. His mother, his brother, his three sisters, Parthenope's husband. Everyone had witnessed Lindsay stumble out of the room like a drunken bat out of hell, and the ensuing silence had been appalling.

'Lindsay's not feeling well,' he told them all. He kept his voice brisk, his face neutral. 'I'm taking her back to our villa.'

Daphne half rose from her seat, her face drawn in a frown of concern. 'Is there something I can do, Antonios?'

'No. She'll be—' *fine* stuck in his throat '—she needs to rest,' he said instead, and turned from the room.

Lindsay was exactly where he'd left her, in the bathroom, her hands braced against the sink, her hair falling forward to cover her face. 'We'll take a car back,' he said and she shook her head.

'I'm not an invalid. I can walk.'

'Even so.' She looked terrible—pale and sweaty, her hair tangled about her face. Seeing her like this made everything inside Antonios tighten like a giant fist. He wanted to protect her, to take care of her, to shout at her.

Why didn't you tell me?

It was a howl of anguish and anger, of guilt and grief, and he swallowed it all down. There would be time for that later, to ask questions and demand answers. Right now he just needed to take care of Lindsay.

He took her arm and led her from the bathroom, guiding and sheltering her, to the front steps of the villa where the car he'd arranged waited, one of the staff acting as driver.

He opened the door and helped her inside the car; she didn't resist. And then, with neither of them speaking, they drove off into the night.

CHAPTER FIVE

As soon as they were back at the villa, Antonios strode to the en suite bathroom and starting running the tub. Lindsay stood in the doorway of the bathroom, exhausted and emotionally drained, knowing Antonios would expect answers and pretty sure she didn't have the resources right now to give them.

'Have a bath,' he said, and dumped half a bottle of expensive bath foam into the tub. 'Then we'll talk.'

A bath sounded heavenly and Lindsay was grateful for the reprieve from any conversation. Antonios left the room and she stripped out of her ruined dress and sank into the steaming water frothing with bubbles, feeling utterly overwhelmed.

For the three months of their marriage she'd kept it together better than that. She'd hidden it better, at least from his family, and even from Antonios. Now, the very first day, the first occasion she'd had to panic, she had. Utterly. She wondered what Antonios's family thought of her now. What he thought of her. She wished she was too tired to care, but the truth was she hated—had always hated—the thought of him knowing her weakness. It was what had made it so difficult to tell him in the first place. Now she felt a fist of fear clench in her stomach at the thought that he knew, even though it didn't matter. They didn't have a relationship any more.

After half an hour soaking in the tub she felt a little better, although wanting nothing but to sleep, and she got out and swathed herself in one of the huge terry-cloth robes hanging from the door. She combed her hair and brushed her teeth and, with nothing left to do, she opened the door, throwing back her shoulders as she went to face Antonios.

He was sprawled on the sofa in the living room, a tumbler of whisky in one hand, the moonlight streaming through the sliding glass doors washing him in silver.

He turned his head to gaze at her fathomlessly as she came into the room; Lindsay braced herself for the questions. The accusations. He spoke only one word.

'Why?'

His voice was so bleak and desolate that Lindsay had to fight back an ache of regret and sorrow. 'Why what?' she asked and he took a long swallow of whisky, shaking his head.

'Why didn't you tell me?'

She sank onto the sofa opposite him. 'I've told you, I tried—'

'I don't recall ever hearing you mention agoraphobia, Lindsay.'

She plucked at a loose thread on the dressing gown. 'Maybe I didn't get that far.'

'And why didn't you? If I'd had any idea of how much you were suffering, I might have understood more. Listened more—'

'Listened more? You didn't listen at all, Antonios. You left for a business trip two days after we arrived in Greece.'

His mouth tightened. 'It was necessary.'

'Of course it was.'

'You never protested—'

'Actually, I did. I asked why you had to leave so soon, and you told me it was important. You practically patted my head before you left. Why didn't you just hand me a lollipop while you were at it?' The words surprised her, yet they felt right. Antonios's gaze narrowed.

'Are you implying that I was patronizing towards you?'

'Oh, well done, you get a gold star. Yes, that's exactly what I'm implying.' The anger she felt now took her by surprise. She was so used to feeling guilty and ashamed about her own deficiency, but this felt cleaner. Stronger. And she needed to be strong.

Antonios was silent for a long moment. 'I didn't mean to be patronizing,' he said at last. 'But I don't see how that has anything to do with you not telling me—'

'Don't you? Can't you see how it might be just a little bit difficult to tell your husband of one week that you have a debilitating condition when all he does is tell you over and over everything is going to be fine, just give it time, and insists you have nothing to worry about?'

'In normal circumstances, that would be true—'

'You think so? You think most wives get whisked off to a country where they don't speak the language—'

'Everyone in my family speaks English.'

'The staff don't. The staff I was meant to *supervise* for a dinner party less than a week after I arrived!'

The skin around Antonios's mouth went white. 'I thought I was giving you an honour, as mistress of the household, to plan—'

'Yet you never asked if I *wanted* to be mistress of

your household. Never asked me what I wanted from life, from marriage.' She shook her head, weariness replacing her anger. 'Perhaps I should have spoken up more, Antonios. Perhaps I should have told you the truth more plainly. But I did try, even if you didn't see it.' She swallowed hard. 'I tried as hard as I could, considering how overwhelmed I felt.'

'Drowning,' he reminded her quietly, and she nodded.

'Yes, it felt like I was drowning. Like I couldn't breathe. Couldn't function—'

'And I didn't see this.' He didn't sound disbelieving, more just wondering. 'Did you have panic attacks like the one you had tonight when we were together?' She nodded, and he shook his head. 'How? How could I have missed that?'

'I tried to hide it, from your family. From you.'

'So you were trying to tell me and hide from me at the same time.'

Which made his aggravation understandable. 'I suppose I was.'

He let out a long, weary sigh and then leaned forward, his head bowed as he raked his hands through his hair. 'Tell me,' he said after a moment, his voice low. 'Tell me about your…condition.'

'You saw for yourself.'

'Tell me everything. Tell me how it started, how you've coped…' He looked up, his expression determined even as Lindsay saw an agony in his eyes. She ached for him, for herself, for them. If only things had been different. If she'd been stronger, braver. If only Antonios had listened more…

Or was it absurd to think things could have been different, that a mere action or word could have changed things for the better? The failure of their marriage hadn't happened, she knew, because of a simple lack of communication. It went deeper than that, to who they both were fundamentally and what they'd expected from life, from love.

But, even if their marriage was over, she could still give Antonios the answers he asked for. Maybe it would provide a certain sense of closure for both of them.

'I was always a shy child,' she began slowly. 'Definitely an introvert. I had a bit of a stammer, and I used to get stomach aches over going to school.' Antonios nodded, his gaze alert and attentive, more so than ever before, and she continued. 'My mother came from a family of famous academics. Her father was a physicist who travelled the world, giving lectures, and her mother was an English professor who wrote literary novels, very well received. I think she thought when she married my father, a mathematics professor, that her life would be like that.'

'And it wasn't?'

Lindsay shook her head. 'My father liked his work, but he didn't want to be some famous academic. My mother dropped out of graduate school when she fell pregnant with me, and I think maybe…maybe she resented me for that.'

Antonios frowned. 'Surely she could have gone back to school, if she'd wanted.'

'Maybe she did go back, eventually,' Lindsay answered. 'I wouldn't know. She walked out on me—on us—when I was nine.'

Antonios's gaze widened as it swept over her. 'You never told me that.'

'I suppose there are a lot of things I didn't tell you,

Antonios.' Lindsay felt her throat thicken and she blinked rapidly. 'I don't…I don't like to talk about my mother.'

'So you became more anxious after she left?'

'Yes—but I was already suffering from panic attacks before then. She used to hold these sort of literary salons—she'd invite a bunch of academics over to our house and they'd talk about lofty things, books and philosophy and the like. It all went over my head. But she'd always call me into the room before bed and try to show me off, make me recite a poem or something in front of everyone. I think she wanted to prove to them she wasn't wasting her life, being a stay-at-home mother.'

'And you didn't like that.'

'I hated it, but I was also desperate to please her. I'd spend hours memorizing poems, but then when I got in front of everyone my mind would go blank. Sometimes I'd start to hyperventilate. My mother would be so disappointed in me she wouldn't talk to me, sometimes for days.' She still remembered sitting at the kitchen table, swamped in misery, while her mother maintained an icy silence, sipping her coffee.

Shock blazed in Antonios's eyes. 'Lindsay, that's awful. Didn't your father notice?'

'A bit, I think, but he was immersed in his research and teaching. And I didn't tell him how bad it was because I felt so ashamed.'

'And is that why you didn't tell me?' Antonios asked quietly. 'Because you felt ashamed?'

'Maybe,' Lindsay allowed. Her feelings about her anxiety and Antonios and their time in Greece were all tangled up—frustration and fear, anger and guilt. And, yes, shame. 'I've worked hard as an adult to control my anxiety, and even to accept it as part of me, but I know back then my mother was ashamed of me.' A lump formed in her throat, making the next words hard to form, to say. 'It's why she left.'

Antonios stared at her, his face expressionless even though his eyes blazed—but with what emotion? Anger? Pity? She hated the thought, even now, of him pitying her. 'How can you say that?' he asked in a low voice.

'My father finally noticed things weren't right when I was eight,' Lindsay continued, squeezing the words out past that awful lump. 'He took me to a specialist and had me examined and diagnosed. And he accepted a position in upstate New York, where I live now, far from Chicago, where we'd been living. My mother felt it was a demotion, and she didn't want to live in some poky town.'

'So she left because of that,' Antonios said. 'Not because of you, Lindsay—'

'I suppose it was the whole package really. The town, the house, the husband, the child.' She took a deep breath and met his gaze, the seventeen-year-old memory as fresh and raw as it ever had been. 'She came to New York to look at the house and college. We all went, and I remember how she walked around the empty rooms. She had this terribly blank look on her face and she didn't say anything, not until my father asked her what she thought, and then all she said was, "This isn't what I expected."' Tears stung her eyes, and one slipped down her cheek. Lindsay dashed it away. 'My father and I thought she meant the house, or maybe even the town. But she meant us. Life with us. It wasn't what she'd expected. We didn't make her happy.'

'She said that?' Antonios asked, his voice sharp with disbelief, and Lindsay nodded.

'She spoke with my father that night. I heard them

from my bed. She said she couldn't cope, living in a place like this with…with a daughter like me. She said she was leaving.'

'Oh, Lindsay.' She was staring down at her lap by that point so she didn't see Antonios move, didn't know he had until his arms were around her and he'd pulled her onto his lap. 'I'm sorry. So sorry.'

'It was a long time ago,' she said with a sniff, but she couldn't keep the tears back, couldn't keep them from sliding down her face as Antonios wiped them away with his thumbs, just as he had back in New York when she'd told him about her father's death. He'd been so tender with her then, and he was so tender now.

'So you blamed yourself,' Antonios said quietly, one hand still cradling her cheek. 'For your mother's abandonment.' He was silent for a moment, one hand stroking her back. 'Were you afraid I might react the same way?'

'I…' She stilled, her mind spinning with that new and awful thought. Had it not just been shame, but fear, that had kept her from speaking honestly? Had she been afraid Antonios would reject her, even leave her if she told him the truth, the whole truth? Maybe some secret, sad part of her had. 'I don't know,' she said slowly. 'I know some deep-seated part of me hates anyone to know. I don't like you knowing now, even though it doesn't matter any more.' Thoughts and memories tumbled through her mind. 'I suppose I felt with you the same way I did with my mother. Wanting to hide my anxiety because I knew it made her angry, yet desperate at the same time for her to see it, to see *me*.'

'And I never saw you.' Lindsay couldn't tell anything from Antonios's flat tone. 'I only thought I did.'

What they'd felt for each other hadn't been real. It was

no more than what she'd been telling him all along, yet it still hurt to hear him acknowledge it. To know how little they'd actually had together.

Antonios was silent for a long moment, one hand still cupping her cheek while the other stroked her hair. 'And so what happened after you moved to New York?' he finally asked.

'Things got worse. I think my father expected them to get better, but with my mother leaving...' She trailed off, then forced herself to continue. 'I started having panic attacks about school—being asked a question, being in a classroom. My father finally withdrew me when I was ten and I was homeschooled. I did all my lessons through a cyber academy, online.' It had been a relief, to leave all the stares and whispers of school, for everyone had realized she was different, that something was *wrong* with her, but it had made for a lonely existence. Her father had tried to be at home as often as he could but he hadn't possessed the resources or sensibility to enrol her in extra classes or activities so she could meet people, make friends. It had just been the two of them, rubbing along together, until he'd died.

'I graduated from high school when I was fifteen,' she continued. 'And started college early, which was hard at first. It made me realize that I had to start coping, that I couldn't hide from life forever. I started therapy and I worked hard to deal with my anxiety. It helped that I was studying mathematics. Numbers have always felt safe to me. They never change.'

'And so you managed for quite a while,' Antonios said. 'Studying and teaching.'

'Academia has always felt like a safe environment to me. I stayed at the same college for my BA and MA and

PhD. I taught a few introductory classes, and I was actually okay standing in front of a classroom.'

'And then your father died,' Antonios recalled quietly.

'Yes. He suffered from early-onset dementia and I cared for him. Life became a bit limited because of that, but I didn't mind.' How could she have minded when her father had given up so much for her? Moved and sacrificed his marriage for her?

'It must have been hard.'

'Yes. And when he died I felt—lost. Adrift. I'd been in the same place for fifteen years but it was as if I didn't know anything any more. So I went to New York to escape everything, even myself, and I met you.'

'And I,' Antonios said after a moment, 'was the ultimate escape. The perfect fairy tale.'

'Yes.'

They were both silent, the only sound the draw and sigh of their breathing. 'I'm sorry I didn't know all of this before,' Antonios said finally. 'I'm sorry you didn't feel you could tell me.'

'I don't know if it would have made a difference, Antonios.'

He turned her on his lap so he could look her in the face. 'How can you say that? You were suffering—'

'I never should have married you,' Lindsay told him, even though it hurt to say it. 'I never should have come to Greece with you. I should have realized it wasn't real. That it couldn't work.'

Antonios didn't answer, and Lindsay wondered if he agreed with her. If she wanted him to agree with her. She felt tired and sad, the relief of having told him the truth coupled with a weary resignation that it didn't, after all, change anything.

'It's late,' he finally said. 'You should get some sleep.' He slid his hands up to cradle her face and pressed a kiss to her forehead. Lindsay closed her eyes, willing yet more tears away. It had been far easier to convince herself she'd never loved Antonios when he was arrogant and dismissive. It was much harder when he was so gentle. 'Thank you for telling me now, Lindsay,' he said softly and wordlessly she nodded. She was afraid if she spoke she would cry. Again.

He stared at her for a long moment, and then he tucked a stray tendril of hair behind her ear. He smiled sadly and Lindsay tried to smile back, but her lips wobbled and, knowing she was far too close to losing it completely, she slid off his lap and hurried from the room.

Antonios stayed in the living room, drinking far too much whisky as Lindsay got ready for bed. He could hear her in the bedroom, opening and closing drawers, the sensuous slide of material as she took off the robe.

He could imagine her, her alabaster skin, so creamy and smooth, the full, high breasts he'd held in his hands and taken into his mouth. Her slender waist and slim hips, those long legs she'd once wrapped around his waist. Her hair as soft and blonde as corn silk, spread out across his bare chest.

They'd been happy together, damn it, even if just for a little while. And yet now he could no longer live in the little bubble of his own certainty. He'd been so damnably certain about how right he was. How *wronged* he'd been. He'd blamed Lindsay for everything, when he hadn't even noticed that she'd been struggling. Suffering.

Drowning.

He poured himself another whisky and tossed it back,

needing the burn of alcohol against the back of his throat, in his gut. Craving the oblivion. He'd been blind before, of course. He'd been ridiculously, wilfully blind when it came to his father. He'd refused to see that anything was wrong, that Marakaios Enterprises was struggling. Just as he had with his marriage.

What the hell was wrong with him? Why couldn't he see what was right in front of his face?

Because you didn't want to see it. Because you were afraid.

Looking back, he could remember moments that should have given him pause. Moments he'd pushed aside because it had been easier. Lindsay claiming she had a headache, her eyes puffy and red. Excusing herself from a party or dinner table with sudden urgency. Yes, looking back, he could see that she'd been unhappy. He just hadn't wanted to see it at the time.

And now? What could he do now to make it better? He'd brought Lindsay back to Greece, back into the spotlight she despised. At least now he could try to make things easier for her. She might need to be here for his mother, but she didn't need to play hostess or be the centre of attention. He'd make sure of that. It was, considering all that had happened before, the least he could do for her.

It was nearing two in the morning by the time he finally made it to bed, his head aching from the endless circling of his thoughts as well as far too much whisky. He stopped in the doorway of the bedroom, his heart suspended in his chest as he watched Lindsay sleep. Her hair was spread out across the pillow, the colour of a moonbeam. She wore a white cotton nightgown with thin straps of scalloped lace, and Antonios could see the round swell of her breasts above the thin material as her chest rose and fell in the deep, even breaths of sleep.

Desire shafted through him, along with an almost unbearable sorrow. It was too late now. Too much had happened, too much hurt and misunderstanding. Their marriage really was over. Lindsay had made that clear.

Wearily, Antonios stripped down to his boxers and slid into bed. It was a wide king-sized bed but it felt too small as he lay on his back, trying not to touch Lindsay even though everything in him ached to pull her into his arms, remind her just how good it had been between them. That, he knew, would be a very stupid thing to do.

Eventually both the whisky and exhaustion overcame him, and he slept.

Lindsay awoke just before dawn, a pale greyish-pink light filtering through the bedroom curtains. She blinked, closing her eyes again as she sank back into the soft, sleepy cocoon of a feather duvet—and a hard body pressed against her own.

Her senses jarred awake even as her mind remained fogged with sleep. She could feel a masculine, muscular leg between her own, a hard chest squashing her breasts. *Antonios.*

Her body went on delicious autopilot, her arms sliding around Antonios's neck as she arched closer to him. Felt the hard press of his arousal against her thighs.

Memories rippled through her mind like reflections in water. Laughing with Antonios. Hugging him, feeling safe and protected and cherished. Making love with him.

She felt one large hand slide from her hip to the dip of her waist to finally, thankfully cup her breast, his thumb moving over the already taut peak.

She gave a breathy sigh of pleasure and Antonios moved her onto her back, his hands seeking her urgently now, lifting her nightgown, finding her flesh. One hand slid between her legs and she moaned and lifted her hips in invitation, wanting and needing to feel him inside her, to experience that wonderful sense of completion and wholeness again.

He was above her, braced on his forearms, poised to slide so deliciously inside her, when the alarm bells that had started to clang distantly in her mind broke into furious peals.

She opened her eyes, stared straight into Antonios's face. He was staring at her with the same expression of appalled realization that she knew she must have on her own.

This shouldn't be happening.

She could feel the tip of his arousal brushing against her and it took everything she had not to arch her hips upwards in invitation.

With a groan Antonios flung himself away from her, rolled onto his back, one arm covering his eyes. Lindsay lay there, her nightgown rucked up to her waist, everything in her aching, demanding satisfaction. With a shuddering breath she pulled down her nightgown and rolled onto her side.

'I'm sorry,' she said hesitantly.

'Don't be.' Antonios lowered his arm and gazed up at the ceiling. 'We both got carried away.' He sat up, throwing off the sheets, and strode, magnificently naked, towards the en suite bathroom. 'We're due at the main house for breakfast with my family,' he said over his shoulder, his tone flat. 'But if it's easier for you, we can have breakfast here and then visit my mother privately.'

His thoughtfulness only hurt her more. 'I think I can manage breakfast.'

He turned to look at her, his eyes narrowed. 'Don't push yourself, Lindsay, on my account.'

'It's fine, Antonios. I know what I'm capable of.'

He nodded in wordless acceptance and disappeared into the bathroom. Lindsay sank back against the pillow. If Antonios had been this sensitive and understanding before, would their marriage have survived? It was a hard question to ask, and an impossible one to answer.

The morning when she'd decided she was going to leave him, her body had felt like a leaden weight, her mind nothing but buzzing emptiness. At that point, after enduring three months of near-constant scrutiny from his family while being routinely ignored by her husband, her anxiety had been nearly all-consuming.

She'd barely been able to drag herself to luncheons and dinners, parties and receptions, all planned for Antonios to introduce his new wife to the local community, to his world. All the while she'd tried to hide the stress-induced eczema on her hands and eyelids, the nausea that had her rushing to the bathroom at inopportune moments, the migraine headaches that came out of nowhere, the light-headedness and shortness of breath that had plagued her every time Antonios took her somewhere public.

The attacks had been worse than anything she'd ever experienced before; she'd been in a strange environment and, far worse, with a man she thought she'd loved but who suddenly seemed like a stranger. She'd been lonely and lost and utterly miserable.

Escaping had felt like her only option for survival. She'd woken that morning and known she no longer possessed the strength, either physically or emotionally, to continue. She couldn't drag herself to one more lunch or dinner, couldn't try to have one more fruitless conversation with Antonios. It had all felt, quite literally, impossible.

And so she'd left. Not telling him she was leaving had been the coward's way out, Lindsay knew, but she simply hadn't had the strength to explain anything any more. She'd told him she needed to return to New York to wrap up some things with her father's house. Antonios had asked her how long she'd be gone and she'd prevaricated, telling him she'd book a return ticket when she was done. He thought she'd be gone a week.

On the plane back to New York she'd felt like a zombie, an empty shell. She'd barely heard the stewardess asking her if she wanted something to drink or eat. She'd simply stared straight ahead, her mind and body going into a kind of emotional and mental hibernation.

Then she'd stepped across the threshold of her father's house; she'd still been able to smell the scent of his pipe and suddenly she'd burst into tears. She wasn't even sure what she was weeping for: her failed marriage, her father, dead just four months, her own weakness that had wrecked so much in her life. Everything.

With a heart that felt like a dead weight inside her she'd typed out the pithy email to Antonios, telling him their marriage was a mistake and she wasn't coming back. He'd called that afternoon and she'd heard the bewilderment and anger in his voice, had felt it when he'd hung up on her. At least she'd chosen to leave, she'd told herself, and then she'd curled into a ball on her bed and slept for fourteen hours straight.

And waded through the next few weeks, trying to summon the strength to rebuild her life. And she had, or at least she'd started to. She'd started therapy again and returned to her research. She'd met up with a few friends who hadn't asked too many questions about her brief failed marriage, and she'd told herself it was enough.

It had to be enough.

Lindsay rolled onto her back and stared up at the ceiling as she heard the sound of the shower being turned on. She imagined Antonios naked under the spray, rivulets of water streaming down the taut perfection of his body.

The body she'd almost just taken into her own, the body she knew as well as her own. The body she missed so much.

Because the little life she'd built for herself back in New York hadn't been enough. Not remotely, not when she'd tasted true happiness with Antonios.

It wasn't real, she reminded herself. *It didn't last.* Letting out a long weary sigh, Lindsay rolled out of bed.

They got ready for breakfast without speaking or even looking at each other. Lindsay showered and changed into a pale green sundress and sandals, plaited her hair into a French braid.

Antonios was wearing chinos and a white linen shirt open at the throat, the light-coloured clothes making his skin and hair seem even darker. He looked magnificent and the sight of him freshly showered, the scent of his aftershave, made desire spiral dizzily inside her again.

Desire she would have to control. Neither of them could afford another encounter like the one they'd had this morning.

His gaze flicked over her as she emerged from the

bedroom but he said nothing and they walked in silence to the main villa.

Just as before, everyone was assembled in the dining room as they arrived, and six pairs of eyes trained on Lindsay as she walked into the room. She felt the speculation, even the censure, and once again her chest went tight.

This time, though, Antonios didn't stride ahead, oblivious. He reached for her arm, steadied her elbow, his body half shielding her from the stares of his family. She glanced up at him in surprise and saw him gazing back at her with that steady strength that had drawn her to him when they'd first met. Antonios had felt like the rock she could cling to in the drowning sea of her own fears and anxieties. He felt that way now, and she was touched by his sensitivity. Despite everything that had happened last night, she hadn't expected it.

After a few seconds her breathing returned to normal and with a little nod she walked forward; Antonios dropped his arm and went to pull out her chair.

'I hope you are feeling better this morning, Lindsay?' Daphne asked as one of the staff poured Lindsay some of the thick Greek coffee she'd learned to drink and even like while she was there before.

'Yes, I think so. Really, I was just tired.'

Ava and Parthenope shot each other significant looks and Lindsay wondered why that remark would set Antonios's sisters off. Deciding not to care, she focused on eating her breakfast of fresh fruit and yogurt with honey, and thankfully the conversation swirled around her without her needing to contribute to it.

'Would you like to go back to the villa?' Antonios asked as they left the dining room. 'I need to work this morning.'

'I suppose.' She could check her email and do some work on her research. She glanced at Antonios, wished she knew what he was thinking about everything. What she'd shared last night. What they'd nearly done together this morning.

Clearly none of it had changed anything between them—but had she wanted it to? The question jarred her because she didn't want to ask it, much less answer it.

'You'll be all right?' Antonios asked when he'd dropped her back off at the villa.

'I have an anxiety disorder, not a life-threatening illness,' Lindsay answered a bit sharply. 'You don't have to coddle me, Antonios.'

'I'm just trying to be considerate,' he returned. 'Since I wasn't before.'

His thoughtfulness made guilt twist inside her. 'I'm sorry,' she said. 'This is hard for me.'

'I know, Lindsay. And I'm trying to make it easier.'

'I don't mean that. I mean having you know about my condition. I hate seeming weak.'

He raised his eyebrows at that. 'You think you seem weak? I think you're strong. Amazingly strong, to have managed as much as you have, and coped for so long.' He smiled with a painful wryness. 'I think you're strong for having been able to hide so much from me, but maybe I was just too blind to see it.'

'I think we were both to blame, Antonios.'

'Maybe so.'

They stared at each other for a moment, regret etched on both of their faces. Then, her heart aching, Lindsay turned to go inside.

She fetched her laptop from her carry-on bag and Antonios retrieved his phone and shrugged on a blazer before heading out once more.

'I'll see you later,' he said and Lindsay watched him go, wishing all over again that things were different between them…and knowing they never could be.

CHAPTER SIX

ANTONIOS SPENT THE morning working in his office but he had trouble focusing on anything. His mind once more was on Lindsay, and all the things she'd told him last night.

As well as what had happened this morning. Dear heaven, but it had felt so good to have her in his arms once again. It had taken every ounce of his control not to slide inside her, not to take his pleasure and give her her own.

And yet what a paltry pleasure it had turned out to be. Good or even incredible sex wasn't enough to make a marriage. And he accepted now that their marriage had made Lindsay miserable. Guilt and grief weighed heavily inside him at the thought.

After Lindsay left him, he'd been so consumed with self-righteous anger. So certain it was all her fault, that he'd done everything in his power to make her happy. He'd bought her clothes and jewels, had showered her with physical affection, had brought her into his home and his family, and he'd thought that had been enough. He knew now it hadn't been, and never could be.

He attempted to focus on work for another hour but thoughts about Lindsay were bouncing around his brain like the little ball in a pinball machine and he finally gave up and headed out into the sunshine of a fall afternoon. He walked back to the villa with no clear goal in mind other than seeing Lindsay again. What he would say to her, he had no idea. What was there left to say?

He came into the cool shelter of the villa, stopping in the doorway to watch Lindsay unobserved. She was sitting on the sofa, her slender legs propped up on the coffee table, her computer on her lap. She was frowning at the computer screen, utterly intent, a few tendrils of hair having escaped her plait to frame her face in white-blonde curls. She was, he saw with a sudden surge of affection, mouthing something silently.

'You look incredibly engrossed in what you are doing,' he said and, startled, she jerked her head up, her body tensing as she caught sight of him.

'Just some research.'

She'd told him a bit about her research before, but Antonios hadn't really understood it. Hadn't tried to, he supposed, because he'd been showing her his life, not having her show him hers. He'd been incredibly selfish, Antonios thought with a fresh bout of recrimination. Incredibly self-centred and arrogant, assuming Lindsay could just drop her life and friends without a thought. He'd felt, he realized, as if he were rescuing her, and he'd liked that, liked feeling like someone's salvation. And instead he'd caused the destruction of her happiness.

'Tell me about it,' he said now, and he came to sit on the edge of the coffee table. He had an urge to reach out and touch her, wrap a hand around the slender bones of her ankle. He resisted.

Lindsay looked up at him warily, her gaze narrowing. 'Do you really want me to?' she asked.

'I wouldn't have asked otherwise.'

'Okay, but you never…' She stopped, shrugging, and then explained, 'At the moment I'm working on maximal prime gap function.'

'Okay,' Antonios said, although he didn't actually know what that meant. Lindsay gave him a lopsided smile, as if she guessed as much, and he smiled back and shrugged.

'I might need you to explain this in plain English.'

'It's all Greek to you?' she teased softly and his smile widened. He was enjoying their light banter. It certainly made a change from the endless arguments they'd had lately.

'Something like that. You must be used to people not understanding your research.'

She gave him a rueful nod and smile. 'Most people don't.'

'So…maximal prime gap function. Give me the low-down.'

She laughed softly, and the sound was the sweetest music to Antonios's ears. He'd missed her laugh, her happiness. Knowing he was causing it now, if just a little, was a balm to his soul. To his heart. Maybe he could use this week to make up for the unhappiness he'd caused her during their marriage. If he could make her laugh again, or even smile…

'Well, you know what prime numbers are?' she said, and he had to think for a moment to dredge up the arithmetic he'd learned as a child.

'A number that is only divisible by itself and one.'

'Yes. The prime gap is the difference between two prime numbers. A maximal gap is the greatest difference.'

'So, for example, the difference between three and seven.'

'Yes, although I'm working with numbers far higher than that—numbers that have yet to be determined if they're in fact prime.'

'And have you drawn any conclusions?'

She shook her head. 'Not yet. I'm still gathering data. But when I have enough I'll start to look for patterns.'

'What kind of patterns?'

'Similar gaps between primes mainly.'

'And what will that tell you?' Antonios asked. 'About...anything?'

She let out a laugh, no more than a breath of sound, her smile turning rueful. 'I know—it seems completely useless to you.'

'Not useless,' he replied. 'But I must admit, as a businessman, I prefer to deal in practicalities.'

'Understandable.'

'So what will the patterns tell you?'

'Well...' Her fingers splayed over her keyboard, a faint frown puckering her forehead. 'Maybe nothing; maybe everything. That, really, is what draws me to number theory. The more research scientists do in physics and mathematicians in number theory, the more they realize how much we don't understand. But the research provides little glimpses into a world of knowledge—a world defined by numbers, and to me it is both mystical and beautiful.' She smiled self-consciously, but Antonios was intrigued.

'Defined by numbers?' he repeated. 'What do you mean?'

'Well, for example, cicadas.'

'*Cicadas?*'

'Yes, you know, like grasshoppers?' She smiled, her eyes dancing with amusement, turning to silver.

'What do cicadas have to do with prime numbers?'

'In the eastern US they only appear after a prime number of years. For example, in Tennessee cicadas have a thirteen-year life cycle. In other places they only appear every seventeen years.'

'And you think there is a reason for this?' Antonios asked, mystified.

'Science has shown us again and again that things in nature are rarely arbitrary. In the case of cicadas, having an irregular life cycle means they're avoiding their natural predator population cycles. So cicadas on a thirteen-year life cycle are less likely to be gobbled up by a frog.'

'How would they know that?'

She shrugged, smiling. 'They wouldn't, necessarily. It's most likely part of natural selection. But I certainly find it interesting. Why have cicadas adapted and other insects haven't?'

'Maybe they're smarter than we think.'

Her eyes danced some more. 'Maybe.'

'Fascinating,' he said, and meant it. 'But the research you're doing, with these huge prime numbers. How does that apply?'

'It doesn't, yet. But with the advances being made in technology and quantum physics, it could in years to come. Understanding the relationships between numbers could be the key to unlocking the universe.'

Her mouth curved in a teasing smile and Antonios chuckled. 'You think so, huh?'

'Actually, I do, in a manner of speaking. But it probably sounds weird to you.'

'Not as weird as it did.'

She laughed and closed her laptop. 'Then my job here is done.'

'Good,' Antonios said. 'Because I thought we could go for a walk.'

She raised her eyebrows, searched his face, wondering, no doubt, why he was being so friendly. He'd been angry for so long. Too long. But he'd enjoyed the last twenty minutes and he wanted to spend more time with Lindsay. Wanted to make her smile again.

'Okay,' she said, and Antonios rose from where he'd been sitting.

'You should put on sunscreen and take a hat.'

'Where are we going, exactly?'

'To the olive groves.'

As a child he'd loved the olive groves that spread across the hillside, all the way to the horizon. He loved the twisted, gnarled trunks of the olive trees, and the pungent smell of their fruit as it ripened. He loved the crumbly earth beneath his feet and the high, hot sun above. And most of all he'd loved walking with his father, feeling important as his father had pointed out the different trees and flowers.

Until everything had changed.

He knew, just as Lindsay did, how a parent could make you feel confused and ashamed. Unloved and rejected.

They walked through the complex of buildings that made up Villa Marakaios, passing the main villa as well as Leonidas's, the staff housing and the central office, before coming to the wrought iron gate with *Marakaios* worked into the iron in curling script above them, in both Greek and English. Antonios opened the gate and ushered Lindsay into the grove.

'So how did your family get into the olive oil business, anyway?' she asked as they walked between neat rows of trees, their grey-green leaves rustling in the wind, the tight cream-coloured buds of their flowers raised to the sun.

'It was my father,' Antonios said, and heard both the tension and pride enter his voice. He had such conflicting feelings when it came to his father. Respect and disdain. Anger and grief. Love and hate. 'He came from nothing,' he told Lindsay. 'His father lived in Athens and worked as a dustman. But my father had dreams and ambition, and he loved the earth. He sweated blood to buy some land, and over the years he expanded it. He decided to grow olive trees for oil because he felt it was something that would always be in demand.'

'And he was very successful.'

'Yes,' Antonios said, 'although not at first. It can be very expensive to make olive oil unless you make it in large quantities using efficient methods. My father struggled at first, but then he was able to buy more land and plant more trees.'

'And so you inherited an empire.'

Antonios's insides tightened with memory. 'Yes,' he agreed. He had sworn never to tell anyone about how the Marakaios empire had been crumbling beneath his feet when he'd been summoned home after his father's heart attack. He wouldn't tell Lindsay. He'd protect his father's memory as he always had, even though it sometimes felt as if he were selling his soul to save his father's.

He still remembered coming home after starting a job in Athens—a job his father had insisted he start because he hadn't wanted him near the family business. Hadn't wanted him to figure out just how badly things were going. Antonios hadn't realized that at the time, though. He'd just felt the rejection.

Just like he had with Lindsay. God help him, he didn't want to be blind any more. He wanted to see what was happening around him, and to help. And he would this week with Lindsay.

'What are you thinking about?' Lindsay asked and Antonios snapped his gaze back to her.

'Nothing.'

'You're frowning.'

He shrugged. 'I was just thinking about all there is to do.'

'Taking time out to go to New York was costly, I suppose.'

'But necessary.'

Lindsay didn't answer and they walked on for a bit, the sun hot on their heads and shoulders even though the air was still cool and crisp. The aromatic scent of the olive flowers wafted up from where they trod over fallen buds.

The grove stretched in every direction, a sea of land and trees that gave him a fierce, almost painful sense of satisfaction. He'd held onto it all, if only just. He might have sold his soul, but at least he'd saved this. Lindsay turned to him with a small smile.

'You look like a king surveying his domain.'

'I suppose I feel a bit like one,' he admitted. 'I am very proud of what my father built from nothing.' And what he'd kept, if only by the skin of his teeth.

Lindsay laid a hand on his wrist, her fingers cool and soft. 'I'm glad you showed me all of this, Antonios. It helps me to understand you.'

He gazed at her, conscious of her hand still on his

wrist, her lovely grey eyes so wide and clear. 'And do you want to understand me?' he asked quietly.

Her eyes clouded and she withdrew her hand from his arm. Antonios felt the loss. 'I…' she began, and then shook her head. 'I suppose there isn't much point, is there?' she said, her lips twisting in a sorrowful smile. 'But I'm still glad.'

Antonios just nodded. He felt emotion burn in his chest, words rise in his throat and tangle on his tongue. Too many memories, too close to the surface. Too much hopeless longing and unsatisfied desire.

Their marriage, he reminded himself grimly, was over.

'We should get back,' he said. 'My mother is hoping to have us over to the main villa for lunch.' He glanced at her sideways. 'Just the two of us. Will that be all right?'

'Fine,' Lindsay assured him. 'I'm all right in small groups of people. And I like your mother, Antonios. I like being with her.' Her expression clouded once more as she turned to him. 'I'm so sorry about her illness.'

He nodded, his chest tightening once more. 'I am, too.'

'I'm…I'm sorry I wasn't there for you when she was diagnosed.' She bit her lip. 'I know I should have been.'

Antonios struggled for words for a moment; the emotions that swooped through him were too powerful and overwhelming for speech. He couldn't untangle one from the other: gratitude and compassion, hope and sorrow. He wished she'd been there. He wished she'd wanted to be there, had been happy there.

'You're here now,' he said. 'That's what matters.'

They started walking back the way they'd come. 'When will you tell your family that we're getting divorced?' Lindsay asked and Antonios tensed.

'When the moment is right. Are you in such a rush?'

'No, but are you really going to keep up the deception for the rest of your mother's life?'

'That won't,' he answered, 'be all that long. The doctors have only given her a few months or maybe even weeks. The cancer has spread, and she doesn't wish to undergo invasive treatment again.'

'Do you want me to tell her?' Lindsay asked quietly. 'I owe you that much, at least.'

'No.' His voice came out too loud, too hard. 'It would only hurt her. Why can't we let her die happy, believing we're happy?'

Lindsay nibbled her lip. 'I don't like lying.'

'I don't either.' And God help him, he'd been doing it for too long. But for a greater good, just like now. 'It would be a mercy for her, Lindsay,' he said quietly. 'Why trouble her in the short time she has left?'

Lindsay gazed at him, her eyes shadowed, and then slowly she nodded. 'All right. But what about your sisters and brother, Antonios? They seem suspicious already—'

'After,' Antonios said, his voice hoarse and raw. 'I'll tell them after she dies.'

Lindsay's face crumpled and she reached out for Antonios's hand, seeming to surprise both of them. She squeezed his hand, her face filled with compassion. 'I'm so sorry, Antonios. Daphne has been more of a mother to me than my own ever was.'

'We'll both miss her,' he agreed, his voice still hoarse. He didn't want to let go of her hand. Didn't want to resort to this careful politeness and wary friendship. Maybe what they'd had before hadn't been real, but it had been good. And maybe they could build something real now.

The thought was like a dagger slipping inside him, slyly finding his heart—and hurting. Because he knew he couldn't suggest such a thing to Lindsay. Not when being here with him had only caused her unhappiness. He owed her her freedom, at the very least.

Lindsay followed Antonios out of the olive grove, reluctant to leave behind the surprising camaraderie they'd shared. She'd enjoyed chatting with him, teasing and sharing, learning about one another. It was more than they'd ever done before during the three months of their marriage. The week in New York had been one of sensual rather than emotional discovery, and then during those months in Greece they'd been like strangers unless they'd been in bed. But today they'd actually felt like friends.

It made her feel both sad and happy at the same time, because while friendship with Antonios was better than the hostility she'd experienced over the last few days, it still made her ache with regret and longing.

They walked to the villa in companionable silence, and then Lindsay went into the bedroom to change. She exchanged her sundress for a pair of linen trousers and a matching sleeveless top, and touched up her make-up and hair.

Antonios was waiting for her in the living room when she emerged and his gaze fastened on her as soon as she opened the door.

'You look lovely,' he said, his voice full of warm sincerity as his gaze swept over her.

She blushed, although she wasn't sure why. He'd told her she'd looked lovely before, had showered her with compliments, but this felt different. And then Lindsay knew why. Because for the first time Antonios truly saw her…and he still thought she was beautiful.

The realization made her understand afresh why she hadn't told him about her anxiety. She really had been filled with shame and fear, terrified that he would reject her or even leave her. She'd convinced herself that she'd tried her best to tell him, but she really hadn't. She hadn't wanted to.

'Lindsay?' He came forward, one strong hand cupping her elbow. 'Are you okay?'

'Yes—'

'You look pale.'

She shook her head. 'I was just realizing how unfair I was to you, Antonios, not telling you the truth. I told myself I'd tried as hard as I could, but I know I really didn't. Because I really didn't want you to know.'

'Between a rock and a hard place,' Antonios surmised with a small sad smile. 'We were doomed, weren't we?'

'I suppose we were.' Which made her feel like bursting into tears. Wanting to hide her emotion, she turned away from him, making a pretence of straightening her top. 'We should go. Your mother will be waiting.'

They walked over to the main villa where Daphne was waiting for them. Lunch had been set out for the three of them in one of the villa's smaller dining rooms, with French windows overlooking a small walled herb garden. Lindsay had never been in the room before and its cosy proportions and atmosphere put her immediately at ease, as did Daphne.

'How are you settling back into life in Greece?' she asked as she took Lindsay's hands in her own thin ones. 'Is it very hard?'

Lindsay swallowed, hating to deceive her, yet knowing as Antonios had said it was both a mercy and kindness. 'Not too hard.'

'And I hope you're treating her right,' Daphne said with a stern look at her oldest son. 'Antonios works too hard,' she told Lindsay. 'He's just like his father that way.'

Lindsay felt the shudder of tension go through Antonios's body and wondered at it. She slid him a glance, but his face was impassive as he held out a chair for his mother.

Daphne took a seat, smiling up at Antonios. 'Evangelos was always working. I used to come into his office and sit on his desk.'

Lindsay let out a choked laugh and Antonios's eyebrows shot up. 'I didn't know that, Mama.'

'Why would I tell you?' she asked with a surprisingly pert look. She turned back to Lindsay. 'But it was the only way to make him stop working.'

'Maybe I should have tried that,' Lindsay joked, then bit her lip as she registered the past tense. Her gaze locked with Antonios and she knew he'd registered it, too.

'It would make for an entertaining change from what's usually on my desk,' he said smoothly. 'Let me pour you some water, Mama.'

This was going to be so hard, Lindsay thought, busying herself with spreading her napkin in her lap. Pretending at a party was one thing, but to someone's face, someone she cared about…

'Let me call for the first course,' Daphne said. 'I'm afraid I don't last for more than a few hours before I need a nap these days.' She smiled apologetically and Lindsay touched her hand.

'I'm sorry…' Lindsay began. 'If there's anything I can do…'

'There is no need for you to be sorry,' Daphne said. 'I've lived a good life, and I'd rather no one made concessions to my condition now. I want to live life as fully as I can for as long as I can.'

One of the staff came in to set the first course before them, a fruit salad with grapes and succulent slices of melon.

'Tell me, Lindsay,' Daphne asked as soon as the staff member had quietly left again, 'do you miss America very much? Did you leave many friends behind?'

Lindsay couldn't help but glance at Antonios, whose face was carefully expressionless. 'Not so many,' she said.

'And your research? Will you be able to finish it here? You are not far from achieving your doctorate, are you?'

'I have a few more months of work at least,' Lindsay answered. 'Most of the research can be conducted from anywhere, as long as I have my laptop.'

'I'm sure you will have to make some trips back to America,' Daphne said, and Lindsay nodded in relief.

'Yes, I will.'

'Not too many, though,' Daphne continued. 'A man and a wife belong together.' She speared a slice of melon, her gaze suddenly seeming almost shrewd. 'Six months apart is a very long time.'

Lindsay threw a panicked gaze at Antonios, not sure how she should answer.

'Lindsay had some business to deal with, back in America,' he said, his voice as smooth and controlled as ever. 'With her house and such things. Her place is here now, Mama, with me.'

'And why couldn't your place be with her?' Daphne countered, a playful smile curving her mouth. 'In Amer-ica?'

Antonios's composure slipped for a second as he

stared at his mother, slack jawed. 'Because I can't run Marakaios Enterprises from America,' he said finally.

Daphne nodded, her playful smile turning down at the corners. 'No,' she agreed softly, 'you can't.'

Antonios pushed his plate away, wishing this meal could be more pleasant for all of them. Deceiving his mother so directly was far more difficult than he'd envisioned, and he could tell Lindsay was finding it hard, too.

As for his mother's suggestion he leave Villa Marakaios…the idea was absurd. He'd poured his soul into the family business, had sacrificed all semblance of a normal life to keep things afloat. He couldn't walk away from it, even if he wanted to.

Thankfully, Daphne moved the conversation to more innocuous matters as they ate their way through three courses, and Antonios was glad to leave contentious matters aside as they chatted simply. He liked watching Lindsay, the way her eyes sparkled when she was amused, the way she tilted her head to one side when she was considering a point. The clear peal of her sudden laugh made him long to make her laugh again. Make her happy again, even if just for this week.

By the time dessert had been cleared Antonios could see that his mother was fading and so he made their excuses, kissing her on both cheeks, as Lindsay did after him, before they left the main villa to head back to their own.

The afternoon air was still and drowsy, the grounds silent and empty in this hot part of the day.

'Are there any more engagements today?' Lindsay asked and Antonios shook his head.

'No, but there will be preparations for the party to-

morrow, and then the actual celebration the day after.'
He glanced at her, wanting to be considerate but knowing she would resist being coddled. 'Will that be all right for you?'

'I think so.'

'I want to make things easier for you,' he said, his manner stilted yet sincere, the awkwardness of it making him cringe inwardly. 'But I know you don't want me to treat you differently, either.'

'You're being very kind, Antonios. I appreciate all you're doing for me.' For a moment she looked as if she wanted to say something more and Antonios felt his heart lurch with fear and hope. Then she shook her head, her eyes shadowed as she touched his hand. 'Thank you,' she said, and walked on to the villa.

CHAPTER SEVEN

LINDSAY TILTED HER face to the sun and closed her eyes, enjoying the warmth—as well as the respite from the preparations for Daphne's party. Even though Antonios had insisted she didn't need to, she had joined his sisters in the villa's main salon to help with the decorations.

Antonios was so clearly making an effort to help her, she felt she could do no less and help him. And if they'd had this kind of understanding before, would it have made all the difference? Could their marriage have survived, or even flourished?

Restlessly, she shifted in her seat, plucked a blossom of bougainvillea that twined its way up the stone wall. That question had been tormenting her in one form or another since she'd told Antonios about her anxiety. Maybe they'd needed to come to the brink of disaster to truly start listening and understanding each other. Maybe they'd needed the heartache and separation to come to a place where they could build something strong and true.

And maybe you're just spinning another fairy tale. Another fantasy.

She pressed the blossom to her cheek and closed her eyes once more. Even if she and Antonios understood each other now, even if they became friends, a marriage still couldn't work between them. She couldn't be the kind of wife Antonios needed, the social hostess and organizer. No matter how much she managed to control her anxiety, the endless social engagements his career as CEO demanded would still defeat her. And what of her own research? She'd told Antonios she could do her research anywhere, which was true. But her PhD would be finished in a few months and she'd already started looking for professorships. Staying here in Greece meant kissing her career goodbye.

Something she hadn't cared about or even considered when he'd asked her to marry him, to come with him to Greece. She'd been so desperate then—desperate to be happy, to leave the sadness of her life behind. But, nine months later, she could acknowledge how incompatible their life goals really were.

Antonios had stated plainly he would never leave Greece. Even if he wanted to restart their marriage, it would mean staying here, doing her best to be the wife he needed, playing hostess and socialite. Roles she couldn't bear.

'May I join you?'

Lindsay opened her eyes to see Daphne standing in front of her, offering her a kindly smile.

'Of course.' She shifted on the bench to make room for her mother-in-law.

Daphne sat down with a sigh of relief. 'Everything aches,' she said quietly, her gaze on the mountains cutting a jagged line out of the horizon. 'I think, when it is my time, I will be ready for the aching to stop.'

'I'm sorry,' Lindsay said quietly. She felt inadequate

for the moment, especially in the light of Daphne's grace in the face of so much suffering and sorrow.

'Knowing you are going to die shortly is, in some ways, a gift,' Daphne said after a moment, her gaze still on the mountains. 'It gives you a chance to set your affairs in order and say things you might have resisted before.' She turned to Lindsay, a surprising humour lighting her eyes. 'Speak the truth of your heart, because it doesn't really matter if you ruffle a few feathers.'

'I suppose,' Lindsay agreed after a second's pause. She had a feeling Daphne was going to speak a few truths now and she had no idea what she'd say in return.

'I know,' Daphne began, choosing her words with care, 'that things went wrong between you and Antonios.'

Shock blazed through her, followed by a deep unease. If she admitted the truth, would Antonios be angry? Was she to lie even now?

'I also know,' Daphne said, patting her hand, 'that Antonios doesn't want me to know. He tries to protect me from so much.'

Lindsay swallowed hard, searched for words. 'He loves you very much.'

'And I love him. I want him to be happy.' Daphne was silent for a moment. 'I think you can make him happy, Lindsay.'

Lindsay shook her head, the movement instinctive and utterly certain. 'I can't. I know I can't.' Too late she realized how much she'd admitted, but her mother-in-law seemed unsurprised.

'Why don't you think you can?'

'Because I'm not what he needs. I can't be the kind of wife he needs.'

'I think,' Daphne answered, 'Antonios doesn't know what he needs.'

Curious now, Lindsay asked, 'What do you think he needs?'

'A wife who loves him. Who believes in him. You love him, don't you?'

'I…' Lindsay shook her head. 'I don't know. I thought I did, and then I thought I didn't. And now…now it doesn't matter.'

'Why not?'

Lindsay bit her lip. She'd said far too much. She'd been startled into more honesty than she'd ever meant to share. 'I only mean because we're already married,' she said feebly and Daphne smiled, as if she knew what a pathetic pretence this was.

'You weren't happy here,' she said after a moment. 'Were you?'

'No,' Lindsay admitted after a second's pause. 'But that was as much my fault's as—'

'A husband's duty is to make his wife happy, no?'

'I suppose a husband and wife should try to make each other happy—'

'Let me say again,' Daphne corrected. 'If a wife is unhappy, a husband needs to address her unhappiness.'

Lindsay swallowed hard. 'Antonios didn't know I was unhappy.'

'Exactly. I could see it and he could not. Because he is just like his father, Lindsay. He only sees what he wants to see.' Daphne let out a long weary sigh. 'Evangelos was a good man and I loved him dearly. But he worked himself to the bone for his business and he closed his eyes to any problems because he could not bear to think of them. Just as Antonios closed his eyes to your suffering because he could not bear it.'

Lindsay blinked, taking this in. It was an entirely new thought, and one she had to sift over for a few moments before replying. 'His eyes aren't closed now,' she said, half-amazed at how honest she was being. 'We've talked about it since I've returned. He knows everything. I'm not sure it makes much difference.'

'Because you still are not happy here,' Daphne said quietly. She sounded sad.

'Because, I told you,' Lindsay said sadly, 'I can't be the wife he needs.'

'And I told you that what he needs is to love and to be loved. That is all anyone needs.'

'You make it sound so simple.'

'No, not simple. Endlessly complicated and difficult.' Daphne smiled, resting one bony hand on top of Lindsay's. 'But worth it, if you both resolve to try. To learn.'

Lindsay swallowed and nodded. She wanted to believe Daphne, wanted to believe love could be that easy. But the question remained: did she want to try again? And, more importantly, did Antonios?

Antonios stared at his brother and tried to mask his shock. 'So you kept this from me?'

'I wanted to make sure it was a definite go,' Leonidas answered, his voice level. The brothers stared at each other, tension simmering in the air.

Antonios glanced back down at the file folder of information Leonidas had presented to him ten minutes ago, much to his stunned amazement. The neat rows of figures and the printed transcript of correspondence showed his brother had been planning this investment in providing luxury bath products to a chain of hotels for a long time. Without telling him a damned thing.

'And it never occurred to you,' he asked, an edge entering his voice, 'to tell me you were thinking about doing this?'

'No, it didn't,' Leonidas answered flatly. Antonios jerked back.

'Do I need to remind you that I'm the CEO of this company?'

'No,' Leonidas interjected, 'you certainly don't.'

Antonios stared at his brother, felt a ripple of shock at the anger he saw there. 'What is that supposed to mean?'

'Exactly what I said. You remind me every day that you're the boss, Antonios. That's why I didn't approach you about this plan. I knew you'd want to take it over.'

Antonios's gaze narrowed. 'As CEO, it's necessary that I—'

'Have your fingerprints on everything? And why is that, Antonios? I am your second-in-command, the Head of European Operations, a Marakaios.' His mouth twisted bitterly. 'He was my father, too.'

Antonios slapped his hand on the desk, the sound loud in the taut stillness of the office. 'Damn it, I do not need this now.'

'Fine. We won't discuss it. Just sign off on the deal and I'll go to our investors.'

'No.' The word came out in a sudden, sharp cry. Leonidas raised his eyebrows. Antonios's jaw tightened. He had, he knew, kept his brother on a short rein because he'd been hiding the extent of the debt their father had amassed. He'd cleared it now, but if Leonidas went to their investors, if he looked at their bank statements or credit history, he would know in an instant how bad things had been. How their father had failed.

And Antonios had promised never to let anyone know.

He'd kept Leonidas busy wining and dining new clients, visiting factories and restaurants, drumming up new business. He'd always handled the money side, but now Leonidas had gone behind his back, set up an entire new deal that he, quite naturally, wanted to close.

And Antonios couldn't let him.

'I'll sign off on the deal,' he said tersely, 'and I'll contact the investors.'

Leonidas's mouth twisted. 'Taking the glory, as usual.'

As if he concerned himself with glory. As if there was anything *glorious* about the debt and despair his father had fallen into, the life Antonios had lived for far too long. 'You can have your name on it,' he said shortly. 'I'll give you credit. But I'll handle the finances and paperwork.'

Leonidas stared at him for a long moment, his face taut with fury. 'Don't you trust me?'

'This isn't about trust, Leonidas.' At least not the kind his brother thought.

'Then why won't you give me more responsibility, Antonios? Damn it, I deserve it. I've worked hard these last ten years—'

'What responsibility do you want?' Antonios snapped, irritation masking his guilt. 'To sign some tedious paperwork, go over a few boring columns?'

'If it's so boring, why won't you let me do it?' Leonidas countered.

Antonios stared at him, hating that they were having this confrontation and yet knowing it had been a long time coming. Fearing he couldn't hide forever. And wouldn't it feel good to come clean, to admit what he'd been covering up, sharing the burden? Lindsay had been honest about her own fears and secrets. Why couldn't he be honest about his?

The desire to unburden himself was so strong he nearly trembled with the force of it. Longed to give Leonidas all the responsibility he craved and more, to walk away from it all, finally free of the shackles of Marakaios Enterprises that had bound him for so long...

Theos, what was he thinking? Appalled, Antonios took a step back, as if he could distance himself from his own thoughts. He could not betray his father that way. It would be a betrayal of himself, of his sense of duty and honour that was at the core of who he was.

'Be happy with what I've offered,' he told Leonidas flatly. 'Because it's all I ever will.'

With a muffled curse Leonidas strode from the room. Antonios pushed back from his desk, striding to the window that overlooked the olive groves. His mind seethed with too many thoughts.

He had never seen his brother so angry before, seeming so resentful of the control Antonios exerted. He'd sensed it, but Leonidas had never spoken so plainly before. Or maybe he hadn't wanted to acknowledge how unhappy his brother was, just as he hadn't wanted to acknowledge how unhappy Lindsay had been. Blind, wilfully blind, as always.

Antonios pressed a fist to his forehead, longing for so much to be different. For his father not to have sworn him to secrecy. For him to have realized the unhappiness around him and sought to change it.

And if only he could change things now. Change things with Leonidas. Change things with Lindsay.

Wearily, he dropped his fist and turned back to his desk. Sometimes change was impossible.

After talking with Daphne, Lindsay went back into the villa, determined to make one more attempt to help with the party preparations. Parthenope and Xanthe were in the salon, debating where to put a display of photographs; Lindsay watched them for a moment before coming over to examine the photos of the Marakaios family throughout the years.

She could pick out Antonios easily—a dark-haired, solemn little boy. For a second she imagined what their child might have looked like and felt an unsettling twist of longing for something she hadn't even truly considered before.

Antonios had wanted to start trying for children right away, but Lindsay had put him off. Attempting to cope with her new life in Greece had been hard enough without adding pregnancy to the mix.

And it was still hard. Too hard to continue. Too hard to try again.

She turned to watch Xanthe and Parthenope continue to wrangle over the display board, their voices raised, their hands moving wildly.

Xanthe caught her looking and put her hands on her hips. 'Do you have a suggestion, Lindsay?' she asked, a faint note of challenge in her voice. Parthenope turned to look at her, too, and even though it was just the two of them Lindsay felt a sweat break out between her shoulder blades.

Damn it, she did not want to go into panic mode right now.

'I'd put it in the corner,' she said, and Xanthe's eyebrows shot higher.

'People won't see it there.'

'It will be in the way anywhere else,' Lindsay countered quietly, 'and a person's gaze is generally drawn to the vertex of an angle, especially a right angle.' She saw the look of incomprehension on the two women's faces and felt herself flush. 'The walls of the room form an angle,' she explained in a half mumble. 'A right angle, with the corner as its vertex.'

They just stared at her, completely nonplussed, and Lindsay turned away. 'Never mind,' she muttered, and everything in her jolted with surprise when she heard Antonios's voice.

'A mathematical proof for putting photographs in the corner. Brilliant.' He came into the room, his smiling gaze trained on Lindsay, rooting her to the spot. 'I knew I needed a reason to have the photo of me as an eight-year-old with knobbly knees put in a dark corner.'

'You could backlight the display board,' Lindsay offered, pleasure rippling through her as Antonios joined her, looping one arm around her shoulders. 'Your knobbly knees could still be on view.'

'You did have knobbly knees, Antonios,' Parthenope remarked as she peered at one of the photos. 'Are they still so knobbly? You always wear business suits now.'

'I'll never tell,' Antonios answered, and slid Lindsay a teasing glance. 'And I trust my wife will keep my secret.'

'My lips are sealed,' Lindsay promised, but inwardly she reeled. Why was Antonios acting so…*lover-like*?

Then it hit her. He was pretending, for his sisters' sake. *Duh.* How could she have forgotten it for even a moment? How could she have wanted something real?

She slipped out from under Antonios's arm. 'I don't

think my mathematical proofs are really needed here,' she said with an apologetic smile for Parthenope and Xanthe. 'I'll just head back to our villa.'

'I'll join you,' Antonios answered smoothly. 'I'd like to rest before dinner.'

Lindsay saw Xanthe and Parthenope exchange knowing looks and inwardly cringed. Outside, she started walking quickly towards the villa and Antonios easily matched her pace.

'It's too hard, Antonios,' she burst out. 'Pretending to everyone. It feels wrong.'

'I know.'

This stopped her short. 'Then shouldn't we come clean? Wouldn't it be easier?'

'For whom? Us? Think of my mother, Lindsay.'

Lindsay bit her lip. 'I think your mother knows. Or at least guesses.'

Antonios turned to her sharply. 'Why do you say that?'

'Because she spoke to me this morning. Privately. And some of the things she said made me think she knows. She knew I was unhappy, anyway.'

Antonios's mouth thinned. 'Which was more than I knew.'

Lindsay stopped to lay a hand on his arm. 'What happened before, we should both put behind us, Antonios. I know we were both to blame. We can accept our guilt and move on.'

Something flared in his eyes. 'Move on?'

'I mean, you know…move on with our lives,' Lindsay stumbled through the explanation. A blush heated her cheeks as she thought what Antonios might have assumed she meant. To move on together.

Antonios didn't answer, just stared at her for a long

moment, his gaze seeming to both test and assess her. 'Have dinner with me tonight,' he said suddenly.

Lindsay stared at him in surprise. 'I thought we were having dinner with everyone, at the main villa—'

'No. Have dinner with just me. Alone.' She searched his face, saw how intent and determined he looked. As determined as he had when he'd asked her out in New York, his playful banter not quite disguising his utter intent to have her go out with him, to have her fall in love with him. And she had. Oh, she had. She'd fallen for him so hard and fast her head had still been spinning a week later, when they'd landed in Greece.

And what did he want now? What did she even want him to want?

'Antonios…'

'Please,' he said softly, and she was lost. As lost as she'd been when he'd given her that achingly whimsical smile of his and said, *What would it take for you to have coffee with me?*

And she'd grinned and said, *A simple please would do.*

And so he'd said it. Tears stung her eyes and she blinked them back, everything in her aching for what they'd had and lost.

And what they could have again?

Hope was such a dangerous thing.

'All right,' she whispered and Antonios's answering smile reached right into her soul.

Antonios paced the living room as he waited for Lindsay to emerge from the bedroom for their dinner. Nerves coiled in his belly and anticipation sang in his blood. He'd planned everything, from the food they'd eat to where they'd eat it, the music that would be playing and the flowers on the table. He wanted this evening to be perfect, and focusing on all the details had kept him from thinking about all the things that could go wrong.

Like Lindsay telling him no.

But that wouldn't happen. He wouldn't allow it to happen. He'd pulled himself back from the brink once before, by sheer force of will and a hell of a lot of hard work. He could do it again. He was, he knew, willing to work hard for his marriage. And it would begin tonight.

'I'm ready.'

He turned to see Lindsay standing in the doorway, looking both uncertain and beautiful. She was dressed in a silvery, spangled sheath dress, her hair loose and tousled about her shoulders.

'You look like a moonbeam,' Antonios said and came forward to take her hands in his. 'Or a Snow Queen, perhaps.'

She gave him a faint smile, and he knew she remembered him calling her that when they'd met in New York. His Snow Queen. For she would, God willing, be his still.

'Where are we eating?' she asked as she glanced around the empty, darkened villa.

'Somewhere private. I made arrangements earlier. It's only a short walk away. Do you have a wrap?'

She held up a scrap of spangled silk and Antonios took her arm in his.

Outside, the night was dark, the air crisp, the sky scattered with stars like a thousand diamond pinpoints in a cloth of black velvet. Lindsay took a deep breath.

'I love the smell of the air here,' she said. 'So fresh and clean. It smells like pine.'

'From the trees on the mountains,' Antonios told her. 'The villagers used to harvest the pine resin.'

'The resin? For what?'

'Well, it's edible,' Antonios told her, 'but I wouldn't advise eating all that much of it. Mainly it was used to make pitch and other adhesives.'

She slid him a smiling glance. 'And you didn't think about going into the resin business?'

'I'm not sure pine resin has all that much value these days, with all the chemical adhesives available now.'

'Did you always want to take up the family business?' Lindsay asked after a moment, and Antonios tensed.

'It was never a question of want.'

'You mean your father expected you to?'

'Of course. He built an empire. He wanted to hand it down to his sons.' And he hated talking about this, about the lies that he knew he'd get tangled up in.

'So you've always worked for Marakaios Enterprises?'

'I worked for an investment management company in Athens briefly, when I was younger. My father wanted me to have some other experience.' That, at least, had been what Evangelos had told him. The truth had been he'd wanted him out of the way.

'And did you enjoy that? The investment management?'

'Yes, I did,' Antonios said, and heard the note of surprise in his voice. He'd never really thought about the work he'd done in Athens, only the hurt he'd felt about being sent away. But the truth was he'd enjoyed it very much. Enjoyed the analysis coupled with risk-taking, and the freedom of not having another man's burden on his shoulders.

'What about you?' he asked. 'Your father was a mathematician. You taught at the same university he did. Did you ever think about doing something else?'

'No. Never,' she answered. 'Mathematics has always been my passion, and I've never been very good at starting somewhere new.' She swallowed and looked away and it occurred to him afresh how difficult it must have been for her to come to Greece, an entirely new place, with him.

And he hadn't made it one iota easier for her. But he would this time. He'd make sure of it.

'Here we are,' he said and, taking her elbow, he guided her into the extensive walled gardens of the estate. They walked in silence along several twisting paths, the gravel crunching under their feet, until they came to a private little garden surrounded by stone walls climbing with bougainvillea, a fountain in its centre, the water gleaming under the moonlight.

Lindsay stopped as she took in the preparations Antonios had made: the table set for two with fine china and linen, candlelight flickering over the silver chafing dishes. A bottle of champagne was waiting on ice in a silver bucket and a recording of a double concerto for violin and cello was playing softly in the background.

'Brahms' Concerto in A Minor,' Lindsay said softly. Remembrance suffused her face; they'd seen the New York Philharmonic play this at Carnegie Hall in New York, after Lindsay had told him it was one of her favourite pieces of music. 'The musical A-E-F is a permutation of F-A-E,' she'd explained to him, amusing him with her mathematical way of looking at everything. 'It stands for his personal motto: *Frei aber einsam.*' Her mouth had twisted as she'd translated, 'Free but lonely.'

Now he understood how those words must have resonated with her. And with him, too, he thought now— working so hard to save Marakaios Enterprises, hiding

the truth from everyone. Until he'd met Lindsay and felt
his soul start to soar.

And it would soar again. Both of theirs would. He
could make it happen.

'This is very thoughtful, Antonios,' Lindsay said quietly. 'And very romantic.'

'That was my intention,' he answered as he pulled out
her chair. She sat down with a whisper of silk and he laid
the napkin on her lap before sitting down opposite her.

Lindsay's gaze was shadowed as she looked at him.
'This is lovely, Antonios,' she said. 'So lovely, but…'

'But why am I doing it?' he filled in before she could
say anything more.

She nibbled her lip, her eyes wide. 'Yes.'

'Because I want to,' he answered her simply. He took
a deep breath, meeting her gaze, knowing his heart was
in his eyes. 'Because I still love you, Lindsay, and I want
you to stay in Greece.' He smiled, or tried to, for her
expression hadn't changed. 'I want us to stay married.'

CHAPTER EIGHT

LINDSAY STARED AT ANTONIOS, saw sincerity blazing in his eyes as his words echoed through her. *I want you to stay in Greece... I want us to stay married.*

I want. I want.

And nothing about what she wanted. What she needed. What she'd felt, all those weeks in Greece. She took a deep breath, felt sorrow sweep through her; she was too tired and sad to be angry. She felt only disappointment at the realization that, as much as he was trying, Antonios still hadn't changed. Still couldn't see.

And yet she wanted him to. Wanted this to work, even though she knew it couldn't. *She* couldn't.

'You're speechless?' Antonios said with a little laugh. 'Say something, Lindsay.'

'I don't know what to say.'

'Say you want that, too, then,' Antonios answered. He was trying to speak lightly, but she could hear an edge entering his voice, signifying what? Irritation? Impatience? She wasn't falling all over herself to say yes.

'Oh, Antonios,' she said finally. She shook her head, and his mouth tightened. 'It's not that simple.'

'I think it seems quite simple. I love you. Do you love me?' He tilted his chin a bit, as if bracing himself for a hit.

Lindsay stared at him miserably. 'I don't know,' she said finally, but she knew it was a lie. She wouldn't feel this terrible, this torn, if she didn't love him. 'I do love you, Antonios,' she said, the words drawn from her reluctantly because she knew they would only make him insist all the more. 'But it's not enough.'

'Of course it's enough.' Triumph blazed through his voice and Lindsay closed her eyes briefly.

Daphne's words had been rattling around in her head all afternoon. *To love and to be loved...is all anyone needs.*

If only that were true. But she was all too afraid it wasn't, at least not for them. Not for her.

'I know what you're thinking,' Antonios said and Lindsay's eyes flew open.

'Do you?' she asked.

'You're wondering how it will work, with your condition.'

She stilled, wondering just how he intended to fix this. Control it, because that was what Antonios did with everything.

'A bit,' she allowed.

'I've thought about that,' Antonios continued, leaning forward, the untouched meal before them momentarily forgotten. 'We can make concessions, Lindsay.'

'Concessions,' she repeated, and knew she hated that word.

'Adjustments,' he amended. 'We'll curtail your appearances at public events. We can live separately from everyone else, in our own villa. We can even limit family engagements, although I hope in time you might come to accept—'

'Stop, Antonios—' she cut him off, unable to listen any more '—just stop.'

He sat back, confusion and irritation chasing across his features. 'I thought you'd be pleased.'

'That you're willing to make so many *concessions*?' she finished and his mouth tightened.

'It's just a word.'

'No, it's not.' She shook her head, slumping back in her seat. 'I don't want you to make concessions, Antonios. I don't want you to have to put up with me.'

'I'm not putting up with you—' he cut her off, his voice sharp '—I told you I loved you. I want this, Lindsay. I'm trying to be considerate.'

'I know you are,' Lindsay said. 'But it's not enough, Antonios. I'd only make you unhappy because I'm not what you want, not really.'

'Maybe you should let me decide what I want.'

'And you really want a wife who hides in the shadows, who can't be by your side?'

'In time—' he began and she shook her head almost frantically.

'No. No. I don't want you to try to *fix* me, Antonios.'

'You said yourself you've worked hard to control your anxiety. I just want to help you.'

Lindsay closed her eyes. 'So I can fulfil a role I never even wanted or asked for.' He was silent at that and she opened her eyes. 'In any case, you'd only become frustrated and disappointed. Because I'd never be good enough.'

'Let me decide that.'

'No, I won't, actually. I won't agree to a half life here that dwindles away to nothing when you decide you're done with me—'

'I wouldn't,' he shot back, his voice rising to a roar. 'I would never abandon a marriage.'

'Like I did?' The hurt spilling from her didn't make sense. She was so angry and so sad, and it felt as if nothing could make things better.

'Like your mother did,' Antonios answered. 'Because life wasn't what she expected. Was that why you left, Lindsay? Because life wasn't what *you* expected?'

She felt the blood drain from her face, empty from her head. 'I can't believe you said that.'

'Damn it, I'm trying to fight for our marriage. To find a compromise. What is so wrong about that?'

'Because the compromise rests on the assumption that I have to stay here in Greece and try to be your perfect little wife,' Lindsay snapped. 'And you never even asked if I wanted that.'

'I'm a traditional man,' Antonios answered tightly. 'Naturally I would expect my wife to have her place with me. And you told me you wanted to go to Greece, that there was nothing left for you in New York.'

'And I've told you since then,' Lindsay reminded him, 'that I was feeling particularly lonely and vulnerable when you asked me. But the truth is, Antonios, I did have a life in New York. Maybe it was a small one, with just a few friends, a little job. But I liked it. I don't want to give that all up just to be a shadow of the woman you want.'

They stared at each other, the anger and tension between them palpable in the cool night air. Antonios threw down his napkin on the table.

'*Theos*, I don't know what I can do,' he muttered, raking a hand through his hair.

Lindsay stared down at her plate as she blinked back

tears. Maybe she was being unreasonable. Unfair. Antonios had created this lovely romantic dinner, was trying to find ways to make her—*their*—life in Greece possible. And she just kept insisting it wouldn't—couldn't—work.

Maybe she needed to give a little. Find a way to make their marriage, their life together possible. Antonios was willing to be flexible; surely she could be, too. She could look into professorships at universities in Greece, or even do some private tutoring. Something. If she loved him she would try, wouldn't she?

Try to be someone you really aren't? Was that what love was?

'I never considered that coming to Greece would be difficult for you,' Antonios finally said, the words drawn from him slowly. 'I was so eager to bring you here, to have you share in my life. Because I was lonely, too, Lindsay. I needed you, even if you didn't think I did.'

Lindsay's throat had thickened so it hurt to get the words out. 'Antonios…'

'And I want you to want to share it,' he continued. 'But you don't.'

Lindsay felt a tear slide down her cheek. 'It's not that simple.'

'Isn't it?' He gazed at her bleakly. 'Isn't it, Lindsay? You don't even want to try.'

Because I'm afraid of failing. Because I'm afraid you'll reject me, hurt me, leave me.

The realization was painful in its clarity. This wasn't even about expectations, or living here, or whether she could teach in Greece. It was about fear—a fear she'd held on to since she was nine years old and her mother had walked out on her because she hadn't been enough.

She was so afraid of that happening again. More afraid than she'd ever admitted to herself.

She remembered when Antonios had asked her to marry him, to go with him to Greece.

They'd been lying on the huge king-sized bed in his suite at the Plaza, their legs tangled together, their hearts still beating fast from the lovemaking they'd just shared.

Antonios had twined his fingers with hers, ran his other hand up her bare thigh, resting it on the curve of her hip. 'I never thought I'd fall in love like this,' he'd told her, his voice husky with emotion. 'I never thought I'd be so lucky.'

Lindsay had blinked back tears as she'd answered, 'I never thought I would, either.'

'We're the luckiest people in the world,' he'd said with a smile before kissing her softly. And she'd agreed with him. She'd felt as if she'd won the lottery when she'd met Antonios. She'd felt like the most loved, adored and cherished woman in the world. After her lonely life, it had been the most incredible feeling.

And it had felt even more incredible when he'd risen onto his knees and taken her hands in his. 'I love you, Lindsay, more than anything. Will you be my wife?'

She'd seen the love shining in his eyes, felt it in herself. She hadn't had to think for so much as a millisecond before answering. 'Yes, Antonios. I'll marry you.'

They'd got married the next day, at a register office by special licence. It had been crazy and impulsive, and maybe that was because they'd both known that if they'd told people, Lindsay's colleagues or Antonios's family, someone would have talked them out of it. Advised them to wait.

And if they had waited?

Maybe they wouldn't be married after all.

But they were married, and they did love each other. And maybe that really could be enough.

'I never felt like I was good enough for my mother,' she told him slowly, haltingly. 'I felt like I always disappointed her, and that made me more anxious than anything else. She used to give me the silent treatment after I'd let her down. Once she didn't talk to me for a week.'

Antonios's face twisted with both sympathy and grief. 'And that was terrible, Lindsay. A terrible, terrible thing to endure.'

'And it affected me more than I'd ever let myself realize,' Lindsay continued. 'But I know now I can never let myself feel that way again. I can never let someone make me feel that way again.'

Antonios's expression darkened. 'And I would never do that to you.'

'But don't you see, Antonios, how it is?' Desperation edged her voice and her hands curled into fists at her sides. 'I don't fit in here. I can't be the kind of wife you need—'

'Maybe you should let me decide that.'

'I don't want you to have to make *concessions*—'

'It was just a word, Lindsay, just a stupid word!' He rose from his chair, took a step towards her. 'I love you. I fell in love with you in New York, on a snowy afternoon. Maybe it was fast and crazy but it was real, no matter what you said or tried to convince yourself of. What I felt for you, what I feel for you now, is *real*.' His voice throbbed with sincerity, the low growl of it reverberating through Lindsay's chest. 'And my love—our love—will be enough. I'll make sure of it. I won't let you down, I swear. I'll listen. I'll *see*.'

He looked so earnest and determined, and she wanted to believe him so badly. Was fear going to keep her from finding her happiness with this man? Would she let it?

'Lindsay.' He rose from his chair, came and dropped to his knees in front of her as he took her hands in his. 'Trust me. Please.'

Trust him. Trust him with her happiness as well as with her fear. With her heart and with her soul.

'You're asking a lot, Antonios,' she whispered.

'And I'll give a lot. I promise.' His hands tightened on hers.

She stared down at him, this proud, passionate man who was on his knees, begging for her. For her to love him. Her throat was so tight she could barely get the single word that she knew she meant, even if she was still afraid.

'Yes.'

He looked up at her, a fierce light of hope dawning in his eyes. 'Yes…?'

'Yes, Antonios, I'll try.'

With his eyes still blazing he pulled her face towards his, catching her up in his arms and then kissing her as if he would never stop.

And she never wanted him to.

CHAPTER NINE

As ANTONIOS'S MOUTH crashed down on Lindsay's, he realized how long it had been since he'd kissed his wife. They hadn't kissed yesterday morning when they'd almost made love. They hadn't kissed, he realized as his tongue plundered the silky depths of her mouth, since she'd said goodbye to him in Greece.

And now she'd said yes. Yes to their marriage, to their love. Yes to him. Triumph and need surged through him and he deepened the kiss, turned it into a demand. He wanted her to give him everything now, not just a hesitant yes from her mouth but a passionate cry from her body. Yes. *Yes.*

In one fluid movement he pulled the silvery dress up and over her head. She gasped softly, her skin pale and pearl-like in the wash of moonlight.

'Antonios...' she whispered, and his name ended on a soft moan as he kissed her again, his hands sliding over her body, remembering the wonderfully familiar feel of her. From the moment he'd first touched her, he'd felt how they fitted, two halves of a whole beautifully joined. Now, as he drew her slender curves towards his, he felt it again, that inalienable rightness of the two of them together. And Lindsay must have felt it, too, for she returned his kiss, her body yielding to his in every way possible.

She shuddered under his touch, his fingers finding her secret places as her head fell forward in surrender, her hair gleaming in the moonlight.

'You love me,' Antonios said fiercely and she let out a trembling laugh.

'I already told you I did.'

'Say it again,' Antonios demanded, needing to hear it. To believe it.

'I love you,' she told him, her voice choking. 'I love you, Antonios.'

And, with triumph roaring through him, Antonios kissed her again.

If he was trying to prove to her how much she loved him, Lindsay thought hazily, he was wasting his time. She knew she loved him. And he set her body on fire. There had never been any question of that.

Already sparks were spreading out from her centre as Antonios kissed his way down her body, his hands cupping her breasts, thumbs teasing the already taut peaks. Need coiled tightly inside her, everything in her straining for the satisfaction only he could give her.

She gasped his name as she pulled at his shirt, craving the feel of his bare skin against hers. Fingers fumbling, she unbuttoned his pants, tugging them down from his hips.

Antonios pulled her onto his lap and she straddled him, his arousal pressing against the soft juncture of her thighs.

The desperate need to have him inside her overwhelmed her, drove out any rational thought. She sobbed his name as he positioned her above him and then drove into her, her legs wrapped around his waist, his name a ragged cry torn from her lips.

Afterwards they remained wrapped around each other, Antonios braced against the stone fountain, Lindsay cradled in his lap with her legs around his waist.

'We look like a Lissajous curve,' she murmured against his shoulder and Antonios eased back to smile wryly at her.

'A what?'

'A figure eight, I suppose,' Lindsay explained. She gestured to their legs: his stretched out and hers pretzeled behind his back. 'A Lissajous curve is the graph of parametric equations that describe complex harmonic motion. It looks a bit like a figure eight.'

'Complex harmonic motion,' Antonios repeated thoughtfully, lightly rocking his hips against hers. 'That sounds about right.'

Lindsay laughed softly and rested her head against his shoulder, breathing in the tangy masculine scent of him. She felt utterly sated, both physically and emotionally. *Complete*. The resistance she'd kept up for so long had been swept away, just as Antonios had swept her away in New York.

She had no idea what the future would look or feel like, and dwelling too long on the possibilities and pitfalls made fear clench her belly. But, no matter how afraid she might feel, she no longer fought against the future. Against Antonios and her love for him. His love for her.

What they shared, she thought as she pressed a kiss against his bare shoulder, was impossible to fight.

Antonios adjusted their bodies so he could look into her

face. His eyes blazed with ferocity and yet his smile was tender. 'No regrets?' he asked softly and she smiled back.

'No. Some reservations, maybe. But no regrets.'

'It will work out, Lindsay. I swear it.'

And she knew that Antonios was the kind of man who would refuse all obstacles. Who would make things happen by sheer force of will. And maybe, for once, that was a good thing.

Tenderly, Antonios scooped her up from the fountain and carried her back to the table.

'Our dinner awaits.'

'I'm naked,' she pointed out, and Antonios gave a negligent shrug.

'I don't mind.'

She laughed, happiness rising inside her like a bubble. 'I'm also cold.'

He let out a theatrical sigh. 'Well, if you must,' he said, and scooped up her underwear and dress. Instead of handing them to her, he dressed her himself, slowly and lingeringly, so by the time he'd tugged up the zip on her dress Lindsay was nearly melting again with desire. 'Later,' he promised, and with one last soft kiss he led her back to the table and, with her heart brimming with happiness, Lindsay sat down to eat. She found she was suddenly starving.

Antonios left the bed, sunlight streaming over Lindsay as she lay tangled amidst the silken sheets, her hair spread over the pillow like a moonbeam. In sleep she looked relaxed and happy, her mouth curved in a small smile, one hand flung, palm upwards, by her face.

Antonios luxuriated in the simple pleasure of watching her and knowing she was his. Finally. Again. *His.*

Last night, after they'd made love, they'd spent several pleasant hours eating their delayed dinner and chatting in an easy way that he wasn't sure they'd ever experienced before, not even in those heady days in New York, when everything had been an odyssey of discovery. Certainly not in Greece, which in hindsight he could see had been marked by strain and silence. This was new, and all the more precious because of it.

They were building something good now, he told himself. Something new and strong. And he would make sure it worked. His mouth hardening in a line of resolve, he turned from Lindsay lying asleep in their bed.

The sun was rising in a bright blue sky, the olive groves sparkling under its light. He wanted to wake Lindsay up before he left for work, make love to her again, but he knew he needed to get to the office. He had a staff meeting in a few hours, and he still needed to talk with Leonidas.

Just the thought of his brother had Antonios's insides tightening in a familiar and unwelcome way. For ten years he'd lived with that tightening, the unrelenting pressure of leading his father's business away from the precipice of disaster while keeping it all from his family.

When he'd met Lindsay in New York and fallen in love with her, it had felt like the first time he'd truly relaxed or been happy. And even though he now had that again he couldn't ignore the tension that ratcheted inside him as he scrawled her a note and walked across the estate to Marakaios Enterprises' offices.

He needed to talk to Leonidas. He hadn't realized the extent of his brother's resentment. They'd been close growing up, getting into similar scrapes on the estate, sharing the usual boyish escapades. United, perhaps, in the alienation they'd felt from their father, who had been consumed by the business he'd eventually run into the ground.

Thinking about his father made Antonios's chest hurt. He loved his parents, his family, and as any Greek man he was fiercely loyal to them. Even acknowledging his father's faults to himself felt like a betrayal and he forced down the stress that felt as if it had a stranglehold on his soul.

'You're late,' Leonidas remarked, unsmiling, as Antonios came into the reception area of the office. Antonios suppressed a flicker of irritation as he walked past his brother into his office, its floor-to-ceiling windows overlooking the olive groves now dazzling in morning sunlight.

'I didn't realize you were waiting for me,' he said. He dropped his briefcase by his desk, shed his suit jacket and sat down before opening up his laptop.

Leonidas stood in front of his desk, arms folded and chin jutting. 'I want more control, Antonios.'

Antonios didn't look up from his laptop. He wasn't surprised by Leonidas's demand, but he still didn't know how he was going to deal with it. 'You're Head of European—'

'Don't fob me off with that,' Leonidas snapped. 'I'm not a dog to be tossed a bone. In the ten years since you took over, I've never had access to financial information. I've never had any true authority. I'm nothing more than a front man who's meant to do the fancy talk.'

'And you're so good at it,' Antonios pointed out, spite spiking his voice even though he'd meant it to be flattery.

'Well, I'm done with being patronized,' Leonidas stated. 'You either give me more control or I leave.'

Anger surged through Antonios and he rose from his chair, one hand flat on the desk as he glared at his brother. 'Are you threatening me?'

'Simply stating a fact.' They glared at each other and in some distant corner of his brain Antonios wondered how it had come to this.

Because your father made it happen.

'I wonder,' Leonidas continued coolly, 'why you insist on hiding the financial information, Antonios.'

'Our accountant is completely up to date—'

'And you never let me in on those meetings. You've never let me so much as look at a spreadsheet. What are you hiding, I wonder?'

It took Antonios a stunned second to realize what his brother was implying. That he was cooking the books, skimming money off the top. It was so far from the truth that for a moment he couldn't speak.

'Don't *ever*,' he finally warned Leonidas in a low voice, 'make such a despicable insinuation again. I've given my life, my soul, to Marakaios Enterprises.'

Leonidas stared at him for a long moment, his jaw tight. 'You're not the only one,' he finally said, and walked out.

Antonios sank into his chair, his mind still spinning, and pulled his laptop towards him. Grimly he clicked the mouse to download his emails and refused to think about what Leonidas had just said.

A couple of hours later he heard voices in the reception area and lifted his head to see Lindsay coming through his door. A wave of relieved joy broke over him at the sight of her; she wore a floral sundress and her hair tumbled loose about her shoulders. She offered him a shy smile as she came in the room and Antonios rose from behind his desk, barely restraining himself from striding across the room and pulling her into a desperately needed embrace.

'I thought I'd see how you are,' she said with a little smile. 'And where you work. I hope you don't mind.'

'I don't.' Emotion bottled in his chest, making his voice sound abrupt. Lindsay frowned.

'Is everything all right, Antonios?'

'Fine. Everything's fine, now that you're here.' Her frown deepened at this but Antonios didn't care. He just needed to touch her. He came round from his desk and pulled her into his arms, fitting her against him, needing her there.

She pressed her hands to either side of his face, twisting to look up at him. 'You seem angry.'

'Just a little stressed. Nothing to worry about.' And to silence any further questions he kissed her, revelling in the honeyed sweetness of her mouth, the instant melting of her response.

He slid his hands down her body to cup her bottom and fit her even more snugly against his growing arousal. She let out a choked laugh.

'Antonios…'

'You know something I've never done in my office?'

'I think I can probably guess.'

He slid his hands under her sundress, fingers finding sweet, warm flesh. He rejoiced at the way she shuddered under his touch, her head falling onto his shoulder.

'Your PA is right outside…' she murmured, but offered no other resistance.

'The door is closed and incredibly soundproof.'

'How do you know?'

He didn't, but at this point he didn't care. 'Trust me,'

he said, and hoisted her onto his desk. Lindsay's lovely eyes widened as he spread her legs and got rid of her underwear with one swift tug. They widened further when he stepped between her legs, stroking her softly as she moaned her response.

'This is crazy,' she murmured, and Antonios slid inside her.

'Crazy,' he agreed, 'and incredible.'

And Lindsay obviously agreed as her body arched under his and she wrapped her legs around his waist to pull him even more deeply inside her.

Afterwards he still didn't let her go, savouring the feel of her, already wanting her again. 'What do you think about going into Amfissa for lunch?' he asked.

Suddenly the thought of escaping the office, the entire estate, seemed like a wonderful and even necessary idea.

'Now?' She peered up at him again. 'But the party's tonight...'

'Right. Of course.' The hope that had seized him for a moment trickled away. He needed to stop by the villa, make sure the preparations were going well, check on his mother. His sisters would expect it. His family needed it.

Lindsay searched his face for a moment, a slight frown puckering her forehead. 'I suppose we could,' she said after a moment. 'For a few hours. I was just in the villa, trying to help your sisters. I think I'm more help to them by just staying out of the way.'

'They can be a bit officious when it comes to party planning,' Antonios conceded with a smile, and Lindsay gave a rueful nod.

'Why don't we go?' she suggested softly. 'Have a date? They can do without us for an hour or two, surely.'

An hour or two snatched from a packed schedule.

They'd had even less the last time they'd been together in Greece, Antonios acknowledged. Work had consumed him and he'd expected, wrongly, for Lindsay to simply slot herself into all that was going on around her.

He wouldn't make that mistake again.

'Let's go,' he said and, taking her by the hand, he led her out of the office.

Lindsay followed Antonios from the office, blinking in the bright sunlight. Ten minutes later they were in his SUV, speeding down the mountain towards Amfissa, the town no more than a cluster of red-roofed, whitewashed buildings huddled against the mountainside.

'I haven't even been in Amfissa before,' Lindsay said a bit ruefully, and Antonios shot her just as regretful a glance.

'I know. I was realizing again how little we actually did together before. That undoubtedly made things even harder for you.'

'Yes. You were busy, though, with work. I understood that.' At least, she'd tried to. But she knew her anxiety had been made worse by Antonios's absence, his total focus on work as soon as they'd returned to Greece.

Antonios flexed his hands on the steering wheel. 'I should have made time. We should have had a honeymoon.'

'Our meeting was our honeymoon,' Lindsay joked and Antonios shook his head.

'We'll have a proper honeymoon after my mother's party. When I can get away.'

'And when will that be, do you think?' Lindsay spoke lightly even as realization was slipping through her in an unwelcome rush. No matter what Antonios had said about things being different now, they surely couldn't be that different. He was still CEO of a company that demanded much of his time and energy. When she'd come into the office this morning he'd looked so grimly focused, so unhappy.

It had surprised and unsettled her, and it made her wonder if Antonios really could work less. If their marriage could work.

Plenty of women had workaholic husbands, she reminded herself. It didn't have to be a deal-breaker.

'Don't,' Antonios said softly, and reached over to link her hand with his.

She turned to him. 'Don't what?'

'Don't start worrying already. We'll make this work, Lindsay, I swear it. We both want it to work, don't we?'

'Yes—'

'Then it will.'

He sounded so confident, so sure, as sure as he had when he'd asked her out, when he'd asked her to marry him. She'd believed in him then, and she chose to believe in him now. At least for an afternoon when they could simply revel in each other's company, an afternoon out of time, out of reality.

And when you return to Villa Marakaios? When life catches up with you, with all of its expectations and demands?

She'd think about that later, Lindsay told herself, and pushed the questions to the furthest reaches of her mind. Today she just wanted to enjoy herself—and enjoy being with Antonios.

Once in Amfissa they strolled down the town's wide main boulevard, taking in the many different shops. Antonios was recognized by many of the townspeople and he stopped and spoke to them all, introducing Lindsay. She could handle small groups of people and everyone seemed so friendly, so interested, that the initial anxiety she felt melted away and she chatted with the different people easily, or as easily as she could considering they spoke different languages.

'Is it all right, meeting all these people?' Antonios asked as they walked away from a local joiner and his wife who had been shopping in the market, and had welcomed Lindsay with kisses on both of her cheeks.

'It's fine,' she answered, and meant it. 'I'm not anxious.' It was different, she realized, having Antonios by her side, concerned and supportive. Different when she didn't have the weight of expectation and potential disappointment on her. Not a magical cure by any means, and she knew she would still be dealing with her anxiety for years to come. But it was better. She felt stronger.

'Let's have some lunch,' Antonios said, and led her down a side street to a small taverna tucked away from prying eyes.

The inside of the restaurant was dim and quiet, with only a few patrons who barely looked up from their meals as they entered. Antonios spoke rapidly in Greek to the owner of the place, and within minutes he was ushering them to a private table at the back of the restaurant. The owner brought them menus, a bottle of spring water and two glasses before quietly disappearing.

'A little privacy never goes amiss,' Antonios said.

'I was fine,' Lindsay protested.

'I know you were. I was proud of you, Lindsay. But I want you to myself now.' He gave her a teasingly lascivious smile and she laughed and shook her head.

'You're insatiable.'

'Only when it comes to you.'

Which felt like some kind of miracle. She'd spent so much of her life feeling deficient and unworthy. Yet Antonios looked at her and saw someone strong, someone beautiful. Someone he loved.

'You know,' she said slowly, 'I think part of the reason I didn't tell you about my anxiety is because I didn't want you to look at me differently.' Antonios waited, eyebrows raised, clearly sensing she had more to say. 'When we met in New York you made me feel so special and beautiful and strong. And I was afraid you'd stop looking at me that way if you knew.'

'I wouldn't—'

'I know that now, Antonios, because you didn't. Because you know the truth and you still love me. You still make me feel special.' She blinked back tears of emotion as she reached for his hand. 'Even more special because you know me completely. I'm not hiding anything from you.'

He squeezed her hand. 'And I pray you never do or feel you have to.'

'I won't.'

They ordered then, and spent the next hour tasting each other's dishes and chatting companionably. Afterwards they strolled through the town, hand in hand as the cares fell away from them both.

Lindsay noticed how much more relaxed Antonios seemed, away from Villa Marakaios—or was it their renewed relationship that had smoothed away the lines of strain from his nose to his mouth and brought the sparkle back to his whisky-coloured eyes?

'I feel like I did back in New York,' she confessed as they sat on one of the stone walls that overlooked the valley, on one of the town's higher winding streets. 'When we first met.'

'That's a good thing, I hope?' Antonios answered, his eyebrows raised, and Lindsay smiled and nodded.

'Yes. Definitely. You seem more like you did in New York.'

'And how is that?'

'More relaxed. Happier.' She paused then asked cautiously, 'Sometimes it seems like work doesn't make you happy, Antonios. Like it's a huge strain.' She waited for him to say something in response but he didn't, just gazed out at the valley with his eyes narrowed.

'I suppose in New York I was free from the concerns of work and daily life,' he finally said, his gaze still on the view. 'It was, as you said before, a time apart.'

'So we need to figure out how to make things work amidst those concerns.'

'And we will,' Antonios said with the same confidence he'd shown in the restaurant. 'All that matters is that we love each other, Lindsay. The rest will work itself out.'

He raised her hand to his lips and kissed it, and Lindsay smiled and said nothing. She wanted to feel as confident as Antonios seemed to be, but worries still nagged at her, made her wonder just *how* things were going to work themselves out. Would Antonios work less? Would he entertain less? How were they actually going to manage the day-to-day of their joined lives?

A short while later they headed back to the car and drove in silence back to Villa Marakaios. Lindsay slid a sideways glance at Antonios as they approached the estate, silently noting how his eyes narrowed and his mouth hardened the moment they drove through the gates.

At their own villa he left her with a quick distracted

kiss, telling her he needed to return to the office before the party that night. Reluctantly, Lindsay headed over to the main villa to see if she could help with the preparations. Antonios's sisters seemed to have affairs well in hand but she wanted to be seen to make an effort, even if she still found her relationship with her sisters-in-law to be one of tension and suspicion.

'Oh, Lindsay, where have you been? Was Antonios with you? Ava's been looking for him—'

'We went out for a bit,' Lindsay answered. 'Is everything all right?'

'Parthenope's been tied up all afternoon with Timon,' Xanthe explained. 'And Ava has decided she can't wear anything she owns and has gone shopping, of all things.' Xanthe rolled her eyes in exasperation.

'Is Timon all right?'

'Just a bit of cold,' Xanthe dismissed. 'But Parthenope was meant to deal with the caterers, where to have them set up, all of that. I've been busy myself with the decorations—'

'I could help,' Lindsay offered and Xanthe looked, perhaps rightly, sceptical. Lindsay straightened, threw back her shoulders. 'What do you need me to do?'

'Well...' Xanthe nibbled her lip. 'The housekeeper Maria is sorting them out in the kitchen, but she's in a flap because she wanted to do the cooking herself. Mama said no, because it was too much. Maria is not as young as she once was.'

'I see,' Lindsay said. 'So you want me to talk to Maria?'

Xanthe nodded in relief. 'Yes, and then show the caterers what to do.' Xanthe turned back to the table she was festooning with large silk bows, clearly itching to keep going with her own work. 'Do you think you could do that?' she tossed over her shoulder.

'Yes, of course,' Lindsay said with more confidence than she felt. She didn't even know where the kitchen was.

She watched Xanthe for a moment, fussing with one of the bows, and then turned and made her uncertain way to the kitchen, opening a few random doors until one of the house staff pointed her towards the large, light room at the back of the house.

The caterers were bringing in large plastic-wrapped trays of hors d'oeuvres, watched over by a silent and surly Maria. Lindsay had seen the housekeeper in passing and had probably been introduced to her on that first awful day, but they'd never had a conversation.

She took a deep breath and approached her. '*Herete*, Maria,' she said as cheerfully as she could. 'Is everything all right?'

Maria just looked at her blankly, and Lindsay realized the older woman did not speak English. And she, unfortunately, had no more than a few words of Greek.

She gestured to the caterers and raised her eyebrows in query, asking haltingly, '*Ti kanete?*' How are you?

In answer Maria let out a torrent of Greek that Lindsay could not begin to understand, but she certainly got the gist of Maria's bitterness at having strangers invade her kitchen. Making soothing noises, she led the woman over to the table in a sunny alcove, and listened with all signs of interest and attention as Maria continued to lament in a language she didn't speak.

Fifteen minutes later, having vented her spleen, Maria seemed somewhat appeased, and with gestures and an absurd amount of miming Lindsay suggested she organize the hors d'oeuvres. The caterers could have a respite from Maria scowling at them, and the housekeeper would hopefully feel she was being consulted.

Twenty minutes later things were going smoothly, and Lindsay felt rather ridiculously proud of herself for coping with it all. She was smiling as she came back to the front house, stopping when she saw Antonios come through the door of the living room, scowling.

'Is everything all right?' she asked, and Antonios jerked his gaze towards her, his face clearing, Lindsay suspected, by sheer force of will.

'Fine. Are things in hand in the kitchen? I just got an earful from Xanthe.'

'Yes, I think so. I was just down with Maria.'

'Were you?' Antonios's eyebrows rose at that, and Lindsay smiled self-consciously.

'I didn't realize she didn't speak English, but we managed all right.'

'That's very good to hear.'

'Shall we go back to the villa?' she asked, and Antonios nodded. Lindsay could still see lines of tension bracketing his mouth and eyes and she stopped in front of him, reaching up to cup his cheek. 'Are you sure you're all right?' she asked quietly.

Antonios closed his eyes briefly, seeming to take strength from her small caress. 'I'm fine,' he said, and Lindsay heard the note of implacability enter his voice. He sounded, she thought, like she used to, claiming things were fine when they clearly weren't.

As she followed Antonios out of the villa, she wondered if he would be as honest with her as she had learned to be with him, and tell her what was going on.

CHAPTER TEN

Antonios stood on the edge of the living room, watching as guests chatted and circulated amidst the staff holding trays of hors d'oeuvres. His mother sat on a chair in the centre of the room, looking weary and yet happy as she held court over all the family, friends and neighbours that had been invited to her name day party.

His gaze moved to the opposite corner of the room where Lindsay stood, looking pale and lovely and amazingly poised, chatting with a guest, a smile making her seem radiant. She was, Antonios thought, the most beautiful and elegant woman in the room.

While they were getting ready, back at their own villa, he'd assured her that she wouldn't need to be the centre of attention and could leave if she felt uncomfortable. Invariably, though, Lindsay attracted attention. She was beautiful, and she was his wife. People wanted to meet her, talk to her, and Antonios had responsibilities of his own. As much as he wanted to, he couldn't hide in the corner, protecting his wife.

Not, he acknowledged with a small wry smile, that Lindsay needed protecting. She'd been more than holding her own so far tonight, chatting with people as they approached her, smiling and laughing. Pride surged through him, mixed with love. She was everything he'd ever wanted in a wife, a partner.

His gaze narrowed as he watched Leonidas come up to her. He still hadn't agreed to give Leonidas access to any of the company's financial information, and he didn't think he ever could, not without betraying his father.

He'd thought, more than once, about telling Leonidas the truth. Sharing the burden. But it wasn't his secret to share. He'd made a promise. A vow. If he couldn't honour it, what sort of man was he?

One whose family is being torn apart by secrecy.

Now, as he watched Leonidas talk to Lindsay, he wondered if his brother intended to put pressure on his wife. Leonidas was so angry and bitter that Antonios wouldn't put such an underhand tactic past him at this point.

Lindsay frowned at Leonidas and every protective instinct in Antonios reared up. The last thing he needed or wanted was his brother breathing his bitter poison into his wife's ear. His mouth set in a grim line, he headed towards his brother and his wife.

Lindsay had been trying to answer Leonidas's questions in a relaxed manner but the more he talked, the harder it was to ignore the edge to his voice.

Are you happy to be back at Villa Marakaios? It's all marital bliss, is it? You and Antonios have everything you want, I suppose? He certainly does.

Lindsay couldn't tell if Leonidas knew the truth of their earlier troubles or if he was simply bitter about what he perceived as his brother's good fortune. What was coming through, loud and clear, was the resentment and animosity he felt towards Antonios.

'Everything all right here?' Antonios asked as he

strolled up to them. His voice was pleasant but his gaze had snapped to Lindsay, and she could see the question in his eyes.

'Fine,' Leonidas answered for both of them. 'Just getting to know my sister-in-law. Wondering what she sees in you.' Lindsay thought Leonidas had meant this as a joke, but it fell rather flat.

'I wonder myself every day,' Antonios answered, his voice light but his face unsmiling. 'Lindsay, there are some people who would like to meet you. The Atrikes family. They're local business owners. Why don't you come with me?' He held out his hand and, with a moment's hesitant glance at Leonidas, whose expression had ironed out to bland boredom, she took it.

'What's going on between you and Leonidas?' she asked when they were alone in a private alcove off the library.

'What do you mean?'

'You clearly don't get along,' Lindsay said bluntly. 'And yet you work together.'

Antonios twitched his shoulders in an impatient shrug. 'Nothing more than a little brotherly competition.'

'Over what?' He just shrugged again, not answering, and frustration fired through her. 'Antonios, can't you tell me? You didn't like it when you were in the dark about how I was feeling, but now you're the same—'

'It's just a business matter—' he cut her off, his tone dismissive '—it will sort itself out.'

'What kind of business matter?'

'Nothing you need to concern yourself about.' He'd kept his voice mild but Lindsay still felt the rebuke. Nothing he wanted to concern her with, he'd meant.

'You're doing so well tonight, Lindsay,' he continued, and dropped a kiss onto her forehead. 'You're the most beautiful woman in the room, the most elegant and poised. I'm proud of you.'

She smiled and turned her face so he could kiss her on the mouth. He did so, lingeringly, and Lindsay knew both of them were thinking about later that evening, after the party, when they could be alone.

'I'm proud of you, Antonios,' she told him. 'You've led your family and your business so well in the absence of your father. So many people have been telling me how you've taken the helm of Marakaios Enterprises without a single misstep.'

Antonios smiled at this, but it was a small, tight smile that didn't reach his eyes.

'We should go. The Atrikes family are waiting.'

A little while later they headed back to the living area, where Xanthe and Parthenope were ushering people towards the dining room, where platters of food were laid out.

Daphne rose from her chair, her hands outstretched towards Antonios. 'Antonios, Lindsay. Come celebrate with me.'

Lindsay came forward and took Daphne's hand, feeling how fragile it was in hers, the skin papery, the bones seeming hollow, like a bird's.

Daphne smiled wryly, as if she noticed Lindsay's awareness, and squeezed her hand. 'Tonight is for happiness,' she said quietly, and her gaze moved to Antonios. 'Yes?'

'Yes,' Lindsay said firmly and gently squeezed her mother-in-law's hand back.

The party lasted until well after midnight, even though Daphne excused herself earlier, tired as she was. By the time she and Antonios returned to their little villa, Lindsay was exhausted, her feet aching.

'I think it was a success,' she said as she kicked off her heels with a sigh of relief. She hadn't had a single moment of true anxiety, at least in part because Antonios had been aware of when she needed to take a step back, have a moment's space and peace.

'I think so,' Antonios agreed. He shrugged out of his suit jacket and undid the knot of his tie. Even though he'd been his charming, confident self throughout the whole evening, Lindsay had sensed his restlessness and tension and it felt like a thorn in her side, in their marriage.

'Are you sure everything is all right, Antonios?' she asked. 'Between you and Leonidas?'

'It's fine,' he dismissed and took her into his arms. 'And the last thing I want to talk or even think about now is my brother. Do you know how beautiful you look in that dress?'

Lindsay glanced down at the pale blue evening gown she wore, the silk rippling in a shimmering sheet to the floor, reminding her of water. She'd never cared much about clothes one way or the other, but she loved the look on Antonios's face when he saw her in something beautiful. When he so clearly thought *she* was beautiful.

'You look gorgeous,' Antonios said in a growl as he pulled her to him. 'But I couldn't stop thinking about peeling it off you all evening.'

Lindsay laughed softly, already breathless with anticipation. 'And will you make that a reality, do you think?'

'I intend to right now.' His gaze blazed into hers as he reached around to her back and slowly, sensuously, tugged the zip all the way down to her hips. The dress fell from her shoulders and, with one tiny shrug, it slid down to her waist.

The style had precluded the wearing of a bra and Lindsay wasn't so generously endowed that she needed one, so now she stood before him, completely bare to the waist, basking in the admiration, the *adoration* she saw in his eyes.

A lump of emotion rose in her throat and Antonios tugged her towards him by the hand. 'What are you thinking?' he asked hoarsely. 'You look as if you're about to cry.'

'I was wondering how I ever could have left you,' Lindsay whispered, her voice catching. 'Even for a moment.'

He pulled her towards him, her breasts colliding with the crisp cotton of his shirt, the friction sending shivery arrows of pleasure ricocheting through her. 'Never again,' Antonios whispered against her hair as he slid his hands up her bare back to cradle her face. 'Never leave me again, Lindsay. Promise. I couldn't bear it.'

'I promise,' she whispered, and then lost herself to Antonios's passionate, desperate kiss.

The next few weeks seemed to pass in a golden blur of contentment and joy: days spent working on her research or walking through the countryside, taking the first steps in getting to know Antonios's family. His sisters were still a little guarded, but they'd thawed when Lindsay had, at Antonios's urging, explained about her anxiety.

Parthenope's face had fallen and she'd pulled Lindsay into a spontaneous hug. 'You should have told us. It would have made such a difference.'

'Parthenope thought you were a snob,' Ava confided and Parthenope pulled away from Lindsay, blushing.

'Ava!'

'Because you're so smart,' Ava continued, shooting her sister a mischievous glance. 'She's jealous, really. I'm the only one who went to university.'

'I got married instead,' Parthenope said, her cheeks bright red.

'I'm not sure a doctorate in number theory is something to be jealous of,' Lindsay said wryly. Her mind reeled from her sisters-in-law's admissions. 'It's not very useful.'

'Antonios told us it was,' Xanthe piped up. 'He said it would help with all sorts of advancements in technology and science.'

'Well, maybe,' Lindsay allowed. The thought that Antonios had championed her research sent a tingling warmth through her.

'We did wonder if you thought you were too good for us,' Parthenope admitted, her face still flushed, and Lindsay's jaw nearly dropped.

'I never thought that,' she said. 'Not once.'

They all smiled at each other, awkwardly and yet with affection, and while Lindsay knew she might not have been what Antonios's sisters had been expecting or even wanting for his wife, she knew they accepted her. A few weeks ago their acceptance would have made her feel guilty, wondering yet again if she should have been honest about her issues when she'd been in Greece before. Now she recognized that she couldn't have been, that both she and Antonios were different people now, capable of different things.

A week after Daphne's birthday party Antonios had

asked her if they could move into the main villa. 'My mother would like us there,' he said. 'And I would like to be there. We'll have our own wing, and you can redecorate as you like—'

His thoughtfulness nearly brought tears to her eyes. 'Of course we can move back to the main villa,' she said.

Yet it was a little strange to be back in the house where she'd once been so unhappy. She walked down the upstairs corridor, her footsteps muffled on the thick carpet, and remembered how she'd run up these stairs, spots dancing before her eyes, everything in her aching, as she'd excused herself from yet another endless social function, Antonios so wilfully oblivious.

In the huge sumptuous bathroom she remembered how she'd locked the door and curled up against the marble tub, hugging her knees to her chest and rocking back and forth as she'd tried to calm her racing heart.

And in the bedroom she remembered how Antonios had brought her such incredible pleasure, and how she'd left him one chilly morning, the grey light of dawn filtering through the curtains as she'd kissed him goodbye and felt her heart break.

So many memories, and she didn't want to linger on them for too long. She wanted to make new memories, have new dreams. Inadvertently, Lindsay pressed her hand against her stomach. They hadn't used protection in the last few weeks, something that made her insides lurch with both excitement and alarm. She knew Antonios had wanted to start a family right away; she'd been more cautious. But now she thought about a baby— Antonios's baby—and a smile spread across her face at the possibility.

Antonios came into the bedroom, resting his hands

on her shoulders as he stood behind her. Both of them were silent, gazing at the wide bed with its cream silk duvet, the shutters of the windows open to the view of the mountains.

Lindsay knew they were both remembering, reliving those last moments. Her final farewell. Then Antonios brushed a kiss against the nape of her neck and it felt like a benediction. They were both moving on from the past.

'I have something to show you,' he said, his breath fanning her skin and making her shiver.

'You do?'

'Come.' He tugged her by the hand down the corridor of their private wing, towards a room Lindsay hadn't been in before. He pushed open the door and then stepped aside so she could enter.

Her breath caught in her chest as she took in the spacious sunlit room: the wide oak desk with the top-of-the-line desktop computer, the comfortable chair, the bookshelves and the huge dry-erase board, just like she'd had in her office back in New York.

'For your research,' he said simply. 'If there's anything else you need, just let me know and I'll get it for you.'

She turned and threw her arms around his neck. 'There's nothing else I need,' she told him as she kissed him. 'Nothing else at all.'

Another week slid by, a week blurred by pleasure and love, and yet not without its moments of disquiet. Antonios still spent all his days and many of his evenings at work, and Lindsay couldn't ignore the strain that etched lines on his face and made him quiet and irritable whenever she asked him about it.

Love was complicated, she reminded herself. *Life* was.

Whatever Antonios was dealing with, he'd tell her in his own time. They could deal with it.

But one night she woke up to an empty bed and, with unease crawling along her spine, she rose and went to their adjoining living area, stopping in the doorway when she saw Antonios standing by the window, one hand braced against the glass.

'Antonios…'

He didn't turn at the sound of her voice. 'I couldn't sleep,' he said, his voice flat and toneless.

'Is everything all right?' she asked. It was the same question she'd asked before, over and over, and as usual Antonios gave the same answer.

'It's fine.'

'Something's going on, Antonios,' Lindsay protested. 'I can feel it. You're unhappy—'

'Just a little stressed,' he corrected, but Lindsay felt it was more than that, deeper than that.

She also knew she wouldn't get any answers from Antonios now. Wordlessly, she went back to bed, lay flat on her back and stared up at the ceiling.

Why wouldn't Antonios tell her what was going on? He'd been hurt that she'd kept so much from him, and he'd never ever noticed she was unhappy. Yet now she was noticing and Antonios didn't seem to want her to.

Sighing, Lindsay told herself yet again to be patient. To trust. They could get through this. She had to believe that.

A month after Daphne's name day party Lindsay received an email from a university in New York City, offering her an assistant professorship of Pure Mathematics. She stared at it in surprise, knowing she shouldn't be so shocked since her supervisor had hinted that her research was being well received by academia in general. But that had been a lifetime ago, when she'd only had her research to think about, to keep her company…

And now? She felt a treacherous flicker of doubt and yearning. She loved being with Antonios, was enjoying this time in Greece…*but for the rest of her life?*

She looked up from her computer and gazed unseeingly out at the pine-covered mountains. She and Antonios had been enjoying a honeymoon period to their marriage, she realized. But even the honeymoon had its bumps, with Antonios's stress over work. And when that phase wore off, when he worked even harder, when the stress and strain of that work took an even greater toll?

Antonios had made it clear he couldn't leave Greece. But what if he needed to? What if working for Marakaios Enterprises, for whatever reason he refused to name, was killing him, destroying his happiness?

What if he needed something different as much as she did—or even more?

The thought was so incredible, so revolutionary, that Lindsay couldn't take it in fully. And maybe it was just wishful thinking because she wanted Antonios's plans to fit in with her own. But she'd tied herself to him and promised to try life in Greece again. She couldn't suggest something else now, not even for his sake. Antonios wouldn't countenance it for a moment.

And, really, she couldn't imagine Antonios anywhere else. This was his home, his kingdom. Yet she also knew she missed the excitement of teaching a class, discussing number theory with students and professors. Being part of a community, however small, of people who were as passionate and excited about mathematics as she was.

Restless and more than a little anxious, Lindsay closed her laptop and headed outside. It was a glorious fall day and the estate gardens were still in full flower. She walked down the winding brick paths that led to different gardens: the walled herb garden where she'd talked to Daphne, the courtyard with the fountain where she and Antonios had reconciled and made love. Just looking at the stone lip of the fountain where she'd wrapped herself around his body made her blush and smile.

She sank onto a stone bench, staring at that fountain, trying to untangle all the feelings that had become twisted up inside her. Hope and fear. Frustration and joy. Anxiety—not for herself, but for Antonios.

'Li-li!' Lindsay turned around to see two-year-old Timon toddling towards her. He'd started calling her Li-li a few days ago, much to everyone's amusement. Now Lindsay reached out and grabbed him by his chubby hands.

'Have you escaped, young man?' she asked, and Timon grinned up at her uncomprehendingly; he was learning both English and Greek, but he understood Greek much better.

'Timon!' Parthenope appeared around the corner, worry replaced by exasperation as she caught sight of her son. She let out a stream of scolding Greek but the little boy just giggled. Rolling her eyes at Lindsay, Parthenope gathered her son up on her lap and sat next to her on the bench.

'You are well?' she asked, a frown settling between her straight brows, and Lindsay laughed lightly.

'Do I not look well?'

'You look worried.' She hesitated then asked cautiously, 'Are things all right between you and Antonios?'

Lindsay stiffened at the implication that Parthenope, and who knew who else, suspected they weren't. 'Yes, of course.'

'Because, you know, when you left for New York he walked around like a raging lion. He pretended he was fine; he wouldn't tell us a thing, but we all knew better.'

Lindsay fought a flush as Parthenope subjected her to a searching gaze. 'Well…things are a lot better than that,' she said after a moment. 'We're working out our problems.'

At least, she hoped they were.

Parthenope laid a hand on her arm as Timon squirmed out of her lap. 'Marriage is not always easy.'

'No, that's what your mother said,' Lindsay said with a small smile. '"Endlessly complicated and difficult" were her exact words.'

Parthenope let out a little laugh. 'Perhaps not quite that bad. But if you both try, it will be good, yes?'

Lindsay saw the hope and concern in Parthenope's eyes and slowly nodded. She sincerely hoped trying was enough. But was Antonios even trying? If he was, surely he would share some of his concerns with her. Maybe, Lindsay thought, she needed to ask him more bluntly. Demand, even, out of her love for him.

She smiled at Parthenope, not wanting to burden her sister-in-law with her private concerns. 'Yes,' she said, 'it will be good.'

That night Antonios stayed late at work, which left Lindsay alone in their bedroom, waiting for him and thinking far too much. At nearly eleven o'clock at night she finally broke down and headed out into the night to look for him.

The air was cool and crisp and she shivered in just her light sweater and jeans as she walked down the deserted drives towards the office building; she could see a single light burning inside.

The front door was open and she slipped silently inside, her heart starting to beat hard. She walked towards Antonios's office; his door was ajar and she stood at the threshold, peeked inside.

At the sight of him her heart lurched with fear, swooped with sorrow. He looked so despairing, his head cradled in his hands, his shoulders bowed.

'Antonios...' she whispered and he jerked up straight, anger blazing in his eyes.

'What are you doing here?'

'I was looking for you.'

'You shouldn't have. You knew I was working.'

She knew his anger was a defence mechanism but it still stung. 'It's nearly midnight, Antonios.'

'I have a lot going on at the moment.'

She took a step into the room, glanced at the computer screen that had been left up, with its many columns of numbers. 'What are you doing?'

He slammed down the lid of his laptop. 'Don't. Don't look at that.'

Lindsay felt herself go cold at the implacable note in his voice. 'Why not?' she asked as reasonably as she could. 'It's only numbers.'

'And you're so good at numbers,' Antonios shot back.

Lindsay jerked back at the sneer in his voice. 'Antonios, what is going on? Why are you acting this way, hiding—'

'I'm not hiding,' he returned in a near roar. '*Theos*, Lindsay, just let me be.' He rose from his chair, pacing the room like a caged lion, one hand clenching in his hair. He looked, Lindsay thought, like a man in torment.

'I don't understand what's going on,' she said quietly. 'And I think I need to.'

Antonios didn't even turn around. 'Trust me, you don't.'

'Does this have to do with Leonidas?' Antonios didn't answer and, filled with frustration, Lindsay walked up to him, put her hands on his taut back. 'Damn it, Antonios, stop hiding things from me. You're making a double standard for our marriage and it's not fair.'

'Don't talk to me about what's fair,' Antonios answered bleakly, and she shook her head.

'I don't understand.'

'I don't want you to understand.' He turned around, clasping her cold hands in his. 'Lindsay, you're right. I am hiding something from you, but I have to.' Anguish lit his eyes and twisted his features. 'Please believe me. This has nothing to do with you, with us. It's just business. Naturally, there are some confidential matters I can't discuss—'

'Confidential matters that are tearing you apart, making you look haunted?' Lindsay finished. 'Making you seem like someone else entirely. Antonios, you're wrong. This has everything to do with us.' She stared at him, watched as his mouth thinned and his eyes hardened. She knew he wouldn't tell her anything now.

Wordlessly, she slipped her hands from his and walked from the room.

CHAPTER ELEVEN

ANTONIOS LISTENED TO the front door of the office close and with a groan he sank back in his chair, raking his hands through his hair. *Theos*, what had he been about to do?

He flipped up the screen of the laptop and watched as the financial figures of Marakaios Enterprises filled the screen. Figures he'd been contemplating doctoring to hide his father's shame—and add to his own. He couldn't believe he'd been contemplating doing something illegal for his father, or at least his father's memory. His father had done his fair share of tinkering with numbers, and Antonios had felt nothing but a sickening disdain. Yet now he'd been about to do the same thing.

He rose from his chair and restlessly paced the length of his office. He felt a need to escape not just the confines of the room, but of his life. Of the promise he'd made to his father, and the shackle Marakaios Enterprises had become to him.

He'd alienated his brother by hiding the truth of his father's actions, and now he'd done the same to Lindsay. He groaned aloud, shaking his head. Somehow this had to stop before it was too late. But maybe it was too late already.

A little after two in the morning Antonios headed back to the villa. Lindsay was already asleep, curled on her side, her knees tucked up to her chest like a child's. Antonios doubted he'd be able to sleep. It had eluded him most nights these last few weeks. Leonidas was barely talking to him, and the tension in the office was palpable, not just to him but to all the staff. And he still didn't know what to do.

He was still staring gritty-eyed at the ceiling when, an hour later, a light yet urgent tapping at the door of the bedroom had every sense springing to alert. Antonios rose from the bed, careful not to disturb Lindsay, and went to answer the door.

'Xanthe—'

'Antonios, it's Mama.' His sister's face was pale and pinched, tears shining in her eyes. Antonios felt as if his heart had stilled for a moment before beginning to thud with hard, painful beats.

'What has happened?'

'She woke up in the night, moaning and in pain. Maria has called the doctor. But she seems…it seems…' Xanthe couldn't go on, tears spilling down her cheeks, and Antonios hugged her briefly, murmuring meaningless words of consolation before he strode down the corridor.

His mother's room was lit only by a bedside lamp and its pale glow threw her features into shocking relief. Antonios knew his mother had been getting more tired and frail in the last few weeks, but the reality of it and her illness hit him now with painful force. The skin of her face was drawn tightly over her bones and she lay back on the pillows, her eyes closed, her breathing shallow.

Swallowing hard, Antonios approached the bed and

perched carefully on its edge. '*Yeia sou*, Mama,' he said softly.

Daphne's eyelids fluttered but that was all. Antonios felt a swooping sensation in his chest, like missing a step. He reached for her hand, noticing how thin her wrist had become, her fingers claw-like. He didn't know what to say; everything felt like a platitude or a lie, so he just held her hand.

After a few minutes the doctor arrived and Antonios stood up, watching as the man checked his mother over, took her pulse and blood pressure.

'Well?' he bit out when he could stand it no longer.

Spiros Tallos straightened slowly and turned to face him. The older man had been the family doctor for two generations; he had set Antonios's leg when he'd broken it, falling out of a tree when he was six.

'She's dying, Antonios,' Spiro said gently. 'But we all knew that.'

'She has not been like this before,' Antonios answered, his voice terse.

'She is closer to the end.'

Everything in him roared in denial. 'How long?'

'It is impossible to say.'

'Guess,' Antonios snapped, and Spiros sighed sadly.

'It could be days, or it could be weeks. There will be good days and bad days, but continued decline.' He gave a little shrug, spreading his hands. 'I am sorry.'

Antonios turned away so the doctor would not see the naked grief on his face; he felt the burn of tears behind his lids and blinked them away rapidly. 'Thank you,' he finally said, when he trusted himself to speak. He cleared his throat. 'Can you…is there anything you can give her, for pain relief?'

'Of course,' Spiros said, and turned back to Daphne. Antonios turned to Xanthe, who was crying quietly. Wordlessly, he drew her into a hug and Xanthe took a shuddering breath, her cheek pressed against her shoulder.

'I know it shouldn't be a shock,' she whispered haltingly, 'but it is.'

Yes, it was. A terrible shock, a grim reality. Antonios closed his eyes, wished Lindsay were here with him. He longed for her quiet, comforting presence, the steadiness and strength he'd always appreciated in her. And yet he didn't want to have to tell her how Daphne had declined.

'Antonios.'

Xanthe jerked out of his arms and he hurried to his mother's bedside. 'Mama…'

'I want…' Daphne swallowed convulsively, her breath coming in shudders and gasps. Xanthe pressed a fist to her lips and Antonios took his mother's hand.

'Don't speak, it's too much for you now—'

She shook her head, the movement violent. 'I want… Leonidas,' she finally managed.

'I'll get him,' Xanthe offered and Antonios nodded his thanks.

Ten taut minutes later Leonidas was striding into the room, his hair dishevelled, his shirt untucked from the jeans he'd hastily put on before coming from his own villa to here.

His gaze snapped to Antonios and then back to his mother and, without a word of greeting for his brother, he sat on the opposite side of the bed and took his mother's other hand.

'Mama.'

Antonios began to rise. 'I'll go,' he murmured. 'You can have privacy…'

Daphne shook her head again. 'No. The two of you here. That is what I want. Together.' Neither Antonios nor Leonidas spoke and with effort Daphne drew her hands together so their hands, clasped in hers, were touching.

'There is too much pain and bitterness between you,' she said, her words coming slowly, her breathing laboured. 'You must make peace with each other now, before it is too late.' A tear snaked its way down her withered cheek. 'Before I am gone.'

Leonidas's hand twitched against Antonios's. They were both, he suspected, itching to pull their hands away, yet they wouldn't for the sake of their mother.

'We're fine, Mama,' Leonidas said placatingly, and Antonios's mouth tightened. *Fine.* He was beginning to hate that word. They were not fine. Lindsay had not been fine. In that moment, nothing, about anything, felt *fine*.

Daphne must have agreed for she shook her head, her hands tightening on her sons'. 'No,' she rasped. 'You have been angry and bitter with Antonios for too many years, Leonidas. It must stop now.'

Years? Antonios blinked, shooting his brother a sideways glance. Leonidas's jaw was tight but he said nothing.

'Don't worry about Antonios and me,' Leonidas finally bit out and Daphne let out a soft cry that tore at Antonios's heart.

'Of course I worry about you,' she answered, her voice choking. 'I know what Evangelos has cost both of you...'

Antonios's whole body tensed and he strove to keep his voice even as he asked, 'What do you mean, Mama?'

She turned her anguished face towards him. 'Making you the CEO—'

'You think he shouldn't have?' The words were out before Antonios could think better of them.

'Oh, Antonios, it doesn't matter what I think,' Daphne said, the words so soft Antonios had to lean forward to hear them. 'What matters is what it has done to you—'

'Done to me—'

'And Leonidas.'

Antonios simply sat and stared, his mind spinning. At least, he thought numbly, his mother hadn't known about his father's debt. For a moment, he'd been afraid she had.

'You must reconcile,' Daphne insisted. 'And be at peace with one another.'

'I—' Antonios began, but Leonidas cut across him.

'We will reconcile, Mama,' he said. 'We will be as brothers should be.'

This seemed to be exactly the right thing to say, for a beatific smile transformed Daphne's tired face and then she sank back against the pillows and closed her eyes. Just seconds later she was asleep.

Antonios and Leonidas remained on either side of her for a moment until, by silent, tense agreement, they rose and retreated to the far side of the room.

'What did the doctor say?' Leonidas asked.

'He said she would continue to decline. It could be days or weeks.'

'But not months.'

'No.'

They were both silent and, despite Leonidas's promise to their mother, neither of them, Antonios noted, was making any attempt to reconcile. Damn it, he hadn't even realized they'd needed to reconcile, at least not before the whole thing with Adair Hotels had blown up.

Leonidas glanced at their mother, lying asleep in bed.

She looked peaceful, despite the agitation she'd shown them both just moments ago.

'Someone should stay with her,' he said.

'I will,' Antonios answered. Leonidas gave him one long, considering look and then nodded. 'Fine. Wake me if…if anything changes.'

Antonios nodded and Leonidas left. He turned back to Daphne, feeling weary in body and soul. Knowing he would not sleep that night, he pulled a chair up to the side of the bed and sat down.

Antonios wasn't in bed when Lindsay woke before dawn. Normally she wouldn't have woken up properly, but the cool expanse of sheet she encountered when she stretched her legs made her whole body jolt with shock.

Then she remembered their argument last night and her heart sank. Had he stayed in the office all night? And how were they going to get past this?

Too awake now even to consider going back to bed, Lindsay paced the elegant confines of the bedroom for a while before curling up in a chair by the window and watching the sun's first pearly rays peek over the mountains, touching the dense forest of pine trees with gold. She wondered where her husband was.

At half past eight the door to the bedroom finally opened and Lindsay sprang from her chair.

'Where were you?' she demanded, her voice coming out in a harpy's shriek.

Antonios looked at her wearily, his face haggard, his eyes shadowed. 'Daphne,' he said simply, and all of Lindsay's petty concerns faded in light of this far greater worry.

'What happened—is she all right?'

Antonios shook his head. 'I need a shower,' he said and, without another word for Lindsay, he disappeared into the bathroom, closing the door behind him.

Lindsay paced the bedroom once more, fresh anxiety eating away at her. She feared for Daphne, for Antonios, who would feel the loss of his mother so keenly, and for their marriage, which suddenly seemed a fragile and untested thing, its foundation rocked by every silence, each argument.

Ten minutes later Antonios came out of the shower, his hair damp and spiky, a towel slung low around his hips. Lindsay stood up from where she'd sunk onto the bed and stared at him, her heart starting to pound.

Wordlessly, Antonios strode towards her and then pulled her, suddenly and urgently, into a tight embrace, his face buried in her neck. Lindsay put her arms around him, hugging him back just as tightly. Neither of them spoke for a long moment, just absorbed each other's uncertainty and pain. This was all the reassurance she needed, she told herself, that Antonios loved her. They would weather these storms.

Finally Antonios eased back, his face bleak. 'It won't be long.'

A lump formed in Lindsay's throat and she blinked back tears. 'Oh, Antonios, I'm sorry.' He nodded, and she sniffed. 'I don't know why it feels sudden—'

'Death is always a shock.' He rubbed his face, clearly exhausted from his night spent in Daphne's room. 'I'm sure she'd like a visit from you.'

'Of course,' Lindsay answered quickly. 'Is she…is she lucid?'

'At times. She spoke, for a little while, to me and Leonidas.' Antonios's mouth hardened at that and his gaze flicked away.

'What did she say?' Lindsay asked quietly, and Antonios shook his head.

'It doesn't matter.'

Lindsay didn't answer because whatever Daphne had said to her two sons was personal, private, and yet…it did matter. Of that she was sure. It was just one more thing Antonios didn't want to tell her. Anxiety churned inside her and Antonios turned away.

'I should get to the office.'

'You haven't even slept—'

'There are things to be done.'

'And what about you and Leonidas?' she blurted.

Antonios swung back towards her, his gaze narrowed. 'What about us?'

Lindsay took a deep breath. 'Antonios, I know you're keeping something from me. Something that is hurting you. I kept something from you, and when I told you it was such a relief. Won't you tell me?'

His face contorted briefly and then he shook his head. 'No. I'm sorry, Lindsay, but I can't. Not…' He took a breath, let it out slowly. 'I can tell you that Leonidas is angry with me, and has been for years.'

'Why?'

'Because our father appointed me CEO. Because I have the authority he wants.' He let out a weary sigh. 'Our mother wants us to reconcile.'

'And have you?' Lindsay asked quietly. Antonios shook his head.

'No, Leonidas left after Mama was settled. And I'm not sure Leonidas and I will ever see eye to eye.'

'And will we?' Lindsay asked softly.

Antonios frowned. 'I told you before. This doesn't affect our marriage.'

'Of course it does,' Lindsay cried. 'All of it does. You think the tension and anger I see in you every day, the bitterness between you and your brother, doesn't affect us?'

Antonios folded his arms, his expression implacable. 'I can't tell Leonidas.'

'Why not?'

'Because I made a promise to my father.'

Lindsay stared at him searchingly, wishing she knew what to say, how to reach across this impasse. Perhaps now, with his mother so near death, was not the time to push.

Slowly she nodded, swallowing hard. 'All right.'

Antonios's expression softened and he pulled her into a hug. 'Thank you for understanding,' he said softly, pressing a kiss against her hair, and Lindsay closed her eyes. She was afraid her understanding wouldn't be enough… for either of them.

Daphne died three days later. Lindsay had been to see her several times, sitting by her bed and talking to her even though Daphne slipped in and out of lucidity. Xanthe, Parthenope and Ava came, too, brushing their mother's thin white hair, holding her hand, singing songs from their childhood.

The process of saying farewell, Lindsay thought, was so important. She'd missed it with her own mother, who had left and never returned, never reached out even once. It had been as if she'd died, or perhaps even worse.

This slow goodbye was painful but necessary, for her as well as for Antonios and his family.

And yet even as the end loomed nearer, and Daphne

slipped deeper and deeper into unconsciousness, death was, as Antonios had said, a shock.

Lindsay was in her study, trying and failing to focus on the research she'd ignored for days, when Antonios came to tell her. She'd pulled up the email from the university and had drafted the first stilted sentences of a reply:

Thank you very much for your email. I have greatly enjoyed my time in the Mathematics Department and am honoured to…

To what? …have been asked? …accept? Her mind churned with possibilities, fears and desires.

'Lindsay.'

She turned from her laptop, her heart lurching into her throat at the bleak and haggard look on Antonios's face.

'Not—'

'Yes.' His mouth compressed and he took a quick steadying breath. 'I was there. So was Parthenope.'

'And the others?'

He shook his head. 'We've been taking it in turns to sit with her.'

'Oh, Antonios.' She rose from her desk and put her arms around him. Antonios pulled her to him as he had before, fitting her body to his. 'I'm so sorry.'

'I know.'

They remained in a silent embrace, needing no words. Then Antonios eased back. 'I'll need to start making arrangements for the funeral.'

'Of course. If there is anything I can do—'

He shook his head and left. Lindsay glanced back at her laptop.

Thank you for your email. I am honoured to…

With a sigh, she closed the laptop and went to find Antonios's sisters.

The funeral was two days later, at the Orthodox church in Amfissa, with a large crowd of townspeople along with all of the family, staff and employees of Marakaios Enterprises. Lindsay saw how Antonios and Leonidas stood apart from each other, their sisters like a barrier between them, as the coffin was lowered into the hard, stony earth.

There was a sombre reception back at the house, painfully reminiscent of Daphne's name day party, yet without her holding court in the centre of the room.

Lindsay helped organize things in the kitchen, glad to be out of the spotlight and knowing Antonios and his siblings needed time together. Her husband, she saw, was still not talking to Leonidas, never mind attempting some kind of reconciliation.

By the end of the day she was exhausted and aching in body and spirit, grateful to retreat up to their private wing. She hadn't seen Antonios for the last hour and had assumed he was closeted somewhere with his siblings.

He opened the door to their bedroom before her hand had touched the knob, causing her to give a small gasp of surprise.

'I didn't realize you'd come up—'

'Yet here I am.' Antonios's voice was clipped, his expression grim. Lindsay closed the door behind her.

'Is everything…' she began, only to have Antonios fill in unpleasantly,

'All right? No, Lindsay, it is not. It is not all right. It is not *fine*.' The last word was spoken in a sneer, a mockery of the times she'd insisted she was.

Lindsay shook her head. 'Antonios, what—'

'When,' he asked, his voice turning savage, 'were you going to tell me?'

Lindsay blinked as he glared at her, his whole body taut with fury, his fists clenched at his sides.

'What...'

'You haven't forgotten, have you?' he enquired silkily. 'The job offer you're so *honoured* to accept?'

Her jaw dropped. 'You read my email—'

'You left it up on the screen. And I'm not going to apologize for some imagined invasion of your privacy when you've been keeping such things from me.' He shook his head, his features twisting with bitterness. 'When were you going to tell me you were leaving, Lindsay, or were you just going to slip away again?'

CHAPTER TWELVE

EVERYTHING IN HIM HURT. Antonios heard his own ragged breathing as he stared at Lindsay and saw the truth in her face. She had deliberately kept the job offer from him.

And why? It felt painfully obvious: because she'd been intending to take it up, to leave him.

Lindsay had gone pale, her breathing shallow. 'Don't have a damned panic attack now,' Antonios growled. 'I won't have an ounce of sympathy for you if you do.'

Her mouth compressed and she swallowed. 'Good to know.'

'Why?' he asked, and heard a world of hurt in his voice, making him cringe inwardly even as fury fired through him. *Theos*, but he'd been here before. Only this time it felt a thousand times worse.

'Why what, Antonios?' Lindsay asked quietly. She had composed herself, and even that infuriated him. She seemed unaffected by his own agony, but then he hadn't been able to read her before, had had no inkling of the anguish she'd tried so hard to hide.

Perhaps he hadn't changed as much as he'd thought and hoped he'd had.

'Why,' he clarified, 'did you not tell me you had a job

offer from a university in New York? A job offer you were thinking of accepting—'

'I haven't accepted it.'

'You're thinking about it, though, aren't you?' Antonios returned. 'In the email you haven't finished the sentence about just what you're *honoured* to do, and why was that? Because you aren't sure.'

Lindsay's face was pale but when she spoke her voice came out calmly. 'No,' she agreed, 'I'm not.'

And somehow her calm admission hurt all the more, and turned his anger into despair. His shoulders sagged and he felt an unbearable weariness sweep through him, making every muscle he had ache. 'And you couldn't even tell me that.'

'I was going to.'

'When?' He shook his head. '*Theos*, what kind of marriage do we have, if we cannot be honest with each other?'

'I don't know.' Lindsay took a deep breath. 'But I'll be honest now, Antonios. I'll tell you exactly what's in my heart because if I don't, I don't think we have a marriage. I don't think there's much point in going on.'

'You always are quick to give up, aren't you?' he said, the words coming out before he could stop them and hitting Lindsay where it hurt.

He saw her flinch but then she composed herself, straightened her shoulders and lifted her chin. 'I'm not giving up. And being honest with you feels like fighting for my marriage, Antonios. For us. It would be easier in some ways to just ignore the things that are hurting you, pretend everything is fine. I did it before, and I'm not going to do it again. Because I love you. Because I want our marriage to succeed.'

He shrugged her words aside, too raw to do anything else. 'So, tell me then. Be honest about whatever it is you have to say.'

'Receiving that email made me realize that I do miss being part of an academic community,' she began. 'Teaching seminars, talking to people who are excited about what I'm doing. But I also knew that I'd committed myself to you, and your life is here in Greece.'

'Such a dilemma,' he cut in, his voice sharp with sarcasm, and she stared at him.

'Are you even going to try to understand?' she asked, and inwardly Antonios cringed.

He was lashing out because he was afraid Lindsay was going to leave him. Just as she'd once been afraid he would leave her. *Theos*, the things you did out of fear.

'I'm sorry,' he said. 'I shouldn't have said that. Please, continue.' He swallowed hard, jammed his hands in his pockets and forced himself to listen without speaking. But if she told him, in that calm and cool way of hers, that she was *leaving*…

'When you brought me to Greece, Antonios,' Lindsay said quietly, 'I was unhappy. So unhappy I didn't notice, didn't even consider, that you were unhappy, too.'

He stiffened, thrown by the sudden change in subject. 'What are you talking about—?'

'I'm talking about how you don't sleep at night. How the moment you drive through the estate gates your whole body tenses and a shadow comes over your face. How you work so hard but you don't even seem to enjoy it.'

Each word felt as if she were stripping him bare, flaying him. He stared at her, shaking his head. 'You're reading too much into something that is temporary…'

'What's temporary, Antonios? This bitterness between

you and Leonidas? That's been going on for years. The stress and strain of your job? I see it now and, looking back, I should have seen it before. You weren't just blind to my anguish, Antonios. I was blind to yours.'

Anguish. The word captured him, felled him. Because he knew she was right and he hated it. Hated it because it meant he'd failed.

'I don't see what any of this has to do with your job offer,' he said finally, his voice flat.

'Because when I read that email I thought of you. I thought of us and how maybe we would be happier, you would be happier, away from here. Away from Marakaios Enterprises.'

Emotion leapt inside him but he refused to name it. 'That's a very convenient justification for following your own desires.'

'Tell me you're happy here, Antonios,' Lindsay answered. 'Tell me you don't want to leave. Tell me this is what you want for the rest of your life.'

'I have no choice,' he said, the words torn from him. 'Don't you see that? My father named me as his successor. This is what I was born to do, what I have to…' He broke off, his chest heaving, his fists clenched.

'Who says?' Lindsay said quietly. 'Why can't you control your own destiny, choose your own life? And choose one that makes you happy?'

'There is such a thing as duty.'

'There is also such a thing as your brother,' Lindsay reminded him. 'Someone who wants more authority, who is already working for—'

'*Theos*, enough.' He flung out a hand to stop her from saying any more. 'Happy or unhappy, my life is here. It has to be here. But if you choose not to share it, then tell me so.'

'I want to share it,' Lindsay answered, her voice trembling. 'Of course I want to, but you don't want to share it with me.'

'Not this again—'

'Of course *this* again! You're unhappy, Antonios, but you won't tell me why. You won't tell me what is going on with your brother, or what happened with your father or anything. How can I help? How can I be your wife, supporting and loving you, when you deliberately shut me out?' He couldn't answer and she stepped towards him, grabbing him by the shoulders. 'I love you,' she told him fiercely, her voice choked with emotion. 'I love you enough to risk everything because I know you can't go on like this. We can't go on. Please, Antonios.' She stared at him, tears running down her face, and the certainty he'd shielded himself with for so long started to crack.

Lindsay had kept a secret from him and he'd felt angry and hurt. Betrayed—as betrayed as when his father had kept the wretched state of the business from him. How could he keep anything from her? How could he perpetuate this life of secrets and lies?

But it's not my secret to tell.

Yet had it been his to keep?

'When I took over the business,' he told Lindsay, the words coming haltingly yet with growing determination, 'I didn't realize—no one realized—that it was in debt. Utterly in debt. My father had a heart attack because he was faced with losing it all.' Lindsay gaped at him and Antonios smiled grimly. 'A shock, no?' he said and she nodded.

'And you didn't tell anyone about this?'

'My father asked, *begged* me not to. Some of his dealings had been…illegal. Criminal.' He drew a shuddering breath. 'Telling my family would have brought such shame to my father. My mother loved him, and my siblings, too. I couldn't bear for their feelings to change, and I knew it would destroy my father. So I worked to get the business back on an even footing.'

She cocked her head, her luminous gaze sweeping slowly over him, and he braced himself to hear recrimination. Rebuke that he hadn't told anyone, that he'd kept it to himself.

'Oh, Antonios,' she said softly, her voice filled with so much love and compassion, 'that must have been so very hard for you. Keeping such a secret for so long, and working so hard.' She shook her head, more tears spilling down her cheeks, and her understanding just about undid him.

'Lindsay, I love you,' he said as he reached for her. 'I know there are a lot of unknowns, a lot of complications, but that is one thing that I know. One thing that it is certain. It is my rock.'

Another tear snaked down her cheek. 'It's my rock, too,' she whispered. 'Loving you. Knowing you love me.'

He drew her to him, needing to feel her soft, slender body against his. 'Then we'll work the rest out,' he murmured against her hair. 'Somehow we'll work the rest out.'

'Antonios.' She pulled away from him. 'It's not that simple.'

'It can be—'

'No,' she answered, 'it can't. I wish it could because it would make things so simple. Just sail along on the certainty of our love.' Her mouth twisted wryly. 'But it's not simple, Antonios. Your mother said it was endlessly complicated. And love is hard work.'

He stiffened, not wanting to hear this and yet knowing in his gut she was right. 'So what are you saying?'

'I'm saying you need to talk to Leonidas. You need to think about what would make you happy, and how our marriage can thrive.'

He tensed, withdrawing from her. 'Is that an ultimatum?'

She stared at him sadly. 'Does it need to be one?'

'This is about your job offer, isn't it?'

'No, Antonios.' Lindsay shook her head. 'It's about so much more than that.'

Anger fired through him, coming so quickly on the heels of the love and gratitude he'd felt. 'Lindsay—'

'I'll refuse the offer if you want me to,' she told him quietly. 'This is about you. And me. *Us.*' She stared at him steadily. 'I wish you could see that.'

And he could see it, Antonios realized. Of course he could. He just hated the thought. He stared at her, the sadness turning down her mouth, the love still shining in her eyes. He hated that he'd made her so unhappy. Again.

'I need to be alone,' he said abruptly and turned from the room.

He walked the length of the estate, ending up in the olive groves, memories of his childhood dancing through his mind. Memories of walking there just a few short weeks ago with Lindsay, when they'd forged this new and fragile foundation of their marriage. He'd fallen in love with her all over again these past few weeks. She'd made coming back here, dealing with Marakaios Enterprises, bearable.

And do you want more from your life than bearable?

Antonios pressed a fist to his forehead and closed his eyes. Lindsay was right. Marakaios Enterprises had been slowly strangling him for a decade. Not just the secret he'd kept from his family, but the whole of it. He was reaching his breaking point and only Lindsay had seen it. Had possessed the courage to confront him.

He would be no less brave. Resolutely, he went in search of Leonidas.

His brother was not in the main villa or his own house; it took Antonios a few stunned seconds to realize Leonidas had gone to the office, on today of all days.

It was dark, twilight having descended without his even being aware of the descent into night, and a few stars glimmered close to the horizon.

A single light shone from the office building. Antonios thumbed the key code and stepped inside. He paused on the threshold of Leonidas's office, taking in his brother's bent head, one hand raked through his hair, the determined yet slumped set of his shoulders.

'It's a little late to be working,' he said quietly and Leonidas looked up, startled, before he gave a shrug.

'The world doesn't stop, even for a funeral.'

For a second Antonios wanted to berate his brother for his callousness, but then he saw the grief in Leonidas's eyes and realized this was how he coped. He was, Antonios thought wryly, starting to see people a little more clearly, thanks to Lindsay.

He took a step into the room. 'I want to talk to you.'

'Oh?' Leonidas eyed him warily. 'About what?'

'About Father.'

He'd spoken quietly, but the two words seemed to bounce around the room, echo in the stillness. Leonidas glanced down at the papers he'd been studying, needlessly rearranging a few.

'What about him?' he asked finally.

Antonios took a deep breath, then plunged. 'Father was deeply in debt, Leonidas. He'd nearly lost it all when he had the heart attack.'

Leonidas's jaw dropped, just as Lindsay's had done. Wearily, Antonios explained it all again: the debt, the shame, the secret.

After a long, taut moment Leonidas pushed away from the desk, turned towards the window. 'You should have told me.'

'I didn't feel I could.' He sounded, Antonios realized, just as Lindsay had when she'd explained why she'd left without an explanation. They were so alike, and yet in such different ways. And they'd taught each other so much. Helped each other so much. 'I realize now,' he told Leonidas, 'I may have been wrong.'

'May have been?'

Temper flared at his brother's obvious sarcasm, but he suppressed it. 'Leonidas, Father made me promise not to tell. He was deeply ashamed that he'd let it get so far. Telling anyone would have felt like a betrayal. It still feels like one now but I recognize that you deserve to know, perhaps more than anyone.' And at least, Antonios thought, his mother had been spared the knowledge of her husband's criminal folly. It was a small mercy.

'I wish he'd told me,' Leonidas said after a long moment. His voice sounded thick. 'I wish he'd seen how much I loved the business, how much I wanted to share it with him. I wish he'd trusted me with that burden.'

'I wish it, too,' Antonios answered. 'I wish there had been no secrets between anyone, ever.'

They were both silent, and then Leonidas looked up and asked, 'So what now? Things will continue on as usual? You'll give me a little more freedom?'

He sounded so cynical, so jaded and yet also despairing, and Antonios knew it was his fault his brother was like that. He'd given him a very short leash.

'No,' he said slowly, and Lindsay's words echoed through his mind. She'd understood him better than he'd ever understood himself. 'That's not what's going to happen.'

Leonidas let out a bitter laugh. 'I see.'

'No,' Antonios said, 'I don't think you do.' He took a deep breath. 'What would you think,' he asked, 'if you became CEO?'

Lindsay paced her bedroom for an hour, until she feared she'd wear down the carpet with her restless tread. It was evening, and everyone from the reception after the funeral had gone. Parthenope would be leaving to return home tomorrow, and the house, Lindsay supposed, would settle into a new and unwelcome normal.

And what about her and Antonios?

She had no idea if he'd accepted or understood what she'd said. No idea if their marriage was teetering on a precipice or about to take off and fly.

She would refuse the job offer, she told herself, as a sign of her faith in him and their marriage. It had been unreasonable of her even to consider it.

Yet her heart still felt heavy as she headed to her study and opened her laptop. The unfinished email was still on the screen where she'd left it, where Antonios had read it. Lindsay scanned the two sentences and then started writing.

I am honoured that you have considered me for this position, but I am afraid that I cannot accept…

'You're not turning down that job, are you?'

Lindsay's hands stilled on the computer keys and then she turned around in her chair, saw Antonios standing in the doorway of her study. He looked both weary and wonderful, and his mouth curved in a slow, tired smile as he took a step forward. 'Because I wouldn't do that, if I were you.'

Lindsay frowned, uncertainty and hope warring within her. 'You wouldn't?'

'No.'

'But…'

'You were right, Lindsay, about everything. About me. About Leonidas. And, most importantly, about us.'

An incredulous smile started blooming across her face. 'What's happened?'

'I told him the truth.'

'Oh, Antonios.' Her smile widened even as she felt the sting of tears. 'I'm proud of you. That must have been hard.'

'It was. But it was also a relief. I suspect you know what that feels like.'

'Yes.' She nodded and he took her hand, drew her up from her chair. 'Thank you for being patient with me,' he whispered against her hair. 'Thank you for loving me the way I needed, even when I didn't think I did.'

'Oh, Antonios.' Her voice was too choked to say anything more, so she just put her arms around him. He held her, stroking her hair, and she pressed into him, revelling in how he managed to make her feel both strong and small.

'So about that job,' Antonios said with a nod towards her laptop. 'What was it exactly, anyway?'

She eased back to eye him warily. 'It doesn't matter—'

'I think it does.'

Unsure of where he was going with this, she gave a little shrug. 'Assistant professorship of Pure Mathematics.'

'Sounds right up your alley.'

'I suppose.' Actually, it involved teaching an advanced seminar on her research topic, but she didn't need to tell Antonios about that. 'I was just about to refuse,' she told him, stopping when she saw he was shaking his head.

'And I told you I wouldn't do that if I were you.'

'Why not?'

'Because I think I fancy the idea of living in America.' Lindsay's jaw dropped. 'What?'

'Leonidas is now the CEO of Marakaios Enterprises.'

'But…' Lindsay's head spun. No matter what she'd told Antonios earlier, she'd never actually believed he would resign.

'I offered him the position,' Antonios explained. 'I realized you were right, Lindsay. Being CEO of Marakaios Enterprises has never made me happy, and I know it's what Leonidas has wanted. He deserves a chance, and I deserve a chance to try something else. To be happy… with you.'

'You've put so much into it, Antonios,' Lindsay said, marvelling at how much he was willing to give up. 'You *saved* it—'

'And now I'm handing it over to Leonidas. But I'm not leaving completely.' He gave her a crooked smile that felt like a fist reaching down and taking hold of her heart. No matter what the future held, she loved this man. She wanted to be with him. 'I've accepted a newly created position with Marakaios Enterprises,' he explained. 'Head of North America and Investment Management.'

'North America…' she repeated slowly, her mind

whirling. 'Investment Management—but I didn't think Marakaios Enterprises even did that?'

'They didn't, but they will, starting with me. I'm opening a new branch of the corporation in finance, in North America. Based in New York.'

She blinked rapidly, shaking her head in disbelief. 'You'd do that for me?'

'I'm doing it for us. Just like you fought for us by confronting me. I didn't want to admit how unhappy I was here. It felt like a betrayal of my father, of my own sense of honour and duty. But you woke me up, Lindsay. You made me realize what I was afraid to acknowledge to myself.'

'Antonios…' Lindsay shook her head, her eyes shining with tears. 'I don't know what to say.'

'Then say yes. Say yes, I'll take the job, I'll go with you, I'll start this grand adventure.' He squeezed her hands. 'Say yes because you love me and I love you and that really is all that matters.'

Just like Daphne had said. Lindsay could almost feel her mother-in-law's presence, imagined her beaming smile. She squeezed Antonios's hands back.

'Yes,' she said.

* * * * *

SOCIETY WEDDINGS

Together with their families

Alessandra Mondelli

and

Christian Markos

*Request the pleasure of your company
at the celebration of their marriage*

May 2015

at 5 o'clock in the evening

*Hotel Parthenon
Athens*

**...but only if Christian can
persuade his pregnant bride!**

❧ SOCIETY WEDDINGS ❧

Dedicated bachelors Rocco Mondelli,
Christian Markos, Stefan Bianco and Zayed Al Afzal
met and bonded at university, wreaking havoc amongst
the female population. In the decade since graduating
they've made their mark on the worlds of business
and pleasure, becoming wealthy and powerful.

Marriage has never been something Rocco, Christian,
Stefan or Zayed were ever after... But things change,
and now they'll have to do whatever it takes
to get themselves to the church on time!

Yet nothing is as easy as it seems...
and the women these four have set their sights on
have plans of their own!

**Your embossed invitation is in the mail
and you are cordially invited to:**

The marriage of
Rocco Mondelli and *Olivia Fitzgerald*
April 2015

The marriage of
Christian Markos and *Alessandra Mondelli*
May 2015

The marriage of
Stefan Bianco and *Clio Norwood*
June 2015

The marriage of
Sheikh Zayed Al Afzal and *Princess Nadia Amani*
July 2015

**So RSVP and get ready to enjoy the pinnacle of luxury
and opulence as the world's sexiest billionaires
finally say 'I do'...**

THE GREEK'S
PREGNANT BRIDE

BY
MICHELLE SMART

MILLS
BOON®

Published in Great Britain 2015
by Mills & Boon, an imprint of Harlequin (UK) Limited,
Eton House, 18-24 Paradise Road, Richmond, Surrey, TW9 1SR

© 2015 Harlequin Books SA

Special thanks and acknowledgement are given to Michelle Smart for her contribution to the *Society Weddings* series.

ISBN: 978-0-263-25061-9

Printed and bound in Spain
by CPI, Barcelona

Michelle Smart's love affair with books started when she was a baby, when she would cuddle them in her cot. A voracious reader of all genres, she found her love of romance established when she stumbled across her first Mills & Boon® book at the age of twelve. She's been reading (and writing) them ever since. Michelle lives in Northamptonshire with her husband and two young Smarties.

Visit the author profile page at millsandboon.co.uk for more titles

To the wonderful sisters in my life:
Jennie, Lulu & Joanne xxx

CHAPTER ONE

CHRISTIAN MARKOS TIPPED the last of his champagne down his throat and immediately refilled his glass.

He'd known today was going to be hard, but hadn't imagined quite how torturous it would be. Not even all the running around he'd done with Rocco that morning, in their seemingly desperate attempt to find the bride, had mitigated it.

Afterwards, he'd stood by the side of his closest friend on the happiest day of his life and all he'd been able to think was how deeply he'd betrayed him.

While Rocco had been exchanging his vows, Christian had been using all his willpower to stop his gaze flitting to Alessandra.

He was still fighting it.

Alessandra Mondelli: Rocco's baby sister. A pretty child who'd grown into a ravishingly beautiful woman. The one woman in the world who was totally off-limits.

Or should have been.

Attired in a long, sleeveless, silk mauve dress, with her glossy, dark-chestnut hair pulled back in a tight chignon, she'd arrived by boat with the radiant bride, the spring sun beaming down on her golden skin.

In his eyes the chief bridesmaid outshone everyone, including the famous supermodel bride.

The last time he'd seen Alessandra she'd been wearing a short, cream lace dress with black beading and a pair of black shoes so high he'd been amazed she could walk in them. But walk in them she had, beautifully, her delectable bottom swaying with every step. That was the last time he'd seen her clothed. The last time he'd seen her properly she'd been burrowed naked under the bed covers in her apartment.

The wedding party had moved from the beautiful gardens by Lake Como and into the Villa Mondelli ballroom. The wedding dinner was over, the evening celebration about to start. He'd made his best man's speech and managed to raise some laughs from the other guests, especially Stefan and Zayed, who'd substituted the speech he'd written with a bluer version. Instead of relaxing, knowing his job was done, Christian was on tenterhooks waiting for the music to strike up.

An American A-list starlet kept making eyes at him, a stunning woman with a body to die for. Just six weeks ago he would have been at her side like a shot. If not her, then one of the other gorgeous women littering this star-studded event already being labelled 'wedding of the century.' Supermodels, lingerie models, singers… It was like being a child in a sweetshop.

If that were the case, then he must have diabetes, because none of the sweets looked remotely tempting.

Except one. The forbidden one.

How could he have allowed things to get so out of hand? He might flit from bed to bed but he never lost control of himself.

To have lost his control with Alessandra…

He could blame it on all the champagne they'd drunk. He could blame it on a lot of things, but all the blame was on himself.

Alessandra had been vulnerable. Try as she'd done to hide it, she'd been a mess, grieving the loss of her grandfather, the man who'd raised her since she'd been a baby and who'd been buried barely two weeks before.

Christian had dropped in at the House of Mondelli, the

world-famous fashion house, on his way back from Hong Kong, expecting to take Rocco out for a night on the tiles, maybe spend the weekend together on his Italian friend's yacht. But Rocco had been in New York and he'd bumped into Alessandra, who'd insisted he take her out instead. Under normal circumstances he would have made his excuses and got back in his jet to fly on to Athens. If he hadn't caught the desperation in her beautiful honey-brown eyes, he would have done just that, not found himself recalling how she'd barely been able to stand during the funeral service.

When they'd set out for the evening, the last thing he'd expected was that they would end up in bed together.

Women came and went in his life on a regular basis. He could only assume that it was the fact Alessandra was someone who was *in* his life, so to speak, that meant he was having a hard job forgetting and moving on. That and the guilt of it all. She might have been the one to instigate the kiss that had led to them making love, but the blame for what followed lay firmly on *his* shoulders.

He should have been stronger.

In the six weeks since he'd seen her, he'd worked hard to push her from the forefront to the back of his mind, enough so that he'd arrived at Lake Como confident he could handle being in her presence without any problems.

He'd taken one look at her and all the guilt had churned itself back up. They'd exchanged a few brief words over the course of the day, the same basic pleasantries they'd exchanged with everyone else, but that was the extent of their interaction. So far, at least. There was still the dance to get through.

Whether he liked it or not, he would have to hold her in his arms one more time.

Stefan said something to him at the exact moment the band started their warm-up. As he spoke, Christian saw Olivia lean in close to press her ear to Rocco's mouth. It was a gesture that reminded him of his dinner with Alessandra, the way she'd leaned into him to hear him speak over the noise of the restaurant; the way her sultry scent had played under his nose...

From the corner of his eye he could see her chatting to the official photographer, the photographer probably getting tips from *her*. Alessandra Mondelli was one of the most famous fashion photographers in the world, a remarkable achievement, considering she was still only twenty-five. She'd made it all on her own. Just as he'd made his name on his own.

Stefan repeated himself; he'd been talking about the charitable foundation they and their friends had formed some years back.

Italian Rocco Mondelli, Sicilian Stefan Bianco, desert Prince Zayed Al Afzal and he had all taken a keen interest in running and raising money for their charity. They were the so-called Columbia Four, although he couldn't recall which of them had dubbed them so. Whoever had come up with it, it had stuck. They'd met during their first week at Columbia University and, as incredible as it was to look back on, the bond they'd formed had been instant. That bond had grown and a good few years later, when it had become obvious all four were heading towards the Forbes World's Billionaires List, they'd formed the charity. Christian was extremely proud of their charity, founded to ensure disadvantaged kids could get the education they deserved but were unable to afford. It felt good for them to be doing something together that didn't involve drinking and bedding as many beautiful women as they could.

They all believed the bond between them to be unbreakable.

But even the strongest steel could be destroyed.

He answered with what he hoped sounded like intelligence but, in truth, what came out of his mouth sounded so unintelligible he could be speaking Martian.

Luckily Stefan's attention was diverted by the band striking up their first song.

The bride and groom glided onto the dance floor to loud applause.

Christian's eyes drifted to his right, back to Alessandra. She was looking straight at him, a trapped expression in her eyes.

His chest tightened.

A powerful slap to his shoulder broke the spell.

'Time to get yourself on the dance floor,' Zayed said, sitting on the empty seat to Christian's left.

Theos. He had to dance with her. Olivia, the bride, had ordered it. The best man and chief bridesmaid…

Alessandra met him halfway, her obvious apprehension mirroring what raced inside him.

It would help if the band were playing one of the usual upbeat tunes that had made them one of the most famous groups in the world rather than the cover of a romantic ballad they were currently warbling.

Gritting his teeth, he walked by her side to the dance floor and took her into his arms.

His heart jolted at the first touch, a dozen memories playing in his mind. Her scent. Her taste…

The back of her dress was low, leaving him no option but to touch her silky skin. It was either that or hold on to her bottom. His hand lay rigid against her bare back, hardly touching her.

Yet, no matter the physical distance he tried to impose between himself and her slender form, his senses filled with Alessandra, her sultry scent playing tricks on him as they moved over the dance floor in a manner more akin to a pair of robots than a couple who'd had a wild night of sex just six weeks before. The stirring that had begun when he'd watched her walk up the aisle and had simmered since took on new life, an ache forming in his groin that he willed away with increasing frustration.

Think of Rocco, he ordered himself, staring at his loved-up friend who was locked in the arms of his equally loved-up wife. Rocco caught his eye and nodded briefly before leaning down to kiss his bride.

That one action felt like a knife in Christian's guts.

What would his friend say if he knew his best man had taken his sister's virginity?

The all-consuming desire he'd felt that night still dwelled in his blood. One night was all he usually needed, all he wanted. Once a woman had been enjoyed, there were no more mysteries to discover, no need for a repeat.

His skin felt as if it were dancing its own tune, his body out of kilter with what his head demanded.

He followed the words of the song they were dancing to, counting down the time to when the obligatory dance would be over. From the stiffness in Alessandra's stance, she was counting down the time too.

When the song finally came to an end and he made to pull away, she tilted her head to look at him, her doe-like eyes staring at him. *Theos*, she was so beautiful, those striking eyes set above a snub nose framed by slanting cheekbones. Her delicious plump lips parted. 'Christian, I…'

Whatever she was going to say was cut short when Zayed tapped her on the shoulder and threw Christian a conspiratorial wink. 'I do believe it's my turn to dance with the beautiful lady,' he said in a voice loud enough for Rocco to hear.

The groom turned his head towards the raised voice, his eyes narrowing before he broke into a wide grin.

It clearly didn't cross his mind that any of his friends would dream of doing anything with the sister he was so protective of.

Sickened with himself, Christian stepped back and forced a smile, mock-bowing. 'She's all yours.'

He waited for Alessandra to make a good-natured but cutting retort about not being anyone's property, but her eyes were stark on his face, a fleeting look of panic flashing over her which she quickly covered. But not quickly enough.

The ballroom of Villa Mondelli had enough waiting staff not to let any guest go thirsty for longer than thirty seconds but Christian wanted to get away from the hubbub of the mingling guests and headed to the bar.

After a shot of bourbon, he turned his head to see her now dancing with Stefan. She looked happy to be dancing with *him*, he thought, taken aback at the strength of his bitterness.

It was only natural she'd been stiff and awkward in Christian's arms. A one-night stand hadn't been on either of their minds when they'd set out that evening.

He'd been her first lover.

That, more than anything, was the thing that refused to dislodge from his mind.

The woman who'd been vilified by the press for an affair with a married man when she'd been a teenager had been a virgin. He'd always suspected there had been more to the story than had been written but the truth had come as a cataclysmic shock.

Whatever the truth, it was none of his business. Alessandra was none of his business. She couldn't be.

He took another shot to clear the bile crawling up his throat and watched Stefan place a hand to her waist. The bile almost choked him to see her laugh at something his friend said in her ear.

Zayed appeared at his side. 'Hiding yourself away, buddy?'

'Just taking a few moments.'

Stefan finished his dance and came over to join them. 'What are we all drinking?'

'Christian's already on the hard stuff,' Zayed said, indicating the empty shot glasses before them on the bar.

Christian hardly listened. Alessandra had left the dance floor. A quick scan of the ballroom found her sitting at a table with a group of people he didn't recognise. She was staring at him.

Their gazes held before he pulled away and fixed a smile on his face for his friends' benefit.

'Who's ready for a shot?' Before either could answer, he waved at the barman to pour them a bourbon each.

The three friends, sitting in a row at the bar, raised their glasses and chanted, *'Memento vivere!'* 'Remember to live,' the motto the four friends *did* live by, and downed their shots.

'I never thought I'd see us at a wedding for one of our own,' Zayed mused, wiping his mouth with the back of his hand. 'I still can't believe Rocco's got *married*. I mean... *married*?'

'Who would have thought he'd fall in *love*?' Stefan said with the same incredulous tone.

Christian grunted and caught the barman's attention for another round.

Call him cynical, but he couldn't help wonder how long it would be before the love they felt for each other turned into something ugly. Because that was what marriage did— turned two people full of hope and love into bitter carica-tures of themselves.

Much safer for everyone's sake to avoid emotional en-tanglement. Christian conducted his own affairs by enjoy-ing the moment and then moving on with the minimum of fuss. He had known before he was in double figures that marriage was not for him.

Zayed swivelled on his stool to cast his eyes over the ballroom. 'There are some hot women here.'

Stefan grinned. 'I noticed that lingerie model giving you the eye.'

'I thought she was an actress?'

'No, that was the other one.'

'I tell you who knocks spots off all these women,' Zayed said. 'Alessandra.'

Christian snapped his head round to stare at him. 'Don't even think about it.'

Zayed raised his hands. 'I'm just making an observation.'

'Well, don't.'

'Man, you know I wouldn't go there. I'd never do that to Rocco— Where are you going?' he added when Christian got up from his stool and made to leave.

'To get some air.'

'You not feeling well?' Stefan was looking at him closely.

'It's been a busy time. I'm probably jet-lagged. Get another round in—I'll be back in a few minutes.'

Instead of going outside, Christian went to the restroom and splashed cold water on his face.

He'd been a paper thickness away from punching Zayed.

Theos, he needed to get a grip on himself.

This was *his* guilt and *his* problem. No one else's.

Back in the ballroom his eyes automatically sought Alessandra out. As he found her, she turned her head in his direction, as if some sixth sense told her he was there. Quickly she turned away.

He thought he was doing a good job of hiding his guilt-ridden inner turmoil. After that one close call of almost punching one of his oldest and closest friends for an innocuous remark, he joined in with the celebration they were there for, drinking, laughing and horsing about, being the same old Christian he always was when with them.

Except, every time he looked, he found Alessandra's gaze upon him. Their eyes would meet for a fraction of a second before jerking away. She certainly seemed to be enjoying herself, though, dancing with anyone who cared to ask, at one point stealing Olivia from Rocco and waltzing her around the floor to screams of delight.

Only when the bride and groom, their hands clenched tightly together, left to head off to their secret honeymoon destination did Christian determine his duty to have been done.

Exchanging bear hugs with Zayed and Stefan, who called him every laughably demeaning name under the sun for retiring to bed so early, he strode out of the ballroom, unable to resist one last glance at Alessandra. For once, she wasn't looking at him.

He was about to climb the stairs to the sleeping quarters when he heard his name called.

Stefan approached him and pulled him into another embrace. 'You are playing with fire, my friend,' he said into his ear.

'I don't know what you're talking about.'

'Sure you do.' He pulled back a little and brought his hands up to Christian's face, slapping both his cheeks lightly. 'You have to end it. *Now.*'

Christian's chest compressed. He couldn't lie to his friend. 'It was over before it started.'

'Good. Keep it that way. For all our sakes.'

Alessandra took a deep breath and knocked on the door. The party was still going strong, a DJ having replaced the band, music pounding through the walls. There were revellers all over the villa but thankfully this wing was quiet and devoid of people.

She waited a few moments before knocking again, louder.

Unless Christian had left without telling anyone, he was in there. The dim light seeping under the door testified to this. She'd casually asked Stefan and Zayed where their fellow musketeer had escaped to. She could only hope she'd imagined the suspicious but pitying look in Stefan's eyes when he'd told her Christian had gone to bed.

Please, God, let him be alone in there.

What were the chances?

She'd been nothing special, just another notch on a bedpost crammed with notches.

Christian Markos travelled with a trail of broken hearts

attached to him ranging from Hong Kong to London. Some sold their stories to the tabloids, tales of short-lived lust before being discarded. Some spoke with bitterness. Most spoke with longing. Most wanted him to break their hearts all over again.

It took an age before the handle turned and the door opened.

Christian stood clad in a pair of jeans. And nothing else.

He blinked narrowing eyes. 'What are you doing here?'

'I need to talk to you. Can I come in?'

His bronzed throat rose. 'That's not a good idea.'

'It's important.'

His firm lips, usually quirked in an easy smile, clamped together. He shifted past her, looking both directions down the wide corridor before ushering her in and swiftly closing the door.

His room was tidy, his tuxedo hanging neatly on the door of the wardrobe. The bed was rumpled; a tablet was on the bedside table next to a half-full bottle of bourbon and an empty glass.

'Are you drunk?' she challenged. This was a conversation she needed to have when he was sober.

'No.' He strode to the window and closed the heavy curtains. 'Believe me, I've been trying to reach that state.'

If only she were in a position to reach that state herself.

'Today went well,' she said, sitting gingerly on the corner chair. She could *really* do with a shot of that bourbon. It would make what was coming next easier to cope with, of that she was certain. 'Rocco and Liv looked really happy.'

Their obvious happiness had had the dual effect of making her heart lighten for her brother's sake and sink at the knowledge it was something she could never have for herself.

Christian propped himself against the wall by the window and crossed his arms over his broad chest. She hadn't really had the opportunity to study his torso in her apartment, and now she could look at it properly she felt the heat she'd experienced that night bloom anew.

Years of rowing and track had honed his physique, his form strong and athletic, his shoulders broad. Fine hair dusted across his bronzed chest and she felt an almost unbearable compulsion to hurtle herself into his arms and take solace in his strength.

Making love to him had been an experience she would never forget. The single best experience of her life.

Try as she had to expel the memories from her head, they'd stayed with her, tantalising her, taunting her with the knowledge it was an experience that could *never* be repeated.

The simple remembrance of his smooth skin flush against her nakedness made her feel as if her insides were being liquidised.

'What did you want to talk to me about?' he asked, cutting the preamble and pulling her back to the present. While he wasn't being unfriendly, there was none of the easy-going Christian she knew. She didn't have to be psychic to know he wanted her gone from his room.

His regret and self-loathing were obvious.

Her heart hammered beneath her ribs, her stomach roiling with nerves that threatened to overwhelm her.

This was all her fault...

'I'm pregnant.'

CHAPTER TWO

THE SILENCE THAT followed Alessandra's stark statement was total.

Christian seemed to deflate before her eyes, as if he'd suffered a body blow.

Which no doubt her news was, she thought miserably.

How she'd kept herself together throughout the day she would never know, her only thought having been that she *mustn't* ruin Rocco and Olivia's special day. *She mustn't.*

She'd spent pretty much her entire life trying to keep herself together in public, the hardest before tonight being two months ago when they'd buried her grandfather. The paparazzi had been out in force. She'd worn dark glasses until they'd entered the church, refusing to give them the money shot they so desired. Even when Sandro, her alcoholic father, had turned up drunk and made that dreadful scene, she'd kept her composure. Christian and Zayed had been the ones who'd calmly approached him and dragged him away.

Christian staggered over to the bed and sat heavily on it, clutching his head.

'Please. Say something,' she beseeched. The back of her retinas burned and she blinked furiously. No matter what happened in the next few minutes, she would not cry. She'd done enough of that.

He fixed his blue eyes on her. 'How long have you known?'

'A while, I guess, but I only took the test a couple of days ago.' She laughed, a hollow sound even to her own ears. 'I took three of them, hoping they were wrong.' At the third positive reading, she'd climbed onto her bed and sobbed.

'Have you seen a doctor?'

'Not yet.' She bit into her lip. It had taken her almost a fortnight to entertain the possibility that her late period might actually mean something, another fortnight before she'd unburied her head from the sand and crossed the threshold into the pharmacy.

She'd never believed she would be a mother. Motherhood went hand in hand with relationships and she certainly didn't believe in *them*.

'But you're certain?'

'Yes.' Once the reality of her condition had sunk into her shell-shocked brain, the tears had stopped.

Inside her, right in the heart of her womanhood, a tiny life grew.

Whatever the outcome of this conversation with Christian, nothing could change the fact that this life—her baby—was a part of her. Nothing could have prepared her for the host of emotions pregnancy would bring. It might be early days in pregnancy terms but already she loved it, this little alien developing within her; knew she would do anything to nurture and protect it. Anything.

Silence rang out, the only sound Christian's heavy breathing. She'd never seen his features—all angles and straight lines forming what had been dubbed one of the most handsome faces in Europe—look so empty.

'I'm so sorry.'

His brows drew together. 'Sorry for what?'

'I screwed up.' She forced herself to look him straight in the eye. 'I didn't take my pill properly.'

He shook his head and expelled a breath through his mouth, running a hand through his cropped dirty-blond hair. 'And you didn't think to tell me that?'

'I didn't know the dangers, not properly.'

'How could you not know? It's basic biology.' He swore under his breath.

'I was put on the pill because my periods were painful, not for the purpose of contraception.'

'You should have told me. *Theos*, if I'd known you didn't take it at regular intervals I would have made certain to use a condom.'

'I am sorry, truly sorry.'

The knuckles of his hands were white. She could see his temper hanging by a thread.

'You can't put this on yourself—*I* can't put it on you,' he eventually said. 'We were both there. I should have had the sense to use a condom like I normally do.'

She closed her eyes, pushing away thoughts of him with other women. 'Christian...I can't do this on my own. I need your support—not financially but in other ways.' Financially she could do it alone. She had her apartment, her career was thriving...

She opened her eyes and looked at his still-dazed face. 'I know I've had a head start getting my head around all this, and that's unfair on you, but I need your word—on your honour—that you'll be there for me and our baby.' Not that she could trust it. He was a man. Men always broke their promises.

All the same, she had to try and put a little faith in him. He was the father of her child. But then, her own father was the worst liar of all. He'd lied to her mother on her deathbed, promising to care for their children, never to leave them. That had been the biggest lie of all.

The only men she trusted were her brother and her grandfather. It had broken her grieving heart to learn recently that her grandfather had had his own dark secrets.

If it hadn't been for his death, she would never have slept with Christian. She'd bumped into him in the House of Mondelli headquarters after she'd had a meeting with the fashion director about a campaign she'd been hired to shoot. Christian had turned up to take her brother out but Rocco had been in New York.

She'd been in a bad place, she could see that now, trying to cope with her grief but not having a clue how to manage it. She'd never known pain like it. It still had the power to lance her.

Christian had presented the perfect opportunity for a night out where she could forget her pain for one evening, so she'd talked him into going out with her instead. Not for a minute had she imagined she would fall into bed with him.

But she had done just that and now she had to pay the consequences.

And so did Christian.

She might never be able to trust him but she'd had enough faith, whatever her state of mind, to lose her virginity to him. That had to account for something.

She wished he would say something. His frame was still but his eyes were alert. She couldn't read them. Couldn't read him.

'When news of the pregnancy comes out the press are going to swarm all over it. I've lived through one scandal and I can't go through that again on my own. I just can't.' Simply imagining going through it all again made her hands go clammy and her stomach churn. How clearly she remembered those awful days when the paparazzi had laid siege to Villa Mondelli, leaving her a prisoner in her own home. She'd never been so scared and alone in all her life. 'If I know I can rely on you for support when I need it, and later on when our baby needs it, I might be able to sleep again.'

Christian's throat rose before he twisted onto his side and grabbed his bourbon and glass. He poured a hefty measure and offered it to her.

She shook her head.

'Of course not,' he muttered, taking a large swallow of it. 'You're pregnant. Did you not drink today?'

'I had a small champagne during the toasts but that's all.'

He got to his feet and headed back to the window, peeking through the curtain.

'Will you support me?' she pressed. For her own peace of mind she needed to know. If he refused she didn't know what she would do other than fall into a crumpled ball. Or maybe join a convent.

No. She wouldn't do either. For the sake of the life inside her, she would endure.

'Will you support our baby and be its father?'

The ringing that had echoed in Christian's ears since Alessandra's pronouncement that she was pregnant subsided.

He gazed at her belly, still flat under the lilac of her dress, not a hint that within it lay the tiny seed of life.

The life they had created together.

His baby.

He was going to be a father.

As this knowledge seeped through him, he thought of his own father, a man who'd left before Christian had been old enough to memorise his features. He had no memories of him, no possessions to place a tangible hold on him. Nothing. Not even a photograph. His mother had burned them all.

If there was one thing he knew with bone-deep certainty, it was that he didn't want a child of his being raised without a father to look out for him or her.

From infancy it had been just him and his mother, a woman whose bitterness ran so deep it seemed to seep from her pores. His father had turned his back on them both and in turn had created the woman she'd become.

Christian would *not* be that man.

He raised his gaze from Alessandra's belly to meet her eyes, a sharpness driving in his chest to see all the fear and uncertainty contained in them. Despite the braveness she strove to convey, her hands trembled, her teeth driving in and out of her plump lips as she awaited his response.

He knew what his response must be.

'Yes,' he said, nodding slowly for emphasis. 'I will support you and our child. But in return I want you to marry me.'

The comb holding Alessandra's hair in place had been digging into her scalp all day, a minor irritation that suddenly felt magnified enough for her to yank it out. She got to her feet, swiping fallen hair off her face.

For a moment she couldn't speak, her brain struggling to find the English she'd spoken like a native since early childhood. 'I know this is a shock for you. I *know*, okay? But marriage?'

'Yes, marriage.'

She shook her head, trying her hardest not to let panic set in. 'Please, don't say anything you'll regret in the morning when you look at the situation with fresh eyes.'

'The morning won't change the situation. You'll still be pregnant.'

'And I still won't be marrying you.'

'Alessandra...' He bit back his rising voice. 'Alessandra, think about it. This is the obvious solution. Marriage will give legitimacy to our child.'

'This isn't the nineteenth century. There's no stigma to children born outside of wedlock.'

His eyes swirled with an emotion she didn't understand. 'Children need and deserve two parents. You know that as well as I do.'

One parent would have been nice in her case, she thought bitterly. Yes, her father was still alive, but he'd never been a real father to her. He'd abandoned her almost from her first breath. By the time of her first birthday, he'd gambled and drunk away their home and had foisted Rocco and her into the care of his elderly father.

She felt as if she'd been blindsided. Marriage was the last thing she'd expected Christian to suggest. The most she'd hoped for was public support for her and their child, and even that had felt like a pipe dream considering she was dealing with the commitment-phobic Christian Markos. He made Casanova look like a monk.

She hadn't allowed herself to hope for anything more substantial, had envisaged her and the baby's future with Christian flitting in and out when it suited him. She'd even prepared her 'please don't introduce our child to a succession of aunties' speech. In her head she'd prepared for just about every imaginable scenario. Apart from the scenario where he demanded marriage.

'Christian, please, be realistic. Marriage is...'

'Something neither of us wants,' he finished for her, meeting her gaze with steady eyes.

How clearly she remembered discussing marriage on their night out together, the night their baby had been conceived. *Fools* had been just one of the many words they'd used to describe people who willingly entered matrimony. They'd even toasted this rare meeting of minds.

'Exactly. Something neither of us wants.'

He finished his drink with a grimace. 'Seeing as neither of us has any intention of marrying in the conventional sense, marriage each other for the sake of our child isn't going to destroy either of our dreams. We won't be making a lifelong commitment to each other, just to our child.'

'But marriage...?'

'Marriage will legitimise the pregnancy and avert any scandal. The press will still swarm over the story, that's a given, but their angle will be softer towards you.'

'Accepting paternity will have the same effect. At this moment, that's all I need. Your acceptance. Everything else can be arranged between us later. There's plenty of time.'

'And what about what *I* need?' he challenged. 'You tell me I'm going to be a father and that you want my support but when I offer you the biggest support I can—marriage—you dismiss it out of hand.'

'What do *you* need?' she asked, now thoroughly confused. 'What will you get out of us marrying?'

'The chance to be a father,' he answered with a shrug. 'I've built up a multi-billion-dollar business and have no one to pass it to.'

She didn't bother to hide her scorn. *'Money.'* The only thing he enjoyed more than bedding women.

His blue eyes flashed sharply. 'No. A legacy. But even if I didn't have the wealth I would still want us to marry. I know what it's like growing up without a father and I will not have my child go through that. I want my child to have my name and know he—or she—is *mine.*'

How did he do it? No wonder he was reputed to be one of the greatest financial minds in the world. Money was what Christian dealt with every day, a world-renowned financial genius advising all the major corporations in all the different sectors.

She'd spent *days* agonising over all the possible details. He'd grasped the situation and dissected all the permutations in an instant. Having only known him as her brother's friend, she'd never appreciated this side of him before.

She appreciated it even less now.

'You can still be a father to our child without marriage.'

'And you can still be a single mother without any support other than financially,' he said, a warning note coming into his voice.

'I've already told you, I don't need or want your money.'

He inhaled a long breath. 'I'm trying to do what's right here. I don't want to force your hand but I have to think of our child. He or she deserves stability—marriage gives that. Or is your freedom more important?'

Christian watched Alessandra suck her cheeks in at his remark. He didn't blame her. Right then he was prepared to say whatever it took to get her to agree.

Theos, an hour ago the thought of marriage would have

made him run all the way to Hong Kong but now here he was, virtually coercing her into marrying him.

'That's not fair,' she said hoarsely.

'Life isn't fair.' He knew that all too well; it was the whole reason he was demanding this from her. 'Marriage needn't be a prison for either of us. You can carry on with your career.'

'How generous of you. You're welcome to carry on with your career too.'

He ignored her sarcasm, understanding the place of fear it came from. If he felt his world had just turned on its axis he could only imagine how it must be for her. She had to carry their baby into the world.

It was their baby he was thinking of. Christian had grown up knowing somewhere out there was the man who had fathered him but who wanted nothing to do with him, his own son. He had never understood why. He still didn't.

It had taken many years for him to accept his father's abandonment as a simple fact of life but as a child it had been a painful knowledge. He would *never* put his own child through that. *His* child would grow up feeling loved and secure with two parents who both wanted nothing more than to love and protect him or her.

Looking at Alessandra rest a protective hand against her still-flat stomach, he could see how deeply she already felt for their child.

Their child. His responsibility. Their responsibility, to be shouldered together.

'When we marry the world will see a united couple…' he started.

'Don't talk as if it's a done deal. Marriage changes *everything*. It's not just two people signing a piece of paper and exchanging a bit of jewellery. There are legal implications.'

'And it's those legal implications I want. I want our child to know their parents loved them enough to create a stable family for them.'

'This is too much.' She got to her feet. He experienced a sharp pang to see her tremble, to witness her keeping it all together, just as she'd done at her grandfather's funeral.

She carried herself so tall it was easy to overlook that she was a slip of a woman. Her glossy hair was sprawled over her shoulders, her golden skin pale.

The last thing he wanted was to hurt her but within him lay a deep-rooted certainty that this was the right path for them. It was the only path.

'I need to sleep on this,' she said, her honey eyes brimming with emotion, her usually accent-less English inflected with her Italian heritage. 'I can't agree to marriage just because you've clicked your fingers. You might change your mind. I've sprung this on you. Everything will look different in the morning.'

There were a dozen threats he could make to ensure her agreement. He bit them all back. He felt bad enough as it was without adding more ill deeds to the slate against him. There was one more thing he could add, though…

'I won't change my mind but you can go ahead and sleep on it,' he said. 'While you're lying in your bed thinking, consider the ramifications if you decide not to take me up on my proposal. If you marry me, scandal averted. If you don't, the press will crucify you and drag your brother and the entire House of Mondelli through the mud with you. Do you really want to go through all that again? Do you want *Rocco* to go through all that again?'

She stilled, stormy eyes locked on his.

'Do you want all the speculation over who the father is? The old scandal being raked up as the world wonders if you've been playing around with another married man?'

'But I never…'

He hated to see the hurt and bewilderment that flashed across her features but he had no choice. For their child's sake he would deploy every weapon in his arsenal to get her agreement. 'You know that and I know that. The rest of the world will believe what it wants to believe and, as it's doing so, the world's eyes will be on *you*.'

'You know how to play dirty,' she said hoarsely, her chest heaving.

'I could never have left Greece without learning how. If you refuse, you will have to deal with the press and the world's attention on your own. I will make no acknowledgement until our baby is born.'

Her throat moved as she swallowed, her eyes blazing their loathing at him. 'Do not think you can blackmail me, Markos.'

'I don't want to blackmail you,' he said, wondering why the sound of his surname being spat from her delicious, plump lips landed like a barb in his chest. 'But you leave me no choice.'

She backed to the door and gripped the handle. 'I'm going to my room now. I'll give you my answer in the morning.'

'There is only one answer.'

'You can still wait on it.'

CHAPTER THREE

HIS HEAD THUMPING, Christian entered the magnificent dining room where breakfast was being served. Alessandra was already there. So too were Stefan, Zayed and a handful of other guests who'd stayed the night rather than retire to their yachts or have their helicopters collect them.

It was little comfort that every person in the room looked exactly how he felt. *Skata.* Like crap.

He might not have been able to get himself as drunk as he'd wanted but his body was punishing him regardless for the quantity of alcohol he'd consumed.

Alessandra's gaze darted to him. Anyone looking at her could be forgiven for thinking she had a hangover too. Only he knew the dark rings under her bloodshot eyes were caused by a different reason.

He doubted she'd had any more sleep than the snatches he'd managed.

Even so, she still had that certain charisma that she carried like a second skin; her hair, left loose to tumble halfway down her back, as glossy as ever.

He took the seat next to Zayed, who was clutching a black coffee as if his life depended on it, and poured himself a cup of his own. He shook his head as a member of staff asked what he'd like to eat.

All he wanted at that moment was hot, sweet caffeine. And a dozen painkillers.

No sooner had he taken his first sip than Alessandra rose,

murmuring something to Stefan, who gave a pained laugh and immediately rubbed at his temples.

He waited long enough not to rouse any suspicion, making innocuous hangover talk with his buddies, before saying he was going for a lie down.

Alessandra's room was in a different wing from where he and his uni friends always slept when they stayed at the villa. He hadn't realised he knew exactly which room was hers until he knocked on the door. After a minute of no response, he nudged it open. It was empty.

Moving stealthily so as not to attract attention, he slipped out of the villa and into the gardens.

After much searching, he tracked her down. She was sitting on the stone steps that led into Lake Como. Only one yacht remained from the handful that had been moored overnight.

She didn't acknowledge his presence.

Today she was dressed in ankle-length tight white jeans and a pale-pink cashmere top, the V plunging down to display a hint of swollen cleavage, the only outward physical sign of the changes taking place within her.

What other changes were taking place within that gorgeous form…?

A stark image came into his mind of the perfection of her breasts, the way they seemed to have been made to fit his hands… If he closed his eyes he could still taste them, taste *her*…

'How are you feeling?' he asked abruptly, forcing thoughts of her naked body from his mind as he sat on the cold stone beside her.

'About as well as can be expected,' she replied after a long pause.

'I never asked last night how you're coping with the pregnancy—physically, I mean.'

Another pause. 'So far I've been lucky. No morning sickness or anything.'

'I've made a few calls and rearranged my schedule so I can stay in Milan for a few days. First thing tomorrow morning, we're going to see your doctor.'

'I've got a shoot to do.' She cast sharp eyes at him. 'And, before you accuse me of being selfish again, I'd like to point out that for me to cancel the shoot would mean a good dozen people's schedules being thrown. We can see the doctor in the afternoon.'

At least she was willing to see a doctor with him. That was a start.

'Does this mean you are in agreement to us marrying?'

She fell silent for a few moments, tucking a strand of hair behind an ear. 'If we marry, we both automatically become our child's legal guardian.'

'I am aware of that.' It was one of the things he wanted—his paternity to be recognised by law. Marriage might be destructive and capable of ruining people but it was the only way he could ensure his child had his protection. For that reason alone he was prepared to do it. For their child's sake, it was no sacrifice.

She stared at him. 'If anything happens to me, you have sole responsibility.'

He felt his blood chill at the sudden solemnity in her tone. 'Why are you talking like this?'

'Do you know how my mother died?' she asked in that same thoughtful tone.

'Rocco never liked to talk about her other than to say she'd died when he was seven.' Alessandra would have been a baby, he realised, doing the maths for the first time.

Her gaze didn't falter. 'She died having me.'

Theos...

'Rocco never said.' He shook his head, trying to digest her words.

'Rocco suffered the most out of all of us.' A faraway look formed in her eyes before she blinked it away and cleared her throat.

'What happened to her?' he asked, rubbing his chin, trying to imagine the Mondelli siblings as they'd been then: Rocco a child of seven, and Alessandra, so fresh and newborn she'd barely taken her first breath before her mother had been taken away from her forever.

He racked his pounding brain, trying to remember the age Rocco had been when he'd gone to live with Giovanni Mondelli, their grandfather. Eight, if he was recollecting correctly, which meant Alessandra had been a year at the most.

She'd never known the love of either a mother *or* a father.

At least his own mother had been there. For all her faults, she'd never abandoned him or reneged on her responsibility as a mother.

'She suffered from severe pre-eclampsia,' Alessandra said, her husky voice soft.

Red-hot anger flooded through him, pushing away the ache that had formed in his chest at learning of the tragic circumstances of her birth. '*Why the hell* haven't you seen a doctor yet?'

'It doesn't affect women until the later stages of pregnancy. For the time being, I'm fine. My mother didn't know what she was dealing with—she'd already given birth to a healthy child without any complications. Medicine has advanced a lot since then and we can prepare for it. The odds of anything happening to me are remote. But—and this is why I'm saying this now, before I agree to anything—if the worst happens then I need to know that you will rise to your legal and moral duty and raise our child.'

'I would *never* abandon our child,' he said harshly. 'I've lived without a father; I know what it's like to wonder where you're from. I will never let our child wonder who I am.'

'My father said that to my mother. He promised he would love and care for us but he broke it—he broke the promise he made to a dying woman. He abandoned me. He abandoned Rocco.'

'I am *not* your father. What he did was despicable. After the way my own father abandoned me, I would never give up my own flesh and blood.'

'I have to trust that you won't be like either of our fathers but I find trusting people, especially men, very hard. If I stay single, then I can nominate the guardian of my choosing.'

If fire could have shot from eyes then what burned from Christian's would have had her in flames.

'I will never allow that,' he ground out. 'I would fight for our child through every court in every land.'

The tension that had been cramping Alessandra's belly throughout the conversation loosened a touch.

She believed him.

Their child would have a father. A proper father.

She just had to hope her trust in this respect wasn't misplaced. For her child's sake, she had to try.

'I'm sorry for being melodramatic. I just need to be sure. We *both* need to be sure. If we marry then that's it—we're married. For better or worse. And, if I agree, I want you to promise that you will be discreet in your affairs.'

His head twisted at her abrupt change of direction. 'My affairs?'

'I'm not stupid,' she said with what she hoped sounded like nonchalance. If she was going to marry him, she would do it with her eyes open.

Christian was an attractive man—oh, to hell with such an insipid description, he was utterly gorgeous. He had the most beautiful eyes she'd ever seen in a man, a real crystal-blue that made her think of calm, sunlit oceans. When he fixed them on her, though, her internal reaction was turbulent; a crescendo of emotions she struggled to understand.

The way he'd made her feel that night…

He was used to women throwing themselves at him. She wasn't so naïve as to believe marriage would tame him. Theirs was not a love match. 'Our loyalty will be primarily to our child but I do not want the humiliation of your liaisons being paraded on the front pages of the tabloids. All I ask is that from now on you choose your lovers wisely.'

He inhaled sharply before expelling the air slowly. If his jaw became any more rigid she feared it would snap. 'Anything else?' he asked icily.

She refused to drop her gaze. 'Only that if we marry I won't be taking your name.'

Now she knew how it must have felt like to be glared at by Medusa. Forget mere fire; she could feel her blood turn to stone under his deadly stare.

'Why. Not?' he asked through gritted teeth.

'Because I like my name and I don't want to have to start all over again. I've spent the past seven years building my career but it's only been in the last few that my name has become famous for my work rather than my heritage and past exploits.' Alessandra wasn't prepared to fool herself. She might be famous at the moment for her photography but she didn't have the longevity that would still make her name roll off fashion editors' lips if she took months off. Her work as a photographer could quickly be forgotten, others taking her place.

More importantly, although this was something she chose not to share with Christian, figuring she'd pushed him far enough as it was, she didn't trust that their marriage would survive. If she was a betting girl, she would give them until their baby's first birthday. By then, Christian would be clamouring for his freedom.

'You can keep Mondelli as your business name but in our personal life you will be Markos.'

'Do not tell me what I can and can't do. Marriage will not make you my keeper.'

'I never said it would. However, one of the main factors in us marrying is to promote stability and unity. Sharing a surname is a part of that.'

'If you feel that strongly about it, you can change your name to Mondelli.'

'That is out of the question.'

'Why? Because you're a man? I never took you for a caveman.'

'It's the tradition of marriage.'

'We're not marrying for traditional reasons. As I pointed out last night, we're living in the twenty-first century. Plenty of couples marry without taking each other's surnames. I'm sorry if this disappoints you but I'm not changing my name. It's non-negotiable.'

'Our child will take *my* name.' He stared at her, the fire in his blue eyes, normally so warm and full of vitality, now turned icy cold. 'That is non-negotiable.'

'I can agree to that,' she said, matching his cool tone. It was one thing refusing to take his name for herself— refusing to let their child take his name too would feel as if she was being cruel for cruelty's sake.

'Good.' The coldness in his eyes thawed a fraction. 'Does this mean—finally—that you will agree to our marriage?'

'After all this you *still* want to marry me?' she asked, a tiny bubble of amusement breaking through the tension. If Christian wanted a wife he could walk all over, she was certain she'd just proved she wouldn't be that woman. She didn't want to be a harridan but she knew she needed to establish the ground rules first. She'd worked too hard to build a life that was all her own to give it up without a fight. For her baby it was easy, but for a man? *No.*

'All I want is what's best for our baby.'

'As do I.' If that meant marrying Christian, then so be it. Rocco had always described him as a man of his word— if she didn't agree, he would refuse to confirm paternity until after the birth. In the meantime, her name would be dragged through the mud again. She would have to cope with swarms of paparazzi hounding her; read the lies that would follow as speculation grew over who her baby's father was; listen to the taunts that would surely rain down on her. She would have to suffer it alone, just as she had the first time.

And it wasn't just she who would suffer. Rocco would too and God alone knew her brother had suffered enough at her hands.

But, above and beyond all that, her baby could be the one to suffer the most. Imagining—*knowing*—what people were thinking of her, were saying about her... It would contaminate her, just like it had the first time. She didn't want that bitterness and despair to infect her innocent baby.

No, whichever way she looked at it, marrying Christian was the obvious, *practical* thing to do. Her head knew it. Soon enough her twisted guts would believe it too.

'How will our marriage work on a practical level?' she asked, stalling the moment when she would have to say aloud the words agreeing to tie her life to this man beside her.

'We will lead our own lives.' His gaze bore into her. 'Our marriage will be private. We can keep separate rooms and lead independent lives so long as we show unity in public.'

'I can accept that,' she agreed.

'But on our wedding night and honeymoon we will need to share a bed.' Christian stared at her without blinking, making sure she understood. Alessandra's approach, blunt as it was, was for the best—neither of them wanted there to be any misunderstandings. They would both enter matrimony with their eyes open but their hearts closed.

Colour tinged her cheeks. 'Surely we don't need to go that far?'

'I want our marriage to be seen as legal in *every* respect. To protect our child from undue scandal and speculation, people must believe we're in love.' He tried to think about their marriage with his business head, consider it as just another merger between two companies. In essence, that was what it *would* be—a merger. The profit would come from the child they would raise together.

He'd craved isolation since he'd been a small child sharing cramped living space with his mother. His homes were his sanctuary, his space. Even his live-in staff had separate quarters.

Alessandra had been the first woman he'd woken next to and felt a tug of reluctance at having to leave.

He couldn't remember ever feeling so greedy for someone as he had that night, when he'd wanted her so badly it had been as if he were consuming her. If he hadn't been concerned that she might be feeling the physical soreness he assumed women must feel after losing their virginity, he would have made love to her all night long.

Her eyes didn't waver although more colour crept over her face. 'When you say you want it to be seen as legal in every respect, are you implying that we need to have sex?'

'No.' His voice dropped, heat unfurling within him as a memory of a dusky pink nipple floated into his mind. A small gust of wind fluttered across them, causing a strand of her hair to stray across her face. Unthinking, he reached out to brush it away. 'But we *will* be married—what couples choose to do in the privacy of their own home is entirely their own business.'

Her throat moved, a subtle movement, but one he recognised.

He leaned in closer. 'When we stay anywhere that is not under one of our own roofs, we will share a bed. What we choose to do in that bed is nobody's business but our own.'

Their marriage would be a merger, yes, but not a business merger. This was going to be a merger of two flesh-and-blood people.

Something pulsed in her eyes and he knew with certainty that she was remembering how good it had been between them.

They had been combustible.

All the supressed memories of that night came back in startling colour.

She'd been wild. Carnal. Eager to please and be pleased, to touch and be touched.

Her arousal had been a living thing…

She cleared her throat. 'And if I choose to sleep and *only* sleep…?'

Then his balls would probably turn blue.

'Then you will be left to sleep.' He let his voice drop further, inching his face closer to hers. 'But, if you choose not to sleep, you won't find me complaining.'

'Is that because you're not fussy about who you lie in bed with?' Her words had a breathless quality to them. He could feel the tension emanating from her.

'No.' He shook his head in emphasis and pressed his lips to her ear. 'It's because you're the sexiest woman I've ever known and I get hard every time I think of how you came undone in my arms.'

He moved back to see her lips part and her doe eyes widen.

'I understand your opinion of my sex life is less than flattering,' he said, thinking that she turned the most beautiful colour when she blushed. 'But, I assure you, I think with the head on my shoulders and not the one in my boxer shorts.'

She swallowed before saying, 'I think that's a matter of opinion.'

'Point proved,' he said. 'But, to prove *my* point, I will not make a move on you until we are legally married.'

Her eyes narrowed but he caught the spark that ignited in them.

'And, of course, you will still reserve your right to say no.' He dipped his head to whisper into her ear again, inhaling her scent for good measure.

All his senses heightened. He could feel the heat from her skin; knew the spark that had drawn them together in the first place was still well and truly alive. 'We're both going to have to make sacrifices for this to work—the bedroom is the one area where compromise and sacrifice are not needed, where our marriage can be about nothing but mutual pleasure.'

She raised a shoulder and exhaled a shuddering breath that sounded almost like a moan. It was a long moment before she next spoke, breaking the charged silence that had sprung up between them. 'I will not have sex with you just because it's expected.'

He pulled away, creating a little distance so he could look at her. 'My only expectation is that, when we're in public, we *both* put on a display of being in love.'

She held his gaze for a fraction longer before blowing out a puff of air and fixing her gaze back on the lake. *'Bene.'*

'So we are in agreement?'

'Yes. We are in agreement. I will marry you.'

It was Christian's turn to exhale. Who would have thought *he* would feel relief to hear a woman agree to marriage?

'It would be best to marry as soon as we can—before you start showing.'

'I don't want to arrange anything until I've spoken to Rocco.'

The mention of her brother's name hit him like a blow: the metaphorical elephant in the room spoken aloud.

'We will speak to him together.'

'It will be best if I speak to him alone. He's my brother.'

'And he's one of my closest friends. He's not going to be happy about this.'

'I would prefer it if he gave us his blessing but if he refuses…' She sighed, a troubled expression crossing her features.

'We will wait until he returns from his honeymoon,' Christian decided, although his guts made that familiar clenching motion they did whenever he thought of what his friend's reaction would be.

Rocco would never forgive him.

He didn't blame him.

Whatever was thrown his way, he would take. It would be no less than he deserved.

He remembered the first time he'd met Rocco, Stefan and Zayed during his first week at Columbia. He'd never left Athens before that, never mind Greece. New York had been a whole new world. He'd felt out of his depth on every level, especially when comparing himself to his new friends' wealth and good breeding. He'd had neither and hadn't been able to understand why they'd accepted him as one of their own.

Even now, a decade on when his own wealth rivalled the best in the world, he still struggled to understand what they'd seen in him.

He was Christian Markos, born a gutter rat without a penny to his name. She was Alessandra Mondelli, born into one of Italy's premiere families. She had class *and* breeding. She could be a princess.

In a perfect world she would marry someone from a similar background. Someone worthy of her.

All the same, they might be from disparate backgrounds but on marriage they had common ground: relationships were not for either of them. In that one respect they were perfect for each other. She would never *need* him or require more than he could give.

And he would never need her.

Messy, complicated emotions would never infect *their* marriage.

CHAPTER FOUR

ALESSANDRA PRESSED THE button allowing Christian into the building and took deep breaths to compose herself.

It would be the first time she'd seen him in ten days.

They'd spent a couple of days together in Milan, seeing her doctor then a private obstetrician. Both had confirmed that she and the baby were in excellent health. She'd known in her guts everything was well but hearing it vocalised had lifted a weight she hadn't been aware of carrying until it was gone.

A scan had been taken, a copy of which they had both taken before Christian had left. She'd spent hours gazing at that picture, making out the tiny head and limbs, so imperceptible she had to rely on memory from where the nurse had pointed. Sometimes, gazing hard, everything inside her would constrict, her throat closing so tight that she had to swallow to loosen it. Her beautiful baby. Her and *Christian*'s beautiful baby.

She hadn't see him since, all their communication coming via daily text messages and phone calls, during which he filled her in on all the wedding plans. He wanted a Greek wedding so it made sense for him to organise it. She didn't think she would have been able to handle getting involved anyway. She was having a hard enough time coping with the magnitude of what she'd agreed to.

She'd known Christian since she was twelve and Rocco had brought the Brat Pack—as she privately called her brother and his little gang of university friends—home for a week-long holiday at the family villa. But she didn't *know* him.

He drank bourbon rather than his national drink of ouzo. He was a snazzy dresser. His brain was lauded around the world. He was completely self-made. He liked rock music. He'd slept with a quarter of the world's most beautiful women, the others being shared out between her brother, Stefan and Zayed. He was used to getting his own way. And that was it. The rest was a mystery. She was marrying a stranger.

Dio l'aiuti—God help her—she would have to share a bed with him on occasion.

And, *dio l'aiuti*, the thought made her heat from the inside.

Ever since that particular aspect of their talk, it had felt as if a glow had been lit inside of her. His lips against her ear, his breath whispering on her skin…the heat it had ignited…

When he entered her apartment, impeccably dressed in a fashionable navy suit and striped pale-yellow tie, her heart made an involuntary skip. It skipped again when she caught his clean, freshly showered scent.

'My apologies for the delay,' he said, leaning in to give her the traditional kiss on each cheek.

Two little kisses; two tiny brushes of his lips against her skin, the hint of his warm breath on her…

The lit glow flickered and pulsated low within her, her body responding to his proximity like a bee to a field of pollen.

'It's fine,' she said, stepping away from him and opening her handbag on the pretext of checking her purse. If he looked at her now, he would see the colour she knew had bloomed on her face scorching up her neck.

Christian had been due at her apartment early that morning. He'd called late last night to say he'd been delayed but would make it to her before lunch. She hadn't been surprised. Men always made promises they had no intention of keeping. They told lies, whether deliberately or not. Even her grandfather, a man she'd thought full of morality, had lied. Only after his death had she learned he'd had an affair decades ago—with her new sister-in-law's mother, no less. If her grandfather could lie to the wife he loved so much, then what hope was there for anyone else?

The only man she trusted was her brother.

She didn't want to think what the cause of Christian's delay could have been.

'How did it go with the doctor?' he asked.

'Good.' She bit back the question of whether he would attend any further appointments with her. It would save him having to lie. It would save her having to pretend to believe it.

'Your blood pressure?'

'Normal. Everything is normal,' she said, anticipating further questions along the same vein. Feeling more on an even keel and in control of her reactions, she closed her handbag and looked at him.

He was watching her closely. 'It wasn't my intention to miss the appointment. There was a crisis at Bloomfield Bank and I had to attend an emergency board meeting.'

'You don't have to account for your whereabouts with me.' She forced a smile. 'After all, it's not as if we're married or anything.' She couldn't deny a tiny bit of the cramp in her belly lessened at knowing he hadn't been with another woman.

He'd given his word not to make a move on her until they married. He'd made no such promise about making a move on another woman.

So long as he was discreet, who he slept with was none of her business.

He laughed, a familiar sound that plunged her back to the meal they'd shared. Of the Brat Pack, he'd always been her favourite, the one she'd privately dubbed 'the Greek

Adonis.' A woman didn't need wine goggles to appreciate the strength of his jaw or the dimples that appeared when he gave one of his frequent smiles.

With wine goggles, though, even the most inhibited of females would be putty in his hands. She, the woman who'd thought herself immune to any man's charms, had been.

He hadn't even tried. A couple of glasses of champagne on an empty stomach and an aching heart and she'd felt her secret attraction towards him, locked away out of reach, escape and bloom. Like the gentleman he was—and he *was* a gentleman in the traditional, chivalrous term of the word—he'd walked her home and right up to her door. She'd been the one to kiss him, not the usual two-cheek kiss but one right on his mouth.

The feel of his lips upon hers, the scent of his skin and warm breath…the effect had been indescribable. It had unleashed something inside her, something craven, a side she'd spent years denying the existence of, telling herself she'd rather die a virgin than give herself to a man.

It hadn't felt like *giving* herself to Christian. *Giving* implied bestowing a favour, not the hot mix of desire and need that had made her desperate for his touch.

She could still feel and taste the heady heat of his breath…

But now she was stone-cold sober, her immunity back in its rightful place. Vivid memories might have the power to jolt her senses but they didn't have the power to knock her off balance. No man would ever have that power. Her body might have a Pavlovian response to him but intellectually and emotionally she was safe.

When they married he could see whoever he wanted. It made no difference to her. All she cared about was her baby. As long as her baby made it safely into this world, nothing else mattered.

Maybe when her baby was placed in her arms, her own place on this earth would make sense.

Maybe then she would lose the feeling she'd carried her entire life that she should never have been born.

Christian sensed a slight change in Alessandra's demeanour, an almost imperceptible straightening of the shoulders and stiffening of the spine.

She was looking good. She always looked good.

With her long hair loose around her shoulders, she wore faded tight-fitting jeans, a pale-blue cotton blouse unbuttoned to the top of her cleavage, a navy blazer and silver ankle boots with a slight heel. Heavy costume jewellery in shades of red hung round her neck and wrists, large, hooped gold earrings in her ears. Alessandra could wear a sack and carry it off, would still have that beautifully put-together air she carried so well.

Her apartment was the same: chic and beautifully put together, the walls and furniture muted but the furnishings bold and colourful. Giant prints of her work hung on the walls, enlarged, framed covers of *Vogue* and all the other glossy magazines she'd worked for.

He knew it would be a wrench for her to leave, but a third-floor apartment in the heart of Milan's fashion district was not a feasible place to bring up a child. He'd raised the subject of her selling it on the phone a few days ago. Her response had been non-committal to say the least.

He'd give her more time to get used to the idea before discussing it again.

'Are you ready to go?' he asked.

She nodded, her plump lips drawing together. 'Let's get this over with.'

Out in the courtyard at the back of the building, where his driver waited for them, her yellow Vespa gleamed from its parking space. 'I hope you're not riding on that thing any more,' he said, nodding at it.

'No,' she answered shortly, getting into the back of the car.

He followed her in, a pang hitting his stomach as he recalled the big beam on her face the one time he'd seen her ride on it—the day of their impromptu date. Another thing pregnancy would force her to give up.

When the car started to move, she turned to look at him, a set look on her face. 'Christian, let me make one thing quite clear. You are going to be my husband, not my keeper. Do not dictate to me.'

He sighed. 'Is this about the Vespa?'

'Yes.'

'I wasn't *dictating* to you. I was satisfying myself that you're not putting our child's life at risk by continuing to ride on it, especially here in Milan.'

'That is exactly what I mean. I don't need you to tell me the drivers here all approach the road as an assault course that must be beaten—I live here. I might not have a penis between my legs but my brain and rationality work perfectly well.'

'I never said it didn't,' he said, keeping his tone even. 'But you must appreciate that it is *my* child you are carrying and it is only right I take an interest in its welfare.'

'But it is *my* life. I will not be told what to do.'

'I am not telling you what to do.' How he held on to his patience, he did not know. 'All I'm saying is that having a child changes things…'

'You think I don't know that?' she said, her colour darkening. 'You think I'm not aware of the responsibility I have to bring our child safely into this world? Do you think I'm not *capable*?'

'Alessandra…' He took a breath and fisted his hands into balls. 'Will you stop putting words into my mouth? You're making assumptions.'

Her shoulders hunched before she flopped her head back and took a long breath. 'I'm sorry,' she muttered. 'I have an aversion to being told what to do.'

'I had already gathered that.'

She cast a sideways glance at him and tucked a strand of hair behind her ear. Her very pretty ear.

'As well as my aversion to being bossed around, I also have a tendency to get grumpy when I'm worried about something,' she admitted, her tone now rueful.

'You're worried about Rocco's reaction to our news?'

'Aren't you?'

He reached for her hand and squeezed it.

'Whatever happens with your brother, nothing will change. You and I will still marry. If he gives his blessing, then that will be beneficial, but if he doesn't then we will handle it together. Okay?' he added when she didn't answer, simply sank her teeth into her bottom lip and tugged her hand free from his clasp.

She nodded slowly, and absently rubbed at the top of her hand where his fingers had rested. 'Rocco is very protective of me. He always has been.'

'You're his sister; nothing will change that.' Christian was doing his best to project a positive frame of mind for Alessandra's benefit but was under no illusion about how hot-headed her brother could be. He knew that if the forthcoming meeting was badly handled, their friendship would be ruined.

Alessandra's lungs had closed up.

The intimacy of the cab, the forced proximity…

Worry about her brother's reaction faded as Christian's oaky cologne filled her senses, moisture filling her mouth and bubbling low in her most intimate area.

She pressed her thighs together and dragged out a short breath. It wasn't enough. She needed air.

There was nowhere to hide.

The traffic outside was atrocious. They were still a couple of streets away from the House of Mondelli, where her brother awaited her. If she were on her Vespa she would be there by now, able to weave in and out of the traffic while turning a deaf ear to the tooting horns.

'Let's walk the rest of the way,' she said. She needed air. She needed to breathe. 'It'll be quicker.'

Christian nodded and pressed the button to lower the partition, telling his driver to stop the car. As they were already stationary, this required no effort on the driver's part.

Alessandra immediately felt better out in the balmy spring air. She loved the sunshine; knew it was the reason her grandfather had left her the villa in St. Barts, so she had a bolt hole to escape to when the gloomy Milanese winter set in. She had no idea yet what she would do with the apartment in Paris he had also left her, but the villa would remain hers until she took her last breath. Which, if the Milanese drivers had anything to do with it, could be sooner rather than later.

They made it to the entrance of the luxurious building without being squashed by any moving vehicles and stepped inside. She smiled at the glamorous receptionists and, with Christian by her side, strode past the large rooms homing all the creative minds that made the House of Mondelli such a success, and through to her brother's office. His door was closed; Gabrielle, his PA, guarded it with her desk like a sentry. She stood to greet them.

Alessandra cast a quick glance at Christian, experiencing the strangest compulsion to grab hold of his hand. He inclined his head and threw a small, encouraging smile. She couldn't read his eyes.

Taking a deep breath, she rapped on the door and pushed it open.

Rocco was at his desk talking into his phone. A smile formed on his lips at seeing his sister, his eyes pulling into a question at seeing Christian follow her inside and shut the door behind him.

He ended the call and got to his feet, sidling round his desk to pull her into an embrace. 'You're looking well, *sorellina*.' Little sister.

'And you're looking tanned. Good honeymoon?'

'*Perfetto.*'

She didn't think she'd ever seen him so happy. 'How's Liv?'

Somehow his face lit up even more. 'She's wonderful.' Rocco moved on to Christian, giving him a bear hug, which he returned. 'What are you doing here?'

'I'm here to see you,' Christian said.

If Rocco heard the serious inflection in his friend's voice he made no sign of it. 'Alessandra and I have a lunch date—are you joining us?'

'Rocco,' said Alessandra, placing a hand on her brother's arm to get his attention. 'Christian is here with me. We have something to tell you.'

Immediately the light in her brother's eyes dimmed, became wary. 'Tell me what?'

Christian shifted slightly and placed an arm around her waist. The gesture felt almost protective. 'We're getting married,' he said, his tone serious.

Rocco shook his head as if clearing his ears of water. 'Married?'

'Yes. We wanted you to be the first to know.'

Alessandra pressed closer to Christian in a show of unity and forced a breezy laugh. If they could make this look and sound as natural as possible, then Rocco should be accepting of their plans. That was what she'd been telling herself for almost a fortnight. 'I want you to give me away.'

Rocco laughed with her, although not at his usual pitch. 'You two are getting married?'

'*Si.*'

'My little sister and my best friend?'

'*Si*! Isn't it wonderful?'

'That's one way to describe it. When did all this happen?'

'We bumped into each other when you were in New York.' She and Christian had agreed to stick with the truth as much as possible. Neither wanted to lie to Rocco. 'Christian had come to take *you* out but, as you were in New York,

I talked him into taking me out instead. Then, at your wedding we spent a bit more time together and realised our feelings for each other had changed.' That was the truth as well. How could someone be just a friend of your brother's if you were carrying his child?

'When do you hope to marry?'

'We've decided there's no point in hanging around so we've set the date for a fortnight. We're marrying in Athens.'

'That soon?'

Christian's hand brushed against her back as he pulled away from her and took a step closer to Rocco.

Neither man spoke.

Suddenly she became aware that the atmosphere in the office wasn't the warm bonhomie she'd intended. It was cold. Icy.

As she looked from her fiancé to her brother, taking in the two sets of lips clamped firmly together, her heart sank.

For all his outward amiability, Rocco hadn't bought a single word she'd said. And Christian knew it.

'Are you pregnant?' he asked, looking at her briefly, his tone casual.

She swallowed, stupidly unprepared for such a question. She placed her arm protectively across her waist.

This time he directed the same question to Christian. There was no denying the menace in his stance. 'Have you got my sister pregnant?'

Christian drew himself up to his full height. It was like watching two silverbacks square up to each other. Both men were equal in stature, both topping six foot by a good few inches, and both kept themselves in extremely good shape.

'Yes. Alessandra is pregnant with my baby and we have agreed to marry. We both want to do the right thing by our child.'

'The right thing by your child?' Rocco snarled, his face ablaze with fury. 'What about my sister? What the *hell* were you doing messing with her in the first place?'

'I'm not going to lie to you,' Christian said, his tone calm but with a hint of steel underlying his words. 'Neither of us meant for this to happen. But it *has* happened—Alessandra is pregnant with my child and I am going to support them both in every way I can.'

'So she was another of your one-night stands? Is that what you're telling me?'

Christian didn't answer, keeping his gaze fixed evenly on Rocco.

'You said neither of you meant it to happen, so I will ask you one more time: was she just a one-night stand to you?'

'Yes.'

If Christian intended to elaborate on his one-syllable answer, his words went unsaid when Rocco's arm shot out like a bullet.

'Rocco, *no!*' But her scream came too late to prevent her brother's fist connecting with Christian's nose, a resounding crack bouncing off the walls on impact.

Christian dropped to the floor with a thump.

Immediately Alessandra fell to her knees beside him. Vivid red blood seeped from his nose.

'What did you do that *for*?' she said, switching to Italian, half-shouting, half-screaming, not looking at Rocco, too busy checking Christian's vital signs. The pulse in his neck pumped strongly, the only blessing she could cling to. She looked up at her brother, who stood frozen. 'Don't just stand there—call for an ambulance.'

Rocco's broad chest heaved, his face a couple of shades paler than it had been when she'd walked into his office. 'He doesn't need an ambulance. He's already coming round.'

He was right. Christian's lips were moving.

'At least get some ice,' she snapped, somehow holding back the tears.

Not sure if she was doing the right thing or not, she carefully lifted Christian's head and placed it on her lap. Being as gentle as she could, she ran her fingers over his hair, not knowing or caring if she was comforting him or herself. Of all the scenarios that had played itself out in her head, this was not an outcome she had prepared for.

She should be getting used to that.

'Are you still here?' she snarled at her brother. 'He needs ice.'

'He needs castration.' He swore loudly. 'You're my sister and he's a playboy—'

'And you're a hypocrite!' she interrupted. 'The majority of the women you've slept with have been *someone's* sister. He's your best friend and you're just as big a playboy as he is.'

'Not any more, I'm not—and I'm not oblivious to those other women being someone's sister, but *you* are *my* sister.'

'No—I *was* your sister. After what you've just done, I will never call you my brother again. I'll walk myself up the aisle. Now, get an ice pack and then you can get the hell out of my life.'

Through the ringing in his ears Christian heard the sound of muffled talking. Arguing.

Was that *Alessandra* speaking so emotively?

Through the lancing pain in his face came the realisation that, yes, it was Alessandra—that it was her warm lap supporting his head, her gentle fingers lacing through his hair, her normally calm, husky voice pitched at a much higher octave than he had ever associated it with.

Footsteps left the room, the door slamming with a close.

He winced as the sound reverberated through his pounding head.

Well, that had gone better than he'd anticipated.

CHAPTER FIVE

BACK IN ALESSANDRA'S APARTMENT, Christian lay on the sofa, holding the ice pack in place to the bridge of his nose.

Eyes closed, he heard Alessandra pour fresh coffee out; listened as she padded over the thick rug and placed their drinks on the glass table in front of him.

Gabrielle had brought the ice pack to him, Rocco himself having disappeared from the building.

His old friend had seen straight through their deception, exactly as he'd known he would.

'You let him hit you, didn't you?'

He opened his eyes to find Alessandra glaring down at him. She'd changed into a short black skirt, the faded jeans she'd been wearing having been covered in his blood. Her golden legs were bare. Gorgeously bare.

He straightened and put the ice pack down beside his mug.

'Are you going to answer me?'

'Yes, I let him hit me.'

'Why?'

'Better to let him get it out of his system now than at the wedding.'

'He's not coming to the wedding. I've told him he's not welcome.'

Even though the movement hurt, he couldn't stop the smile forming. 'You don't mean that.'

'Don't I?'

'No, you don't.' He knew how close the Mondelli siblings were.

'I told you, I don't like being told what to do. I've had it up to here with my brother thinking he can run my life.' She slumped onto the single sofa and rubbed her eyes, smudging her make-up. 'Did you know I always refused to do any work for the House of Mondelli?'

'I was aware of that—Rocco always said he thought it was a shame, as your fashion shoots are some of the best in the business.'

'He said that?' A look of pleasure flashed over her, quickly replaced by another grimace. 'A few months ago he asked me to do all the photography for the new launch he was working on. For the first time, I said yes. I thought our relationship had reached the stage where he regarded me as his equal, as Alessandra Mondelli, not just as his little sister. I wanted to be employed for the quality of my work, not out of nepotism. I should have known better. He still thinks he knows best and can ride roughshod over my feelings.'

She made a noise that sounded like a choking growl and slumped on the sofa, bending her head forward, her long hair falling like a sheet before her until she tossed her head back and sighed. 'I love my brother but he has to accept I'm not a child any more. I'm an adult. I make my own decisions. He doesn't have to like them but he has to at least respect them and if he can't do that then he can keep away.'

'Our news was a shock to him. He'll come round.'

'I don't care if he does.' She blinked rapidly and swallowed. 'So much for averting a scandal; how long do you think it'll be before the press learns he hit you?'

'There's no need for the press to know anything.'

She arched a perfectly plucked dark brow. 'We were seen by at least a dozen people leaving the House of Mondelli, you with an ice pack stuck to your nose. Have you looked in the mirror?' She didn't give him the chance to reply.

'You've already got two black eyes forming. How are you going to explain that away?'

'I wear exceedingly dark sunglasses. No one will see my eyes.'

'That's not even funny.'

Seeing she was working herself into a state, he leaned forward and spoke forcefully. 'There will be no scandal. We will cut the press off at its head.'

'How?'

'By announcing our marriage. We will send out a press release today.'

She pulled a face. 'If we announce it now, the press will go into a frenzy.'

'They will,' he agreed. During their many phone conversations over the past ten days they'd discussed how to handle the press and had agreed to delay notifying them until a week before the wedding, at which point Alessandra would join him in Athens. All the guests they planned to invite could be relied on for their discretion. 'But it will be a controlled frenzy and give them something to write about that should, hopefully, supersede any rumour that may come about your brother hitting me. You will have to travel to Athens with me...'

'Absolutely not.'

'You've already agreed to join me there.'

'But not for another week.'

'It will be safer for you. Here, you're too exposed. The paparazzi can doorstep you.'

'I don't care.' Eyes blazing, she folded her arms across her chest. 'I can't go anywhere. I have work commitments. Lots of them. It's been hard enough trying to rearrange my schedule for the wedding and honeymoon but at least I've been able to give the editors and fashion houses I freelance for some notice. For me to come to Athens today means letting them all down at the last minute.'

'What's the alternative? For you to stay here in Milan to

face the press on your own? You wanted my support and I am trying to give it to you.'

'Why do I need to leave? Why can't you stay here?'

'I need to be in Athens. I have important business commitments coming up this week.'

'Are you saying your commitments are more important than mine?'

'No.' Swearing, he gripped hold of his mug. 'Yes.'

Looking at her, he could see she was fighting the urge to punch him in the face just as her brother had done.

Such passion.

On the surface, Alessandra Mondelli was the epitome of cool sophistication. Scratch beneath it and the passionate, sultry woman emerged like a vibrant butterfly emerging from a chrysalis.

Knowing he was the only man to have experienced that passion made his chest fill.

Her passion was *his*. All his.

One day, soon, he would sate himself in her arms again. He knew it and she knew it too; he could see it in the way the pupils of her eyes dilated when their gazes met, the way her breath hitched when they brushed against each other.

She still wanted him.

The thought of them sharing a bed again made his loins tighten and the dread of their forthcoming nuptials taste sweeter.

She would be his again.

For now, though, all thoughts of making love would have to wait. He'd given his word not to make a move on her until after their wedding and he intended to keep it.

'In the future we will arrange our schedules to accommodate both our obligations, but in this instance I'm afraid my commitments *are* more important than yours.'

One of Greece's major banks—one that had weathered the worst of the financial crisis—had been plunged into serious financial trouble and had called on Christian for help and advice. So many of his compatriots were struggling; it was like a constant pain in his chest. He'd been there once: impoverished. Desperate. He gave his assistance gladly.

'That's just…'

'There is another alternative,' he said, knowing perfectly well it was an alternative she would dismiss out of hand. 'You can stay at Villa Mondelli. The press won't be able to touch you there, not with all the security measures that have been put in place.'

'What, with my brother? I would rather stay in a convent.'

'Those are your options: stay here alone to deal with the press you hate so much, stay with the brother you've just disowned or come to Athens with me where the press can't touch you.'

'Then I stay.'

Theos, give him patience. The woman was even more stubborn than her brother. 'And deal with the press alone? When you hate them so much?'

'At least I know their comments will be kinder than they were before. I'd much rather they harass me by asking questions about our wedding than harass me by telling me who the latest person to call me a slut is.'

'They did that?' He'd seen much of the coverage, knew she'd had a rough time with the press, but had had no idea they had stooped so low as to tell a vulnerable teenager what despicable names people were calling her.

'That was then. I'm perfectly safe here in my apartment—the press can't get past the concierge.'

'Who are these people who called you a slut?' His brain refused to move on from that piece of information. When he learned who had said such insulting words towards her, he would hunt each and every one of them down. He would make them pay.

The sheer violence of his thoughts shocked him.

All his life he'd used his brains to better himself, only using his fists when it was a choice of fight or flight.

The kids in his neighbourhood had roamed the streets of Athens in packs while he had spent his precious free time with his head buried in books, determined to educate himself out of that life. They'd seen him as a freak.

Often they had lain in wait for him. Between the ages of ten and sixteen he'd been beaten up on average once a month. Always he'd fought back, sometimes more successfully than others. Then, aged sixteen, he'd experienced a monster of a growth spurt, growing six inches in six months. He'd also found himself an early-morning job at the fish market lugging heavy boxes of freshly caught mackerel and sardines. He'd filled out physically to match his new height.

He'd no longer been the skinny, bookish kid and the bullies had known it. After one particular fight, when he'd broken the nose of the ringleader and blackened the eyes of two others, they'd left him alone.

He hadn't wanted to hit anyone since then. Until now.

How could *anyone* call Alessandra a slut?

'Too many to name.' She answered his question with a shrug.

'How could they say such things? You were a child.'

'I was seventeen. Old enough to know better.'

'Do not tell me you blame yourself?'

'Only in the respect that I swallowed Javier's lies.' Her eyes pierced right through him. 'I should have known not to trust the word of a man.'

'Not all men are liars.'

'Aren't they?' She didn't elaborate. She continued staring at him with the same piercing expression.

'No!' he said forcefully.

'With the exception of my brother, all the men *I've* ever known have been liars. Trusting Javier cost me everything. My grandfather turned into my jailer, the few friends he'd permitted me to have turned their backs on me because their parents didn't want me corrupting them and Rocco had the humiliation of reading untrue, lewd comments about his baby sister. I'm sorry, but I will never trust you, Christian. All I can do is try and have faith that your indiscretions will be discreet.'

'I will never humiliate you or disrespect you.' He rose from his seat, ignoring the throbbing pain across the front of his face, and crouched on his haunches before her. Placing a hand on her neck, he rubbed his thumb over the soft skin.

Theos, one touch of her softness, one inhalation of her scent and his body responded, his groin tightening as memories of burying himself inside her assailed him.

'You are going to be my wife.' He spoke the words slowly. 'If you do not believe anything else, believe that that means something to me. I will take my vows seriously.'

'I'm sure Javier said the same thing to his wife.'

Christian swore and inhaled deeply.

Alessandra leant forward, matching the intensity of his stare, close enough for his oaky, masculine scent to swirl around her.

His hand was still pressed against her neck, heating her skin. For a moment she lost her train of thought, suddenly pulled back to that night two months ago, his naked body covering hers…

She blinked herself back to the present, grabbing onto his hand and lacing her fingers into his. She squeezed. 'When Javier's wife saw those photos of her husband kissing a girl half his age, she must have thought her heart was breaking.'

Those dreadful, incriminating pictures.

Her brother and grandfather had taken a business trip together to New York for a long weekend. The Mondelli housekeeper had taken the day off. Alessandra and the man who was supposed to be giving her private tuition in maths over the long summer holiday had had the villa to themselves for the very first time. They could have done anything.

It had been her suggestion that they go out for lunch at a

nearby hotel, famed for its discretion. Javier didn't live locally. No one would know him.

She'd *longed* to do something as a normal couple, not have to keep her feelings hidden away, and this had been the perfect opportunity. She'd believed him when he'd said they had to keep their love a secret until she turned eighteen and finished her schooling.

How grown up she'd felt, walking hand in hand with her would-be lover. How naïve she'd been.

They'd dined in the fine hotel restaurant using *her* allowance to pay the bill, oblivious to the fact that half a dozen paparazzi had swarmed the lobby, awaiting the rumoured arrival of one of Hollywood's most eligible bachelors.

While she'd been blithely oblivious, they'd recognised her in an instant. The photos they'd taken, published the next day across the whole of Italy, had been incriminating. Her and Javier holding hands, stealing kisses that looked a damn sight worse than the chaste kisses they'd actually been.

That was the last time she'd seen the coward. For a whole weekend, while her brother and grandfather had been in New York, she'd had to cope with a siege of paparazzi on her own. Those reporters had been there to witness Javier's wife arrive at the villa and bang on the door until a guilt-stricken Alessandra had answered it, her fulsome apology ready on her tongue. She'd never had the chance to say the words. As soon as she'd opened the door, Javier's wife had spat in her face, slapped her and called her a *puttana*— a whore. The press had caught every frame for posterity.

By the time her brother and grandfather had returned the damage had been done.

'Why didn't you ever put your side across?' Christian asked. If he felt any pain in his fingers he didn't show it, allowing her to continue squeezing tightly, as if he knew it to be an outward measure of the fury and pain recalling that awful time provoked.

'I wasn't allowed. Rocco and *Nonno* closed ranks.' She attempted a laugh. 'They were furious with me.'

'Why? Your tutor took advantage of you. If they were furious with anyone, it should have been him.'

'They *were* furious with him for taking advantage of me, but it didn't change the fact that I'd been sneaking around with a man almost twice my age. They forbade me from speaking to the press, saying I'd caused enough shame on the family name.' Even if she'd chosen to defy them, by the time she'd got over the shock that had rendered her virtually mute the press had moved on to its next victim. Alessandra Mondelli's affair with a married man had been old news. No one had cared for her side.

Christian disentangled his fingers from her grip and muttered another curse as he got to his feet.

The place where he'd rested his hand against her neck suddenly felt cold.

She shivered and rose to her feet to stand before him. 'If I leave with you today, my career will be ruined. No editor or fashion director will ever trust me again. It's the only thing I've got to hold onto, the only thing that gives my life any meaning.' How could she expect him to understand that? Her career was all her own. It had taken everything she had to get her name taken seriously and pull herself out from the cloud of scandal.

'And what about our child? Or does he or she not come into it?'

'Don't twist it like that. When our baby is born everything is going to change—I know that, and I'm preparing myself for the change it will bring, but right now I'm healthy and capable of working.'

'I'm not happy about this. You can't take risks with your health.'

'I don't expect you to be happy about it, but ultimately the decision is mine, so please don't patronise me about the health aspect—you were there when the doctor said I should live a normal life.'

He threw his hands in the air and shook his head, not bothering to hide his anger or frustration.

She continued speaking before he could open his mouth to argue any further. 'I will hire a bodyguard for when I leave the apartment—I promise I will protect our baby.'

'*I* will hire a bodyguard for you,' he insisted, looking only slightly mollified. 'And I want your word of honour that if at any time you feel in any kind of danger you will call me immediately.'

'I promise.'

He appraised her with narrowed eyes for a moment longer before inclining his head. 'Then I will have to trust you to keep to *your* word.'

She certainly deserved *that*.

Welcome to Athens.

No sooner had Alessandra stepped off Christian's private jet than two bodyguards appeared from nowhere. They took her luggage and escorted her to the waiting car with its bullet-proof, blacked-out windows.

A week ago she would have thought this overkill. She'd thought her brother was a pain when it came to being over-protective. Rocco had always been protective of her. After Javier, he'd become even more controlling. Her grandfather had been even worse. He'd withdrawn her allowance and curtailed her freedom, which had always been limited, to the point of non-existence. She'd returned to her private all-girls school when the holidays had finished to find he'd given strict instructions not to let Alessandra leave the grounds under any circumstances. This had been particularly humiliating, it being her final year, the school year when more adult freedoms were permitted. But not for her. All trust between her and her grandfather had broken down irrevocably.

She'd spent years breaking free and now, just as her life

and freedom were hers and hers alone, she found she was pledging herself to a man with the same controlling instinct she had spent so long kicking back from.

Christian had over-protectiveness down to an art.

He hadn't merely employed a bodyguard for her, he'd employed an elite squad of hardened ex-soldiers.

Unfortunately they didn't come with personalities, all having been highly trained never to crack a smile or share banter. In the safety of her apartment building she could forget all about them, but the second she stepped outside they would materialise.

As much as she found their presence stifling, she was grateful. She'd never imagined the paparazzi could be any worse than when she'd been seventeen. She'd been wrong. Eight years ago it had been mostly the Italian press with a handful of Brits thrown in. This time their number included Greeks—lots of them—Americans, French… She swore she'd even heard a Japanese voice throw questions at her. She'd known her engagement to Christian would generate a frenzy but had not been prepared for such madness.

The granddaughter of the great Giovanni Mondelli, a man of such stature he was regarded like royalty; the sister of Rocco Mondelli, the man credited with dragging the House of Mondelli kicking and screaming into the twenty-first century, a man who'd recently married one of the most famous supermodels in the world; Alessandra Mondelli, the former scandal-hit teenager who'd become one of the world's leading fashion photographers: for such a woman to be marrying the self-made Greek billionaire, the whizz of the financial world with the movie-star looks… For the press it was a dream combination.

For Alessandra it was a nightmare. She consoled herself that at least she wasn't being called a slut any more. She'd kept her dark sunglasses on and answered only one of the hundreds of questions that had been thrown her way over the past week.

'Are you looking forward to the wedding?' someone had asked.

'Of course,' she'd replied with what she hoped was an enigmatic smile.

She hadn't been the only target. Christian, his sunglasses permanently attached to his face too, had also been mobbed. As had Rocco, who ignored every single question. Rumours had started circulating in the past few days about the punch, a new frenzy ensuing.

Relieved to be away from the madness, she leaned back in the leather seat and gazed out at Athens, the city that would play a huge part of her life from this moment on.

She'd heard it referred to as 'the cradle of Western civilisation.' Even if she'd been unaware of its history, she would have recognised it. It had seeped into the walls, some pristine, some falling apart at the seams. With ugly apartment blocks and majestic buildings, it was a city that managed to be cosmopolitan yet obviously ancient and historic. A city of contradictions.

For the first time she felt something akin to excitement bubble in her veins.

She had six days in this city before she exchanged her vows. From worrying that she would be bored stuck in a place where she knew no one, she now saw a huge opportunity. If she could ever get anywhere. At this rate, she would be lucky to make it to the hotel before the sun set. She'd thought the traffic in Milan was bad…

Eventually, they came to a road with manned security gates that opened slowly and led to an enormous white building with pillars either side of the huge entrance. It was as though she was staring at a palace that had been home to the Greek gods themselves.

A fleet of staff was by her side within seconds of the car coming to a stop, her luggage whisked away while she was taken through to the marble foyer.

'Don't I need to sign in?' she asked when a woman, who

identified herself as the general manager, offered to take her straight to her room.

'No, *despinis*,' the woman replied. 'Everything is taken care of.'

Christian's work, Alessandra told herself, her belly tightening at the thought of seeing him again. She'd been so busy over the past week that she'd hardly had the time to think of him on anything other than a practical level. Her dreams, though, had been…disturbing. Enough that merely to think of him made her bones feel as if they'd been through a blender.

Pregnancy hormones. That was all it was, she told herself—pregnancy hormones playing with her emotions.

'Where are all the other guests?' she asked, following the manager to the lift.

'Today, you are our only guest. The others will be arriving from tomorrow.'

How strange. She'd never known a hotel to have only one guest before.

Her suite was one of two located on the top floor. She guessed the other had been reserved for Christian.

Stepping into it, she couldn't help the little thrill that ran through her at the opulent marvel of marble and the stunning views. The back window had a direct view of the Parthenon.

Over the years she'd stayed in many luxurious hotels but the lavishness of this suite had a magical quality to it.

'Will you require lunch in your room or would you prefer to eat in the restaurant?' the manager asked.

'I think I'll eat on my balcony.' She had a quick skim of the menu and selected a tomato salad with crusty bread. Nothing fancy, just something healthy to keep her going until Christian joined her that evening…

The same tightening in her belly happened as she thought of him again, her heart rate speeding up to a thrum.

CHAPTER SIX

AFTER A LAZY afternoon spent by the swimming pool, unwinding after a full-on week of work and the morning's travels, Alessandra was stepping out of the shower when the phone in her room rang out.

'*Ciao?*'

'Good evening, *agapi mou.*'

A tingle fluttered up her spine to hear his rich tones.

'Hello, Christian,' she said, keeping her voice formal. 'Does this call mean you're here?'

'It does. Can you be ready in a couple of hours?'

'Why?'

'I'm taking you out for dinner.'

Trying hard to dampen the excitement fluttering low in her stomach, she opened the large wardrobe where a maid had hung all her clothes. Amongst them was her wedding dress.

Her intention had been to buy the first dress that fitted and didn't make her look like a hag. Her intentions had gone to hell. Her brain had tried to hand over the cash in the first boutique but her heart had overruled it. It wasn't until the fourth boutique that she'd found The One, the dress that had made her heart want to burst with delight.

She didn't know what she'd been thinking when she had then parted with a large sum of cash for the lacy white lingerie she'd selected to wear with it.

No, that was a lie: she *did* know what she'd been thinking. She'd been thinking of Christian.

For now she selected a khaki shirt-dress that fell to mid-thigh. She stared with longing at her five-inch-high red Manolo Blahniks but ended up disregarding them for black strappy sandals with a more reasonable three-inch heel. She had a little life inside her to think of and to totter on sky-high heels was asking for trouble.

She wondered if her own mother had faced such trivial conundrums in her pregnancies. So many questions she would never hear the answer to.

She would give anything for one day—one hour, even—with her mother. One hour to be held in her arms, to inhale her scent and hear her voice.

She prayed her baby never grew up having the same longings: so many hopes and fears, a mountain of them. All that mattered was getting her baby safely into this world.

Accessorising with beaded orange jewellery and dangly ruby earrings, she'd just applied a second coat of matching ruby lipstick when she heard a rap on the main door of the suite.

She pressed a hand to her chest, a sop to trying to control her heart that had galloped at the first knock.

Opening the door, her stomach plunged to see Christian so tanned and gorgeous before her, dressed in a silver suit, tieless, the white shirt unbuttoned at the neck. She'd kissed that neck, remembered vividly its taste…

Their eyes met; there was nothing said for the breath of a moment before she stood aside to admit him.

'You're looking good,' he said.

'Thank you,' she said, striving for breeziness.

'Are you ready?'

'Let me get my bag and we can go.' The expansive room seemed to have shrunk in the space of seconds and she was glad to escape, if only for a moment.

In the sanctuary of the bedroom, she sat on the corner

of the bed and took some deep breaths. *Keep it together, Alessandra.*

Keep it together?

At Rocco and Olivia's wedding she'd been too worried about informing Christian of his impending fatherhood to read too much into the raging emotions sleeping with him had provoked. She'd assumed that, once she'd shared the news, her equilibrium would be restored. She hadn't thought for a minute it would become more unstable around him, an instability that seemed to increase with every moment spent with him.

She *would* keep it together. She would. She was a pro at it.

Getting to her feet, she grabbed the gold clutch bag off the dresser and strolled back into the living area. Christian was leaning against the dining table, doing something on his phone. As soon as he saw her, he pressed the button to turn the screen off and quickly put it in the inside pocket of his blazer.

'Everything okay?' he asked.

She mustn't question. It was none of her business. *None* of her business.

Javier had always been secretive over his phone: hiding to answer calls; speaking in hushed tones so she couldn't overhear him; telling her it was other private students who deserved his discretion. Naïve idiot that she was, she'd believed him, had never imagined for a moment that the reason his phone never left his person was because he was married to a woman who'd lived through one of his affairs before and checked on him constantly.

If Christian wanted to be secretive, then so be it. She had no emotional claim on him. He had no emotional claim on her.

She forced a smile. 'I couldn't remember where I'd left my bag.' What was a white lie in the scheme of things? She couldn't tell him his appearance had left her feeling so off-kilter she'd needed a moment to catch her breath and her thoughts.

'Where are we eating?' she asked, following him out of the door.

'At Titos, a French restaurant near the Panathinaikos Stadium.'

'French?'

'It is considered the best restaurant in Athens.'

She raised her brows. 'Can't we go somewhere...Greek?'

'This is the most exclusive restaurant in Greece. The waiting list is eighteen months long.'

She pulled a face. 'I like fine dining as much as the next person but, truly, you can't relax somewhere like that. Please, just for tonight, can't we go somewhere normal? You live here—you must know the place that serves the best Greek food.'

Something flickered in his eyes.

'You *do* know somewhere! Please, take me.'

'It's nothing special,' he said, his voice guarded.

'Good! Nothing special is exactly what I'm in the mood for. Plus, if we eat somewhere nondescript, the less chance we have of being spotted by the paparazzi.' They would be circling the city looking for them. They were nothing if not tenacious.

After what seemed an age, Christian gave an abrupt nod. 'I know a little taverna in Pangrati, a decent area of the city.'

She beamed. *'Perfetto.'*

They both nodded at the reception staff as they left the hotel and got into the waiting car.

'Can we walk some of the way?' she asked once they were enclosed in the back.

Christian stared at her, remembering how on their night in Milan she'd insisted they walk to the restaurant, happily tottering in the black stilettos that had displayed her slender yet shapely legs so well.

The dress she wore now showed them off too, golden thigh close to his…

He preferred to walk too. He'd especially enjoyed walking with Alessandra, the refreshing conversation, her obvious femininity without demureness. He'd enjoyed everything about that evening. He'd enjoyed everything about that night. Except for the guilt that had almost crippled him, especially the next morning.

It felt even worse now. Not only had he got her pregnant but he'd lost his friend. He could cope with that if he didn't feel so damn responsible for Alessandra and Rocco's estrangement. Even if he couldn't fix his own relationship with Rocco, he was determined to fix theirs.

'The driver can take us a little further in and then we'll walk the rest.'

'*Eccellente*. I want to see as much of your home city as I can.'

'There's plenty of time for that. In the meantime, how have you settled in? Do you have everything you need?'

'I'm finding it all a little strange,' she admitted. 'I assumed the hotel would be bursting with guests.'

'Usually it would be.'

'Did you have all the other guests kicked out?' She was only half-joking.

'Not exactly. Alternative accommodation was found for them. Hotel Parthenon is for the exclusive use of our wedding party for the next week.'

'However did you manage that?'

'It wasn't difficult. I own the place.'

Her brows knitted together in confusion. 'Seriously?'

'I assumed you knew.'

'I thought your business revolved around finance.'

'On the whole it does, but in Greece it's different. Greece is my home. I love my country but its economy is a mess. Anything I can do to invest and bring money into it, I will.' Hotel Parthenon had been an obvious place for him to start. He'd discovered it six years before, a shabby, run-down two-star hotel situated on a prime site. He'd paid over the odds for it then set about transforming it, employing local builders and architects to renovate it into the seven-star luxury hotel complete with heliport it was today. Its growing reputation meant it was fully booked all year round.

'I like that,' Alessandra said, nodding her approval. 'I always think people are too keen to disregard their roots.'

'That's easy for someone like you to say.'

'What do you mean?'

'You were born with every advantage. Your roots are something for you to be proud of.'

'You think?' Her eyes flashed. 'Please, tell me, what advantage did I have when my very existence is the reason for my mother's death?'

Shocked, he momentarily lost his voice. 'You can't believe that?'

Confusion flitted over her features as if she'd shocked herself with her own words. 'It's the truth,' she whispered.

'Ochi!' No.

'Si. My mother died so I could live. If I hadn't been conceived, she would still be here.'

A coldness lodged in his stomach. 'But *you* wouldn't be here. We wouldn't be sitting here now. Our child wouldn't be growing in your belly.'

Her eyes held his, a slight wobble in them, as if she were trying desperately not to let whatever driving emotion had caused her outburst to gain any further hold.

He could kick himself. 'I apologise. When I said you were born with every advantage, I meant it in the respect that you were born a Mondelli.'

Alessandra swallowed back bile. She didn't know where her outburst had come from. It was an outburst that had lived mutely on her tongue since she'd been a young girl made to feel as if she should be grateful for the privileges of her life. As if the fact she'd grown up with money could hide the circumstances of her birth and the knock-on effect that still echoed in Rocco's and her lives. Their father's life too, weak and spineless though he was. He'd effectively thrown his life away because he hadn't been able to cope without his beloved Letizia. Nor forgetting her grandfather, her *nonno*, who'd spent the last twenty-five years of his life raising his grandchildren while his own son and heir drowned in bottles of alcohol.

All those ruined lives. Ruined dreams. Rocco ripped away from the mother he'd worshipped. And for what? For *her*? Was one life really a fair exchange for so much misery?

'No, I'm the one who should apologise. You're right. Being a Mondelli is a privilege. I've been given every material advantage.'

'I didn't mean to imply that you were spoilt. I appreciate the Mondelli name has been a mixed blessing for you.'

'And the Markos name?' she said, glad to be able to turn the conversation onto him. 'Has that been a mixed blessing for you?'

He raised a shoulder. 'The Markos name is nothing special. It doesn't stand for anything.'

'Yes, it does. It stands for hard work, determination and guts.'

'Guts?'

'Rocco told me you got into Columbia on a scholarship. That alone tells me how hard you've had to work to get where you are.'

'We all have our crosses to bear, whatever background we're born into,' he said quietly. He tapped on the dividing window. Amidst a hail of tooting horns, the car came to a stop. 'We will walk from here.'

The taverna was exactly what Alessandra had been hoping for. Set off the beaten track, its marble tables with checked paper table-cloths were crammed inside and out, every one of them taken. Inside, a man played an accordion, the music only just audible above the raucous noise of the patrons, while pictures of celebrities lined the walls in haphazard fashion above empty bottles of wine with melted candles rammed into them.

Just as she was thinking they would never get a table, a balding man of about sixty wearing a white apron stretched around possibly the largest pot belly she'd ever seen ambled over to them, his arms outstretched. In a flurry of Greek, he pulled Christian into a tight embrace, slapping kisses on his cheeks, all of which Christian returned before stepping back and putting an arm around Alessandra's waist.

'Mikolaj—Alessandra,' he said, before adding, 'Mikolaj doesn't speak any English or Italian, *agapi mou*.'

Her offered hand was ignored as she was wrenched from Christian's hold and yanked into Mikolaj's embrace, which finished with an affectionate ruffle of her hair, much as if she were a child.

A small table materialised for them against the far wall. Mikolaj pulled the chair back for her, fussing over her until he was certain she was sitting comfortably—although how comfortable anyone could be when crammed like a sardine was debatable. He plonked a laminated menu in front of her then ruffled her hair again for good measure before disappearing into the throng.

Christian took the seat opposite. The table was so small his long legs brushed against hers. She waited for him to move them but realised there was literally nowhere else for them to go unless he twisted to the side and tripped up all the waiting staff.

She craned her neck around, trying to ignore the heat brushing up her legs. 'This place is wonderful.'

He raised his eyebrows. 'You like it?'

She nodded. 'This is exactly how I imagined a Greek restaurant to be. You can feel the energy—you don't get that in high-class restaurants.'

His eyes crinkled. Seeing it made her realise how tense he'd been up to that point. Although unfailingly polite, a barrier had been put up. Was it being here, in his home city, that had caused its construction? Or had she been so wrapped up in her own problems that she hadn't fully appreciated the effect their situation was having on him? Or a combination of both?

'The best thing about this place apart from the food?' he said. 'It's tourist-proof—all the people in here are locals.'

'Don't tell me you own it?'

'No. This is all Mikolaj's.'

'Is it always this busy?' It was a Monday evening, hardly the busiest night of the dining week.

'Always.'

Alessandra looked down at the menu. It was all in Greek.

'I can recommend the *stiffado*,' Christian said. 'Beef stewed in a wine and tomato sauce. The stuffed courgettes are good too.'

'Can I have both?'

He laughed. 'You can have whatever you like. It's all good.'

'Have you eaten everything on the menu?'

'A dozen times each.'

'No wonder Mikolaj treated you like his long-lost son.'

Before he could respond, a waiter appeared at their side, notebook at the ready.

'Shall I order us a selection of *meze* to start with?' Christian asked.

'You know all the best stuff,' she answered with a grin. Already the bustling, warm atmosphere of the place was easing the tension within her, making her relax in a way she hadn't since she'd taken the pregnancy test. 'Go ahead.'

She had no idea what he ordered, the waiter making squiggles on his note pad before bustling off, immediately to be replaced with Mikolaj, who carried a carafe of red wine and a jug of iced water.

'Do you want any wine?' Christian asked, knowing better than to tell her not to have any.

'I'll stick to water, thanks,' she said, her cheeks quirking as if she knew what he'd been thinking. As soon as they were alone again, she asked, 'How do you know Mikolaj? I'm guessing it's more than you being a good patron.'

'I have known him since I was small child.'

'Is he an old family friend?'

'Something like that.'

Her doe eyes were fixed on him with unashamed curiosity. 'Something like what?'

'My mother and I used to live in a room in the attic,' he supplied, adopting the tone he used to denote the end of a subject.

Alessandra ignored his tone and raised her eyes to gaze at the ceiling. 'You lived in the attic *here*?'

'Yes, here. My mother was a childhood friend of his. When we were kicked out of our old place, Mikolaj and his wife gave us the attic room.'

She looked back at him, her pretty brows drawing together. 'One room? For the both of you?'

'Yes.'

'That must have been hard.'

'You have no idea,' he said, more harshly than he'd intended. In those days, Mikolaj had been barely scraping a living for himself and his own family. If not for his incredibly generous heart, Christian and his mother would have lived on the streets. The attic room was given to them for free in exchange for his mother working in the kitchen. She'd been paid a share of the tips. It was all Mikolaj had been able to afford.

When Christian had made his first significant trade, a deal that had earned him a hundred thousand dollars, he'd sent Mikolaj a cheque for half the sum.

Looking back on those early years, it hadn't been the

poverty that had been the hardest to bear. The biggest cross had been living with his mother and her poisonous tongue.

Theos, but he didn't want to imagine Alessandra losing the spark that made her such a passionate, vivacious person and turning into one of the Furies, as his mother had. He wouldn't wish it on anyone but especially not her.

'Do you ever see your father?'

'No. He left when I was a baby.'

She leaned her elbows on the table and rested her hands on her chin. 'That must have been hard too.'

'It was hard for my mother, not me. I don't remember him.' He no longer wanted to remember him, although he had as a child, had been desperate to know any detail his mother could spare. As all her details had been disparaging at best, nothing concrete, he'd let his mind fly free to construct him. His father was a superhero who had gone to save a galaxy far, far away—unable to send his mother any money by dint of being in a galaxy far, far away. When that galaxy was saved, he would swoop back to Athens, and the little attic room his wife and son shared, and rescue them.

That fantasy sustained him for a few years until around the age of seven, when he'd overheard a conversation between Mikolaj and his eldest son. They'd been talking about Elena, Christian's mother.

'She can't help the way she is,' Mikolaj had said. 'When Stratos left her for that woman, it poisoned her. He packed his stuff and left her with no money when the boy was only six months old.'

Christian had tuned the rest of the conversation out. It had been enough to convince him all his mother's disparaging comments about his father were true. From that moment on, he'd no longer fantasised about his father. Stratos Markos was never going to swoop in to save them. That would be Christian's job.

CHAPTER SEVEN

'HAVE YOU EVER tried to find your father?' Alessandra asked a short while later, her eyes filled with curiosity.

'What for?' he dismissed. 'Why would I want to involve myself with a man who abandoned his wife and child?'

'I get that,' she said, pulling a face.

He closed his eyes. 'Your father is an alcoholic and a gambler. He was incapable of looking after you. He didn't abandon you. He's always been a fixture in your life. There's a difference.'

She laughed contemptuously. 'I thought you knew my background. My father dumped me on his father before I was a year old. Rocco took care of me from the moment I left hospital. My father wanted nothing to do with me—he still doesn't. He's never been there, not for any of the significant events in my life. My first Holy Communion, my Confirmation, the time I represented Milan in the under tens' gymnastics,' she said, ticking the events off on her fingers. 'He wasn't at any of them. The few times he's bothered to join us as a family, he won't speak to me. He's never *looked* at me. I was there, I was present and still he didn't want me. So don't try and make out I can't understand what it was like for you, growing up without a father, because my father abandoned me too, and, worst of all, he abandoned Rocco.'

He and Alessandra were like two peas but from pods grown in very different gardens, Christian realised. They'd both been abandoned by the people who should have been there for them. For good or ill, it had shaped them both. The distrust and avoidance of love and relationships.

They were more alike than he'd ever suspected.

Colour had heightened across Alessandra's high cheek-bones, her eyes ablaze with furious passion, the honey-brown a darkened swirl. He'd seen that swirl before, when she'd been pressed against the wall of her apartment.

Theos, she had felt unbelievably good in his arms, as if her contours had been shaped especially for him.

He regarded her carefully, pushing away thoughts of her naked: the way she had wrapped those lithe legs around him and clung to him, as if trying to burrow under his skin. Those same legs were pressed against his at that very moment...

The V of her dress had dipped, exposing the top of her golden cleavage, below which lay breasts that had become plumper since their time together.

What did they look like now? Did they still taste so sweet...?

This had to stop. Right now. Imagining them in bed to-gether was what had got him into all this trouble in the first place, sitting in that Milanese restaurant, fascinated by her plump lips, imagining them over his...

He would not touch her again until they were legally man and wife. He'd given her his word. He might have screwed things up but he was determined to do the right thing from here on in. On paper, his track record with women was less than complimentary. Given that and her own history, he could understand why Alessandra would be untrusting. It was down to him to prove himself to her.

Theoretically, it should be easy. Christian loved sex—what red-blooded man didn't?—but he'd never allowed his libido to run his life. With Alessandra... The longer she kept those gorgeous doe eyes fixed on him, the more his blood swirled with the need to consume her again. Every-thing about her spelled temptation, from the glossy chestnut hair that begged to have his fingers run through it to the toned golden arms his hands itched to trace. Every time she opened her mouth to speak, drink or eat, he would watch those beautiful lips and ache to press his own to them, to feel the heat of her breath merge with his.

Soon. Soon she would be his again.

'At least you had Rocco,' he said softly, thinking he would have given anything for a sibling when he'd been a child. It hadn't been until he'd met his fellow Columbia Four that he'd realised what had been missing in his life: true friendship.

'Emotionally, I had Rocco,' she conceded. 'But he's seven years older than me. By the time I was eleven he was at university, thousands of miles away. My grandfather loved me but he had no experience of raising girls and preferred to leave me in the hands of the household staff.'

'Our lives have been very different,' he said, choosing his words with care. 'It's pointless comparing them. You have lived yours and I have lived mine.'

'How has it been different?' she pressed, leaning forward.

'It just was.'

'But how?' A troubled look flitted over her face. 'Christian, we are marrying in five days. I don't want to marry a stranger.'

He reached for his wine and took a swallow. 'You, *agapi mou*, come from a world of glamour and money. You have no comprehension what it was like for us. We were so poor that for a whole year I went without shoelaces—trivial in the scheme of things but imagine it for a minute. I arrived at university with only one change of clothes. I was the child people like you pretended not to see.'

Alessandra was like one of those mythical creatures he had watched swish past this very taverna's front while he'd swept the floor. Unobtainable. Better than him. Better than he could ever be no matter how much money was held in his bank account.

Angry colour stained her cheeks, and she opened her mouth, surely to argue with him, before she visibly controlled herself. The outrage that had sparked in her eyes softened. 'Maybe you're right that I can't understand what your childhood was like. But I would like to try.'

He didn't *want* her to understand. Christian wanted her to remain untouched by the deprivation and misery that had sucked his mother down a black pit, turning her into a bitter woman who, even if presented with a glass three-quarters full would still regard it as being a quarter empty. All the riches and success in the world hadn't been enough to earn his mother's love.

He had no memory of the happy, vibrant woman Mikolaj assured him she had once been. Love that had turned sour had soured *her*, marking her with such blackness that nothing he'd done had been enough to turn it into a lighter shade of grey.

He didn't want that for Alessandra. Never for her.

Alessandra needed protection from it before it infected her too.

'We've had a good response from all the wedding invitations,' he said, deliberately and overtly changing the subject.

One hundred and fifty invites had been couriered across the world. It seemed even heads of state could drop commitments when it suited them and, with all the hype already surrounding their 'whirlwind courtship,' as the press was dubbing it, their wedding was shaping up to rival Rocco and Olivia's as Wedding of the Century. One of the British glossies had offered one million pounds for exclusive rights. They had, politely, ignored the offer. He liked that Alessandra hadn't been tempted to accept, one of the many ways she differed from all the other women he'd been with.

But wasn't that the reason he'd been with those women? Because he could see the pound signs ringing in their eyes and so knew there was absolutely no danger they could ever develop anything like a healthy—or unhealthy, depending on your point of view—attachment to him? He hadn't needed to protect those women from himself.

Her eyes sparked again before she sank back into her seat, gazing at him with a thoughtful expression.

'All but a handful have replied and all in the affirmative,' he added.

After too long a beat, she asked, 'What about Rocco? Has he replied?'

It had been at Christian's insistence that her brother had been invited. Left to Alessandra, he would have been ignored, something he knew she didn't mean, her pride and anger doing the talking for her. It would break her heart to walk up the aisle of the chapel in the grounds of the hotel without her brother on her arm.

'No,' he admitted reluctantly. 'He hasn't replied yet.' And neither had Rocco responded to the dozen emails and text messages he'd sent to him, entreating him not to abandon his sister. Rocco hadn't replied to a single one of them. He'd ignored all the messages and calls from Stefan and Zayed too.

The Columbia Four had been broken, just as he'd known they would be.

At least Stefan and Zayed were coming to the wedding. He would need his friends there. But not as much as Alessandra needed her brother.

If he had to get on his bended knee and beg, he would get Rocco to their wedding.

'I sent a bridesmaid dress to Olivia,' Alessandra blurted out, her cheeks staining with colour.

'Have you heard back from her?' he asked hopefully. If anyone could get through to Rocco, it would be his wife.

She shook her head. 'I didn't expect to. Her loyalty is with Rocco, not me.'

Conversation paused when a waiter arrived at their table laden with plates of steaming food.

Once they had helped themselves to a little of each *meze*, Alessandra said, 'Are many of your family coming?'

'I don't have any family.'

She looked confused. 'What about your mother?'

'I haven't invited her.'

'Why not?'

'We do not want my mother at our wedding.'

'Why not?' she repeated.

'Trust me.' He dipped some pitta bread into the hummus and popped it into his mouth, leaving her in no doubt that, as far as he was concerned, this thread of discussion was over.

Her eyes glittered with incredulity, as if to say, *trust you*?

Instead of arguing with him, she took a drink of water and allowed him to steer the conversation to innocuous small talk about music they liked and films they had both seen and enjoyed. Their tastes were surprisingly similar.

Theos, she was so easy to talk to; she had a way of fixing her honey eyes on him and making him feel he was the only man to exist in the world.

To know he was the only man to have tasted her delights and to imagine tasting them again made him feel as if he had heated syrup running through his veins. It wasn't just the contents of his trousers that stirred to be with her—everything felt heightened.

In that respect, the day of their wedding couldn't come fast enough.

The hotel was in silence when they returned. For the first time Christian regretted having the entire complex to themselves. There was no one—other than the handful of duty staff—to distract his attention away from Alessandra.

His fiancée.

She'd taken the hint and stopped digging for information on his past, although something in her eyes had warned him not to expect her silence to last for long. Instead, they had relaxed into easy conversation, just as they had on their one real date together. As on that night in Milan, he'd found his eyes drawn to her lips. They fascinated him. *She* fascinated him.

What was it with this woman? he wondered as they climbed the private lift to the top floor. His awareness of her was off the charts. His body reacted to everything, from the way her mouth moved to her husky laugh, to the way she smoothed her hair back to keep it from her face.

Alessandra's eyes had been as firmly fixed on him as his had been on her. She hadn't drunk any alcohol but he recognised the signs of inhibitions loosening. Just as they had that night in Milan.

He would not act on it. Not tonight. Not until they were legally man and wife.

Man and wife.

Three words he would never have put together with himself and, he knew, Alessandra would never have put with herself.

If he were being honest, he would have to admit that, if someone had put a gun against his head and said he had to choose one woman of all the women he'd been with to marry and have a baby with, Alessandra would have topped the list. All the other women had been fun and flirty but without an ounce of substance. Exactly the way he'd liked them. No commitment, no emotions. No chance of them falling in love and that love turning into bitterness.

Alessandra had a fun and flirty streak in her but she also had substance by the barrel. Her emotions were right there on the surface, no pretence, no subterfuge and, *Theos*, she was sexier than any mortal had a right to be.

He'd spent half the evening fantasising about those luscious lips.

They reached the door to her suite.

'Thank you for a lovely evening,' she said, leaning against the wall by the door. Her eyes were wide; even under the soft lighting he could see the dilation of her pupils.

'It's been my pleasure.'

And it had been.

He didn't want the evening to end.

What was there to stop him leaning in for a kiss?

Nothing.

Except he'd given his word that nothing physical would happen between them again until they were legally married and he would keep that promise even if his testicles exploded with frustration.

'Are you working tomorrow?' She rubbed a hand up her arm, the movement pushing her breasts together. The image of dusky pink nipples immediately floated into his mind and with it came the thickening of his blood he was fast associating to feeling when with her.

He had to assume it was a simple case of forbidden fruit tasting sweeter. Like the child in the sweet shop who had no money and salivated over every piece of delicious confectionery on offer.

'Yes. Some of our guests are arriving in the evening. I should be back to greet them with you.'

'I guess this will be the first public display of our love and unity,' she said, an ironic smile whispering across her face.

He palmed her cheek and rubbed his thumb over the soft skin. He could do that much without breaking his vow. 'Can you handle it?'

'Can you?'

'For the sake of our child, yes, I can.'

Her eyes held his. She raised a hand and pressed it to his fingers still resting against her cheek. 'Then I can too.'

Alessandra was certain he was going to kiss her. She recognised the look in his eyes, the desire in them that darkened the blue. She'd seen that look before, right before she'd pressed her lips to his in her apartment...

He stepped away before either of them had the chance to act on it, dragging his thumb down her cheek one last time.

'Sleep well, *agapi mou*,' he said, bowing his head, then turning on his heel and striding down the corridor to his own suite.

She didn't know if the breath she expelled was one of relief or disappointment.

After yet another unsettled night, Alessandra got out of bed early, not long after the sun had begun to rise.

Showering quickly, she shrugged on a short, lime-green sundress and slid her feet into a pair of wedged espadrilles, then grabbed her camera and headed out of her suite. As she made her way up the corridor, she passed Christian's room.

Was he still sleeping?

He'd been as good as his word yesterday, arriving back from his busy day twenty minutes before their first guests had arrived. They'd spent the evening glued to each other's side, laughing and joking. At one point he had leaned in to whisper into her ear.

'I think we're convincing them,' he'd said. At least, that was what she thought he'd said, the feel of his hot breath against her skin turning her brain to mush in less than a second.

Dio, what was he doing to her?

Was it any wonder she couldn't sleep?

She'd spent years believing marriage and babies would never be in her future. Sexual relationships had been consigned to the same void: not for her. No messy emotions to contend with, no lies for her ears to disbelieve, no truths for her eyes to avoid. Once the dust had settled with the fall-out over Javier's lies, she'd come to the conclusion that living a life of solitude was the best for her.

Other than her brother, she'd effectively been alone since birth. Her grandfather had controlled every aspect of her life, from the food she ate to the clothes she wore to the friends she was allowed—but always remotely, Alessandra another tick on his daily to-do list, his directives adhered to by the many members of the Villa Mondelli staff. She'd *longed* for someone to want to be with her for her, not because they were paid to be or because she'd passed some kind of wealth and social standing test, but for *her*. She'd truly believed Javier had seen beyond the surface but it had been a lie that had shattered her.

All the protections she'd placed around herself since those awful, lonely days were crumbling at the edges.

In three days she would be pledging her life, her future, to Christian Markos. How could she keep her emotions in a box if she had to share the bed with him occasionally?

One night: that was all it had taken. She'd watched him sleep, her chest clenched so tightly she'd fought for air.

She needed air now.

She wandered to the end of the corridor and climbed the stairs that led up to the roof terrace.

Their wedding was three days away but already a huge transformation was taking place for the party they would be having there once the nuptials were done. White tables and chairs were laid out to the specifications of their wedding planner. She stared at what was to be the top table, a sharp pang lancing her as she thought of sitting there without either her grandfather or her brother by her side.

A part of her wanted to call Rocco, was desperate to hear his voice. But she would not. Christian still bore the remnants of the punch Rocco had given him, the black eye now a pale yellow, but still evident if you looked closely enough. Unless he was prepared to apologise and accept her marriage, he could stay away.

Forcing her thoughts away from her brother, she headed to the back of the terrace, the part that overlooked the huge gardens. Far in the distance sat the whitewashed chapel they were to marry in. It gleamed under the morning sun, as if it were winking at her. She readied her camera and fired off a couple of shots.

She much preferred taking photos of people but one day

she wanted to be able to show her child everything about their parents' big day. She'd been nine when she'd stumbled across her own parents' wedding photos. Until that time she'd never believed her father had *ever* smiled, not once in his whole life. But, of course, it had been the pictures of her mother that had meant the most to her.

Whenever she was asked the question of who her biggest influences were as a photographer, she always said Annie Leibovitz and Mario Testino, but in truth it was her parents' wedding photographer. He had brought them to life in a manner that had touched her deeply and made her see them as people in love.

She wondered if Christian had photos of *his* parents' wedding day and if he ever looked at them.

Christian. It disturbed her how badly she wanted to know everything about him, to understand everything that made him tick, everything that had shaped him. The pieces were coming together but it was like a semi-filled photo album with pictures missing.

Resolve filled her. She looked at her watch. If she hurried, she should be able to catch him before he left the hotel for his first appointment of the day.

CHAPTER EIGHT

Minutes later she knocked on his door, her camera still slung round her neck.

She sensed movement behind the door before it opened, sensed him peering through the spyhole.

And there he stood, skin damp, hair wet…and with nothing but a towel wrapped around his hips.

'Sorry; I've caught you at a bad time,' she said, having to fight to get her vocal cords to work properly and not stammer.

'Not at all. Come in.' He stood aside to admit her into his suite.

She stepped past him, moistening suddenly dry lips.

Dio, was he naked beneath that towel?

Her arid mouth suddenly filled with moisture.

'Is there a reason you've come to my suite so early, *agapi mou*?' he asked, a smile playing on his lips, as if he knew exactly what was going on beneath her skin.

'No.' She blinked sharply. 'Yes. Do you want to get dressed before we talk?'

'I'm good.'

'Please?'

'Does the sight of me undressed disturb you?'

'It makes it hard for me to think straight,' she admitted, wishing she could think of a decent lie.

'That is good.'

'It is?'

'The thought of you naked makes it hard for me to think straight too. So, we are even.'

'You think of me naked?' Did she *have* to sound like a breathless imbecile?

The smile dropped. He closed the distance between them and inhaled deeply.

His voice dropped to a husky whisper. 'All the time. I've just thought of you while I showered, imagining you sharing it with me.'

She swallowed. Was he suggesting what she thought he was…?

His lips brushed against her earlobe. 'Until we are legally married I will have to satisfy myself with memories of our night together in Milan.'

Her skin fizzed beneath the warmth of his breath while heat such as she had never experienced surged through her, settling in the V of her thighs. He stepped closer still and placed a hand on her thigh, close enough that she could feel his erection jut through the cotton of his towel and press against her belly.

She tilted her head back and gazed into his eyes. It was there, that desire: stark, open, unashamed.

What would he do if she were to loop her arms around his neck and kiss him? If she were to clasp his towel and yank it off him…?

He must have read her mind for his lips brushed against her ear again. 'Anticipation makes fulfilment taste so much sweeter.'

She pulled away. 'Do you know that from experience?'

A strange look came into his eyes, a half-smile tugging on his lips. 'Only in a professional sense. I look forward to finding out if it's as sweet when it comes to us making love again.'

'I thought you said it would depend on whether I wanted anything to happen,' she said, her voice hoarse.

'And it will.' Now his eyes glittered, no mistaking the

feeling behind them. 'But we both know the anticipation is driving you crazy too.'

While Alessandra stood there, unable to deny what he'd said, too full of the heavy, pulsating thickness swirling through the very fabric of her to think clearly, Christian strode into the bedroom of his suite.

'So, what did you want to see me for?' he asked, disappearing from view.

Forcing her brain to unfog itself, she followed him to the door but stopped at her side of the threshold.

She took a moment to compose herself, but that very composure almost fell to ruins when he emerged back in view, now wearing a pair of black boxer shorts that only enhanced his strong physique.

He opened his dressing-room door and disappeared again, re-emerging moments later with a pair of grey trousers on. Looking at her, he slipped his arms into a pale blue shirt. 'Alessandra?'

'Sorry.' She put her hand to her mouth and cleared her throat. 'I just wanted to discuss the guest list.'

'Everyone has accepted.'

'Apart from Rocco?'

He nodded, his mouth tightening.

She watched as he deftly did the buttons of his shirt up.

'I think you should reconsider inviting your mother,' she said.

He didn't react, other than a slight narrowing of his eyes.

'It doesn't feel right, us marrying without you having any family there.'

'You haven't invited your father,' he said pointedly.

'That's because my father is an alcoholic who likes to pretend I don't exist. She's your mum—wouldn't she *want* to see her only child get married?'

'Just drop it. She's not coming and that's final.' He tucked his shirt in and pulled the zip of his trousers up.

'No. I won't drop it. If you won't invite her then can you at least tell me why?'

His mouth set in a forbidding line, he reached for the silver tie on his bed and walked over to the mirror on the wall, his back to her. He met her eye in the reflection.

'No. I can't.'

'Why not? Christian, we're getting married in three days. You know everything about me and my past—what is so bad that you don't want me to meet your mother? Are you ashamed of her or something?'

'*Or something* about sums it up,' he said grimly. 'But, no, I'm not ashamed of her.'

'Really? Because it looks like you're ashamed of her from where I'm standing.'

His nostrils flaring, his jaw clenched tight, he knotted his tie. 'Can you not take my word for it?'

'I'm sorry, but no.' This was too important a topic to back down from.

He must have seen something in her reflection that made him read the stubbornness of her thoughts. He shook his head angrily. 'If it means that much to you, I will show you.'

'Show me what?'

He straightened his shirt, then turned back to face her. 'I'll take you to meet her. You can see for yourself why I don't want my mother anywhere near our wedding.'

The car came to a stop outside an immaculate two-storey house in a quiet Athenian suburb.

No sooner had the engine been turned off than Christian got out, not bothering to wait for the driver to open the door for him.

The entire drive had been conducted in silence, Christian sitting ramrod-straight, only the whiteness of his knuckles betraying what lay beneath his skin.

It was a demeanour Alessandra had never seen from him before. It unnerved her.

That he'd cancelled his first appointment of the day had unnerved her even more; that, and the grim way he'd said, 'Let's get it over with.'

It was with a deep sense of dread that she followed him out of the car and up the small driveway.

A tall, thin woman with short white hair appeared at the door, lines all over her weathered face, her thin lips clamped together in an obvious display of disapproval.

Wordlessly, she turned on her heel and walked back inside, leaving the door open for them to follow.

The house itself was pristine, a strong smell of bleach pervading the air.

There was nothing homely about it. What could have been a beautiful home was nothing but a carcass, sanitised functionality at its best.

If Elena Markos could speak English, she made a good show of hiding it. She made no show of hiding her disdain for Alessandra, refusing her hand when Christian introduced them, and looking through her when Alessandra said, *'Hárika ya tin gnorimía,'*— 'pleased to meet you'—a phrase she'd practised with the girl who'd brought breakfast to her suite that morning after Christian had grudgingly agreed to bring her here.

They gathered together in the immaculate kitchen, where the stench of bleach was even stronger. No refreshments were offered.

Alessandra might as well have been invisible. All of Elena's attention was on her son. She was speaking harshly to him in quick-fire Greek, whatever she said enough to make the pulse in his jawline throb. When he replied, his answers were short but measured. At one point he seemed to be the one doing the talking rather than the listening, his words making Elena dart her blue eyes to the stranger in the midst, a sneer forming on her face.

In all her twenty-five years, Alessandra had never sat in such a poisonous atmosphere as this, or felt as unwelcome.

There was something almost unhinged in Elena Markos's demeanour. Her eyes were the same blue as Christian's but were like a frozen winter morning without an ounce of her son's warmth.

Simply imagining being raised by this woman made her skin feel as icy as Elena's eyes. But Christian couldn't leave it to imaginings. He'd lived it, every cold, emotionless second.

Was it any wonder Christian eschewed any form of emotional entanglement when *this* was what he'd grown up with?

Her mind flitted back to their many conversations at Mikolaj's taverna. She'd said the name Markos stood for guts and determination but had not appreciated then exactly how great his determination must have been, not just to drag himself and his mother out of poverty but to keep his humanity.

Mikolaj. She recalled the obvious affection between the two men. Surely it was from this man Christian had learned to form real human bonds? It soothed her to know he hadn't been completely alone in his childhood.

So much for the couple of hours Alessandra had anticipated spending there. After twenty minutes, Christian took her hand and said, 'We're leaving.'

'Already?'

'Now.'

Elena glared at them, her eyes like lasers.

When they reached the door to leave she gave what Alessandra assumed was supposed to be a laugh.

'Fool girl,' she said, her accent thick. 'Marry fools. He kill you heart.'

Alarmed and not a little scared, Alessandra nodded weakly, squeezing Christian's hand so tightly her blood screamed for circulation.

Nothing was said until they were back in the car and moving, both pressed against their respective doors.

'What did you think of my mother?' Christian asked, amusement and bitterness both vying for control in his voice.

Alessandra was unable to do anything but raise her shoulders and blow air out of her mouth.

That had to be the most surreal experience of her life, like stepping into some parallel universe where poison ivy grew instead of roses.

'Do you understand now why I don't want her at our wedding?'

'I think so.' She shook her head some more. She could still taste the acrid atmosphere, overwhelming even the cloying bleach. 'What did she say to you?'

'The usual. That I'm a useless son for leaving it so long between visits; that her house isn't good enough for her; that the house is too big for her, that it's too small, that her car is getting old. The usual.'

'You bought the house for her?'

'It's the third house I've bought for her—the other two didn't *match her needs*. I buy her a new car every year. I give her a large allowance. It's never enough. I could give her my entire fortune and it wouldn't be enough. If she came to the wedding, she'd spend the day complaining. Nothing would be good enough for her, and when she isn't complaining she'll be telling all our guests about my no-good bastard of a father who broke her heart and deserves castration without anaesthetic.'

His father's desertion and betrayal had shattered her. Whatever love had once resided in his mother's bones had been destroyed, leaving nothing but the toxic shell of the woman she must have once been. Christian understood it, could see how she had become like that. Stratos Markos hadn't just walked away from her, he had walked away from the child they had created together—that was how little she had meant to him. He had wanted no part of her, so worthless that their baby meant nothing to him either.

'Has she always been like this?' she asked, her husky voice stark.

'All my life. She thinks all men are like my father—that's what she was saying to you when we left, that you're a fool to be marrying me and that I'm going to break your heart.'

Alessandra's shock was palpable. 'She said that about her own son?'

'She also said it would be kinder for me to rip your heart out now—you forget, *agapi mou*, that I am my father's son, something she never lets me forget. In my mother's world, all men are liars and cheats, especially those with the name of Markos.'

Her doe eyes widened, full of sympathy. 'You're not to blame for your father's actions.'

'I know that.' But right then he didn't want to hear any platitudes. A coldness had settled in his chest, bearing down on him.

It was always the same after he visited his mother. Regardless of the heat outside, inside all he felt was compressing ice.

'And it's not fair for her to label all men as bastards because of the misdeeds of one.'

'But do you not believe that yourself?' he said roughly. 'That all men are scum?'

She swallowed, her eyes dimming as if in confusion. 'I don't hate men, I just don't trust them.'

What would it take to get her to trust *him*? If she'd taken him at his word he would never have had to bring her here.

He wished he could demand it of her, as if trust were like a tap that could be turned on and off at a whim.

After a long pause, he said, 'We're lucky we both know how destructive love can be. We won't fall into the trap our parents fell into. Our child will never have to deal with parents whose love has turned to bitterness and recrimination.'

Their child wouldn't have to deal with his or her parents

loving each other at all. All the love would be reserved for their child and only their child.

He exhaled slowly, waiting for the chill in his chest to lessen but it continued to cling to him like a thick, cold fog.

He hadn't expected anything different from his mother; he was more or less immune to it. It had been witnessing Alessandra's visible shock at it all that had really set the cold in, had brought the old feelings and memories hurtling back.

The empathy shining from her eyes had been too much.

He'd never introduced his mother to any of his friends or lovers before. His mother had her own special compartment in his life. He'd long ago accepted that she wouldn't change, that no matter how he succeeded in life it would never be enough for her. Even the news of being a grandmother had failed to elicit a smile. She would never love him.

Far from repelling Alessandra, his mother's behaviour had elicited her sympathy, her empathy: towards him.

He didn't want her pity.

She was getting too close; he could feel it.

Any closer and she'd be able to see the gutter rat who lived in the blackness of his heart.

Christian's driver dropped Alessandra back at the hotel before taking Christian to his offices.

A dozen more guests had arrived while they'd been at his mother's house. It amazed her that so many super-wealthy and famous people were able to drop their commitments for what was essentially a free holiday, but surprisingly their presence worked in her favour, distracting her thoughts from their visit to Christian's mother.

Every time she closed her eyes she saw the laser glare of Elena Markos's eyes and she wondered how Christian had endured living with such coldness.

That he had dragged himself out, turned it around and made something of himself only added to what had been a slowly growing admiration towards him. That admiration had now accelerated.

Although she was suffering a large dose of guilt for forcing the issue, she was glad they'd gone. Her understanding of the man she was going to marry was growing by the day.

She spent the rest of the day mingling with their guests, some of whom she actually knew, lazing by the pool, playing cards, drinking non-alcoholic cocktails. It was fun, but she wished Christian could be there to enjoy it too. He worked so hard, just like her brother.

Maybe he would kick back and relax when they went on their short honeymoon. She hoped so. He deserved it.

She headed back to her suite late afternoon and had a long soak in the sunken bath, already looking forward to the evening meal which Christian had said he'd be back for.

As she slipped into a red tunic dress, she realised that there hadn't been a single minute when she hadn't thought of him. The thought was like a jolt, enough to make her hands tremble, making it hard for her to apply her make-up.

She'd just regained her equilibrium when there was a knock on her door.

And there he stood, wearing the same suit she'd seen him change into that morning in his suite but with the tie removed and the top three buttons of his shirt undone, exposing the top of his bronzed chest.

Finding him there sent a huge surge through her, making her heart pump and her pulses race. *Dio*, the man was divine. In *all* ways.

'I thought I should let you know I'm going to New York,' he said as he stepped into her suite.

'Okay. When's that?'

'I'll be leaving for the airport in a few minutes.'

His words had the effect of making her heart sink to her knees. 'Are you kidding with me? You're leaving *now*?'

Dio l'aiuti, was he getting cold feet?

'It's only for a couple of nights—I'll be back Friday evening.'

She forced her voice to remain calm. 'We're getting married on Saturday.'

'I'll be back in plenty of time.'

A little distance was all Christian needed. Distance away from Alessandra, time to clear the coldness on his chest that still hadn't shifted. Time to track her brother down and force him to listen.

'I thought we were supposed to be putting on a united front?'

'We have been. Our guests will understand.'

'But these are *our* guests. I've completely rearranged my schedule to be here this week so we can entertain them together and convince them that we're the real deal.' The brightness of her welcome had cooled considerably.

'This is my life, Alessandra. I warn you now, there will be plenty of occasions when I have to fly off at a moment's notice.'

She eyed him, lines appearing in her brow. 'And what if *I* have to *fly off at a moment's notice*? Will you show me the same latitude?' The challenge was there, from the jut of her chin to the tone of her voice. 'I have a career of my own too, remember?'

'Our marriage is going to take time to shake down,' he conceded, wishing he could be in his jet *right now*. He didn't want to deal with her anger or acknowledge the suspicion emanating from her eyes. That was not what they were about. They were two individuals able to lead their lives to their own needs, not justify their whims and absences to each other. He shouldn't feel any guilt. 'We will find a path that suits us both.'

She nodded slowly but when she spoke her voice was fractionally warmer. 'So long as you don't expect all the compromise and sacrifice to come from my end.'

'I don't expect that.'

'Good.' After a moment of silence, she jerked her head in another nod. 'Have a safe trip.'

He mimicked her movement. 'I'll see you at the chapel.'

CHAPTER NINE

ALESSANDRA STARED AT her reflection. She'd been primped and preened by an army of beauticians and now she was ready.

Ready?

She would never be ready. Not for this.

But it had to be done.

She had to marry Christian and she would do it alone.

Sebastian and Zayed, who had arrived together the night before, had both offered to give her away. She'd been touched by the offers but had declined. They were there for Christian, not her.

There were only two people she would have wanted to walk her down the aisle and one of those was dead. The other hadn't even had the courtesy to respond to his invitation.

She straightened her spine. It wasn't as if this would be a real marriage. This wedding was going ahead for one reason and one reason only: their baby. That was what she needed to focus on. It was *all* she should focus on—not Christian or the way he'd flown off to New York at a moment's notice. Or her suspicions that there was more to his impromptu trip than business. Or those horrible hours waiting for him to return while the cynical part of her brain had thrown taunts that he wouldn't be coming back, that he'd abandoned her. Just like her father had.

Do. Not. Trust.

She *had* to trust him with regard to their child. She had to.

Christian was not her father. And he hadn't abandoned her. Right at that very moment he stood in the chapel waiting for her. Exactly as he'd said he would be.

The relief she'd felt late last night when he'd called to say he was back in Athens had been so powerful it scared her to remember the physicality of her reaction.

It was simply relief that he hadn't humiliated her by standing her up, she insisted to herself. Nothing more than that. Nothing.

She checked her watch. It was time. In approximately one hour she would be married. Christian would be her husband.

She watched her reflected cheeks flush, her blood heating at the remembrances of their one night together, the night that had led to this very moment. Vivid memories of it played in her dreams every night, teasing her, haunting her.

People always said you couldn't miss what you'd never had and in the sexual aspect of her life that had held true. Now that she *had* tried it…

But it wasn't sex on its own that she wanted, that her body responded to. It was sex with Christian. Whether it was the alcohol loosening her inhibitions or something else undefined, he'd awoken her. He did things to her.

Before she'd put her wedding dress on, she'd stepped into her lacy white knickers, imagining him sliding them off; had put her lacy white bra on, imagining him unclasping it; had rolled the silk white stockings up her legs, imagining his strong fingers trailing over her skin as he slid them off.

Dio, how many times had she picked up her phone to call him before slamming it back down? Too many to count.

He'd called her a couple of times, though, conversations that had left her feeling all knotted yet incredibly warm inside. There was something about his voice that set tiny little bolts darting through her skin…

She hadn't been able to shake the feeling that he was hiding something from her, though.

Per favore, not another woman.

Do. Not. Trust.

How she could she trust him? She didn't know how.

She did know that she wanted to. She wanted to believe he would treat her with respect, that maybe one day…

A rap on her door jolted her out of the trance she'd worked herself into.

It was probably a member of staff, come to escort her to the chapel. The sweet girl who brought her breakfast every morning had been shocked when Alessandra had told her she would be walking to the chapel alone.

Always alone.

How she wished she'd swallowed her pride and called her brother and begged him to come. Deep inside, a part of her had believed he *would* come, that he wouldn't leave her to do this alone. That he'd forgive her.

This was his flesh and blood growing in her belly, the very reason she and Christian were prepared to take this ultimate step.

Alone or not, she should have left already.

Her stomach clenched.

She gazed at the French doors.

She didn't have to do this. She could step out onto her balcony, unfold the emergency stairs and escape. Everyone was at the chapel. The staff was busy organising all the celebrations. It could be ages before anyone realised she wasn't being traditionally late.

She pictured Christian's face when he realised she'd stood him up.

She couldn't do that to him. Alessandra knew all about humiliation and would never intentionally inflict it on someone else, least of all him.

And what would their innocent baby say when, at some

point in the future, he or she learned what their mother had done to their father?

Another rap on the door reminded her that someone stood on the other side waiting for her.

Hurrying over, she opened it, pulling a smile onto her face that dropped as soon as she saw who it was.

Dressed in a morning suit, stood her brother.

For a moment she didn't say anything.

Then she burst into tears.

Christian stood with Zayed and Stefan at his side, his two best men—or, as they were called here in their shared role, his *koumbaros*—eyes fixed on the chapel door.

Where was she?

It was traditional for the bride to be late but half an hour? If Stefan hadn't taken his phone from him after Christian had texted her to say he was at the chapel, he would have called and demanded to know where she was.

A face in the congregation caused him momentarily to lose track of his thoughts.

There in the third row sat Mikolaj, an enormous beam on his face. Beside him sat his wife, Tanya, and three of their seven children.

Alessandra must have invited them.

His stomach curled.

She'd done that for him.

Christian nodded a greeting to them but was unable to return the smiles.

Where was she?

The priest continued to smile reassurance but Christian could see the doubt now plaguing his jovial demeanour.

At least the chapel belonged to the hotel and thus was owned by him. They would wait.

Another ten minutes passed. Just as his guts were really starting to churn, the door swung open and there she appeared, the sunshine illuminating her in a golden glow that made the white of her dress sparkle.

It was like gazing at an angel, a moment so beautiful that the relief that should have overwhelmed him faded into nothing, leaving only wonder.

The sound of Pachelbel's *Canon in D* began, played by the string quartet hired for the occasion.

Alessandra walked towards him, an ethereal smile on her face, her steps slow.

His eyes fixed solely on her, it took a good few beats before he registered the arm she held on to.

Rocco had come. He hadn't abandoned his sister. Christian's trip to New York had paid off.

Behind them walked Olivia, stunning in emerald green.

As the bridal party stepped closer to him, a lump formed in his throat that grew larger with every one of Alessandra's steps until she was there before him.

Unlike most brides, who pinned their hair up into an elaborate creation, she'd left hers loose, tumbling around her shoulders in dark chestnut waves. She looked amazing. Her dress a work of art: thin lace-embellished straps with tiny diamonds curved down and across her cleavage like a heart, the sheer material wrapping around her waist to showcase the flare of her hips, then floating to the floor and resting in a white circle.

He looked for a sign of apprehension but none was there. Her beautiful honey-brown eyes, artfully made-up, were clear. Remarkably clear.

He reached out a hand, and as she took it he caught Rocco's eye. The look he gave said: *she's all yours now. Hurt her and you will spend the rest of your life paying for it.*

He'd never understood the full weight of what 'giving the bride away' meant until that moment.

From here on in, the role of her protector passed to him, an antiquated sentiment, but one he felt keenly.

Alessandra would never be his possession but for good or for ill they would be bound together.

The service was anticipated to last around an hour. For the congregation, it no doubt dragged. For Christian, time accelerated, the moment to exchanging their vows speeding up until it was time for them to make their promises to each other—not a requirement of the church but something they had agreed upon between themselves for the benefit of their guests.

He said his first, then Alessandra recited hers, her husky voice true and strong, her Greek practised and flawless. The look in her eyes, fixed on his, was full of meaning. It was a sight that made his chest feel as if a weight had been placed inside him, squeezing down.

There was no time to consider it as now was the time for what was, to many Greeks, the most important part of the ceremony: the crowning. The priest blessed the two floral-wreath crowns, then Zayed took the lead, passing the crowns back and forth over them three times before carefully placing them on their heads.

Finally they were done.

It was time to kiss the bride.

He searched again for her apprehension. It was still missing, a smile playing in the corner of her delicious lips. Lips he hadn't felt upon his since the night they had conceived the child that grew in her belly. Lips he'd spent the past couple of months dreaming of.

Swallowing away the lump in his throat, he placed a hand to her still-slender hip and leaned down. Her small hand reached up to rest on his lapel.

He closed his eyes and pressed his lips to hers, just the breath of a kiss, but enough for the softest mouth he'd ever known to reawaken more memories of their night together and make his pulses race.

When the kiss ended, the congregation, no doubt led by Mikolaj, burst into applause. Alessandra grinned, her whole face smiling, her happiness transparent. She placed a hand on his shoulder and straightened to whisper into his ear, 'Thank you.'

He knew without her having to explain that she was talking about Rocco.

'Thank *you*,' he whispered back.

She'd brought Mikolaj to their wedding. Christian hadn't thought he wanted him there, thought he hadn't wanted any associations with his past. He hadn't appreciated how much it would mean. He'd thought having Stefan and Zayed there would be enough but, no matter how close they all were, Mikolaj had been there his entire life. He was family. Knowing he and Tanya were there to witness it all warmed him right down to his toes.

A sharp pang of regret rent him that his mother wasn't there to witness this day too. But, unlike Mikolaj, his mother would have taken no joy from it. The opposite, in fact.

One look at Mikolaj's beaming, proud face showed how much being there meant to him.

Alessandra had done that for him. Before he could consider what that actually meant, she kissed him, a kiss containing more than a hint of promise. That promise was reflected in her sparkling eyes.

The coldness that had remained within him since their visit to his mother suddenly lifted, pushed out by the desire this beautiful woman—his bride—elicited in him.

For a moment he was tempted to say, to hell with the reception, and whisk her straight off to his suite.

A knowing look played on her beautiful features, a look that said *just a few more hours and I will be yours.*

And she would be—his. Every inch of her.

A short time later they left the chapel, officially husband and wife.

Most of the non-Greek guests had brought confetti to throw over them, but Mikolaj and Tanya had come prepared, handing out paper cups full of rice to throw, as was the proper tradition in Greece.

Amidst howls of laughter, thousands of hard grains were chucked over them from every possible angle. Zayed and Stefan got hold of him and tipped a cupful down the back of his morning suit, rubbing them into his back for extra effect.

The official photos were taken in the grounds before the chapel, and then the entire wedding party headed back to the hotel for the proper celebrations to begin.

The terraced roof of the hotel had been transformed. An abundance of balloons and beautiful flowers covered the entire perimeter, the Parthenon clear in the distance, but close enough that from certain aspects it felt as if you could reach out and touch it.

The day had turned into something magical.

All Alessandra could think was how much work and effort Christian had put into making this a special day for them. Sure, he'd outsourced it all, but he'd been the one to do the outsourcing.

All she'd done was buy her dress. And lingerie…

Crying in her brother's arms had had the effect of clearing her head.

Rocco had urged her to abandon the whole thing. He and Olivia would take care of her.

Alessandra didn't need taking care of—her baby did. Christian was her baby's father. They belonged in each other's lives.

She'd washed her face and reapplied her make-up and then, when she'd looked back in the mirror, the truth had been reflected back at her in startling clarity.

She was committing her life to Christian and their baby. It was time to embrace it for all their sakes.

Done with taking pictures of her husband and their

guests—it truly was a photographer's dream here—she put her camera back into its case and sat back down at the top table.

Staring at him now—holding court with Zayed, Stefan and Stefan's date, Clio, on the edge of the dance floor—her heart clenched, packing into a tight little ball.

Christian must have felt her gaze upon him for he met her eyes, raising his glass of champagne to her.

She raised her lemonade back, her skin dancing as if his gaze had physically touched her.

He said something to his friends which made them all laugh. It pained her that Rocco refused to join them, keeping his distance in the far corner of the room with Olivia and an earnest A-list Hollywood superstar. Her brother had spelled out in no uncertain terms that he was there to do his duty and nothing else.

Her suspicions about Christian's trip to New York had been correct—he *had* gone there with an ulterior motive. But her fears had been wildly off the mark. He hadn't gone to meet up with a secret woman. He'd gone in an attempt to make her brother see sense and attend their wedding.

He'd turned up at their New York home and told her brother in no uncertain terms that Alessandra needed him. When he'd left, Olivia had taken up the cause, essentially bullying Rocco into attending.

Knowing Christian had done that for her...*è stato incredibile*.

She only wished Rocco would see what an amazing thing it was too. To her knowledge, he hadn't exchanged a word with Christian all day.

Whatever his reasons, and however great his reluctance, she was glad he'd come. More than glad. She hoped with all her heart that one day he would come to accept them and accept that their marriage was the right thing for all of them. He might infuriate her but he was her brother and she loved him.

Christian weaved his way through the dancing guests and took his seat at the top table beside her. 'How are you feeling?' he asked, leaning back into his chair.

'Perfetto.' She smiled. 'This has all been amazing, *grazie mille.'*

He slung an arm around the back of her chair. 'It is my pleasure.'

The sound of rotor blades in full motion caught their attention.

'Paparazzi,' he spat, getting back to his feet and kicking his chair back. Immediately he pulled his phone from his pocket and dialled a number, speaking into it with a low voice packed full of menace.

'I had arranged that no helicopter fly within a mile of the hotel today,' he explained tightly when he finished his call, his face taut. 'I will not have our wedding day turned into a circus.'

She shrugged. 'They're tenacious. It was to be expected.'

'They're like locusts.' He laid his palms on the table, his face stark with anger.

Not wanting all the good feeling ruined, she raised a hand to his face and palmed his cheek. 'Thank you.'

The blue in his eyes darkened, his frame stilling. 'For what?'

'For trying to keep them away from me.'

His nostrils flared a touch. He didn't answer, simply stared at her as if trying to peer into her mind.

She gazed back, drinking him in, the heat inside her—so constant when with him—bubbling beneath her...

And then he dipped his head and covered her mouth with his, holding it there, not moving, just breathing into her, warm champagne-scented air filling her senses until he gently slid his mouth across her cheek and brushed his lips against her ear. 'Soon, *agapi mou*, I will do more than just kiss you.'

Her insides melted. Her heart racing at a gallop, she was about to grab his hand and beg him to whisk her away to somewhere private when Zayed joined them, announcing his presence by slapping Christian hard on the back.

'Come on, newlyweds, it is time for the Kalamatianos,' he said, referring to the traditional wedding dance adored by all Greeks. Over his shoulder, Mikolaj and Tanya grinned and waved, already tapping their feet in anticipation.

She was so glad she'd gone behind his back and invited them. It hadn't sat well with her, knowing he would have no one from his childhood there. Knowing Christian was happy she had done so lightened her further.

It made her feel all warm and fuzzy inside, thinking they had gone behind each other's back to bring someone important to their big day.

Soon she was on her feet with Christian in the centre of the dance floor, each holding an end of a scarf that had been thrust at them. With traditional Greek music playing, Zayed and Stefan chivvied everyone up to form a circle around them, the guests linking hands and, following Mikolaj and the other Greek guests' example, swirling around them like a circling snake, shouts of, *'Opa!'* ringing out.

Alessandra had the time of her life. When the Kalamatianos was over, everyone, including the bride and groom, stayed on the dance floor. They danced together, slow songs, fast songs, their hands entwined, their eyes only for each other.

She wanted the wedding and all the good feelings it evoked in her to last forever, to hold on to this moment for as long as she could. Contrarily, she wanted it to end now, wanted the sensuous promise ringing from Christian's eyes to become reality.

Soon…

Soon it would be time to retire to his suite and begin their newly married life in a manner that sent heat surging through her just to think about it.

Christian opened the door of the suite and, keeping hold of Alessandra's hand, closed it behind them.

'Someone's been busy,' he observed, burrowing his face into the nape of her neck. At long last, he was free to touch her and taste her and do all the things he'd wanted to do for so long the ache in his groin had become a permanent part of him.

His suite—*their* suite, now all of Alessandra's possessions had been moved in while their celebrations had been going on—had been decorated. Flowers were artfully arranged in vases, rose petals had been scattered over the bed and a bottle of champagne sat in an ice bucket next to two champagne flutes.

'Clichéd but very romantic,' she said, twisting round to face him.

All the dancing had left her cheeks flushed and her eyes alive with pleasure.

He wanted those eyes glowing with pleasure for a different reason.

Gripping her hip, he pulled her to him and snaked his arm around her waist.

He gazed down into those striking eyes and those moreish lips. His to taste.

She was his to taste.

As he bent his head to claim her mouth, she darted gracefully out of his clasp, laughing softly. 'Not yet.'

'You're making me wait?' he said, his words coming out with an animalistic growl.

'I'm going to freshen up. Remember, *anticipation makes fulfilment taste all the sweeter.*' She sashayed to one of the bathrooms, flashed him a smile full of promise and locked the door behind her.

* * *

Alessandra applied a touch more lipstick then tightened the sash of her silk white robe.

Who needed alcohol?

Desire pulsed through her, making her pulses race uncontrollably.

She hadn't expected that a ring on her finger and a signed piece of paper could make her feel so different but it did.

Christian was the only man she'd ever truly wanted.

She remembered the first time she'd met him, when she'd been twelve and Rocco had brought the Brat Pack to Lake Como for a break. How young and naïve she'd been, still believing in love and romance. She'd taken one look at Adonis and her heart had skipped into her mouth.

He'd hardly noticed her existence.

Looking back with the benefit of hindsight on her ill-fated tryst with Javier, she could see it was the flattery she'd responded to, not *him*. She'd swallowed all his lies because she'd been flattered a man, not an immature boy, was showing an interest in her.

With Christian, it was the man himself she responded to.

She dabbed some perfume behind her ear and onto her wrists and left the privacy of the bathroom. It was time to see her husband as his wife.

CHAPTER TEN

WHEN ALESSANDRA EMERGED from the bathroom and closed the door softly behind her, the only sound Christian could hear was his own heartbeat. Drumming. Thundering in his ears.

He'd stripped naked, shedding his clothes in front of the mirror, staring closely at his reflection.

He didn't know what it could be but he felt different.

He looked the same. The desire he felt for his beautiful bride still burned deep inside him.

But something had changed.

Now he sat in the huge bed, leant back against the headboard, the bed sheets draped across his lap, a dim light glowing. And she was here with him, her dress removed, only a white robe covering her beautiful figure.

Slowly she stepped to him until she reached his side.

'Take your robe off.' He could hear the thickness in the timbre of his voice.

Her hands trembled, but a knowing smile pulled at her lips. She tugged at the sash of her robe and parted it, letting it drop to the floor.

Christian couldn't have torn his gaze away if he'd wanted to.

He didn't want to.

He wanted to capture this moment so he could replay it forever.

Theos but she was more beautiful than he remembered,

the white of her lacy lingerie contrasting against the golden hue of her skin.

Her breasts were swollen, the bra pushing them up to display her cleavage, only just hiding the dusky nipples he remembered so well.

Sitting upright, he extended a hand to grip onto her curved hip, sliding a finger under the strap of her suspender belt.

He ran his other hand up the soft swell of her belly, only slightly thickened since he'd last seen her unclothed.

She dropped a hand onto his shoulder, a cloud of her sultry scent releasing and filling his senses. He'd never known a scent like it, so perfectly matching its owner, a sweet yet musky fragrance, with depth.

He traced his hand back down her belly and clasped hold of her other hip, tugging her to him.

Inhaling her scent deeply into his lungs, he pressed a kiss into the curve of her neck, felt her quiver.

The ache in his groin, that constant state of affairs whenever he was with her, magnified by a thousand, his entire body coming alive to her sweet touch and even sweeter taste.

Using gentle manipulation, he pulled her onto the bed facing him, so she straddled his still-covered lap.

Her eyes darkened and swirled, arousal and desire burning strongly.

The first time they'd made love he'd plunged into her without a thought. His shock at discovering she was a virgin had been masked by concern that he'd hurt her. Her breath had hitched, a tiny mew escaping her throat. He'd held her tightly, stroking her hair, her body, raining kisses over her face until he'd felt her relax, seen her pupils dilate…

She'd been so responsive to everything he'd done to her, so eager to give in return.

She'd been a revelation.

And now he got to experience and taste her all over again.

But this time there would be no pain. Only pleasure.

Wrapping an arm around her and cradling the back of her head with his other hand, he pulled her flush against him and slanted his mouth over the soft, plump lips he'd spent the past two months dreaming about.

She sighed into him and rested her hands on his shoulders, her nails digging into him as her lips parted to allow his tongue to sweep into her warmth.

He stroked her back, up and down, exploring the silky skin anew, then down her sides to the top of her stockings.

She broke the kiss, nuzzling her mouth against his jaw and down into his neck, her hair tickling him.

'You taste divine,' she murmured, the first words she'd uttered since she'd left the bathroom.

Her compliment made his chest heave.

He speared her hair and tugged it back gently so he could look into her eyes. '*You* are divine.'

A small, almost shy, smile spread across her face, and she leaned forward to kiss him, deeply, passionately, her hands crawling up to his scalp and holding on to it.

He found the clasp of her bra and undid it. She released her hold on him, enabling him to pull the straps down her arms and discard the bra on the floor beside him.

When they'd made love the first time, he'd been enraptured with her breasts, their size, their taste, the way his hands could cup them perfectly, everything about them. Pregnancy had swollen them. He didn't know if it was a trick of the light but her dusky nipples seemed darker than he remembered, contrasting against the paleness of her breasts.

He was the only person in the world who knew Alessandra's breasts were the palest part of her body.

It was because his child was growing inside her that these small, subtle changes were taking place.

Using his hands to lift her a touch, he dipped his head and captured one of those beautiful, dusky nipples in his mouth.

Alessandra moaned and ran her fingers through his hair, arching her back to thrust her chest forward and into him.

He flattened a palm against the small of her back to steady her, his free hand roaming until he found the clasp of her suspenders. Before he released it he stroked the exposed flesh above the stockings. Her skin felt better than any material ever could.

When he played with the clasp he was shocked to find himself all thumbs, the deftness he'd acquired over the years gone. It was as if he'd never tried to undo a suspender belt before.

Spearing her hair again, he kissed her, filling his senses with her sultry, sweet taste, driving all thoughts from his mind.

Frustrated at the suspender belt, he tugged at a stocking and felt the material rip in his fingers. He grabbed the material of the other and did the same, then clasped her bottom and leaned forward, using his strength to lay her flat on her back. The movement caused the bed sheet to fall from his lap, freeing his erection which brushed against her thigh, sending deep pulsations firing through his blood, his loins, everywhere.

He sat back to gaze at her, noting everything, from her short, shallow breaths to the jutting of her erect nipples.

Unable to resist, he kissed her again, hard. Alessandra's arms looped around his neck, her legs lifting to hook around him, clasping him to her.

'Not yet,' he murmured, kneeling upright.

She pouted and raised herself onto her elbows. Her breaths came in shallow pants.

'Soon,' he promised, leaning forward to kiss her neck and push her flat again.

A sound like a purr came from her as he kissed his way down her chest and belly and slipped a hand round her back to undo the clasp at the back of her suspender belt. Discarding it, he flattened a hand over her thigh and caught the top of the ripped stocking. Slowly, he pulled it down, past her knee, over her calf and down to the delicate ankle.

'I've dreamed of you doing that,' she said, her husky voice almost breathless.

She'd dreamt of him...?

In response, he leaned down to press a kiss to her now bare foot, then followed the trail he'd just made with his hands with his tongue, darting licks and kisses all the way up to her inner thigh and up to the very heart of her. Pressing his mouth onto her knickers, he inhaled deeply, the scent of her heat almost making him dizzy with desire.

Checking himself, he gritted his teeth before gripping hold of her remaining stocking and slowly sliding it off.

Now she was naked save for her lacy knickers. He took a moment to stare at her, taking every inch of her in.

She was perfect.

She was *his*.

The look on her face was something to be savoured, a knowing yet shy quirk of the lips.

She levered herself up until she knelt before him, face to face.

'My turn,' she whispered, her eyes sparkling.

For such a slight woman she had a hidden strength, able, with a push of her hand, to shove him onto his back.

She laughed softly, taking hold of his wrists and pulling them up and over his head.

This had to count as the single most erotic moment of his life: Alessa straddling him, pinning him down, her swollen breasts brushing against his face. Every time he made to capture one in his mouth, she would move just out of reach.

Her teasing was deliberate, as was the way she strad-dled him, positioning herself on his erection. Every time she moved out of the reach of his mouth her crotch rubbed the length of his erection, the material of her knickers pre-venting any penetration.

She leaned down to kiss him on the mouth, still holding his wrists.

With a simple flick he could be free from her clasp.

Instead, he kissed her back, succumbing to the delights she wanted to bestow on him.

Her soft mouth pressed along his jaw then she released her hold on his wrists and slowly made her descent. No part of his chest was left unkissed or unstroked, his skin alive under the trail she made.

When she reached his groin she completely ignored his erection, her mouth working around it, her hands cupping his balls while her tongue darted out to taste them.

Her movements were clumsy, a sign of her inexperience, but this only added to the eroticism of the moment.

This was all for him.

Her tongue flickered onto the base of his shaft.

A powerful bolt shot through him, a groan escaping his lips.

He gripped the bed sheets in his fists and clenched his teeth even tighter, finding a spot on the ceiling to focus on.

For a moment he'd been certain he was going to come.

'Is something wrong?' she asked, stopping what she was doing to look at him, her eyes clouding with doubt.

Speech wouldn't form. He shook his head and sat up, leaning forward to clasp her cheeks and pull her into another kiss. In a tangle of arms and legs they collapsed together, Alessandra beneath him, devouring each other with their mouths.

He tugged at her knickers, pushing them down her hips, using his thighs and legs to pull them down. When they reached her ankles she kicked them off then wrapped her legs around him, raising her bottom so her heat rubbed against his erection.

And then he was inside her, burrowed in her tight heat, the relief giddying.

The first time they'd made love he'd been blown away

with how deeply he'd felt everything, every touch, every movement magnified.

This was something else completely.

Slowing their kisses, he began to move, keeping his groin ground to hers.

Her soft moans fired him, her kisses fuelled him, her roaming hands and fingers burning through his skin.

He opened his eyes to find her gazing at him in a dazed wonder.

Reaching for her hand, he brought it up to rest by the side of her head and clasped it tightly, kissing her with renewed passion as his thrusts deepened. It was as if he'd fused into one with her.

He felt rather than heard her come. Her grip around his erection thickened and tightened, her lips freezing on his, her only sound a tiny, almost breathless mew.

He was hardly aware of his own release. His senses were too full of Alessandra, watching every last moment of her climax.

Finally spent, he burrowed his face into her neck, careful not to put too much weight on her belly, and savoured the most delicious warmth he'd ever known spread through him.

The heavy weight of sleep soon came to claim him, and he shifted his weight off her. She followed his movements and settled into the crook of his arm with a contented sigh.

He awoke a few hours later. The suite was in darkness, a sliver of moonlight shining through.

Alessandra was draped over him, breathing deeply, her hair tickling his neck and chin. He smoothed it down, marvelling at its silkiness.

He tried to doze but sleep refused to return.

How could he sleep with so much racing through his mind? When there were so many emotions racing through his chest, it was a struggle to catch his breath.

The first time he'd slept with her, in her apartment in Milan… He'd struggled for thoughts and breath then too.

This was much worse.

He'd felt her getting too close in Mikolaj's restaurant, that feeling she could see through the veneer of his skin and through to the heart of him. That feeling had been compounded after the visit to his mother's house. He'd retreated to New York partly to talk sense into Rocco but mostly for space to compose himself in preparation for his new life.

Marriage wouldn't change anything, he'd convinced himself. He would compartmentalise Alessandra's presence in his life just as he did with his mother. They would live together but they wouldn't *be* together.

Making love to her again… Something had come alive inside him. He'd felt it uncoiling when they'd exchanged their vows but with everything going on that day had put it to one side. Now it, whatever *it* was, had uncoiled and bitten him, hard enough that it felt like a physical pain.

Before he could hope to decipher it, she roused in his arms, pulling herself up enough to kiss him, deeply, passionately, awakening in an instant.

He responded as if he'd been lying there waiting for her to wake, groaning when she slid onto his already hard length.

Doing nothing but hold on to her waist to support her, he let her take the lead. The moonlight bathed her, letting him watch as she took her pleasure, watch the lips that parted, the eyes that glazed. Her soft moans deepened until she ground herself onto him. He felt her release as deeply as he felt his own, revelled in the pulsations that seemed to draw his own orgasm into unquantifiable realms.

Afterwards, when he thought she was falling back into slumber, she pressed a kiss to his chest.

'I could get used to this,' she said, her voice sleepy but tinged with a smile.

And tinged with something that sounded like hope.

His eyes opened with a jerk.

He remembered the look in her eyes when they'd exchanged their vows. Now he knew what it had been: hope.

Alessandra had hopes for their future as a married couple.

She was changing towards him—she *had* changed towards him.

And with that change came the realisation that he could forget sharing a bed with her when they both wanted it.

Unless he kept a proper distance from her, he would soon have the power to hurt her.

Carefully he disentangled himself from her arms and got out of bed.

'Where are you going?' she mumbled.

'To get a drink. Go to sleep. I'll be back in a minute.' But he knew his words were a lie even as he spoke them.

He needed to protect her.

He needed to protect her from himself.

Alessandra slipped into her robe and headed to the bathroom where she could hear the shower running.

Her skin flushed to think of joining Christian in there, lathering his gorgeous body…

She stretched for the third time, shaking the lingering sleepiness off, and turned the door handle. It was locked.

She tried the handle again and still the door didn't budge.

She didn't know why—what experience did she have of men in a sensual sense?—but it surprised her that he might want his privacy whilst he showered. After the things they'd done to each other…

The flush on her skin deepened, penetrating through her flesh and down low, erotic memories of what they had done together, making her glow from the inside out.

It had been even better than she remembered. The alcohol during their first time might have been enough to loosen her inhibitions but it must have dulled her senses a fraction too.

Or maybe it was because this time there was something real between them that surpassed mere lust.

All Alessandra knew was that she wanted nothing more than to spend the day in bed with him. The only thing to spoil her memories was awakening to find his side of the bed empty.

Instead of waiting for him, she dived into the adjoining bathroom and deliberately kept the door ajar, an open invitation for *him* to join *her*.

After a good few minutes of soaping herself under the powerful walk-in shower and washing her hair, boredom kicked in.

She dried herself quickly, rubbed the towel over her hair and moisturised her face.

She made to leave the bathroom, pausing at the last moment to put her robe back on, not yet confident enough to walk around stark naked in broad daylight.

The door of the bathroom he'd been using was open. Masculine scents mingled with the steam of the shower, filling the empty bedroom.

Maybe he was ordering breakfast for them.

She wandered through to the main living area of the suite and found him at the dining table—fully dressed and working on his laptop.

He looked up and flashed a quick smile. 'Good morning.'

She nodded slowly, caught off-guard to find him working. For surely he must be working? He hadn't even donned casual clothes but wore a white shirt and blue pinstriped trousers.

'Are you planning on wearing that to Marrakech?' she asked. They were due to fly there later that afternoon for a four-day honeymoon.

An uncomfortable look spread over his face, quickly gone, but there long enough for her chest to sink down to her feet.

'I'm afraid we will have to take our honeymoon another time,' he said calmly, looking back at his laptop. 'An emergency has come up.'

'Another one?'

He threw her a smile that was clearly intended to bestow patience when all it did was make her want to throw something at him.

'You know my job is all about finance. When financial problems hit companies, prompt action is needed.'

'I appreciate that. What I don't get is why it has to be you—why can't someone else step in and act as saviour?'

'There is no one else.'

Her eyes narrowed in suspicion. 'What about our honeymoon and the way it's supposed to convince the world we're in love?' Why did her heart clench to say that?

'I joined the board of an Athens shipping company last month in an advisory capacity. One of my staff has been going through the accounts and has discovered a large hole in the company's finances. Unless we plug that hole in the next two days, fifty thousand people will not receive their pay cheques. That's fifty thousand people who will struggle to pay their bills, their mortgages, feed their children. We will go to Marrakech at a later date.'

How could she argue with that? She couldn't, not unless she wanted to sound like the most selfish person in the world.

She eyed him coolly, trying to decide if the whiff of duplicity she detected was real or the workings of a tired, disappointed mind. Four days in Marrakech with nothing to do but laze under the sun and make love had sounded like heaven.

She didn't dispute the crisis he'd described was real. What she did dispute was his assertion that he was the only person in the world able to resolve it.

Throwing a tight smile, determined not to show her disappointment, she said, 'Seeing as you're going to be busy,

I'll return to Milan. There's a lot of stuff there I need to be getting on with.'

'No, you will stay here in Athens with me.'

'Are you giving me an order?'

He sighed. 'If you return to Milan on your own, the day after our wedding, suspicions will be aroused. People will understand the postponement of a honeymoon because of a financial crisis. This is Greece; the whole country's in crisis. They will not understand a new wife who is not at her husband's side during it. We need to live together full-time as man and wife for a few months to keep the doubters at bay. We already agreed this.'

Alessandra's teeth were clenched so tightly against the metaphorical kicking they'd just received that she had to fight to prise them apart.

Suspicions would be aroused?

That was one way to bring her back down to earth.

While she fought the despondency crashing through her like a wave, she fought even harder to keep her composure.

This was a timely reminder that theirs was not a real marriage. The romance of their wedding day— what Christian had done to get her brother there, the wondrousness of their love-making—all must have combined to set off some new hormones within her that made her look at Christian in a fuzzy light.

Dio, she must have been cast under a spell.

She blinked rapidly to clear the fuzzy light, wishing she could clear the churning in her belly with the same ease.

'Okay, I'll stay in Athens with you, but remember I've a shoot scheduled for next Thursday so we need to be back in Milan for that.'

He bowed his head. 'I'm sure that won't be a problem.'

'Good.' She didn't add that should a 'problem' occur she would fly to Milan and do her work regardless. 'I'm going to order some breakfast. Do you want anything?'

'Just a pot of coffee, thank you.'

Christian watched her pick up the suite phone and place their order then turned his attention back to the screen in front of him.

His eyes wouldn't focus.

After the incredible night they'd shared he'd been expecting much greater resistance from Alessandra about the postponed honeymoon, had braced himself for the worst.

If he hadn't seen the flare of despondency in her eyes he would believe her understanding and calmness at the situation was genuine.

As much as it hurt him to hurt her, he knew it was for the best.

He *had* to put their marriage on the footing they had originally agreed.

There were women who could separate love and sex. He no longer believed Alessandra to be one of them.

The hope he'd seen in her eyes as they'd exchanged their vows and then the hope he'd heard in her voice after they'd made love…

What did he, the gutter rat from Athens, know about love?

All he knew about it was that it broke hearts and destroyed people. It had destroyed his mother and Alessandra's father.

He wouldn't know how to love or show love if he tried. All he knew was how to make money. A woman like Alessandra deserved so much more.

Physical distance wasn't enough. He needed to put emotional distance between them too. Now. Before he hurt her.

If he allowed their sexual relationship to develop, her feelings would likely develop too while his…

He'd never had a proper relationship before. Never. He had no idea how long it would take for boredom to set in, when the thrill of making love to the one woman would abate and he'd be looking for a new challenge.

If her feelings grew stronger whilst his decreased, the pain it would cause her would be immense.

He had to nip it in the bud now. For both their sakes.

CHAPTER ELEVEN

CHRISTIAN'S HOME WAS a pebblestone villa in a private enclave of Athens, set away from the hustle and bustle of the city. Surrounded by acres of green land, the villa itself was found by means of a private driveway; indeed, the one word that sprang to Alessandra's mind as she got out of the car was *private*. They could be anywhere. They could be nowhere.

The villa was beautiful, there was no denying that—picture perfect—but the silence was deafening. Villa Mondelli had been much the same, the majority of her childhood spent in its splendid isolation. She'd adored the infrequent trips to Milan Rocco would take her on when he was home from university—loved the noise, the smells and the bustle of the big city, that feeling of being a small cog in a big wheel where all the tiny component parts jostled together nicely to make the big picture.

They'd left the hotel after breakfast, waved off by their remaining guests. She'd forced a bright smile, forced jollity.

On the drive to his home he'd explained in more detail what he was working on. She'd tried hard to be sympathetic and understanding about the importance that the situation be speedily resolved. That did nothing to prevent the underlying resentment.

She was used to workaholics. She'd been raised by the various nannies her workaholic grandfather had employed for her. Her brother was of an identical mould.

But she was one hundred per cent certain that, if such a situation had occurred hours before Rocco's honeymoon, he would have put Olivia first. At the very least he would have discussed the matter with her and taken her input before making a decision.

The big difference was that Rocco loved Olivia. She was his world.

All Alessandra was to Christian was the vessel carrying his child, married to secure his heir and avert a scandal. Love did not and never would feature in it, no matter what foolish feelings had been stoked on her wedding day.

Against her better judgement she'd allowed hope to rear its head.

Sex was a dangerous game to play. It evoked feelings that had no business being conjured.

In future she would make love with her body and detach her mind. Somehow. She was certain it could be done. Lots of other women were able to do it so why should she be any different?

The vows she'd made had been given honestly but for the sake of the little life growing in her belly, not for herself.

It would be wise for her to remember that and stop letting her hormones off the leash.

Christian followed her out of the car and walked her to the large front door, the driver tasked with bringing her luggage in.

A woman who Alessandra judged to be in her mid-forties opened the door to greet them. Christian introduced her as Evanthia, his head of housekeeping.

Evanthia took Alessandra's extended hand, uttered a friendly greeting in Greek then stood back so they could enter.

The interior was every bit what the average person would expect a bachelor billionaire's home to look like: lavish. Ostentatious. Cold. All vaulted ceilings, white walls and lots of marble.

The reception area where they stood led through to an enormous open-plan living space. While she stood at the threshold, craning her neck to take it all in, Christian and Evanthia had a quick conversation.

'I need to go,' he said to Alessandra a few moments later. 'Evanthia will show you around and show you where your room is.'

'Where *my* room is?' she interrupted, snapped out of her musings about his interior decoration.

He nodded. 'If you're not happy with it then let Evanthia know and she can move you to a different one.'

'Oh.'

He looked at her with calm eyes. 'Is there a problem?'

She forced her own eyes to be bright and wide. 'Not at all.'

'Then make yourself comfortable—this is your home now. It is doubtful I will be back before the evening but you have my number if you need me for anything.'

With that he left, leaving Alessandra feeling as if a rug had been pulled out from under her.

They were to have separate rooms.

That meant they would be sleeping in separate beds.

Her reality check that morning when he'd cancelled their short honeymoon hadn't been a reality check enough.

The talking-to about having sex with her body and not her heart now sounded presumptuous and silly, even if she'd only been talking to herself.

Silly, silly Alessandra. When would she learn?

She placed a hand to her stomach, refusing to let the swell of hopelessness pull her down.

Evanthia said something in Greek, beckoning for Alessandra to follow her.

Time to pull herself together.

All her love would be reserved for her baby.

With many gestures, Evanthia gave her the tour: the huge living area with its 'hidden' library, a bar nestled in a cut-out section of wall and a dining area with a table that could fit two dozen comfortably. She was also shown the enormous kitchen, the indoor swimming pool and the gymnasium that would put any private member's club to shame. Through a back door she was shown two outdoor swimming pools and a lawn tennis court, then it was time to head upstairs. They climbed one of three sets of winding stairs and walked along a landing that overlooked the living area, a four-foot-high length of impossibly clear Perspex barrier there to stop anyone plunging headfirst to the first floor.

Her room was at the far end of the landing. Her luggage had been placed inside.

'Clothes,' Evanthia said, pointing at an internal door. Alessandra opened the door to find a dressing room.

'I do?' Evanthia asked, picking one of the suitcases up.

'I can do it,' Alessandra answered with a smile. 'Thank you for the offer.'

Evanthia started talking, gesturing wildly.

Not having the faintest idea what the housekeeper was saying or what her gestures meant, Alessandra smiled and nodded politely. Eventually Evanthia bustled off after making gestures Alessandra thought might have indicated food.

As soon as she was alone in her room she set about unpacking, hanging her clothes in the empty dressing room.

A dressing room that would only ever contain feminine clothes.

Silly little Alessandra, she thought, folding into drawers the new underwear she'd brought expecting her husband to remove them.

She could wear bloomers and he would neither know nor care.

At some point in the preceding weeks she'd allowed herself to believe their marriage could be like a small nursery garden that, with some care and attention, might—just might—bloom into something substantial. Something real.

She'd even allowed herself to believe that Christian could

be someone in whom she could trust, not only with her baby but with *her*.

Christian had taken all those little seedlings and ripped them up, a reminder that he'd never wanted the garden in the first place. He'd put her subtly but firmly in her place.

So why had he made love to her on their wedding night? Out of duty? To consummate it and make it legal?

No. He must have made love to her because she was there and he could. She could have been any woman in that bed.

It was her own lack of sexual experience that had failed to recognise it for what it was.

Did he expect them to sleep together again or was that it?

Her cheeks burned just imagining asking that question. The humiliation of his answer would be too much.

But it hurt so much to know that an experience she'd found so special and fulfilling had been all one-sided. Christian had been going through the motions, his tenderness part of those motions.

He probably had sex with all his lovers in the same way. Why did she think she was so special that Casanova Markos would want to share a bed with her more than once? She'd shared two nights with him; she should feel special. She'd had a one hundred per cent higher success rate than his other women.

She rubbed her itchy eyes and chided herself. Christian wasn't doing anything they hadn't previously agreed. She had to accept things as they were, not as she now wished they could be.

Their marriage would be like the green land surrounding the villa. Flat and one-dimensional and not a single different colour in sight.

Alessandra hovered the photo over the place on screen until she was happy with the position then clicked to release it. She stared for an age, trying to think of a witty caption to go with it. Inspiration struck. She typed it in, clicking the save button at the exact moment Christian stepped into the hidden library.

She'd heard movements, had assumed it was members of the household staff.

She hadn't for a minute thought it was her husband actually returning home at what would be regarded by a normal person as a decent time.

How she wished her pulses didn't race at the mere sight of him.

'What are you doing?' he asked, leaning against the oak desk she'd appropriated for her purpose.

'A wedding montage.' She made sure to keep her tone neutral. 'I'm making what is basically an electronic magazine with pictures of all the people who were there to share our happy day.' How she stopped her tongue curdling over 'happy day' she didn't know. 'When it's done I'll email it to all of them as a keepsake.' She would also print and frame a copy and hang it beside her bed where it could be a daily reminder that her life with Christian was a sham, a marriage for appearances.

It felt good to have something to occupy her. Since their wedding three weeks ago, they'd travelled to Milan together for a few days so she could do her prearranged shoot and meet her obstetrician, flown on to Hong Kong where they'd stayed in his penthouse apartment—in separate rooms—for a week then travelled to London for a day's shoot. They'd been back in Athens ever since.

Having no work to occupy her here, she'd spent a day sightseeing, undetected by any paparazzi. Far from being able to enthuse about all the ancient relics at the Acropolis, she'd felt lonely surrounded by couples and groups of people all chattering happily together.

Christian's home was so remote and her grasp of the Greek language so weak that the chances of making any friendships were almost impossible. At least his apartment in Hong Kong was central, allowing her plenty of freedom to explore and occupy herself.

Being in Athens reminded her too strongly of being back at Villa Mondelli, when her grandfather had always been too busy working to take any notice of her. Rocco had been of the same mould. She'd learned as a child that moping about didn't change anything. Keeping busy was the solution to curbing isolation. As a child she would bury her head in books, draw pictures and practise her gymnastics. She'd needed something, a project here in Athens, to keep the isolation at bay and it had been while going through the photos she'd taken on their wedding day, trying hard to look at them objectively and not through maudlin eyes, that inspiration had struck.

'May I look?'

'It isn't finished yet—I'm about two-thirds done, but help yourself.' She pushed her chair back to give him access to her laptop. She didn't push back far enough, catching that gorgeous oaky scent that made her mouth water.

She closed her eyes in a futile attempt to curb the longing sweeping through her at his proximity.

In three weeks he hadn't once attempted to seduce her, not even with his eyes, as he had done so many times before they'd made their vows.

One night had been enough for him to bore of her sexually. Okay; two nights. But they'd been months apart.

If only she could get her body to believe it was bored of him too.

Time would curb it, she told herself. Eventually his lack of interest would creep through her like a pollutant and she would be able to stop tossing and turning throughout the night, wishing he would come to her.

After three weeks of no physical attention she accepted that wasn't going to happen.

It had done nothing to cure her longing.

'This is incredible,' Christian said, clicking his way

through the pages she'd created. 'The glossy magazines would pay you a fortune to get hold of your memory stick.'

'I'm sure they would,' she agreed drily.

Silently she congratulated herself on another coherent conversation with him.

It would have been easy to slip into self-pity after his rejection.

She would not do that. She would not infect her baby with negativity.

In fairness, he hadn't lied to her. On the contrary, their marriage was shaping up to be exactly how they'd devised when they'd first agreed to it.

She only wished she'd known how heartsick it would make her.

Pushing her chair farther back, she got to her feet. 'Are we still going out tonight?' She refused to make assumptions. He might have only popped home for a fleeting visit between appointments.

Christian worked ridiculous hours. Even in Milan, where they'd stayed so she could work, he'd holed himself up in the spare room of her apartment, which he'd turned into a bedroom-cum-office, working until the early hours and joining her for an evening meal before disappearing again.

'Yes. We don't need to leave until eight. There's plenty of time.'

They were going to a party at the British Embassy, their first official function as man and wife.

She looked at her watch. 'I suppose two hours is adequate time to get ready for a night out.'

'You suppose?' he echoed with a droll tone.

Christian put his cufflinks on then slipped into his tuxedo jacket and straightened his black bowtie. He would do.

He headed downstairs and poured himself a small shot of bourbon.

It had been a hard few weeks and now he was looking

forward to an evening out. Yes, it would be a networking evening, but with Alessandra by his side it would be bearable.

It was strange to think of himself merely enjoying a woman's company for company's sake but with Alessandra he did. Until their impromptu date, all his dealings with women had been for two reasons: business, at which he refused to blur the lines between personal and professional; and pleasure, the women he dated with the sole intention of bedding them. He'd enjoyed the time spent with them but it had been a means to an end, the end being in bed naked.

Alessandra was the first woman he'd gone on a date with whom he'd had no intention of bedding. He'd found her wildly attractive but she'd been so off-limits he'd curbed that side of his thought process with her. After a few glasses of champagne had loosened them both up, he'd found himself wildly fascinated by *her*, the mind beneath the beautiful face, not just the body beneath the dress she'd worn.

For the first time, he looked back on his behaviour before he'd met Alessandra with a sense of shame.

How many women had he bedded in his thirty-two years?

He couldn't even hazard a guess.

He'd hopped from bed to bed without a second thought.

For the first time, he considered he'd been running, not hopping. Running as fast as he could.

Alessandra was the only woman whose bed he'd run from without immediately hopping into another.

From their first night together until she'd approached him at Rocco and Olivia's wedding, there had been no one else. There still hadn't been.

He hadn't promised fidelity to her. So long as he was discreet, he could bed whomever he chose.

The problem, as he was learning, was that just because he could act like a kid in a sweetshop, his taste at that moment was for only one particular sweet. That sweet went by the name of Alessandra.

He didn't believe he'd ever worked as hard as he had these past three weeks. He'd always been a hard, diligent worker but since his university days he'd always ensured there was time for fun.

The only fun he wanted now came in a slender package with a mane of glossy chestnut hair. There were times, especially late at night, when he heard movement from her room, when he would fight to remind himself why he couldn't allow their relationship to be anything but platonic.

In his eyes, she was a princess.

He was a gutter rat.

He wasn't good enough for her.

He would only bring her misery.

Better to keep things platonic for both their sakes *and* for the sake of their unborn baby.

It was harder than he'd ever imagined.

He straightened as Alessandra descended the stairs, the jewellery she wore around her wrist clanging against the railing she lightly gripped.

She never failed to take his breath away.

Tonight she wore a floor-length turquoise silk gown with only one long sleeve, gold and diamond beading around the neck line that slashed under her bare arm. The material layered like descending waves down to her feet, displaying her slender curves but hiding the slight burgeoning of her waistline. Tonight her neck was bare, the only complementary jewellery a chunky Egyptian bracelet and a pair of gold teardrop earrings. Her hair had been swept up into an elegant knot, her eyes dramatically darkened, her lips conversely painted a nude colour.

The Egyptian bracelet only accentuated the idea of an Egyptian queen having sprung to life.

An ache formed in his chest, a much different ache to the one coursing through his loins.

That bare, golden arm and shoulder were her only real

bits of bodily flesh on display but the effect on him was as dramatic as if she'd walked down the stairs naked.

His mind filled with visions of peeling the dress from her…

He swallowed the imagery away and stepped forward to her, being greeted with a cloud of her sultry perfume in return.

'You're beautiful,' he said.

She smiled. '*Grazie*. You look good yourself.'

Alessandra had always found men wearing dinner jackets attractive—there was something so sophisticated and suave about the look—but Christian made other men's attempts look like little boys playing dress-up. There was something about the way he filled it that made her pulses skip and her skin tingle.

If they had a proper marriage she would at least have the anticipation of ripping it off him when they got home…

Stop it, she scolded herself. Thoughts like that did nothing for her private mission of gaining immunity against him.

And nor did the darkening of his eyes, that look as if he wanted nothing more than to rip her clothes off too.

A rush of warm heat pooled in the apex of her thighs, so deep and sudden her legs weakened.

It was a look she hadn't seen in three weeks.

Any immunity she might have managed to attain was ripped away in one fell swoop.

CHAPTER TWELVE

CHRISTIAN'S DRIVER PULLED up outside the embassy. No sooner had the engine been turned off than the door was opened for them and they were ushered out of the car amidst a hail of flashbulbs from the waiting paparazzi, who'd been tipped off that they were attending.

As they crossed the threshold of the historic building, Alessandra almost jumped out of her skin to feel Christian place his hand on the small of her back.

It was the first time he'd touched her since their wedding night.

It's for the paparazzi's benefit, she told herself.

When he clasped her hand into his much larger one, threading his fingers through hers, the nerves on her skin tingled with warmth, her fingers yearning to squeeze their possession.

Keeping a firm grip of her hand, he steered her around the room, introducing her to various bankers, investors and their partners and spouses.

She found it hard keeping track of names. Every time Christian's body brushed against hers, her heart would skip and her mind would lose its train of thought.

When a waiter passed carrying a tray of canapés, she pounced, glad of a decent excuse to drop her husband's hand.

It wasn't just money and finance people wanted to talk to them about, though; many were keen to discuss the wed-

140

THE GREEK'S PREGNANT BRIDE

ding, eager for the intimate details the press had only been able to guess at. They'd released a couple of photos to the media in the hope that having something publishable would help them lose interest.

'They should give everyone name tags,' she said after a few hours of small talk and endless canapés. Christian had noticed her springing lightly on her aching legs and, insisting she rest for a few minutes, had borne her off to some empty seats in an alcove.

A smile tugged at his lips. 'It would make life easier.'

'How many of these people do you actually know?'

'Far too many of them.'

'You don't sound very enthusiastic.'

'Finance doesn't always attract the most charismatic of people.'

'It attracted you.'

'You think I'm charismatic?'

'You know you are,' she said with deliberate dismissal.

'Is that a compliment?' he asked, raising a brow in bemusement while his beautiful eyes glittered.

'Take it however you want.' She smiled at a passing woman they'd spoken to earlier, the wife of a diplomat. She couldn't help but notice the woman's gaze linger a touch too long on Christian.

Did she think he was charismatic?

Christian had more charisma than anyone she'd known. People were drawn to him. *Women* especially were drawn to him and it wasn't the sole result of his good looks. She doubted the size of his bank account had much affect either—the magnetism he carried came from him.

'Then I will take it as a compliment.'

'Why finance?' she asked, her interest piqued. 'Of all the jobs and careers out there, why go that route?'

The bemusement dropped, the warmth in his eyes cooling. For a moment she thought he was going to ignore her innocent question.

Instead, he held her gaze. 'When I was a small child, every night before she slept my mother would get the few drachmas she had to her name, place them in front of her and count them.' He spoke slowly and concisely, as if he were thinking carefully about his answer. 'I think she hoped that if she counted them enough times they would magically double. The only time I was ever able to make her happy was if I found a stray coin and brought it home to her.'

He shook his head, distaste pouring off him. 'She worked so hard but we were so poor she couldn't afford to pay for my school books. We had food in our belly from Mikolaj—whatever was left over from the day before—but there was no money for anything—not birthdays, not Christmas, not anything.'

Alessandra swallowed, the familiar ache forming in her belly that always came when she thought of his childhood. She hated imagining what he'd lived through.

His gaze bore into her. 'I was obsessed with people like you.'

'Me?' she queried faintly.

'I would see men and women like you, people who were clean and wore beautiful clothes, and wonder why we were so different, why the clothes my mother and I wore were falling into rags. Then I realised what the difference was: money. They had it and we didn't. So that became my obsession. Money. I was determined to learn everything about it: how to earn it, how to make it grow and how to keep it so that my mother and I too could be clean and wear beautiful clothes.'

'You certainly realised your dreams,' she said quietly. 'Did you have to study hard for it or did it come naturally to you?'

She thought back to her own single-sex education and how she had resented the strictness, rebelling by refusing to pay attention or do homework until it had become likely she would fail all her exams. If she'd applied herself a bit more, her grandfather would never have felt the need to employ a private tutor to help her catch up. Javier would never have entered her life. Who knew how different her life would have been if she'd never met him?

Would she have stayed a virgin until the age of twenty-five?

She hadn't been ready for sex with Javier but with hindsight it was because she'd known, even without being aware of his wife and children, that a sexual affair between them was wrong. The balance of power had been too one-sided, in his favour.

But Javier was her reality. She didn't know if she would have stayed a virgin until the age of twenty-five if she hadn't met him because that would have been a different Alessandra, not the Alessandra she was today.

'I studied every hour I could,' Christian said, adopting the same quiet tone as she. 'I must have been ten when I realised education was the only way either I or my mother could escape.'

'I'm so sorry,' she said softly after a long silence had formed between them.

'For what?'

'I don't know.' She raised her shoulders, wishing she could articulate the shame churning within her. She recalled the little rant she'd had in Mikolaj's taverna when she'd put Christian in his place about him not having a monopoly on childhood pain and abandonment.

At least she'd always had clean clothes and fresh food. Materially she'd had everything she could have wished for; the things she'd been denied were to stop her being spoiled and not due to a lack of finances.

After the mess that had been her relationship with Javier, her grandfather had used money—her allowance—as another means to control her. No allowance meant no money; no money meant she stayed prisoner in the villa without the means to bring any more shame to the good Mondelli name.

A prisoner?

What a self-absorbed brat she had been.

Christian's whole life came into sharp focus. No more potted snapshots of her Adonis, the hard working but poor scholarship student, the small child sharing a mattress in a cramped attic room with his harridan of a mother...

Now the snapshots formed a whole picture. Formed the man before her; everything it must have taken for him to drag himself out of the slum. Two decades of suffering before he'd had the opportunity to shower daily.

What must he think of her, the spoiled little rich kid? *She* knew she'd never been spoiled but in comparison to Christian she might as well have been Imelda Marcos. So her grandfather had been a workaholic and happy to pass the actual raising of his granddaughter to the female staff of his household? At least she'd never doubted his love. So he'd cut off her allowance? Oh, boo hoo. Her grandfather had been teaching her a lesson. Without it she would never have felt compelled to get herself a job, would never have answered the advertisement to be a photographer's assistant and taken the first steps on the career she loved.

She'd been self-sufficient ever since.

She might not have had a mother or a father but she'd had her grandfather, strict as he was, and her brother, as protective as he was. Things might be tense at the moment but Rocco would always be there for her.

Christian hadn't had any of that. Mikolaj had been there as best he could but with a business to run and seven kids of his own to raise it hadn't been enough. Christian had basically been alone until he'd established the strong friendship group with her brother, Stefan and Zayed. A friendship that had been destroyed because of her.

'Your mother...'

'What about her?' he asked tersely.

'However crazy she makes you feel, you must love her very much.'

He breathed deeply. 'I respect what she did for me as a child. She could have abandoned me but she didn't. I do my duty towards her and will never abandon her. But love? She poisoned any notion I ever had of love.'

As Alessandra digested this, a silver fox of a man came over to join them in the alcove, a German she recalled Christian telling her was head of one of Europe's major private banks.

'Have I introduced you to my daughter?' he asked, indicating a woman of around the same age as Alessandra who was hovering behind him.

'I don't believe so,' Christian answered.

Silver Fox pulled his daughter to him. 'Kerstin, this is Christian Markos and his wife, Alessandra.'

Kerstin's eyes gleamed as she leaned in to kiss Christian's cheeks, lingering to whisper something in his ear. A tall, blonde, impossibly glamorous and beautiful woman, she reminded Alessandra of old Hollywood. Her kisses to Alessandra were quick and perfunctory, the first thing that caused the word *bitch* to float in Alessandra's mind.

'Kerstin graduated a few years ago from your Alma Mater,' Silver Fox said when the introductions were complete.

'You studied at Columbia?' Christian asked with interest.

'I did,' she said with a knowing smile.

So she had brains as well as beauty?

'I seem to recall your father saying something about it, but that was quite a few years ago,' he mused. 'Are you planning on following in his footsteps?'

'*Ja*—when Papa retires the plan is for me to take over his role.'

'That's something I wanted to talk to you about,' Silver Fox said, addressing Christian. 'Kerstin and I feel she needs to expand her horizons. We would like you to taking her under your wing for a year or two so she can learn directly from you different aspects of our business.'

Over my dead body.

'That's an interesting idea,' Christian said, turning his attention directly to Kerstin. 'What are you hoping to learn from me?'

'Everything!' Thus said, Kerstin proceeded to discuss in great detail what she hoped to achieve under his tutelage, most of which went straight over Alessandra's head. This wasn't through a lack of understanding on her part, more to do with the raging burn in her brain that glowed so brightly, nothing else could penetrate.

If she had claws she would scratch Kerstin's eyes out without a second thought.

With a snap, she knew who Kerstin reminded her of and why she'd taken such an instant dislike to her.

She reminded her of all the women she'd ever seen photographed on Christian's arm.

His interest in her—the way he leaned in closely to hear what she had to say, the obvious interest in his expression—was all so clear a highly polished window couldn't have been more transparent.

Feeling everything inside her clench, she forced her ears to tune in to the conversation.

Now it really did fly over her head.

When it came to financial matters, the most Alessandra ever needed to know was the amount in her personal and business bank accounts and what income and outgoings she had. When she heard the word *securities* banded about in all earnestness, the only thing her brain conjured up were her bodyguards.

She wasn't stupid; she knew that. But finance was its own separate language, one she didn't know how to translate.

Kerstin did. Kerstin spoke fluent finance.

Alessandra placed a hand on her belly as if by covering it she could protect the tiny life within from the thoughts raging through its mother's head.

By marrying her, Christian had deprived himself of a marriage that would be far better suited to him.

Kerstin would be perfect. She had the physical attributes he so desired—Alessandra doubted any man would get bored of making love to *her*—but, more importantly from her husband's point of view, there would be no juggling of time, no compromise. Kerstin would flit into his life as if she'd been born there and then, when her father retired, she and Christian would take over the running of his bank together.

Dio, now her brain was running away from her. She couldn't make it stop.

They'd been in the woman's company for twenty minutes and already Alessandra had mapped her entire future out for her.

Christian had never wanted to marry. He'd given up his freedom for their baby. He was trying to accommodate the mother of his baby into his life as well as he could.

He might never have wanted to marry but he *did* want children.

If he'd met Kerstin tonight as a single man, would he too have grasped what an ideal wife she would have made for him?

They'd have been perfect together, could have made beautiful babies over a set of spreadsheets then whispered sweet nothings about the world of finance into each other's ears until the early hours of every morning.

'Are you okay?' Christian asked quietly, breaking into her runaway thoughts.

She swallowed and jerked a nod. 'I think I have indigestion,' she said, uttering the first thing that came into her mind.

His blue eyes studied her, a question mark in them.

'I must have eaten too many *spanakopita*,' she expanded, referring to the mini filo-pastry pies stuffed with spinach and feta she'd taken a liking to. At her last count she'd eaten eight of them.

Her appetite had deserted her now. Her stomach felt so tight she doubted anything would go down.

'Would you like to go home?' Did he have to look so concerned when she was playing an imaginary game of marrying him off to someone else? A more suitable someone else.

'No, I'll be fine.' She forced a smile. 'Carry on with your conversation—I need to visit the bathroom.'

A few minutes later, after a sharp talking to herself in the privacy of a cubicle, she was washing her hands when Kerstin walked in.

The hot, burning feeling in Alessandra's brain immediately started up again.

'Is something the matter?' Kerstin asked.

Dio, now Christian's future imaginary wife was looking at her with concern.

'Not at all.' She forced another brittle smile.

A knowing expression came into Kerstin's eyes. 'My sister have a baby soon. You are the same, *ja*?'

'How can you tell?' Not only was she beautiful and intelligent but also psychic.

'My sister has had many babies,' Kerstin said with a laugh.

'Please don't tell anyone,' Alessandra beseeched. 'We're not ready for the world to know.'

'All those men chasing you with their cameras…is not nice.'

Beautiful, intelligent, psychic *and* empathetic?

Had a more perfect woman ever been born?

Kerstin looked openly at Alessandra's belly. 'I think you hide it for not much longer. Soon you will show.'

She stated the latter with such certainty that for a moment Alessandra was tempted to ask exactly how much later, right down to the hour.

Instead she fought back the sudden spring of hot tears welling in her eyes.

Kerstin saw them too and placed a comforting arm around her shoulder. 'Your hormone will feel better soon.'

Alessandra gave a shaky laugh, accepting the tissue Kerstin magically produced.

At least she had one advantage over the beautiful German woman. Her own English was much better.

'You're very quiet,' Christian said. They'd been in the car for ten minutes since leaving the embassy and Alessandra had spent the entire time gazing out of the window.

She'd become increasingly quiet since their wedding. It was only tonight, when she'd been her old, sociable self, that he'd realised quite how withdrawn she'd become.

Was he the cause? Had his mother's prediction already started coming true?

He wanted to reach out to her and find out what troubled her but didn't know how.

She raised a shoulder—the bare shoulder he'd spent the evening trying not to stare at. It had been an effort of epic proportions that had failed. That one naked limb had acted like a beacon to his eyes. The rest of her had acted as a beacon to his senses.

Holding her hand, feeling her warm, slender body brushing against him…

All the good work he'd done in recent weeks building a distance from her had crumbled.

Theos, he *ached* for her. Ached to possess her all over again with a burn so deep it was like fighting through treacle fog to remember why he had to keep his distance.

'Are you going to take Kerstin on?' she surprised him by asking.

'I haven't decided.' On paper Kerstin was an ideal candidate for his ever-growing empire, having the perfect qualifications and aptitude. Her father was a long-standing, respected member of the finance community. Yes, on paper she was ideal.

But he hadn't imagined the tension emanating from Alessandra when he'd been talking to her. He didn't want to do anything that would make his wife uncomfortable.

'I think you should.'

'What? Take her on?'

Alessandra turned her head to look at him. Her features were still, sombre, even. 'She's perfect.'

It was too dark to read her eyes.

'If I were to take her on in the capacity she and her father have requested, she will do a lot of travelling with us,' he stated carefully.

'She will do a lot of travelling with *you*,' Alessandra clarified. 'In another month or so, we can stop zigzagging the world together. Our schedules will thank us for it,' she added drily.

'Let us consider that in another month,' he said, his mouth filling with an acrid taste at the thought of travelling without Alessandra by his side. The acridness turned sweet as he thought of how travelling made her sleep. How many hours had he spent these past few weeks on his jet, taking advantage of her oblivion to study her sleeping form, reminding himself over and over why he could only look at her? *Theos*, he wanted to touch her so badly.

She raised her shoulders in a sign of nonchalance, a smile playing on her lips. It was too dark to tell if her eyes smiled too. 'I do think you should consider taking Kerstin on. Every billionaire should have a decent protégée.'

'I thought our child would be a good candidate as my protégé.'

'It will be a long time before our child is old enough for that. Consider Kerstin as practice.'

'That's not a bad idea,' he mused. Taking Kerstin under his wing would certainly strengthen the ties between himself and her father, Gregor, a very powerful man in the

European banking world. To take Kerstin under his wing would put Gregor in his debt. Debts of a personal nature were their own form of currency.

Under normal circumstances, he wouldn't hesitate. As Alessandra had pointed out, Kerstin was perfect. She was highly intelligent, multilingual and already had an excellent grasp of his business. His job would involve fine-tuning that grasp.

Moonlight seeped in the windows, the light bouncing off Alessandra's bare arm, giving it a silver glow.

That naked arm. How could any man concentrate on anything for longer than a few seconds with that in his eyeline?

All it made him think of was the rest of her naked too.

Do not think of her naked.

It was hard enough sitting in an enclosed cabin in the back of a car with her without bringing memories of her beautiful naked form to his mind's eye.

Self-enforced celibacy clearly did not agree with him.

How could any man cope with celibacy whilst living with such temptation?

He gave a silent prayer of thanks as his driver turned the car into the long driveway.

They were home.

In silence they entered the villa. The live-in staff had long since retired to their own quarters for the night.

Tiny nightlights glowed from the reception through to the living area and up the stairs, bathing Alessandra in a dim light that magnified her sultry beauty.

The ache in his groin, far from diminishing as he'd valiantly willed it to do in the car, increased, his arousal spreading from his loins...

That damn bare arm...

She paused at the bottom of the staircase to look at him. 'Thank you for a nice evening—'

'You have enjoyed yourself?' he cut in, delaying the time she would climb the stairs and head to her room.

'I wouldn't go that far,' she answered with a wry smile. 'It was hardly a night of music and dancing but it was a lot less stuffy than I expected.'

'That's good. I don't want you feeling uncomfortable when we go to these functions.'

She nodded, looking away. 'Well, good night.'

He inclined his head in return, fighting to keep his feet from crossing the marble floor to her. 'Good night.'

Holding on to the rail, she climbed the stairs and crossed the landing to her bedroom. Only when she reached her door did she turn her head to look back round and gaze down at him.

Then she disappeared inside her room, closing the door firmly behind her.

CHAPTER THIRTEEN

ALESSANDRA'S PHONE VIBRATED in her pocket. Grimacing, she fired off a couple more shots then carefully let go of her camera, which she kept around her neck. 'You can change into the next set now,' she said to the model standing in front of the white board, wearing nothing but a pair of skimpy knickers and bra.

She'd spent the past three days working on a shoot for a well-known lingerie brand. With a waist that seemed to be thickening by the day, spending days with semi-clad underwear models was not doing a great deal for her ego. Her pregnancy would soon be obvious to everyone.

She pulled her phone out, her heart skipping to see Christian's name flash up. She read his message:

Just landed. How long are you going to be?

She fired off a quick reply.

A couple of hours. Meet you at my apartment.

When they weren't physically together, most communication between them was done via messaging. She'd steered it that way. The first time he'd called after the embassy do a month ago, her hands had gone clammy just to see his name flash up in the screen. She'd stared at it until it had gone to voicemail, wiped her hands and written a quick message back, apologising that she'd missed his call. He'd messaged straight back. The next few times she'd done the same—avoided the call and then messaged him. Since then, he'd taken to messaging her without bothering to call. It made it easier for her. Having his rich tones play directly into her ear made more than her hands clammy.

Shoving her phone back in her pocket, she forced her concentration back to the skinny model, who'd changed into another lacy number with the help of an assistant, uncaring of who in the studio saw her fully naked.

'Left arm in an arc above your head please,' she said, lifting her camera back up to her face.

When the final frame was taken she packed her camera away, had a quick chat with her assistant, who was happy to pack everything else up, and left the building.

Soon she was nodding at the concierge and climbing the stairs to her apartment, grabbing the extra seconds gained by not using the lift to compose her thoughts and get her emotions in check.

Only three days apart, the longest since they'd been married.

She'd hoped the distance would be good for her.

Christian sat at the dining table, cradling a coffee and eating a bowl of pasta.

'I saved you some,' he said by way of greeting. 'I thought you might be getting hungry.'

Alessandra had taken her health seriously from the moment she'd realised she was pregnant but since she'd entered the second trimester, she'd become fanatical about her diet.

Food and calorie intake she could control and she did so rigidly, making sure everything she ingested was as nutritionally perfect for her baby as it could be.

It was the only thing she could control. Everything else seemed to be slipping through her fingers.

'How was Hong Kong?' she asked, walking over to her little office space in the corner which was a little too close to the dining table than she liked. Being in Milan made it harder for her to tune Christian out. The apartment she'd always thought of as wonderfully spacious seemed to shrink whenever he was there with her.

God knew she was trying to keep her distance from him, trying to be as unobtrusive as possible.

Thankfully her work load had increased. The days she wasn't on shoots were spent developing the results, spent in meetings with directors whether in person or via conference calls; being busy.

Conversely, Christian's workload had seemed to abate. He now made it home at a decent time most evenings.

Now it was Alessandra holing herself away, burying herself in work. Avoiding him as much as she could.

It was the only way she could keep herself sane.

She'd never imagined marriage would be so hard emotionally, a feeling exacerbated at Stefan's wedding to the beautiful Clio a couple of weeks ago. It had been a wonderful occasion but watching them exchange their vows had brought everything back about her own wedding day and the hope she'd been foolish enough to allow through.

She'd never imagined she would feel so emotional towards him.

'No problems,' he said. 'The contract was signed.'

'How did Kerstin get on?' Good. Her voice was normal as she spoke the German's name.

'Very well. She's staying in Hong Kong for a few days.'

Kerstin had started working for him a couple of weeks before. Right at the exact time as Alessandra's nutrition control had taken on a life of its own.

Typically of Christian, as soon as he'd decided on a course of action he implemented it immediately. He'd decided they should marry—a month later it was done. He'd decided to employ Kerstin—a fortnight later she was his new protégée.

'That's good.' Taking a seat at her desk, she fired up her laptop.

'Are you working?'

'We don't have to leave for half an hour.'

'I wanted to talk.'

'About?'

'We need to start looking for a proper house here in Milan. One we can raise a child in.'

She shrugged. 'Go ahead.'

'I've spoken to a property agent.'

'Naturally.'

'I've shortlisted a couple of homes we can look at after we've seen the obstetrician.'

She could feel his eyes upon her as she placed her memory stick into the side of the laptop. Her hands trembled.

'We need to get moving on this,' he continued. 'I've asked the agent to provide a valuation for this place too.'

She snapped her head round to stare at him. 'I don't want to sell it.'

His eyes narrowed. 'We agreed…'

'No, *you* agreed. I'll let you know when I'm ready.'

Christian counted to ten in his head, fighting to keep his features neutral.

He pushed his bowl across the table and got to his feet. 'We should leave now.'

'We've plenty of time.'

'It's always good to be ahead of the traffic.'

He didn't want to argue with her, especially not prior to their appointment with the obstetrician, but if he stayed another minute in this damned apartment he would go crazy.

He'd given her carte blanche to redecorate all his homes to her own taste so she would come to think of them as her homes too, and what did he get in return? Nothing.

This was Alessandra's apartment, not his. She had no intention of ever making it *theirs*.

It probably wouldn't bother him so much if not for the

fact that the distance between them now came from *her*, a state of affairs that had grown since the embassy function. Even at Stefan's wedding she'd been distant, when normally she thrived at social events.

If he'd thought she was happy with the status quo it wouldn't disturb him so much but, whenever he looked in her eyes, all he saw was unhappiness. When she was with him, she withdrew into herself. He was doing everything in his power to bring her spark back but she resisted at every turn. There were times when he thought he saw glimmers of it, generally if a magazine was released with her photography in it or if they passed a billboard she'd created—her face would light up like an enchanted child's.

It pained him to see her so withdrawn. It unnerved him. It reminded him too much of how things had been with his mother, when nothing he did made any difference to her mood.

Today, he was determined to get to the bottom of it—he would learn whatever it was troubling her and fix it, whether she wanted to talk about it or not.

She must have seen the no-nonsense light in his eyes for she pursed her lips together, slapped the lid of her laptop down and grabbed her handbag.

'Let's go, then.'

All was good with the obstetrician. Alessandra was healthy. Her blood pressure was normal. Their baby's heartbeat was strong. Yes. All was good. Christian always left those appointments feeling lighter.

The good feelings dissipated quicker than normal this time. They'd visited a number of homes in excellent parts of Milan, all large enough to raise a football team, if they so wished, with rooms to spare. Alessandra's interest had been minimal. Grudging.

It only added to his intuition that something was seriously wrong with her.

'Let's get something to eat,' he said after the third viewing. Maybe she was tired.

She didn't argue. 'Where do you want to go?'

He was about to suggest somewhere quiet where they could talk but had a flashback of their date and the trendy restaurant she had led them to. The lively atmosphere there had certainly played its part, along with the alcohol, in loosening them up. Maybe it would have the same effect on her again. 'Let's go to Nandini's.'

He shook the agent by the hand, promised to be in touch soon and waited for Alessandra to get into the back of the waiting car.

Instead she met his eye. 'Can we walk? It's not far.'

He gazed down at her feet. Only small heels on the black boots she wore. Almost practical. Ever the fashionista, though, she wore a black-and-white drop-waisted minidress. The gap between the hem of the dress and the top of her boots was tantalising him to the point of distraction.

If anyone looked closely or from a profile view, they would see the hint of a burgeoning bump beneath it.

They walked in silence down the bustling streets, past tourists and locals alike, gazing through windows at the glamorous wares of the now closed shops, and into a narrow street packed with cafés and bars. People sat on tables outside, smoking, eating, drinking and enjoying the weather.

When they'd dined in Nandini's that last time, it had been a Friday evening and the place had been full of people ready to let their hair down after a hard week of work.

Tonight, a Wednesday, it was much quieter. Even the music was on a lower setting, no longer loud enough to burst your eardrums.

A waiter took her jacket then showed them to their booth. She slid onto the long leather seat with obvious relief.

'Are your feet hurting?' he asked.

'A little.' She opened the menu. 'I've been on them all day.'

'Then why did you want to walk?' It made no sense to him. That was why he had a driver at his disposal at all times.

Alessandra shrugged. 'I like walking.' She didn't add that she couldn't face sitting in the back of the car with him any more.

She'd felt his irritation at her attitude to the beautiful homes they'd been shown round. And they *were* beautiful, palatial in size and structure, the kind of homes any little girl dreaming of being a princess would love to live in. But those little girls also dreamt of living in their palatial homes with their princes, not with the man who'd married them so he could have legal rights to their child.

It wasn't that she worried he would bawl her out for her ungrateful attitude—God alone knew, she wished she'd been blessed with acting genes so she could fake pleasure for him—because he didn't bawl her out over *anything*. She knew when she displeased him, though. He might not verbalise it, keeping his anger contained within him, but it was there in his eyes and the tone of his voice when he wasn't quick enough to curb it.

She wished he *would* bawl her out. At least it would show he felt something for her, that she was worth expending some hot air arguing with.

The main reason she hadn't wanted to sit in the back of the car with him was because spending time alone with him had the effect of turbo-charging her emotions. It would be easier to contain if it were just sexual feelings but it ran so much deeper than that. Whenever they listened to their baby's heartbeat, she longed to reach out to him and clasp his hand, to unite for those few magical seconds.

Sitting alone in the back of the car with him, his hard, warm body so close…

She wanted to reach out and grab more than his hand. She wanted to climb onto his lap and nuzzle into that strong neck that smelled so good, taste the smooth skin…

Far from the distance she'd imposed lessening these long-ings, it had only increased them. She needed proper physical distance, and not just emotional distance, because keeping only an emotional distance wasn't working. The three days apart they'd just had were nothing. Three months might do the trick.

At least tomorrow she had an overnight trip to London without him.

They ordered their meals and drinks, both opting to go straight into the main course. While they waited, they chewed on breadsticks and made idle small talk.

She remembered that first date, here in this restaurant. They'd had to sit close to each other to make themselves heard. They'd talked about anything and everything, their conversation easy.

Tonight it felt as if she were dragging barbed wire from her throat.

As was normal, Christian's phone vibrated at regular intervals.

'You should answer it,' she said upon the fourth vibration.

He shrugged. 'Whoever it is can wait.'

'It might be important.'

His eyes fixed on hers. '*This* is important.'

'*Si*, food is very important,' she answered, as if making light of it could evaporate the growing tension.

A bowl of butternut squash and spinach ravioli with strips of crispy pancetta and flakes of parmesan was placed before her. She didn't know which dish she liked the look of more, hers or Christian's *cotoletta alla Milanese* which looked equally divine.

'Would you like to try some?' He held up his fork, a good helping of breaded cutlet on it.

'No, no, you eat it.' Quickly she forked a delicate raviolo into her mouth, dropping her eyes away from his thought-ful expression.

'Are you still travelling to Tokyo next week?' he asked,

referring to a fashion shoot she'd been booked for for one of Japan's up-and-coming fashion houses. She was looking forward to the trip. Five whole days away from him.

'I was thinking I'd meet up with you there,' he added. 'I've some clients in Tokyo I need to touch base with.'

'Don't rearrange your schedule on my behalf.' Never mind the distance she wanted to take advantage of, he'd made enough sacrifices for her. If all his sacrifices had been purely for the baby's sake, she could have lived with it. But they weren't. He'd made sacrifices for her too. The more she thought of them all, the more nauseous it made her feel.

'I want to,' he said, his voice dropping.

'I think the press are convinced about our marriage now,' she said, keeping her attention firmly on the bowl of food before her. 'I haven't been stalked for days.'

'I'm surprised they haven't picked up on the pregnancy yet.'

'So am I.' It was only a matter of time.

'I will still travel with you. I don't like the thought of you being away for a week without me.'

'It's only five days, not a week,' she corrected. 'I've been travelling with my job since I was eighteen. I'm perfectly capable of looking after myself.'

'You weren't my wife then. Is there something wrong with me wanting to spend time with you?'

Yes, she wanted to scream. There was everything wrong with it. Every minute they spent together made her heart hurt even more that their marriage could never be real, that the love she felt for him could never be reciprocated...

Love?

Where had that thought sprung from?

Amore?

Frantically she fought with herself to deny it, to refute the obvious.

Dear God, had she really fallen in love with her husband?

No. She couldn't be that foolish. She wouldn't be.

In a flash, she remembered the first time she'd seen him, sitting with the rest of the Brat Pack in her brother's den, drinking beer and watching football.

Little Alessandra had taken one look at the blond Adonis and immediately pictured him on a white horse coming to rescue her from the tower where the evil witch held her.

A young girl's crush, that was all it had been. She'd had plenty of them: pop stars, film stars—her bedroom walls had been littered with posters of her favourites. Christian had seemed as remote to her young self as they had been.

Whenever she'd studied the tabloids with stories and pictures of him, and whoever was the latest woman hanging off his arm, she'd felt a funny tugging deep in the pit of her belly. She'd never understood the feeling or what it meant. But now she did understand it.

Her heart had belonged to Christian from that first look.

She'd never imagined any of the pop stars or film stars rescuing her on a white steed. Only Christian.

He hadn't rescued her. He hadn't saved her. All he'd done was unlock her heart.

She'd always wondered how his women could swallow his lies, had assumed he *must* have lied to them to get so many of them into his bed.

He didn't lie. He didn't need to. Women wanted him regardless. *She* wanted him regardless.

She always had.

'Alessandra?'

She darted her eyes to him.

'Is something the matter? You've gone very pale.'

She shook her head with vigour, part in denial and part to clear the burn scratching the back of her retinas. 'Will Kerstin come to Tokyo with us?'

'I don't know. I haven't thought about it.'

'Have you slept with her yet?' The question escaped before she could contain it.

'*Ochi!* What kind of question is that?'

'An obvious one.'

'No, I have not slept with Kerstin, and I am insulted you would think I have.'

'Don't be insulted. It's only a matter of time.'

A dangerous silence followed.

When she looked at him, Christian's eyes had darkened and fixed on her, a pulse throbbing at the junction where his earlobe met his jaw.

Not taking his eyes from her face, he put his knife and fork together on his half-eaten meal and dabbed at his mouth with his napkin, which he then screwed into a ball and released onto his plate.

'Get your things together,' he said, rising to his feet and throwing some euros onto the table. 'We're leaving. I'll wait outside for you.'

She watched him retreat, her heart hammering so hard she could feel the beats in her mouth.

Even her legs were shaking, her whole body one mass vibration of cold fear and misery.

Their waiter appeared with her jacket. 'Is something wrong with your meal?' he asked anxiously.

'No, it's delicious. My husband's remembered an appointment, that's all.'

As promised, Christian stood outside on the pavement with his arms folded.

His car pulled up in front of them. Christian didn't wait for the driver to get out, opening the back door himself and indicating for Alessandra to get in.

She waited until the car was in motion before attempting to apologise. 'I'm sorry if I…'

'I am not prepared to have this discussion in the back of a car,' he said grimly.

'But…'

'Ochi!' he said with such finality she clamped her lips together lest she say anything else.

CHAPTER FOURTEEN

ONCE INSIDE THE APARTMENT, Alessandra hurried to hang up her jacket and remove her boots. 'I'm going to make myself a camomile tea. Do you want anything?'

'No.' Christian's answer was curt. She could feel his anger rippling beneath the surface, just as it had on the drive back from the restaurant when he'd sat beside her with arms folded so tightly she could see the muscles bunched beneath his shirt.

Now his hands were rammed firmly into his pockets.

She headed straight for the kitchen area and with shaking hands filled the kettle. Camomile tea, while not the most palatable of hot drinks, was famed for its calming abilities. Maybe it would help soothe the tumult of emotions shredding her.

Dio l'aiuti, she loved him.

'I'm struggling to understand some things,' Christian said in a tone calm and reasonable. She could hear the undercurrent of wrath beneath it, though. 'I took Kerstin on at your behest.'

Keeping her back to him, she took a teabag from the container. 'You wanted her anyway.' How could he not? Kerstin was *perfect*. She was everything that she, Alessandra, was not. For a start, Kerstin would never be so careless about contraception. If Christian was to have a family with the German woman it would be because they both chose it and not out of a sense of duty.

'Not in the way you're implying.'

'You should.'

'What should I want? To *sleep* with her?'

Did he really expect her to believe his incredulity? This from the man who hadn't touched her, his wife, since the night they'd exchanged their vows. He hadn't laid a single finger on her.

'Why not? She's a beautiful, intelligent woman.'

'Yes,' he agreed. 'That doesn't mean I want to have sex with her.'

'Of course you do. She's exactly your type, all long legs and blonde hair.' Deliberately, she tossed her hair back and flashed a smile. *Hold it together, Alessandra, please; just a few more minutes, keep it together, then this conversation will be over and you can breathe again.* Her fingers dug into the palm of her hands so tightly she could feel her nails pierce the skin. 'Honestly, Christian, I think you're mad for *not* wanting to sleep with her. She's perfect for you.'

'I'm married to *you*. I chose *you*.'

His words cut through her, slicing through her heart and deep into her marrow.

Lies. Lies. Lies.

'You chose me?' she asked slowly, her ears ringing, her heart thundering so hard it reverberated through her skin.

'You know I did. I made my vows to *you*.'

Alessandra twisted round so quickly Christian could have sworn she'd performed a pirouette.

The smile she'd been wearing since their return to the apartment had been nothing but a mask that now ripped away to reveal the savagery beneath the surface.

'You *chose* me?'

'Alessandra...'

'You chose me?' Her husky voice rose with every syllable. Before he knew what was happening, she'd grabbed her cup and thrown it at the far wall. White china exploded upon impact, large chunks flying onto the wooden floor, smaller shards landing like darts around the larger pieces.

'What the...?'

'You didn't *choose* me. You didn't choose to be my husband; you chose to be a father.' Her face was dark with colour, her eyes wild, feral.

He strove for composure. '*Parakalo*. Please, *agapi mou*, I need you to calm down.'

'Do *not* call me that. Whatever it means, *you* don't mean it.'

'It means—'

'I don't care what it means!' Her voice had risen to a scream. 'You want me to calm down? Don't you like me throwing cups? Well, how about plates? Is that what Greek housewives do when their husbands don't want them? Do they throw plates?'

The bowl of pasta Christian had been eating out of earlier, which had been left in the sink, went flying the same way as the cup. Without pausing for breath, she swung open the door of the cupboard that contained all the crockery.

'Alessandra, that's enough,' he commanded.

'Don't tell me what's enough.'

He lunged for her before she could throw the plate she'd taken hold of, grabbing her wrist with one hand and relieving her of the plate with the other. 'I said that's enough.'

Heart pounding, blood surging with adrenaline, he kicked the cupboard door shut, flung the plate on the work surface then pressed her against it, using his strength and height to trap her.

She pushed against him furiously, bucking. '*Bastardo!* Let me go.'

'I will let you go when you've calmed down.'

'I am calm!' she shouted.

'Listen to me,' he said, trapping her face in his hands, forcing her to look at him. 'I do not want to sleep with Kerstin. The only woman I want to sleep with is you.'

Her eyes raged with so many emotions he didn't know where to begin counting them. '*Bugiardo*. Liar.'

'When have I ever lied to you? Name one instance.'

'I...' Her voice trailed off, became smaller. 'You don't want me. You've rejected me since we married.'

'Not want you? Can you not feel how turned on I am?' He laughed cynically. As if she could fail to feel his erection pressed against her abdomen.

That was what happened when you were starved for the woman you wanted more than you'd thought humanly possible. One touch and the body turned to lava, no matter how inappropriate the situation or how vainly you tried to control it.

'I thought I was doing the right thing.'

Her plump lips parted, closed then parted again. 'Why?'

The solitary word came out as a breathless rush, but air did escape, warm, sweet air that filled his nostrils and penetrated down, burrowing through his skin, his veins, down into his arteries and pumping through him in a great rush of need.

Why? All he saw were those lips, luscious invitations to sin.

Why?

He no longer knew. All he knew for certain in that moment was that if he didn't feel those plump lips on his again he would never know the answer to anything.

He crushed his mouth to hers.

There was no resistance.

A tiny, guttural noise came from her throat and she melted into him, weaving her arms around his neck, her nails scraping the nape of his neck, her mouth moving beneath his as she kissed him back, kissing him with a violence that made the heat deep within him enflame and his heart beat like a thousand drums had been let loose within him.

Still devouring her with his mouth, he raised her onto the work surface, her legs parting to wrap around his waist.

Her hands were everywhere, yanking at his shirt to loosen it from his trousers and burrowing up, her small fingers sweeping up his chest, marking him with her heat.

Theos, but she felt amazing.

He found the zip of her dress, was about to tug it down, when Alessandra suddenly wrenched her mouth away from his, pressed a hand to his chest and pushed.

'No,' she said, her tone biting. 'Do not try and distract me by trying to have sex with me. I am not a toy to be played with and then discarded.' She slid down onto the floor and glared at him. Her chest heaved. 'You were going to tell me why you've rejected me since our wedding night.'

Christian raked a hand through his hair, trying valiantly to stem the pumping of his blood. Her taste was there on his tongue, under his nose.

Theos, he wanted to be inside her.

Taking deep breaths, he turned away to rummage through a cupboard. Weeks ago she'd brought a bottle of bourbon to keep in her apartment for him, a gesture that had touched him. A gesture he was now thankful for as a method of numbing his heightened body a fraction.

He'd been on the brink of losing his control with her. Again.

He poured himself a measure and downed it before facing her.

She leant back against the work surface, arms folded across her chest.

This was what he'd wanted just ten minutes ago. For them to talk. For her to tell him what was troubling her. Was it really the lack of sex within their marriage that had caused it? Or something deeper?

What he hadn't expected or wanted was for her to demand the conversation start with him.

'We married for one reason and one reason only,' he reminded her.

'Our baby,' she supplied flatly.

'Yes. For our baby. It's the only reason we married. We did not marry for ourselves. I became concerned that your feelings for me had developed beyond mere convenience.'

Her eyebrows shot upwards. 'You were concerned about my *feelings*?'

'Alessandra…you are an incredibly sexy woman. I would have shared your bed every night since our wedding but I didn't want you mistaking good sex for real emotions.'

'Why would you have thought that? Because I'm a woman and incapable of separating my emotions?'

'No.' It was the light and hope in her eyes when she'd looked at him at their wedding. It was the desolation he'd caught glimpses of these past few weeks.

Alessandra rolled her eyes but there was a definite tremor in her voice. 'And you wonder why I don't want to sell my apartment? Where else am I supposed to go when our marriage falls apart?'

'That is not going to happen. There is no reason for us to fall apart provided we stick to our original agreement.'

'And what if our original agreement doesn't suit me any more?'

A cold chill swept up his spine.

'This is my *home*,' she continued. 'You talk about wanting to leave a legacy for our child? Well, this place is *my* legacy. It's the only thing that's all mine, that I can leave. I'm not prepared to give it up for a man who can't commit to a real marriage.'

'We have a real marriage. Real to us. We both meant our vows.'

'No, we do *not*. Our marriage is no more real than a winged unicorn.'

'Where is all this coming from?' he demanded. The thumping in his ribs no longer had any connection to desire or lust. Fear knotted in his guts but he knew not what the fear was of. 'You knew the score from the start—it's what we agreed on. It's what we both wanted.'

'But now I want something else. I want something more.' Alessandra had seen the way Rocco and Olivia were together. If her brother could find love and be happy...

She had found love too. The problem was she had found it with her husband.

'More? What kind of *more*?' He spoke as if it were a dirty word.

'I want *everything*. I want a husband to sleep with every night, not just for sex but to curl up to. I want to wake up every morning and know that the man I love loves me in return and doesn't regard me as a means to an end. I want it all.'

Christian looked as if he'd been sucker-punched. 'Have you met someone else—is that what all this is about?'

'No.' She stared at him, willing him to understand.

She couldn't hide any more. This was the point of no return. Time for her to lay her cards on the table and see where it took them, for good or ill. 'There is only you.'

She watched as his powerful body froze, the only movement coming from his blue eyes which darkened and pulsed, the look in them as if he were seeing her for the very first time.

'Please, say something,' she beseeched.

'For the love of God—Alessandra, that is not what our marriage is about.'

Her heart lurching so violently she feared she would be sick, she brushed past him, reached for the bottle of bourbon, poured a measure then thrust the glass into his hand.

After he'd downed it and slammed the glass on the work surface, she stood before him and gazed right into his eyes. 'Can you ever love me?'

His face went so white it would have been comical had the situation not been so serious.

'Neither of us believe in love. It's what makes us so compatible.'

How she wished she could have a proper drink too. Just as well she couldn't—the aroma of bourbon playing under her nose made her belly recoil. Or was that terror of where this conversation was going?

Retreat wasn't an option. Not any more. Their time had come.

'This is all your fault,' she said starkly, holding his eyes, refusing to let their hold drop. 'When we married, all I felt towards you was a severe degree of lust. If we'd kept it at sex, I probably would have been fine—lust is intransigent. It would have fizzled out eventually.' But as she spoke the words, she realised them to be a lie. She'd already been in love with him.

'Instead, you withdrew physically,' she continued. 'But you've been…good to me. You look out for me but don't try and inhibit or stifle me. You're supportive and enthusiastic. You made me trust you.'

Something flickered in his eyes at her utterance of the word *trust*. She hardly believed it herself but it was the truth. Somewhere along the line she had begun to trust him. She'd fought it and fought it but it had crept up on her all the same. Just as her love for him had.

'If I'm such a good guy then what is the problem here?'

'This pregnancy has changed me. *You've* changed me. I deserve love and all that it can give. And so do you.'

'Do you hear what you're saying?' he asked roughly, his eyes wild as he took a step back. 'All this crap about love when we both know all it does is destroy people.'

'*No, it does not!* Love only destroys if the person allows it. My father allowed it and so did your mother. We don't have to be like them.'

'You're right—we don't. And we won't. People who take the risk are weak and foolish and I am neither of those things. I thought you were better than that too.'

'Then I must be weak and stupid.'

'I can't be the man you think you want,' he warned. 'I have no capacity to love and, even if I did, I've grown up seeing how dangerous it can be and the knock-on effects it has on everyone else.

'Where are you going?' he demanded when she suddenly turned away and headed for her bedroom.

'To pack.'

'For where?'

'London.'

'Your flight doesn't leave until the morning.'

'I'll see if I can get a sooner one.' She flung her wardrobe doors open, pulled out her small carry-on case and placed it on the bed.

He didn't love her.

He would never love her. He wouldn't even try.

'Can you call me a cab, please?'

'You're not going anywhere. Not until we've talked this through.'

'We're talking it through right now.' She selected some clothes and placed them neatly in the case, then dug her phone from her pocket and pressed the app that would send a taxi straight to the apartment building. 'We can stay married until the baby is born, so you can have the legal rights you want, and then we can divorce. I'm sure we can find an amicable solution to custody—'

She started to zip her case but Christian wrenched it from her, whipping it away and hurtling it to the floor with a slam. She didn't think she had ever seen him so angry. Not that *anger* was the correct word for the wildness surrounding him.

She could hardly blame him. She was destroying the future they had planned. But that had been a future before she'd fallen in love with him.

He gripped her shoulders. 'We made a promise to each

other and our child to be a family. You're breaking that promise. I will not agree to any divorce.'

'Why are you being so unreasonable?' she demanded, her own temper rising back up. 'You're still going to get what you want. You're still going to be a father.'

His hands slid off her shoulders and balled into fists. 'Why are you doing this?'

Because I love you. And I know you will never fall in love with me. And to continue living with you knowing I will never have your love will eventually destroy me just as it destroyed your mother and my father. But not to their extent. Never to their extent. Our child will never suffer for it, I swear.

But the words went unsaid. If she thought for a second there was a chance that in the future his feelings could develop as hers had, she would say them.

What kind of idiot fell in love with a man incapable of returning it?

Had she been fool enough to hope his feelings would change as hers had? *No*, she hadn't been stupid enough to think that. But still she'd fallen for him.

'What do you think the press are going to say when they learn our marriage barely lasted two months?' he asked, his voice cold and terse.

'Let them think and write what they like. I have finally grown an immunity to them.' Three months ago, the thought of them crucifying her for the whole of Italy's delectation had made her want to vomit. Now...let them write what they liked. The fear she had felt of the press since she'd been seventeen had gone. She didn't know when it had happened, only that it had.

She was an adult. *She* controlled her life, not the press.

'And what about when our child grows up and reads about it?' he snarled.

'Then we will tell our child the truth. There's been enough lies.'

Every feature on his face was taut but his eyes were hard. 'If you're so determined to go, then go. Take the time to think. When you get back we can discuss this like rational adults and find a way to thrash out a marriage that suits us both.'

'There's no way thrashing anything out will change my mind. We're over.'

He got back to his feet and strolled past her and into the spare room. *His* room. He'd never wanted to share hers. He shut the door behind him with a slam.

Blinking back tears which served no useful purpose other than to blind her, Alessandra scraped her hair into a tight ponytail, carried her suitcase into the living area and quickly gathered her work stuff together.

Dio, Dio, Dio, get me out of here before he comes back out. Please, before my strength deserts me and I throw myself at his feet and beg for his love.

She left the building and walked straight into a media scrum.

Dozens of paparazzi swarmed her, closing in, leaving her trapped between them and the door she had already closed.

'Alessandra, when is the baby due?'

'Alessandra, how do you feel about becoming a mother?'

'Alessandra, was the baby planned?'

She never got the chance even to think of a response or a way to escape. The door behind her flew open with such force she lost her footing. Were it not for the strong arms there to catch her, she would surely have fallen. As it was, Christian gathered her to him, protecting her with his strength, and marched her and her luggage deftly through the mob and into the back of the waiting cab.

Her last glimpse of him was when he tapped the top of the car to indicate the driver should leave, turned on his heel and marched back through the swarm, parting it as if he were Moses and they were the Red Sea.

* * *

Christian poured himself another bourbon.

He should check himself into a hotel and out of Alessandra's apartment. She'd spelt out in no uncertain terms that this was her home. Not theirs. His homes weren't enough for her.

He wasn't enough.

Did it really matter if they divorced? He'd still have his legal rights with regard to their baby. He would still be a father. Alessandra would never deny him access; that he knew with as deep a certainty as he knew anything. She would do the right thing by all of them.

So why did it feel as if his world had toppled upside down?

And why did he feel so full and nauseous?

He finished his drink and poured another. The bottle was now empty.

Yes. Time to leave.

The freedom and space he'd always cherished so much but had gladly sacrificed for his unborn baby was his again to do with as he pleased.

Under normal circumstances he would hunt down Rocco, Stefan or Zayed and talk them into a night out. But these weren't normal circumstances. Not for any of them. Rocco would sooner spit on him than see him. Stefan had recently shocked them all by marrying Clio—he hadn't seen that coming—while Zayed was spending increasing time in Gazbiyaa, preparing to take over the throne.

All their lives were changing.

He went to grab his briefcase, which he'd left by Alessandra's corner office. Instead of picking it up and leaving, he found himself sitting at her desk, flipping through the portfolios of her work.

As much as he admired all her work, it was their wedding album he spent the most time looking through. These were the unofficial ones taken by Alessandra, a timeline from the start of their wedding week, when their first guests had arrived, right up to the moment they'd got on the dance floor for the Kalamatianos. His lips quirked to see a picture of a particularly beautiful but notoriously moody actress smiling for the camera with something black in her teeth.

His heart jolted when he turned the page over to find a montage of photos of the same face. All different angles, all different moods: some smiling, others distant, a couple frowning... One in particular held his attention. The face was staring directly into the camera, a wide, relaxed grin on the face, a soft yet suggestive look in the eyes, as if the person wanted nothing more than to take the photographer to a private room and make love to them.

Not have sex.

Make love.

The subject of the photographs was him.

Christian pulled up outside Villa Mondelli. Turning off the engine, he stared at it in the same way he had stared at it as a poor eighteen-year-old boy on the cusp of becoming a man. He'd seen lavish splendour before, had walked past the mansions in the most affluent parts of Athens vowing that, one day, he too would live in a home like these. Villa Mondelli was the first of that particular type he'd actually been invited into. Not only invited to cross the threshold but to stay there for a week—and many more weeks later on throughout his life, but of course at the time he wasn't to know that. The Mondellis had welcomed him, Stefan and Zayed into their home and treated him *as if he were their equal*, as if he were more than a dirt-poor gutter rat raised by a single woman with callused hands.

Now, fourteen years later, with homes every bit as opulent as the villa and wealth beyond his dreams, he still felt that same tug in his heart. But this tug was for Alessandra.

When he'd first visited he'd been full of envy for the

people who lived there, brought up with such easy wealth. Or so it had seemed to his eyes.

Alessandra had lived in this house almost her whole life, brought here when her father had lost his own house and abdicated responsibility for his children onto his own father. Alessandra had been a baby. She'd grown up feeling responsible for her mother's death, shunned by her father and raised by an often austere man who'd thought his child-rearing days long finished with. Her only source of love had been her older brother whom, despite all her grumbles at his interfering, she worshipped. For much of Alessandra's life in this home, that same brother had been absent, away in the US studying, graduating to become a workaholic.

More often than not, her only company in this vast house were the staff, people sharing a roof with her because they were paid to.

All the envy he'd felt fourteen years ago had gone, replaced with the sad knowledge that even the richest of people could lead the poorest of lives.

Look at him. He, Christian Markos, was now regarded as one of the richest men in the world. He had all the wealth and all the trappings such wealth brought, but in his heart he was still poor.

It was only now, at the age of thirty-two, that he'd discovered the path to true richness.

He hadn't even placed a foot on the bottom step when Rocco answered the door.

Christian looked up at him. 'I'm here to see Alessandra.' He hadn't seen her in a fortnight. They'd exchanged a couple of text messages. She'd agreed to meet him in Milan for her next obstetrician appointment, but until then she wanted some space.

He'd needed space too, to get his head together. To get his heart together.

Rocco looked him up and down. 'And what if she doesn't want to see you?'

'Has she said that?' A puff of relief escaped from him. His hunch had been right. For all Alessandra's proclamations that she'd rather live in a convent than stay with her brother, this was the first place Christian had looked when she'd failed to return to her apartment after her Tokyo trip.

He'd been there waiting for her.

A long pause. 'No. She doesn't need to.' Rocco made no effort to move.

'Either let me in or I let myself in.'

Now Rocco's face did show some animation, a snarl flitting over it. 'You enter my home when *I* say you do.'

Christian had had enough. He was there to see his wife, not debase himself by getting into a fight with his brother-in-law. Raising himself to his full height, he climbed the steps and stood eye to eye with him. 'I know Alessandra is your sister but she is *my* wife and the baby she is carrying in her womb is mine—*mine*—and I will fight with every breath in my body to protect them. I am going to see her whether you like it or not, so, are you going to let me the easy way or the hard way?'

He couldn't believe it had come to this, two old friends squaring up to each other. If he wasn't so heartsick about his wife there would be some room in his heart to mourn the death of a friendship he'd valued so highly and had hoped, until this precise moment, could one day be mended.

To his surprise, Rocco's stance relaxed a fraction. He looked him over, nodding slowly, his eyes thawing. 'She's in the summer room.'

Christian waited for the catch. When no catch seemed forthcoming, he headed off in the direction he remembered.

'Memento vivere,' Rocco called out.

The words made him pause in his tracks. He turned his head and supplied, 'Remember to live.'

Finally a smile attached itself to Rocco's face. 'The best life to live is with the woman you love, *si*?'

He agreed with a nod. 'Living without the woman you love is no life.'

Rocco laughed. 'My sister is going to run rings around you.'

'She already is.' As quickly as Christian's cheeks raised up into a quick grin, he felt a fragmented piece of him re-attach itself.

Now to find his wife and see if all the other broken pieces could be fixed too.

He found her curled up on the daybed, a cross between a *chaise longue* and a sofa, reading a glossy magazine. Beneath the simple black dress she wore, he could see the definite rounding of her belly, safely protecting their baby in its confines.

He would give his life to keep Alessandra and their baby safe from harm.

She glanced up, her eyes widening to see him there. 'Christian.' Her voice sounded hoarse. 'What are you doing here?'

'I've come to bring you home.'

She raised a brow. 'Home?'

'Home. With me. Where you belong.'

Sighing, she put the magazine down and swung her legs round, dipping her head. 'I told you I wanted some space.' Her words were muffled behind the sheath of her hair that had fallen in front of her face.

'You've had enough space from me to last you forever.'

'Nothing's changed…'

'Everything's changed.' Crouching down on his haunches before her, he gently swiped her hair away and placed a finger under her chin.

Her gaze met his for a brief moment, honeyed eyes wide with pain.

'Answer me one question. Do you love me?'

'Are you trying to humiliate me? Is that why you've come here?'

'I found the pictures you took of me.'

Her mouth curled in bitterness. 'Then you already know the answer.'

'I want to hear it from your lips.'

'Why? Let me have *some* dignity, please.'

'Because I've never heard the words before.'

A glimmer of shock passed over her. She sat up straight and looked at him—really looked at him. 'Never?'

'Never.' Not from his mother. Not from any of the scores of women he'd had throughout the years, which wasn't surprising, considering he would leave before the beds had cooled. 'Please, *agapi mou*, if the words are true then say them.'

She'd lost so much colour he feared she would faint. But that was not Alessandra's style. This was not a woman who wilted under pressure. Her lips clamped together, her eyes brimming with tears, he watched her fight to stop from falling.

'Shall I make it easy for you?' he said quietly. 'How about if I were to tell you that I love you? Would that make it easier for you to say the words?'

Her chest hitched as she gave a sharp nod, still not speaking.

'I love you.'

One solitary tear did break free, trickling down her cheek. He wiped it with his thumb.

'I've spent many hours these past couple of weeks looking at those photos you took of me. You see something in me no one else can. The thing I never wanted you or anyone to see.'

'What thing?' she whispered.

'The man inside. The gutter rat who grew up feeling dirty and unworthy and unlovable.'

'You're *not*…'

He placed a finger to her lips, though the sound of her outrage warmed the coldness inside him. 'I've been fighting to stop you getting too close since before our wedding night because I knew you were so near to seeing what's inside me. I thought it would repel you as it does my mother. I knew when you spoke of love in our apartment what you were trying to tell me, but I refused to listen. I didn't think I deserved your love. I was scared that to fall in love with you would be to destroy you—and you, Alessandra Mondelli, whom I so wish would be Alessandra Markos, are the most precious person in the world to me. Without you, I am nothing. I accept that I'm not good enough for you...'

'Will you *stop* saying that?' She dug her nails into his skin. 'You are not a gutter rat. You are...*everything*. Everything you've achieved with your life, everything you've done... If anyone's undeserving, it's me.'

'To me, you are a princess. You deserve all the richness this world can bring, *agapi mou*, and I will do everything in my power to give it to you—if you'll let me. I love you and I don't want to live another day without you.'

Alessandra felt a whoosh of air leave her body. He loved her?

He loved her?

He loved her!

He placed her hands to his chest. She could feel his heartbeat thrumming wildly beneath his shirt. 'I thought I could compartmentalise our marriage in the same way I compartmentalise my relationship with my mother. She lives in a corner of my life, safely hidden away from everyone so she cannot hurt me or anyone else. I told myself I would marry you to become a father and not a husband but I was wrong—I wanted you as much as the baby and was desperate to make you mine. I tried to compartmentalise you, not because I was scared of hurting you, but because deep down I knew *you* had the power to hurt *me*.'

'I have the power to hurt you?' she whispered, gazing at the man she loved so much.

'More than you could ever know. Throughout my childhood I wanted nothing more than to make my mother proud and for her to love me. The power she had over me, the power to hurt me… I swore no one else would ever have that power. But then you came into my life and nestled straight into my heart and there was nothing I could do to stop it. I used to fear that falling in love with someone would curse them, make them turn into her. But you could never be like her. She took her heartbreak and bitterness out on me. You would never do that to our child. There hasn't been anyone else since that first night we had and I know there never will be. Only you.'

He brushed a thumb over her lips. 'I was desperate for you to sell your apartment, not because I thought it made sense in any way but because I felt excluded from it.' He allowed himself a crooked smile. 'I was jealous of an apartment.'

She leaned forward and rubbed the tip of her nose to his, unable to believe this was really happening.

From feeling as if she would never feel the sun on her face again she could feel its beams spread through her.

He loved her!

'I was also afraid that if you had a bolt hole to escape to you would be more tempted to use it,' he continued. 'I should have guessed you would use this place as your bolt hole.'

'I couldn't face being in the apartment without you,' she confessed. 'So I turned up at Rocco's door claiming asylum.'

He laughed. 'He must have been delighted to know we'd fallen apart.'

'No,' she said thoughtfully. 'When he realised I was actually in love with you, the chip he'd been carrying went. He became my brother again.'

His lips were so close to hers. She craned her neck forward, suddenly desperate to feel them upon her, to be cradled in his embrace but he gripped her neck at the side, gently but with enough firmness to stop her moving.

'So, you do love me?' For the first time she saw his vulnerability.

'Yes. I love you. With everything I have.'

She'd hardly finished speaking before his mouth crushed hers, his essence filling her with such sweetness the tears really did fall.

'Oh, my love,' he said, wiping her tears away. 'I never want to see you cry.'

'They're happy tears,' she said with a sniff. 'You're not the only one who's always felt unworthy—I've spent my whole life feeling like a poisoned chalice, put on Earth to destroy anyone who gets close to me.' She stroked his cheek. 'I wanted you to employ Kerstin because I thought she was the perfect woman for you.'

Incredulity spread over his face. 'You were trying to *engineer* me being with her?'

'I thought she could make you happy. You wouldn't have to compromise your time or sacrifice…'

Her words were cut off by a hard, possessive kiss.

'You're perfect for me,' he said when he pulled away, cradling her cheeks to gaze into her eyes. 'Just you. We've both made sacrifices. I would make them again a thousand times over.' He bowed his head and brushed his lips against hers. 'I love you. You're my world.'

'And you're my everything,' she answered softly.

For the first time Alessandra felt a tinge of sympathy for her father, who had gone so off the rails when he'd lost the love of his life. After a fortnight without Christian, she had a little insight into what he must have gone through. She would never be able to forgive him, not for the way his actions had so hurt Rocco—and they had hurt her brother more than her because Rocco remembered a time when their father was a loving man who had adored his small family—but a whole chunk of the bitterness she felt towards him fell away.

'I love you, Christian.'

'Always.'

'Always.'

And they did.

EPILOGUE

'IT'S A GIRL!'

Alessandra didn't know who was the most excited at the giving of the news—the obstetrician or her husband, who announced it in unison while the midwife held the baby—her daughter—up for a few brief seconds before the cord was cut and they whisked her away to clean her up

Christian was back at the top of the table, bed or whatever it was she was laid upon, raining kisses all over her face, muttering prayers and thanks in Greek, English, Japanese, Cantonese and any other language he could conjure.

'You are wonderful,' he said into her ear in a reverential fashion.

'You're pretty wonderful yourself.' She laughed, stroking his hair.

It felt good to laugh.

It felt even better when they placed her daughter on her, allowing a little skin-on-skin time before whisking her back off for swaddling.

'Look in my bag,' she whispered.

'Why?'

'Just look. There's an envelope in the side pocket.'

Doing as he was bid, Christian tore the envelope open and studied the document inside.

After long moments he faced her, his eyes brimming with so much emotion it was like looking into an overflowing bucket.

'Thank you, *Kiria* Markos.'

'You're welcome *Kyrios* Markos.'

It was a document making official Alessandra's name change from Mondelli to Markos.

This was her gift to him, her statement to them both as much as to the world that they were a unit. Their love was for keeps. Cut one and both would bleed. Their baby made them a family. She wanted their little family all to have the same name.

'There is one little problem.'

'Oh?'

He reached into his back pocket and pulled out an envelope.

Inside was a document making official Christian's name from Markos to Mondelli.

Thus, when their swaddled baby was handed to them properly to begin their journey as a family, the first thing their daughter heard was the sound of her parents' laughter.

As beginnings went, it couldn't be bettered.

'Three, two, one, drink!'

In unison, Christian and Rocco raised their glasses to their mouths and downed their shots.

'To Letizia Markos,' said Rocco, picking up his next shot.

'To my beautiful baby,' Christian agreed. 'And to my beautiful wife.'

'Three, two, one, drink!'

Christian had already celebrated the birth of his baby with Rocco, Zayed and Stefan four months before.

Tonight it was Alessandra's turn. She was having her own version of wetting the baby's head in the bar next door with her sister-in-law and some other friends. He suspected theirs would be a much more civilised affair than his had been. But not by much.

Thinking about it, he realised Alessandra hadn't drunk

any alcohol for well over a year, what with the pregnancy and then the four months of breast-feeding she'd done.

Her tolerance would be minimal.

Theos, and she'd insisted on wearing her five-inch heels.

He was all set to bolt out of the bar and hover over her like her own personal guard when Rocco called the barman over for another round.

'Now we need to drink to baby Mondelli,' Rocco said with a knowing look.

'Baby Mondelli?' It took a moment for the penny to drop. 'Olivia, she is…?'

Rocco couldn't hide the beam on his face. 'Yes. I'm going to be a father.'

'That is wonderful news!' Embracing in a manly fashion, the two men then downed their final shots, got to their feet, walked out of the bar and into the next one, both eager to be with the women they loved above all else.

* * * * *

Look out for the next instalment of
SOCIETY WEDDINGS:
THE SICILIAN'S SURPRISE WIFE
by Tara Pammi
Coming next month!

Read on for a SOCIETY WEDDINGS Exclusive!

Deleted Scene

ALMOST ELEVEN AND the streets were packed, the evening balmy. As they passed loud party-goers, all Alessandra could think was that her night was almost over.

Every step took her closer to her apartment.

Soon she would be left to nothing but her thoughts.

Such awareness. All she could feel in her skin was him. He walked beside her, so near yet so far.

For the first time that evening, talk between them became stilted, a real tension having sprung up, an air of anticipation hanging, ready to be grabbed hold of.

Was it her imagination or had Christian's pace slowed too?

However slowly they walked, they arrived at her apartment much too quickly.

'Are you coming up for coffee?' she asked, pressing the code to enter the building.

He shook his head. 'I'll walk you to your door and then head to my hotel.'

Compared to the noise of the Milanese streets, the building that housed her apartment was quiet. So quiet, she could hear her own heartbeat.

The security guard ordered the lift and in painful silence they rode up to the third floor, Christian beside her, his strong jaw clenched.

'Are you sure you don't want to stay for coffee?' she asked softly, looking at him as she unlocked her door. 'Or more champagne? I've a bottle in the fridge.'

A pulse along his jawline throbbed, his Adam's apple rising and falling. 'I need to go.'

'Well…thank you for a lovely evening. It's been fun.'

He nodded, looking over her shoulder into her apartment. She'd left a light on in the main living area, a warm glow permeating through the vast space.

She leaned forward onto her toes, placing her hands onto his shoulder, moisture filling her mouth as she anticipated the customary kiss goodbye. 'Good night, Christian.'

His chest rose, and his lips clamped together, a deep breath expelling from his nose. He placed a hand loosely on her hip. 'Good night, Alessandra.'

She placed her lips to his cheek, breathing in his scent, the champagne and bourbon that played on his tongue, her skin delighting to feel his mouth brush against her own cheek, their faces moving in sync to kiss the opposite cheeks.

What would those still firmly clamped lips feel like against her own? she wondered, moving her mouth to press lightly against them and discover for herself.

He didn't move, his breaths coming even deeper, his body as rigid as a board.

The fingers holding her hip tightened, a subtle movement that enticed her to press herself closer so all that separated them were the clothes they wore.

She felt the slightest of softening in his unyielding form, enough to embolden her further to slip her fingers beneath the collar of his shirt and gently graze his smooth, warm skin, her lips still chastely placed against his.

A guttural noise came from his throat, a groan that reverberated through her skin and seeped down low, right into her pelvis.

She scraped the nape of his neck with her nails, breathing

him in more deeply, his masculine scent filling her senses in the most delicious way.

And then the statue came to life, his hand rising to clasp the back of her head in a firm, hard grip, his lips parting. Then he was kissing her, kissing her with a violence that made the pulsations deep in her core enflame and her heart beat like a thousand drums had been let loose within her.

The Wedding Breakfast Menu
from Christian and Alessandra's wedding!

MENU

APPETISERS
Crabmeat Charissa
Spinach and Feta Spanakopita (V)

FIRST COURSE
Steamed Shrimp Served on a bed of Fresh Seaweed
with a Cocktail Sauce and Lemon Wedges
Fresh Bread Rolls

Chilled Pea Soup (V)
Fresh Bread Rolls

INTERMEZZO
Lemon Sorbet

MAIN COURSE
Stuffed Leg of Lamb with Pepperoncini Peppers
in a Red Wine Rosemary Jus
Served with Rice Pilaf and Roasted Vegetables

Vegetarian Souvlakia Skewers (V)
Served with Rice Pilaf and Roasted Vegetables

DESSERT
Trio of Chocolate Marquis,
Mango Mousse Cake and Passion Fruit Cake
Served with Chocolate Sauce and Mango Fruit Purée

Coffee

The Chocolate Fondue Fountain will be available to all
guests throughout this happy occasion

MILLS & BOON®

It's Got to be Perfect

* cover in development

When Ellie Rigby throws her three-carat engagement ring into the gutter, she is certain of only one thing. She has yet to know true love!

Fed up with disastrous internet dates and conflicting advice from her friends, Ellie decides to take matters into her own hands. Starting a dating agency, Ellie becomes an expert in love. Well, that is until a match with one of her clients, charming, infuriating Nick, has her questioning everything she's ever thought about love…

Order yours today at
www.millsandboon.co.uk

MILLS & BOON®

The Thirty List

* cover in development

At thirty, Rachel has slid down every ladder she has ever climbed. Jobless, broke and ditched by her husband, she has to move in with grumpy Patrick and his four-year-old son.

Patrick is also getting divorced, so to cheer themselves up the two decide to draw up bucket lists. Soon they are learning to tango, abseiling, trying stand-up comedy and more. But, as she gets closer to Patrick, Rachel wonders if their relationship is too good to be true…

**Order yours today at
www.millsandboon.co.uk/Thethirtylist**

MILLS & BOON®

MODERN™

POWER, PASSION AND IRRESISTIBLE TEMPTATION

A sneak peek at next month's titles…

In stores from 15th May 2015:

- **The Bride Fonseca Needs** – Abby Green
- **Protecting the Desert Heir** – Caitlin Crews
- **Tempted by Her Billionaire Boss** – Jennifer Hayward
- **The Sicilian's Surprise Wife** – Tara Pammi

In stores from 5th June 2015:

- **Sheikh's Forbidden Conquest** – Chantelle Shaw
- **Seduced into the Greek's World** – Dani Collins
- **Married for the Prince's Convenience** – Maya Blake
- **For Revenge or Redemption?** – Lucy King

0515/01